PRAISE FOR
FRANCES MENSAH WILLIAMS

'One of my go-to heart-warming authors.'
—Dorothy Koomson, bestselling author of *The Ice Cream Girls*
and *I Know What You've Done*

PRAISE FOR
THE SECOND TIME WE MET

'I loved this novel! There was so much to love about it. A big, bold, beautiful rollercoaster of a book, in which the main characters are a modern-day fairy-tale couple . . . The story kept me turning the pages . . . Adorable read.'
—Judy Leigh, bestselling author of *The Old Girls' Network*

'Plenty of laugh-out-loud moments . . . and Williams's exploration of the British class system is on point. This is sure to charm.'
—*Publishers Weekly*

STRICTLY FRIENDS

ALSO BY FRANCES MENSAH WILLIAMS

The Second Time We Met
From Pasta to Pigfoot
From Pasta to Pigfoot: Second Helpings

The Marula Heights romance series:

Imperfect Arrangements
River Wild
Sweet Mercy

STRICTLY
FRIENDS

Frances Mensah Williams

LAKE UNION
PUBLISHING

This is a work of fiction. Names, characters, organizations, places, events, and incidents are either products of the author's imagination or are used fictitiously. Any resemblance to actual persons, living or dead, or actual events is purely coincidental.

Text copyright © 2023 by Frances Mensah Williams
All rights reserved.

No part of this book may be reproduced, or stored in a retrieval system, or transmitted in any form or by any means, electronic, mechanical, photocopying, recording, or otherwise, without express written permission of the publisher.

Published by Lake Union Publishing, Seattle

www.apub.com

Amazon, the Amazon logo, and Lake Union Publishing are trademarks of Amazon.com, Inc., or its affiliates.

ISBN-13: 9781542038898
ISBN-10: 1542038898

Cover design by The Brewster Project

Printed in the United States of America

For Chux, with love.

PROLOGUE

The clouds hovering over Brighton beach were even greyer than the overcast skies they had left in London. Watching the lone figure standing by the shore spinning stones into the foaming waves, Ruby scarcely registered the sound of the screaming seagulls overhead or the crash of high waves on to the weathered stone barrier of the secluded stretch of shore.

Waiting alone on the cold, damp pebbles with the wind whipping her long black braids into a frenzy, Ruby finally allowed her tears to flow unchecked, feeling their warmth slide down her frozen cheeks. The short dress she had thrown on in her rush to get to Griffin wasn't designed for sitting on a stony beach, and she shivered as the icy wind sliced through her puffa jacket and thick tights. As she watched Griffin toss the last stone in his hand and then bend over, clasping his knees as though struggling to control his emotions, Ruby's tears fell faster, and she gulped back the loud sobs fighting to escape her chest.

You need to let it out, Rubes. After all, this was why Griffin had brought her here today. This was their special place, and she knew he was hoping that maybe, just maybe, out here on this deserted stretch of beach, she would allow herself to scream out the emotions she had been too shocked and too numb to release since turning up at his front door that morning.

He turned and walked back towards her, and Ruby quickly wiped her face with her sleeve. Whatever pain Ruby felt, Griffin always felt it too and she couldn't bear to add to the torment he still carried from his mother's death.

He dropped down to sit next to her, the pebbles shifting under his weight, and reached for her hand, rubbing its icy coldness between his own. She felt the tears well up once again, and this time she let them run freely, her chest heaving with silent sobs.

'It's okay, Rubes. You can let it out. I'm here,' Griffin said softly, and she stared down at their intertwined hands, noting the contrast between his light brown complexion and her deeper brown skin.

After a moment, Ruby exhaled with a long, shuddering sigh. 'Why did he leave me?' she asked baldly, unable to hide the anguish in her voice. Just saying the words was destroying her but she had to face the truth and try to make sense of what had just happened. Deep down, she'd always known she wasn't enough, but after almost four years with Kenny she had finally started to believe she could be.

'He didn't love me, did he?' she persisted, turning to meet his gaze squarely.

A shadow crossed Griffin's face and he looked away, releasing her hand and raking his fingers through his cropped black curls.

'I-I don't think that's why,' he stammered helplessly, and she could feel his body trembling. He was clearly still in shock from her news and when his eyes finally met hers, she felt a pang of guilt at the pain she saw reflected in their depths. Griffin was her best friend and the person she trusted more than anyone in the world and, after reading the note Kenny had left on the kitchen table, her first reaction had been to jump into a cab and rush to Griff. But although he wouldn't have wanted it any other way, Ruby also knew better than anyone how badly Griffin was struggling with his own changed circumstances.

'I'm sorry, Griff. You've got enough to deal with already and it's not like any of this is your fault. You were right all along. Mum, Dad, Auntie Pearl . . . *everyone* was right! I was an idiot to think it would last.' She heard the huskiness in her voice, and she exhaled deeply, watching the cloud of warm breath quickly disperse into the freezing air. 'Mum and Dad will be furious with me. They always said I'd rushed into things with Kenny, and now he's proved them right.'

'Rubes, you'll get through this. You've got me, and I'll always be here for you.'

'Kenny said he'd always be here for me, but he's not any more, is he?' she countered bleakly, her heart cracking inside her. '*Why* didn't he talk to me instead of just disappearing? We have a *child!* How do I tell Jake that his father's left me – left *us*? What am I supposed to do now?'

Griffin threw his arm around her and cradled her head against his shoulder as the tears streamed down her face and her body convulsed with agonised sobs.

'I don't know, Rubes,' he whispered. 'He's gone, but you'll always have me. I *promise.*'

SIX YEARS LATER . . .

PART ONE

LIMBO

PART ONE

1

If she tried hard enough, Ruby realised, she really *could* tune out the sound of the red-faced man talking at her from behind his desk. Like pressing the mute button on a TV remote, she had the power to cut off the irritatingly nasal drone of Jake's headteacher. Just by focusing on the glasses perched on a nose with enlarged pores like seeds on a colourless strawberry, she could block his words from reaching her ears—

'Mrs Lamont?' Mr Hinton glared at her over the top of his frames.

Oops, how did that slip through?

'*Miss* Lamont,' Ruby corrected him automatically. *How many times must we go through this charade?* Sending her son to a Catholic school with quaint, old-fashioned ideas had always been a risk, but no-one had warned her that quaint included refusing to recognise the concept of an unmarried parent.

'*Mrs* Lamont . . .'

Apparently, Mr Hinton knew how to tune out people too, Ruby acknowledged with a silent *touché*.

'I hope you have taken on board what I've just said,' Mr Hinton continued, his pale blue eyes searching hers for confirmation that his words had registered. 'Jacob's behaviour is becoming a matter of great concern to us at St Martin's.'

Hearing Jake's name galvanised Ruby into defensive mode. No-one threatened – or even *hinted* at threatening – her son while she had breath in her body.

'*Mr* Hinton,' she said, leaning forward in her chair and deliberately stressing his title to show that at least one of them could get people's names right. 'Jake is eight years old. Of *course* he's going to get upset if some nasty boy tries to take the piss – excuse me, teases him about his dad. What I don't understand is why Jake is the villain of the piece here instead of that little – erm, the other student?'

Mr Hinton was clearly not used to having his authority challenged. He took a deep breath, his face growing redder, and Ruby sat back, satisfied. *Hah! Bet you wish now that I* hadn't *been paying attention.*

'I don't think you realise quite how serious this is, Mrs Lamont,' he snapped, before launching into an extended lecture on the importance of truthfulness in children and the risks involved in turning a blind eye to Jake's lively imagination.

Ruby sighed inwardly and mentally reactivated the mute button. *Why must everything be so bloody difficult?* Mr Hinton's bristling outrage at her audacity in talking back to him was nothing new. She'd lost count of the times when simply being five feet and eleven and a half inches tall provoked someone – usually a man – to react like a pack leader whose status was under threat. No matter how calmly Ruby spoke, she was still labelled as intimidating. But then, as Griffin had pointed out, it wasn't her fault – or her problem – if some people felt apprehensive about engaging with a tall, athletic Black woman with wide shoulders, strong thighs, and abs you could bounce tennis balls off. Although, he'd added less charitably, her gobby mouth allied with all the above could also explain why some people felt somewhat unnerved until they got to know her.

None of which, Ruby mused, was any comfort in dealing with the irate teacher who, unfortunately, held her son's fate in his hands. After a few moments of watching Mr Hinton's lips articulating words she refused to hear, Ruby absently scanned the wood-panelled walls of the headteacher's imposing office. Her gaze fixed on a display of framed certificates on the wall behind him and directly above a large picture of a smiling Mr Hinton shaking hands with a man dressed in ceremonial robes and wearing a heavy gold chain.

The sound of loud throat-clearing penetrated Ruby's contemplation and she returned her attention to Jake's headteacher.

'—Mrs Lamont, let me be quite clear. We pride ourselves on our values here at St Martin's, one of which is honesty. If Jacob transgresses or resorts to violence once again, we will be forced to exclude him from our school community. I really cannot condone any behaviour that puts our students at risk.'

Ruby generally scorned anything she considered mawkish or sentimental, but the one area of her life where this rule didn't apply was her son. From the moment Jake's tiny newborn fist had reached out to grab her finger, he had burrowed into her heart and lodged himself at its centre. There was no question she would stop a bullet or leap in front of a speeding bus to save him, and Mr Hinton's implied threat to her son's future was one provocation too far. Incensed, Ruby stood up and crossed the short stretch of carpet between her chair and the headteacher's desk. She rested her hands on the edge of his desk and leaned forward, not missing the instant widening of the man's eyes or the way he shrank back into his chair to widen the space between them.

'So, let me understand this,' she said. 'You've dragged me out of my extremely busy workplace this afternoon to tell me that you think my eight-year-old son is a *risk* to your school because he stood up for himself this morning when some little shit shouted – in front of *everyone* in the playground – that Jake was lying about his father and is secretly an orphan? Are *those* the values you consider acceptable within your school community?'

The headteacher flinched at the fury seeping through Ruby's quietly spoken words and his eyes darted nervously around the room. While she had him on the ropes, Ruby pressed home her advantage.

'Isn't it bad enough that Jake's father isn't around without the poor kid being tormented about it? Please explain to me how this type of behaviour fits in with the charitable Christian environment I thought St Martin's was supposed to offer my son.'

Mr Hinton's indignation subsided like a balloon suddenly losing air and Ruby watched as his flushed cheeks returned to a pale pink. She almost felt sorry for him. Almost, but not quite. *He* wasn't a confused little boy whose father had left home one day and never returned. *He* wasn't a gifted young artist who drew haunting sketches in the hope that when his father finally did come home, he'd be so impressed with them that he would stay. No. Mr Hinton was a grown man who, Ruby would bet, had never needed to make sense of why his own father didn't want to stick around.

'Please sit down, Mrs Lamont.' Mr Hinton spoke without bluster and Ruby returned to her chair with a pang of trepidation. Not for the first time, she silently cursed Kenny. Six years on, the shadow of her former partner's abrupt departure from their lives continued to loom large and was now threatening to ruin Jake's life. Mr Hinton might be a pompous cultural dinosaur, but Ruby couldn't afford to push him too far. St Martin's was a highly sought-after school, and its location only a short walk from their house in Blossom Street made it easy for Ruby to drop Jake off in the mornings and for Auntie Pearl, who lived with them, to pick him up after school. Even more importantly, St Martin's after-school art club came with expert tutors who were guiding Jake to develop his impressive drawing skills, and her son would be devastated if he had to leave.

Ruby's despair was mirrored on her face and, after studying her for a moment, Mr Hinton unfolded his arms. 'Look, Mrs Lamont, I have also communicated with Oliver Marshall's parents and made it clear their son's behaviour was unkind and completely unacceptable.' Remarkably, his tone had switched, and it sounded almost as if he were pleading with her. 'Our ethos at St Martin's is to support everyone, whatever their circumstances, to fulfil their abilities. Jacob is a talented student, and his artwork is remarkable for his age. Nevertheless,' he added quickly, 'while young Oliver's behaviour was reprehensible, it did not justify Jacob's actions and I cannot condone violence.'

Mr Hinton sounded sincere and, mindful of her need to keep the teacher onside, Ruby relaxed her shoulders and forced a reassuring smile she was far from feeling. 'I certainly don't condone violence, either' – *unless it's against that bastard, Kenny,* she thought silently – 'and I appreciate you speaking to Oliver's parents. Believe me, I loathe any form of deceit and this certainly isn't the Jake I know. I'll have a strong word with him when he gets home today.'

The headteacher nodded and stood up, glancing towards the closed door of his office to make it clear the meeting was over. 'Thank you for your understanding, Mrs Lamont, and I can assure you we will be keeping a close eye on young Oliver as well.'

The 'as well' almost did it, but Ruby bit her tongue and quickly shook Mr Hinton's outstretched hand before grabbing the coat from the back of her chair and striding out of the office.

2

Leaving the school through its old-fashioned wrought-iron gates, Ruby stood on the pavement for a few moments, gulping in the cold air while deciding on her next move. The chilly October wind whistled past her ears, and she shook her long braids loose to frame her face and warm her ears before drawing her heavy wool coat up around her throat. She was in no mood to go back to the office and Priya, her assistant, could easily cover for the rest of the day. Jake wouldn't finish school for another couple of hours, and after thirty minutes in Mr Hinton's company, Ruby was in desperate need of a mug of tea and a few of the remaining Bourbon biscuits in the kitchen cupboard.

Ruby glanced at her watch. Auntie Pearl would no doubt be on the sofa engrossed in the daytime television shows that had become her favourite activity since her retirement. Only months after Kenny's disappearance, Ruby's life had been further devastated by the sudden death of her parents in a car accident. Without ever being asked, Auntie Pearl – her mum's twin – had quietly moved into their Blossom Street semi one day between her nursing shifts, taking charge of a struggling Ruby and two-year-old Jake. When Ruby had once fearfully asked her aunt how long she was staying, Auntie Pearl had brushed away the question.

'Looking after you and Jake is what Opal would have wanted. My darling sister and Neville didn't get to watch their grandson grow up, so I'm going to do it for them.'

A sudden blast of cold wind jolted Ruby back into the present. She dashed off a quick text to Priya and dropped the phone back into her bag. Thrusting her chilled hands into her coat pockets, Ruby started down the road, her long legs eating up the short distance between the school and her house.

◆ ◆ ◆

'*Ru-bee!* Is that you?'

Ruby grinned and slammed the door behind her, resisting the temptation to shout, 'No, it's an axe murderer!' Making flippant comments to an elderly woman who took everything literally was not a clever idea.

'Hi, Auntie Pearl,' she called, using the toe of one boot to ease off the heel of the other. Tugging off the other boot, she hooked her coat on to the rack behind the door and made her way to the living room. 'I had to leave work to go to Jake's school for a meeting with the headteacher. You'll never guess what that child has—'

Ruby broke off abruptly at the sight of a woman sitting next to her aunt on the sofa. The woman was dressed in jeans and a lemon-yellow jumper. Her long blonde hair was dishevelled and judging from her blotchy, tear-stained face and the striped cotton hanky in her hands – which Ruby immediately recognised as one of Auntie Pearl's – she had been crying. A full mug of tea with the steam still rising sat on a side table next to the visitor, and the television volume had been lowered to a hum.

Standing in the doorway in her socks, Ruby shifted uneasily while racking her brains to remember the name of the visitor now staring at her accusingly through red-rimmed eyes. It was only a couple of weeks since she'd been out clubbing with her, along with Griffin and a group of their friends. But the polished, slightly stuck-up woman with a thick, glossy mane and posh drawl that she remembered was a far cry from the resentful-looking one on the sofa. Unfortunately, Griffin's girlfriends came and went so quickly it was hard to keep track. *It's not Janine; she was a few months ago. Monica was last month . . . Think, Ruby! What the hell was . . . ? Shirley!*

'Shirley!' Ruby exclaimed, throwing an apologetic smile at her aunt as she moved into the room. Remembering the possessive way in which the girl had clung on to Griffin at the club, Ruby had a shrewd idea of what was going on here, and her heart sank. But whatever Griff had been up to, it really wasn't her aunt's headache.

Auntie Pearl, however, didn't seem the slightest bit put out. She gave her visitor's shoulders a comforting squeeze before picking up her own mug, filled to the brim with milky tea, and fixing her gaze studiously on to the television. Her body language made it clear the woman was now Ruby's problem.

'It's Shir*lee*, not Shirley,' the woman snuffled in response to Ruby's greeting.

Ruby stared at her in bafflement. 'Isn't that what just I said?'

'No! The emphasis is on the second bit, not the first.'

About to argue, Ruby took one look at the frown that had suddenly appeared on her aunt's face and swallowed her words. She returned her gaze to Shirlee's red-rimmed eyes and the handkerchief clutched in her hand and suppressed the sigh bursting for release. Although it wasn't their usual practice to find their way to her house, it wasn't hard for Ruby to work out why this woman was here and in such apparent distress.

Trying to buy time while she figured out how to deal with the situation, Ruby walked over to Auntie Pearl and dropped a kiss on the soft, dark cheek so much like her mum's. She gently dislodged

Indie, the plump cat curled up in the armchair next to the sofa, and sat down.

'So, um, what brings you here, Shir*lee*?' she asked gently, tucking her braids behind her ears as she leaned forward attentively.

'It's Griffin, of course! He – he's finished with me!' Shirlee wiped her nose with the hanky, and seconds later burst into sobs.

Ruby watched helplessly as a flood of tears cascaded down the woman's face. 'I'm so sorry,' she said humbly, sounding as contrite as if she was the one who had done the finishing with. 'What happened? I thought you guys were getting on well.'

Shirlee wiped away the tears and blew her nose hard. 'So did I! Griffin took me to dinner at an amazing restaurant in Chelsea last night and we had a brilliant evening. He got us a cab to go back to his place, and on the way I suggested that we go away together for the weekend. I thought spending more time alone would help us really connect as a couple and give us space to plan our next steps together. But then he – he said it was a bit soon for all of that. So, I told him I'm not getting any younger and I think it's important to let any man I'm seeing know that I'm after a commitment. Before I knew it, he'd told the driver to take us to my flat instead, and then he went all quiet on me. When we got to mine and I tried to kiss him goodnight—' She broke off as fresh tears tumbled down her cheeks. 'He – he said he didn't want to lead me on and that he wasn't ready for that kind of com— commitment and it was probably best if we didn't see each other any *mo-oore*!' She ended with a sound that combined a sob with a loud snort.

Ruby grimaced and absently reached for the brimming mug of tea Shirlee had left untouched, taking a couple of sips while she mulled over the woman's predicament. After her earlier confrontation with Mr Hinton, Ruby wasn't in the best frame of mind to clear up a Griffin-shaped mess and smooth things over for yet another woman who had fallen too quickly and too hard for her commitment-phobic best friend.

'Shirlee, I feel really bad for you about what's happened, but I don't understand why you're here.'

Auntie Pearl grunted and took a long sip of her tea. Baffled, Ruby glanced at her, wondering why her aunt – never usually lost for words – had apparently taken a vow of silence.

Shirlee dabbed her eyes with the damp scrap of cotton. 'I was too upset to think straight and your aunt said I could wait here until you finish work. I wanted to see you because you're supposed to be his best friend. I thought you might be able to talk to him and get him to change his mind.'

'*Me?*' Ruby's voice rose with incredulity. 'I'm sorry, but have you *met* Griffin?'

It never ceased to amaze her that anyone, particularly the women who dated him and had presumably seen first-hand just how pig-headed he could be, imagined that Griffin was amenable to taking orders or doing anything he didn't want to. Deciding to overlook Shirlee's belligerence in view of her obvious distress, Ruby softened her tone. 'Look, I know you're upset, but there's nothing I can—'

'Oh, *please*!' Shirlee cut in, glaring accusingly at Ruby while balling the limp handkerchief in her palm. 'Whenever I'm with Griffin, it's always Ruby-this and Ruby-that. If anyone can make him change his mind, it's *you*. From what I've seen, he doesn't so much as sneeze without checking in with you first.'

Auntie Pearl grunted again, but Ruby was too stunned by the unfairness of Shirlee's accusation to react. How the hell had Griffin's bad behaviour suddenly become *her* fault? But despite Shirlee's aggressiveness she still felt bad for the girl, and if Griffin had been in the room with them, she would have cheerfully thumped him – assuming Shirlee didn't get there first.

Shirlee trained narrowed eyes on to Ruby. 'I asked you that night we went to the club, and I'll ask you now. If Griffin's so obsessed with you, why the hell aren't the two of you together?'

Ruby could feel her levels of sympathy for the woman plummeting, but before she could respond Shirlee waved a dismissive hand. 'And please don't tell me that silly story again about how the two of you kissed behind the bike shed when you were fourteen or whatever and how it was *so* awful you knew you'd only ever be friends.'

Feeling more than a little aggrieved by Shirlee's dismissive attitude – and embarrassed at having secrets she'd drunkenly confided to allay Shirlee's fears blurted out in front of Auntie Pearl – Ruby maintained a stony silence. Undaunted, Shirlee continued to argue her case, eventually grinding to a halt with a petulant, 'If you told him to make it work with me, he *would*!'

'Shirlee, I can assure you that I have *never* interfered in Griff's relationships!' Ruby protested, appalled at the prospect of being dragged any further into her friend's messy love life. 'Yes, Griffin and I are close but, trust me, he makes his own decisions about his . . . um, affairs.'

As far as Ruby was concerned, any observations she might have occasionally made about Griffin's taste in women was only the candid feedback any good friend would offer and in no way amounted to interference. After all, no-one could argue that Belinda, the stunning bodybuilder with a massive tattoo of a rose on her thigh who he'd met at the gym, hadn't proved Ruby's concerns right when she demanded Griffin tattoo her likeness on to his chest to prove he cared for her. Or that Ruby's suspicions about Marsha – the gorgeous flight attendant with the flawless cocoa-brown skin and bee-stung lips who Griffin had met on a flight to Zanzibar and dated for a month – were unfounded after the woman turned up at Griffin's apartment with two suitcases and her fluffy Pomeranian in tow.

However, notwithstanding Shirlee's patent hostility, Ruby couldn't help feeling bad for her. Griffin's lackadaisical attitude to women was a reminder, if Ruby ever needed one after Kenny's actions, that romantic relationships were a complete waste of time. Putting down the mug of tea she'd been cradling, Ruby tried her best to sound conciliatory. 'Again, I'm sorry things have ended this way, but to be fair, you *did* know Griffin's reputation when you started seeing him . . .'

She tailed off at Shirlee's outraged expression and bit back the words hovering on her tongue. *Oh, come on!* As much as she sympathised with Shirlee's heartbreak, there couldn't be a single woman under the age of forty left in London who didn't know Griffin Koinet's reputation as the romantic equivalent of the plague – easily caught, and tough to recover from.

'To be honest, I don't even know why I bothered coming here.' Shirlee drew in a deep, shuddering breath and exhaled, her shoulders slumping in resignation. 'I mean, it's not like you ever wanted me to be with Griffin, is it?'

Without waiting for an answer, Shirlee stood up and turned to Auntie Pearl with a tight smile. 'I'm sorry to have disturbed you and I'm grateful to you for letting me in and being so kind. Thanks for the tea, although' – she glanced at the half-empty mug on the side table and threw a venomous glance in Ruby's direction – 'it rather looks like that was taken away from me too.'

As she stalked out of the room, Auntie Pearl gestured furiously to Ruby to follow her. Gritting her teeth, Ruby scrambled out of the armchair after Shirlee, catching up with her at the front door and watching helplessly while the woman shrugged on her coat and flipped out her hair. As Shirlee reached for the handle and pulled opened the door, Ruby gave it one more try.

'Shirlee, wait!'

Slowly Shirlee turned around, and Ruby winced at the scorn in the puffy-eyed glare directed at her. *This is* not *my fault, dammit!*

Shirlee's lips, pinched into a pink slash that stood out against the pallor of her skin, appeared to disagree, and Ruby scrabbled to find the right words.

'Look, why don't you call Griffin and tell him how you feel? I know he really likes you and maybe you just took him by surprise when—'

'If he *really* liked me,' Shirlee echoed sarcastically, 'I wouldn't be standing here in the first place, would I? Tell you what, Ruby, why don't you just go out with Griffin yourself and spare the rest of us from being treated like crap!'

With that, she walked out and slammed the door behind her.

3

Reeling from the unwarranted verbal attack, Ruby stood in the hallway staring at the closed door in bewilderment while trying to process what had just happened. After a couple of minutes, reluctantly conceding that any hope Shirlee would reappear and accept Ruby's innocence was highly unlikely, she slowly padded back to the living room, where Auntie Pearl, remote in hand, had turned up the television volume.

Taking no notice of her aunt's self-righteous expression, Ruby returned to the armchair and crossed her legs, staring unhappily at her candy-striped socks while she brooded over Shirlee's explosive visit. It was hard not to feel wounded by the other woman's naked dislike when she wasn't the one responsible for her distress, and Ruby reached for the mug of tea she had appropriated and took a long sip.

Abandoning her silence, Auntie Pearl pressed the mute button on the remote, and looked hard at Ruby. 'Now, you know I'm not one to say I told you so—'

Ruby spluttered, promptly choking on the tea. There were few things her aunt loved better than pointing out when she had been proved right.

Auntie Pearl scowled and waited for Ruby's coughing fit to subside before continuing. 'I've been telling you for years that one day that boy's troubles are going to end up on your doorstep.'

As much as Ruby hated to admit it, this time Auntie Pearl was right. It was one thing to work your way through every eligible woman in the city; it was quite another to have the righteous anger of said women visited upon your innocent best friend. Suddenly furious at having been forced to bear the brunt of Griffin's behaviour, Ruby burst out, 'Wait until I see Griffin! I don't know what's wrong with the man and why he insists on behaving like such a – a – man-whore!'

'*Ruby!*' Auntie Pearl looked so shocked that Ruby hastily mumbled an apology. Using bad language in front of your elders was a cultural taboo ingrained from Auntie Pearl's early years in Ghana, and almost forty years of living in London had yet to change that.

'I'm sorry you had to deal with Griffin's nonsense, Auntie Pearl,' Ruby added, genuinely contrite. 'Shirlee was in the car when Griffin dropped me at home after we'd all been out a couple of weeks ago, and I suppose she remembered where I live.'

Recalling Shirlee's parting words, Ruby felt her hackles rise again. 'You know, I understand she's upset, but can you believe the *nerve* of her attacking me because things have gone pear-shaped with Griffin? I mean, for God's sake, what was the woman even thinking? Who in their right mind brings up "the next step" with a man you've been seeing for less than a month? Really, who *does* that?'

Auntie Pearl inhaled so deeply her nostrils flared. She opened her mouth, and then as if thinking better of whatever she had intended to say, she reached for her tea and took a sip. Replacing the mug on the side table, she adjusted the colourful headscarf wrapped around her short, greying curls and settled back into the sofa.

'Never mind about that poor girl for now. I want to know why you're home so early. What's this about Jake being in trouble again?' She tutted loudly. 'I do not understand what is going on with the child!'

23

Indie slunk back into the living room and hopped up on to Ruby's lap, and Ruby stroked her fur while she thought back to the meeting with Mr Hinton.

'Apparently, Jake's been telling everyone that his father's a spy and he had to disappear to protect us from a group of terrorists he's tracking down. During break this morning, one of the kids in his class started teasing Jake and called him a liar in front of everyone in the playground. Then the boy – his name's Oliver – started shouting that Jake's father is dead and he's an orphan. Some of the kids began to laugh, and Jake . . . well, Jake punched the boy in the mouth.'

Auntie Pearl sat bolt upright, her face creasing with worry as Ruby relayed the details of her meeting with Mr Hinton.

'Auntie Pearl, I honestly don't know what to do about Jake. This is the third time in as many weeks that he's been pulled up at school for making up stories, even though I've *drilled* the importance of telling the truth into him since he could speak. I get that he's curious about his dad, especially now he's getting older, but I don't know what more to tell him. I mean, other than Kenny's letter telling me where to find him, it's not as if he's bothered to stay in touch. The man's been gone for years and lives halfway across the world. I haven't got the first idea what he's up to these days!'

Auntie Pearl's eyes turned back to the silent TV screen, where a man in white shorts was running along a beach with a young boy around Jake's age, while a smiling woman looked on.

'A boy needs his father,' Auntie Pearl observed in a low voice.

Ruby followed her aunt's gaze and grimaced at the picture-perfect family on the screen. 'Loads of boys succeed without a father. Besides, Jake's got Griffin. He's an amazing godfather and we've managed without Kenny for years. We don't need him now!'

'I know how close they are, but it doesn't change the fact that Griffin is not his father. I understand you have no interest in seeing – that man—' Auntie Pearl broke off and wrinkled her nose in disgust, and Ruby bit back a grin. Even after all these years, Auntie Pearl still couldn't bring herself to utter Kenny's name.

'No-one can blame you for never wanting to see *him* again after what he did, but you are a mother, and you need to think about what's best for your son. You know where the man lives and, as hard as it might be, I think you should let Jake meet his father. Trust me, darling, once the boy sees the real thing, he won't need to make up these silly stories.' She reached across to tickle Indie's neck as she lay sprawled across Ruby's lap, and the cat looked up for a moment to lick her lips before laying her head back down.

'Yeah, well, maybe Kenny doesn't *deserve* to know Jake!' Ruby retorted.

Her aunt sucked her teeth impatiently. 'Now look, you know as well as I do how important it is for Jake to stay at St Martin's. He was doing very well before all this nonsense started and he loves going to Art Club. If the school excludes him for misbehaviour when all he's doing is acting out because he's curious about his father . . .' She tailed off with an ominous '*hmm*' and turned back to the television.

Ruby followed her gaze, watching the man sweep his son up into his arms and run along the shore, splashing them both as he darted in and out of the water. The boy, his mouth open in laughter, had his arms around his father's neck and was clinging on tight.

'I haven't spoken to Kenny since he left, and I don't have a clue how to get to Sorrel Island,' Ruby said eventually. Even to her own ears her objection sounded pitiful.

Auntie Pearl snorted in disbelief. 'You're on the internet all day, aren't you? How hard would it be to find out?'

'It's not just that,' Ruby parried. This wasn't simply about geography. Kenny had behaved abominably for reasons she still didn't understand. Surely it would be irresponsible of her as a mother to bring such a man back into her son's life. 'Auntie, he's hurt Jake once before by abandoning him, so why would I give him a chance to do it again?'

25

Auntie Pearl's face took on the look of fondness blended with exasperation she normally reserved for shooing Indie off her spot on the sofa. 'Because, Ruby, sometimes in life you must take a chance. If things go wrong, Jake will have you by his side to protect him. But if, by some miracle, that man can make amends with his son, would you honestly want to stand in the way?'

Increasingly alarmed by the unexpected turn of the conversation, Ruby desperately sought for straws to clutch. 'But – but – going out there would mean taking Jake out of school for . . . I don't know . . . *weeks*! And there's also my job to consider. I've used up almost all my holiday this year and while Fi might give me a week off at a pinch if I begged, Sorrel Island's miles away and there's no telling how long it would take to sort things out between Kenny and Jake once we got there.'

Her aunt pursed her lips and picked up the remote, changing the television channel. She kept her gaze fixed on the screen as the opening credits to her favourite antiques show began to roll. 'Jake can keep up with his schoolwork remotely. Everyone's used to it now, and from what you've said Mr Hinton will probably be too relieved you're sorting things out for Jake to object.' She glanced at Ruby and raised a caustic eyebrow. 'And as for your Miss Dolly Parton, that woman owes you a lot more than a week off! Do you think she could have made such a success of her business without all the extra hours you've put in over the years?'

Despite feeling appalled at the prospect of searching for her ex-partner, Ruby smiled at the reference to Fi, her long-time boss and longer-time friend. With her petite frame, tiny waist and impressive breasts, Fi was a dead ringer for the country music star, a resemblance she cultivated with carefully teased ash blonde hair, tight-fitting clothes, and her trademark scarlet lipstick. Fi's commercial savvy, however, defied her doll-like appearance. Over the past few years, she had built a thriving communications consultancy, hiring Ruby initially as her PA, and now as Office Manager.

'Fi's not just my boss; she's one of my best friends. Which is why I wouldn't want to take the pi—' Auntie Pearl frowned, and Ruby cleared her throat. 'I mean, presume on our friendship. She has a business to run, and with the company growing so fast, it's all hands on deck.'

Auntie Pearl waved aside the objection with an impatient tut. 'Now you listen to me, Ruby. My daddy adored Opal and me. We were his precious twin gems and he made sure we knew there was nothing he wouldn't do for us. Opal named you Ruby because you were *her* precious gem, and you've never had to wonder if your father loved you because Neville worshipped you from the moment you were born. Jake doesn't have those types of memories, and until he meets his father face to face, he's always going to feel like a part of him is missing.'

'But what if it all goes horribly wrong?' Ruby agonised. 'I mean, we don't even know why Kenny left the country! What if he's involved in something awful or – or *criminal* – and I'm going to put Jake in harm's way?'

'Jake's not the only one who needs answers,' Auntie Pearl muttered, but Ruby, caught up with imagining the direst possible repercussions of getting entangled in Kenny's life, let her aunt's words go right over her head. As she opened her mouth to raise another objection, Auntie Pearl cut in.

'Ruby, love, you really don't have a choice. If you want to kill off the fantasy, you've got to show the boy the real thing. When Jake sees for himself what he's been missing – or not missing, in the case of that man – he will snap right out of all these delusions.'

Taking in the disconsolate expression on her niece's face, Auntie Pearl's voice softened. 'Darling, let the boy meet his father. It's time.'

4

Jake's class emerged from the building and trooped into the noisy playground in single file. Spotting his mother leaning against a pillar a few feet away, Jake gave an excited shout and ran over, throwing himself against her.

'*Oof!* Hello to you, too!' Ruby laughed.

Jake wrapped his arms tightly around her waist and she stooped to drop a kiss on his soft curls before he could object. She scooped up the battered backpack he had dropped in his haste and slung it over her shoulder, raising her thumb in an OK gesture to Jake's harassed-looking class teacher scanning the playground filled with waiting parents and checking off the names on her list.

'Wait, how come *you're* picking me up today, Mum?' Jake demanded. 'Why aren't you at work – and where's Grandma Pearl?' His initial excitement at seeing her disappeared and she could see the worry lurking in his wide eyes and suddenly serious expression.

Jake's tendency to catastrophise was another thing she blamed on Kenny's abrupt departure from their lives. After losing his father and doting grandparents within the space of a few months, Jake's response had been to cling to Ruby, Auntie Pearl and Griffin. Leaving him at nursery had proved a daily battle and it had taken months before Jake eventually settled. His anxiety had persisted as he grew older and, constantly fearful of bad things happening to those he loved, he would imagine the worst and then feel as despondent as if it had already occurred. Convinced that anything he grew to love would either run away or die, Jake refused to pet or even engage with Indie, despite the cat's best efforts.

'Grandma Pearl's fine,' said Ruby reassuringly, before he could get worked up. 'I took the afternoon off so I could pick you up because I've got a lovely surprise for you. Come on, let's get out of here and I'll explain everything.'

Ruby's cheery tone restored her son's smile, and she wrapped his trailing scarf around his neck and steered him away from a group of boys playing football and towards the school gates. They started down the road, but after a minute Jake stopped in his tracks and looked up at her through narrowed eyes.

'This isn't the way home. Where are we going?'

'I thought I'd treat you to a hot chocolate at the café on the high street – if you want one, that is?'

'*Cool!* Can I have mine with whipped cream?'

She ruffled his hair and grinned. 'Absolutely!'

◆ ◆ ◆

Ruby was still smiling twenty minutes later as she watched Jake peer into his half-empty mug, oblivious to the streaks of chocolate smeared liberally around his mouth. She had yet to meet anyone who tackled hot chocolate with as much focus as Jake.

'So, how was school today?' she asked, before taking a cautious sip from her cup of steaming black coffee.

'Fine,' Jake replied, his attention still on the contents of his mug. His preferred strategy was to save as much whipped cream as possible to eat by itself and after gulping down a mouthful of his drink, he tilted the mug carefully to gauge how much liquid was left under the top layer of melting cream.

'Well, that doesn't tell me very much. You had Literacy today, didn't you? What did your teacher say about the Black History Month class project?'

Jake spared her a quick glance. 'Everyone's got to choose a Black person and write about why they're inspiring.'

'Okay, that sounds interesting. Any idea who you'll choose?'

'I told Miss that I'm writing about my dad because he's very famous and he inspires lots of people.'

Ruby winced. 'We've talked about this, Jake. Making things up is wrong. You *know* how important it is to always tell the truth. Look at the trouble you got into at school last week. If you hadn't said those things about your father—'

'But everyone teases me because I'm the only one in my class who doesn't have a dad,' he said defiantly.

'You *do* have a dad. He just happens to live in a different country. He's a real person, Jake – you don't have to make up stuff.'

'I do, if I don't know anything about him,' Jake retorted, and Ruby sighed, unable to argue with his logic. Why couldn't he still be the baby she could swaddle in a shawl, hold in her arms, and nuzzle, knowing he was safe from the cruelty that came with the outside world? When Kenny first left, Jake had cried for his 'dada' for weeks until one day, as if tired of hearing his father would come home soon, he had simply stopped asking. Ruby had welcomed the reprieve from giving assurances she couldn't fulfil, and as Jake grew older, he seldom raised the subject of his absent father. Until, that is, he'd started bringing home sketches from Art Club, convinced they would impress a father he could barely remember, and making up stories about the man that grew more far-fetched by the day. The past few weeks had proved that the years of not talking about Kenny didn't mean Jake had forgotten him. But no matter how much Ruby wished it were so, Jake was no longer a baby, and her job now was to help him navigate a crisis he wasn't responsible for creating.

'Listen, buddy, I understand what it's like to be different to everyone,' she said gently. 'When I was in primary school, I was the tallest person in my class. Some of the kids made fun of me all the time and called me names like "the giraffe". So, believe me, I know what it's like to be teased constantly and how awful it makes you feel inside.'

Jake put down his mug and looked at her solemnly. 'That was really mean of them, Mum. It's not your fault that you're tall.'

Ruby nodded, surprised at how much the memory of those childish taunts still hurt. Towering over the rest of her class in junior school hadn't helped endear her to the popular boys, and even in secondary school when the boys had shot up in height, she'd always felt like a lanky giant compared to the other girls.

'I know, but sometimes good things come out of horrible situations. Do you know that me being tall was how Uncle Griffin and I became friends? We were in the same class at secondary school, and he was one of the very few boys who was taller than me. One day we had a supply teacher for one of our lessons, and when I put my hand up to answer a question, the teacher pointed at me said, "Yes, you. The big girl in the back." So then, Uncle Griffin jumped up and said, "That's really *rude*! And she's tall, not big!" He got a detention for talking back, and I waited for him after school to thank him for sticking up for me. So then he walked me back home and we became best friends after that.'

Jake returned his attention to slurping the remains of his hot chocolate, and Ruby observed the tiny frown of concentration between his brows with a pang. Her son was turning into a miniature version of Kenny, and it broke her heart that his father couldn't see how sweet and handsome his boy had grown to be.

Well, that's why we're doing this, Rubes. Get on with it.

Ruby took a deep breath and tried to keep her tone upbeat. 'So, listen, buddy, remember I said I have a surprise for you?'

31

'Mmm-hmm?' Jake murmured, spooning the thick cream left in the mug into his mouth.

'*Soo* . . . how would you feel about not going to school for a few weeks?'

His hand stilled and he looked across the table at her, his dark eyes huge in his chocolate-smudged face. 'Why? Won't they let me go to St Martin's any more? I said sorry to Oliver for hitting him, Mum. Honest!'

'No, sweetheart, it's not that,' Ruby said hastily. She should have realised Jake would go straight to the worst-case scenario, and the last thing she wanted was to ramp up his anxiety. 'You've just been saying you don't know anything about your dad, and I know that's why you keep making up these stories . . . Jake, put your drink down and look at me.'

He thumped his mug on the table, his face set into a stubborn expression that was the spitting image of Kenny's. Jake's striking resemblance to his father was a constant reminder that it would never be possible to ignore Kenny's existence, and Ruby pushed aside the unwelcome thought to focus on the task in hand.

'Jake, I understand why you've been struggling lately, and Grandma Pearl and I have been trying to work out the best way to help. We've talked about it and we both think it's time you met your father.'

Jake looked at her, puzzled. 'But you said he lives a long way away.'

'He does. After he – he, er, left here, he moved to an island in the Caribbean. It's called Sorrel Island. So, we'll be going there to find him. It's a very long journey by plane, but it will be an amazing adventure for you – for both of us, actually. I've spoken to Mr Hinton about it, and he's given me permission to take you out of school for a few weeks. Your teachers will put a learning plan together and you'll have to do schoolwork every day while we're gone so you don't fall behind.'

The last spoonful of cream in his mug was forgotten as Jake absorbed her words. In silence, he traced the handle of his teaspoon over the pattern of the wax table covering and after a few moments he asked hesitantly, 'Will Uncle Griffin come with us?'

'No, buddy, it's just you and me.'

'But I *want* him to come!' Jake pouted. 'He makes everything fun.'

Yeah, cos he's a big kid himself. Prudently keeping her thoughts to herself, Ruby picked up her napkin and reached across the table to wipe Jake's face. 'So, what do you think? You haven't seen your father since you were a little boy. Are you excited about finally meeting him?'

He jerked his head away in protest at her attempt to clean him up and stared down at the table.

'Jake?' she urged, when the silence stretched out, unnerved by his lack of reaction to such momentous news.

'But what if he *still* doesn't like me, Mum? That's why he left us, isn't it?' Jake said finally, his voice so quiet it was barely audible.

'*No!* Absolutely not!' Ruby stared at him, horrified. 'Why would you even think that?' It had never occurred to her that in the absence of any explanation for his father's disappearance, Jake would blame himself.

Jake looked up and Ruby's heart felt like it was shattering into tiny pieces at the naked pain in his eyes. Seeing her little boy look so wounded, she wouldn't have been responsible for her actions if Kenny had been within arm's reach.

Jake shrugged, as if no longer sure what to believe. He pushed his mug aside and planted his elbows on the table, his chocolate-stained face cupped between his hands. 'But if it wasn't my fault, Mum, why did he leave us?'

Ruby leaned forward to stroke his hair, and this time he didn't pull away.

'I don't know, buddy.' She sighed and blinked back the unexpected tears prickling her eyes. 'That's what we're going to Sorrel Island to find out.'

5

'You're doing *what*?' Fi's aquamarine eyes were wide in horror, her heavy eyelashes fanned out against her porcelain complexion like thick black spiders.

If the visitor's chair in Fi's office had offered enough space, Ruby would have squirmed in her seat at her boss's reaction to Ruby's – admittedly abrupt – announcement. But Fi's taste in office furnishings was much more suited to her own petite frame, forcing Ruby to face the fallout from her bombshell news head on.

'I'm really sorry, Fi, but like I said, I'm resigning,' Ruby muttered. She ducked her head to avoid the accusatory gaze following the gobsmacked response.

'Why?' Fi demanded. Her gravelly voice, the legacy of smoking twenty cigarettes a day throughout her twenties and thirties, sounded even more like ground glass than usual. 'Have you found another job? How *could* you—?'

Ruby's head jerked upwards. 'No! *Of course* I haven't found another job! Okay, that sounds stupid.' She paused to take a breath. 'What I mean is, I'm resigning because I need to take Jake away and I can't say how long we'll be gone. I'm sorry, I should have chosen my words a bit more carefully instead of just blurting it out like that. The thing is, I've used up almost all my holiday entitlement for the year and it's not fair to mess you around when I don't know when I'll be back. I can't do my job remotely and, besides, I'll be busy with Jake, so . . . Well, I don't see any other way round it. I've got enough savings to tide me over for a while and I'll just have to look for another job when we return.'

Fi slumped back into her chair and exhaled loudly. 'Bloody hell, you had me going there for a minute! I really thought you were planning to leave.'

'I *am* planning to leave.'

'No, Rubes, you are not! Now, tell me what's going on and how I can help.'

Fi's tone brooked no argument and after a moment of silent resistance, Ruby reluctantly started talking. Initially trying to keep her explanation brief, she quickly found herself blurting out everything that had taken place over the past couple of weeks.

'—and even after the incident with that kid, Oliver, nothing I say seems to be getting through to Jake. When I picked him up from his friend's house on Saturday, Archie's mum said Jake told them his dad was away training for a passenger flight to Mars. You should have seen the look of total pity on her face . . . I was *mortified*! Given the chance, I'd send Kenny to Mars in a heartbeat, but things are seriously getting out of hand. My up-until-now perfect son is getting into trouble at school and telling ridiculous lies about his father to anyone who'll listen! If I don't nip this in the bud, who knows where all this will lead?'

'So, you're going to drag the poor boy halfway around the world to meet Kenny,' Fi said flatly when Ruby paused for breath. 'Are you sure that's wise? The man hasn't bothered to be a dad to Jake for, what, *six* years? What makes you so sure that bringing them together won't make matters worse?'

'I'm not,' Ruby confessed, gripping the arms of the visitor's chair as she tried to shift into a more comfortable position. 'Seriously, Fi, would it kill you to get a decent-sized chair in here?'

Ignoring her boss's narrowed eyes, Ruby continued. 'Quite honestly, if I had my way, neither my son nor I would ever lay eyes on Kenny again. He did a truly crappy thing leaving us the way he did, but it doesn't change the fact that he's Jake's dad. I'll be right there to protect Jake if it turns out Kenny isn't responsible enough to have a relationship with his son but, Fi, if there's even a minuscule chance that meeting his father will help, then I don't have a choice. Sorrel Island is miles away but, like Auntie Pearl says, if Jake doesn't see the reality for himself, he's always going to create a fantasy version of the man.'

'So, your Auntie Pearl is obviously fine with you going off into the sunset, but what about the gorgeous Griffin? What does he have to say about this?'

Ruby frowned. 'What do you mean? There's no reason he gets to have an opinion about it.'

'*Puh-lease*,' Fi snorted. 'You two are practically joined at the hip. He surely can't be too happy at the idea of you sodding off to the other side of the world in hot pursuit of your ex?'

Ruby shook her head impatiently. 'Griff is my best mate, but that doesn't give him the right to decide what I do or don't do. Besides, he adores Jake, and I know he would want me to do whatever makes the boy happy.'

'All of which means you haven't told him yet,' Fi said, her tone distinctly sceptical. She picked up a sheet of paper from her desk and made a show of reading it, and then tossed it back on to the desk and cocked her head curiously.

'I generally try to mind my own business, but I'm going to ask anyway because it's been niggling at me for years. How come you and the gorgeous Griffin aren't' – she raised her hands in air quotes – '*together*? You've always insisted you're just friends, but have you two honestly never been an item?'

Ruby burst out laughing. 'Don't be funny! Griffin and I have been best friends since we were teenagers. Listen, that boy has never been short of girls fawning over him – which is probably why he gets through them like a hot knife through butter! Trust me, I've never felt any desire to join the list.'

'Ye-es, but you two are *so* close. Are you saying you and he never even *considered* . . . well . . . you know?'

Ruby shook her head, wondering why people found it so hard to believe it possible to have a best friend of a different sex. Fi's quizzical expression didn't budge and after a moment, Ruby sighed. 'Okay, there *was* this one time when we were about . . . fifteen, I think? I don't know what got into us – probably the cider he'd sneaked out of his mum's house – but we were hanging out together and Griff kissed me. I had braces on my teeth at the time, and he came at me out of nowhere. Our teeth clashed and— Urgh, it was awful!' Ruby giggled at the memory. 'We were both so appalled we agreed on the spot that it would *never* happen again.'

'So, you're strictly friends?'

'Indeed, we are,' Ruby agreed cheerfully. 'I know some people find it weird – even Kenny struggled to get his head around it at times. I think it's partly why they never got on. Of course, it didn't help that Griff thought I'd rushed into things with Kenny, and didn't hold back from telling me so. That time was probably the closest Griffin and I ever got to falling out.'

Fi stared at her thoughtfully. 'You know, Rubes, I've never been able to get my head around why Kenny just disappeared.'

'Yeah, well, that makes two of us. It just goes to show how badly you can misjudge someone.'

'So, as far as you could tell, things were okay between the two of you? It's just so weird how one minute he was like this loving partner and proud dad, and then the next minute . . . *poof!* In my experience – and that includes both my marriages – when relationships fall apart, there's usually been heaps of arguments, slammed doors, and chilled silences. You and Kenny weren't secretly at each other's throats behind closed doors, were you?'

Ruby shifted uncomfortably, thrown by the question. She hated thinking about Kenny. Dredging up a past she couldn't do anything to change had always felt like a waste of time, and analysing her failed relationship was something she generally avoided. But Fi was clearly not going to drop it, and it was hard to tell her to mind her own business only minutes after resigning and leaving her in the lurch.

'No, of course we weren't. I actually thought things were pretty good between us. We wound each other up at times, but, yeah, we were – well, *I* was – happy. He worked hard and loved partying and having a good time. Coming here from Trinidad, he had a big network of friends, and I think he knew every Caribbean hotspot in London. Like any couple, we had our differences. Kenny was way more touchy-feely and romantic than me and he could get possessive – which was annoying – but I'd always made it clear I would never drop my friends just because he and I were together.'

'*All* your friends or just one in particular?' Fi murmured, smoothing her bouffant blonde curls and fixing Ruby with a shrewd stare.

'Can we get back to the reason I'm here,' Ruby said pointedly. 'I've just handed in my resignation, so can we please focus on how we're going to find my replacement?'

Fi leaned back in her chair and folded her arms. 'You are *not* resigning, and that's that! When are you planning on taking this crazy trip?'

'As soon as possible. I can't risk Jake getting into more trouble. Besides, if I leave it too long, I'll bottle it cos, truth be told, I really can't bear the thought of seeing Kenny again.'

'Fine. You can take an unpaid sabbatical for as long as you need, and we'll work out how to cover your role while you're gone. If it means bringing in a temp, then so be it.'

Seeing Ruby's troubled expression, Fi's voice softened. 'Rubes, you've been by my side every day since I started this business, and no-one's worked harder than you to make it a success. You're not just my office manager, you are family, and I can't do without you. So go off and do whatever you need to do for Jake, and we'll hold the fort while you're gone.'

Ruby sat quietly as the memories stirred by Fi's impassioned words came flooding back. As a single mother facing redundancy from a job that she'd hated and a supervisor she hated even more, Ruby had struggled to find a role that offered enough flexibility to cater to the demands of a clingy two-year-old. In hiring Ruby to join her fledgling company, Fi had thrown her friend a lifeline in more ways than one. Slogging alongside Fi to build her dream business from an idea into a successful communications company had allowed Ruby to literally work her way through the pain of Kenny's disappearance and the loss of her parents. Fi, for her part, was only too grateful for the long hours Ruby put in to work and always made a point of waving Ruby off to Jake's special school assemblies, sports days, and other occasions with a blithe 'Just take the time, for goodness' sake!' Although Ruby had never felt taken for granted, this was the first time that Fi, who was possibly even less sentimental than Ruby, had been so open about how much she valued her.

'I honestly don't know what to say,' Ruby admitted. Although Jake would always come first, she had been dreading this conversation with Fi and the reality of walking away from a job she loved with a team of people – many of whom she had hired – who were not only colleagues, but friends.

Fi's scarlet-tinted lips widened into a wry smile. 'I mean it, Rubes. You've been there for me through all my disasters, so it's only fair I do the same for you.'

Ruby hauled herself out of the chair. 'I'd give you a massive hug, but I'm worried I'd break you.'

'Ha-ha, very funny. I wish you would stop putting yourself down all the time. You are tall, not a bloody monster!'

'Says the tiny blonde bombshell who has every man she meets dying to tuck her into his jacket pocket,' Ruby scoffed.

'Whatever,' Fi muttered. 'Oh, and can you contact a couple of the recruiters we use and tell them we need a temporary office manager as soon as?'

'Okay, boss.' Ruby nodded. She walked towards the door and hesitated before turning back. 'You know, you *could* give Priya a chance at doing my job and just get someone else in to help her with the admin.'

'Priya?' Fi looked doubtful. 'I dunno, Rubes. I'd rather have someone I can have a go at without feeling guilty. Just the idea of Priya giving me wounded looks with those huge brown eyes of hers . . .' She tailed off with a shudder. 'Urgh! It would be like shouting at Bambi. Besides, is she tough enough to handle the account managers? I need someone who can keep them in check and make sure they don't pad their expenses. They know better than to give you grief—'

'That's because they're terrified of me,' Ruby interjected with a wicked smile. 'Don't underestimate the power of towering over every one of them.'

Fi tutted impatiently. 'There you go again! No, don't give me that look – *that's* what intimidates people, not your height. I don't scare easily, as both my ex-husbands can attest, but even I get a teensy bit terrified of that frown.'

Ruby's mouth dropped open in outrage. 'I can't believe you just said that! Do you *know* how awful a stereotype it is when you call a Black woman intimidating?'

'Noelle's Black and she's never scared me,' Fi said airily. 'This isn't about horrible stereotypes, it's about *you* and how you'd rather scowl at people than smile in case anyone has the audacity to think you're a walkover. It's got nothing to do with being Black and everything to do with the fact you don't trust anyone.'

Ruby's indignation was replaced by shock. *Where the hell did that come from?* Momentarily stunned into silence, she opened the door. Then, she shut it again.

'Fi, I *do* trust people . . .' Her voice tailed off as she heard herself sound less than convincing.

'Really? Let's see. When did you last go on a date, then? No, don't bother trying to rack your brains because it was two years ago, and the reason I know is because I'm the one who set it up. I'll also remind you that you blocked the poor bloke on your phone the very next day.'

Ruby pulled a face. 'Yeah, well, that's because I hadn't wanted to go out with him in the first place. Let me remind *you* that not only did you threaten to sack me if I didn't go, you also conveniently omitted to tell me he was only five foot six.'

'Well, Paul's a lovely man – as you'd have found out if you'd given him half a chance. But, no, you won't allow yourself to trust anyone and be happy.'

'Happiness is overrated,' Ruby said breezily. 'Besides, as hard as it is for you to believe, I don't need a man to complete me or any of that romantic guff people seem to think is real life. I've got my incredible son, a job I love, and friends who – when they're not interfering in my life – are absolutely brilliant, thank you very much.'

'If you say so,' was Fi's sardonic response. 'By the way, don't go getting any funny ideas about leaving me while you're out in the tropics. I'd like us to have a chat about promoting you when you get back. With our overseas business expanding so quickly, I want to move marketing out from sales and I'm going to need someone to run the team. Marketing has always been your passion and you've been involved in loads of our campaigns – not to mention you know the company and our services inside out. It would mean working closely with sales, and with Nick and the tech team, and you'd have to beef up your digital skills, but I think you'd be perfect for the role. Think about it while you're away, will you? It would mean a good bump in salary.'

Ruby grinned. 'Sounds brilliant. Bloody hell, I should resign more often!'

Fi looked pointedly at her watch and then tapped on her keyboard with a perfectly manicured finger. 'I'll talk to Priya, but I still want you to brief a couple of recruiters in case I'm not convinced.'

This time, however, Ruby was determined not to let Fi have the last word. 'Priya will do a great job of managing the office, and you should have faith in her. It's only because she looks like a puff of wind would blow her away that no-one realises the girl is as tough as old boots.'

'No surprise you two get on so well, then,' Fi muttered.

Ruby's expression didn't shift, and Fi was the first to drop her gaze. 'Fine. Send her in and I'll have a chat with her. If, by some miracle, Priya does as good a job as you say she can, I'll consider letting her take over as office manager when you come back. But, Ruby, if I'm willing to give her a chance, then maybe it's time to take your own advice and give others a chance. You're too young and too bloody gorgeous to shut down any chance of love. I know what Kenny did to you was unforgiveable and I totally get how that's put you off relationships, but not every man is going to be like *him*.'

Ruby stared at her wordlessly, and Fi pulled her laptop closer and peered at the screen. Reaching for her glasses, she perched them on her nose and, without glancing up from her computer, added crisply, 'You can close the door on your way out.'

6

Ruby shivered and pulled her coat tightly around her to ward off the cold salty wind gusting in from the sea. Flocks of seagulls circled overhead; their high-pitched cries caught up in the sound of waves crashing on to the stretch of deserted beach. Although the sky was an ominous dark grey with heavy rolling clouds, the rain forecast for the afternoon had held off so far.

Ruby ducked her head to avoid the icy wind and fought to keep her balance as she struggled over the wet pebbles in her thin-soled high-heeled boots. Persuading Griffin to come with her to Brighton beach in this weather now seemed a less than clever idea.

She stopped to catch her breath and a strong gust of wind sent her long braids swirling around her. Pushing her hair back, she glanced across to where Griffin was crouched over the pebbles a few metres away and watched as he picked out a stone and weighed it in his palm before standing and spinning it into the waves in a single fluid movement. The pebble sliced into the water with barely a hint of foam, and when Griffin turned around and pumped his fist in triumph, Ruby laughed, thankful Jake wasn't with them. In the interminable battles between Jake and his godfather as to who could spin pebbles with the least amount of foam, she was invariably dragged in as referee.

Thinking of Jake reminded Ruby of why she was standing on a freezing-cold beach in October. Having lost his own father at a young age, Griffin had always despised Kenny for choosing to leave Jake fatherless and, despite what she'd said to Fi, Ruby *had* feared Griffin would talk her out of travelling to Sorrel Island to track down Kenny. But now, with Mr Hinton's blessing and a study plan in place for Jake for at least the next month, there was nothing Griffin could say to change her mind, and she couldn't justify keeping her best friend in the dark any longer. With their flights booked and confirmed, she and Jake were leaving in less than a week, and Ruby was running out of time to break the news.

'Hey! Earth calling!'

Lost in thought, Ruby hadn't registered Griffin walking towards her until he was within reach.

He knitted his brow at her obvious confusion, and she couldn't help noting how even a frown couldn't detract from his almost perfect features. There was really no mystery as to why so many women found Griffin irresistible. His hazel eyes were striking against his light brown complexion and the square jaw and razor-sharp cheekbones wouldn't have been out of place on a magazine cover. The curly black mop of his teenage years was now closely cropped waves, while his youthful lankiness had – courtesy of intense gym sessions and a black belt in Taekwondo he'd picked up along the way – morphed into broad shoulders and a muscular physique that his zipped-up padded jacket couldn't conceal.

'Sorry, I was miles away,' Ruby said. 'Can we get out of this wind? It's so cold my lips have gone numb! I wore my thickest leggings but it's still bloody freezing out here.'

She pushed back her errant braids and looked around for shelter, but all she could see was a row of brightly coloured beach huts, all of which were padlocked.

45

'There's a bench over there – next to the blue hut.' Griffin pointed to the one furthest away and started walking towards it. After a few paces, he turned to watch Ruby plodding slowly behind and, with an exasperated shake of his head, he retraced his steps and extended a hand.

'Come on, slowcoach. I don't know what you were thinking, wearing heels to the beach.'

'I *always* wear heels,' Ruby retorted breathlessly, grabbing his hand, and puffing as she tried to keep up with his long strides. Even in her heels, Griffin was almost three inches taller. 'They make me feel good and the extra inches come in handy for staring down any idiots that get in my way.'

'Whatever,' he laughed, tugging her along until they reached the bench. Ruby threw herself on to it and stretched her legs out in front of her to relieve her aching calves while she caught her breath. The beach hut provided a barrier against the strength of the wind, and for a few minutes they sat in silence, watching a flock of screeching seagulls fly in formation along the shoreline.

'Rubes, what's this about?' Griffin asked quietly. 'I know you didn't make me come out here in this weather for a fun beach trip, so I'm guessing it's something serious.'

The feeling had returned to her frozen face and Ruby gnawed on the inside of her lip and stared at the scuffed toes of her leather boots while she tried to find the right words. Now the deed was done, she sorely regretted not having said anything sooner. They had vowed never to keep secrets from each other, and Griff would rightly be furious with her for keeping such a momentous decision from him.

Oh, just tell him, Rubes!

Griffin nudged her gently in the ribs. 'Come on, what's up? You've been acting weird for the past couple of weeks, and you've had a face on you since we set foot on the train. You know you can tell me anything. Are you sick? Is that it?'

He sounded matter of fact but when she turned to face him, she saw the fear lurking in his eyes and mentally kicked herself. Griffin wasn't stupid, and of course he would have known something was wrong when she suggested a trip to the beach without Jake on an arctic Sunday afternoon. While the seaside was their happy place, she should have remembered the beach also held memories beyond their day trips with Jake.

The beach was where Griffin had brought her on the day Kenny left, hoping she would let out the emotions frozen inside her from the moment she'd read the letter lying on the kitchen table and realised she and Jake were now on their own. It was also where, fifteen years ago and on the day of his mother's funeral, Ruby had brought Griffin and watched with her heart in her mouth as he finally broke down. Emerging from the dry-eyed shell of grief he had crawled into since Marilyn's death from cancer, it was on this same stretch of beach where Griffin, screaming into the wind before collapsing into helpless sobs, had finally released the pain of losing the woman who had been both mother and father to him for most of his life.

Recalling that moment, Ruby inhaled sharply and looked him squarely in the eye. 'No, Griff, I'm absolutely fine. I promise.'

'Then, what? Is it Auntie Pearl or . . . not – not Jake?' He didn't hide his alarm and Ruby placed a reassuring hand on his arm.

'No! Well, yes . . . but it's not anything bad,' she added quickly. Wasting no more time, she recounted everything that had happened over the three weeks since the meeting in Mr Hinton's study. Giving the occasional nod, Griffin listened without interruption, and when Ruby eventually ground to a halt, he stared straight ahead without speaking.

'I'm really sorry I didn't tell you what was going on at the time,' she said after the silence had stretched into minutes. 'Don't be angry with me, it's just—' She broke off and raised her hands helplessly. '*Say* something, Griff! It's been a really tough decision to take Jake out of school and I'm dreading the prospect of going in search of Kenny.'

Griffin looked at her thoughtfully for a moment and then jumped to his feet. 'Come on, it's too cold out here to think. Let's go to the diner. I'm starving, and we can talk properly inside.'

◆ ◆ ◆

Half an hour later and minutes before the threatened rain started pelting down, they were sitting across from each other in a booth in Jake's favourite restaurant. The diner, a few minutes from the beach, was done up in 1950s style with framed black-and-white vintage posters of pop stars on the walls and a red-and-silver jukebox pumping out a steady stream of rock'n'roll. The steamed-up windows blocked out the dreary weather, while the warmth of the diner provided welcome relief from the bitingly cold wind. Although it was well past lunchtime, the place was humming, and waiting staff moved swiftly between tables to deposit heaped platters of sizzling steaks, French fries, onion rings, and an impressive variety of stacked burgers.

'So, are you doing this for Jake or for yourself?' Griffin asked, taking a huge bite of his double cheeseburger. He chewed vigorously and tossed back a couple of fries for good measure.

Ruby watched him, torn between fascination and horror. 'How do you fit so much food into your mouth at one time?'

Griffin swallowed hard and took a long sip from the pint glass of lager next to his plate before answering. 'Don't change the subject. Do you want to find Kenny for Jake or for you?'

Ruby speared a forkful of the crispy chicken salad she had ordered and then dropped her fork back on to the plate. 'Okay, I'd be lying if I said I didn't wonder at the time why Kenny just upped and left, but it was too painful to dwell on. I thought I'd put it all behind me until this business with Jake started. Now—' She broke off with a shrug. 'This *is* about my son, but maybe it's also a bit about me.'

She chewed slowly as she watched Griffin plough through the pile of French fries on his plate and then said pensively, 'Fi had a go at me at work not too long ago. She said I've given up on love because I don't trust anyone, and maybe she's got a point – though there's no way I'm telling *her* that. But the truth is I haven't had a relationship with anyone since Kenny, and that can't be right.'

Griffin's hands stilled over his plate. 'You've always said you're happy as you are. I had no idea that's how you felt.' He hesitated. 'Maybe you just haven't found the right person yet?'

'At this rate, I don't think I ever will,' she said wryly. 'Fi reckons I'm way too fussy, but you know I don't do short guys and it's not like there's a queue of six-foot-plus men waiting out there to take me on – even if I wanted them to.'

Ruby jabbed distractedly at a piece of lettuce on her plate. 'Can I tell you something that's been nagging at me ever since Fi said that? I feel like if I don't find out what drove Kenny away, I'll never properly move on. Everything that's happened with Jake is also making me realise how – I don't know . . . how *stuck* I've become. It's like being in emotional limbo, because until I know what went wrong with Kenny, I can't trust myself not to mess up another relationship. I mean, if I couldn't even *see* that things were so bad between us that he had to leave—'

She paused as she took in Griffin's expression and tilted her head. 'What's that look for?'

'What look?' He reached for the half-empty bottle of ketchup on the table and poured it liberally over what was left of the chips.

'I don't know . . . you looked funny for a second. Is there something you're not telling me?'

Griffin studied her for a long moment and then shook his head. 'No, of course not.'

Ruby's eyes narrowed into a laser stare. '*Griff?* No secrets, remember?'

'No secrets,' he echoed with a small smile. 'Although you can talk after keeping so many yourself. Why didn't you just tell me what you were planning?'

'I don't know,' Ruby admitted with a sigh. 'I feel like I'm doing the right thing, but it doesn't stop me from going back and forth in my mind about it. I suppose I was worried you would think it was a crazy idea, which would have given me an excuse not to go, which wouldn't be fair on Jake, and . . .' She tailed off with a grimace.

Griffin put down his fork and leaned back against the padded, red faux-leather upholstery. 'Rubes, if you've been putting your life on hold all these years because of Kenny, then it's not fair on you either. Auntie Pearl's right: it's time you found out what happened with Kenny.'

He took a long sip of his beer and put the glass down with a decisive thump. 'Who knows, the truth might set everyone free.'

Before Ruby could respond, their waitress, a cheery petite blonde with a perky high ponytail, appeared at their table and pulled a notebook from the pocket of her black-and-white checked apron. 'Can I get you two lovebirds anything else to eat?'

Although the question appeared to be directed at them both, the girl's eyes were firmly fixed on Griffin.

'I'd love another order of chips, er . . .' Griffin's eyes zeroed in on the waitress's name badge. 'Suzie, right? Oh, and' – he nodded in Ruby's direction and then winked – 'me and her? Strictly friends.'

Suzie blushed and tossed her ponytail before giving Griffin a smile that made it clear there was more on offer than was on the menu. Ruby concentrated on her chicken salad, totally unbothered by the silliness of girls who threw themselves at her flirtatious friend at every opportunity.

'You're going to need more than a couple of hours in the gym to get rid of the amount of food you're getting through here,' she remarked pointedly when the waitress moved away.

'I'm sure I can find a more interesting way to burn off the calories.' He flashed a wicked grin and dredged the few remaining chips in the pool of ketchup on his plate before devouring them and wiping his fingers on a paper napkin. 'So, what did Kenny say when you told him you were coming?'

'I haven't told him yet. At least, not directly.'

'Hold on, isn't that a bit risky? How do you even know he's still there?'

'Do me a favour, I'm not *that* daft,' Ruby said, trying not to sound defensive. She knew she had to speak to Kenny, but she was still struggling with the idea and didn't need reminding.

'First of all, he promised he'd let me know if he ever left Sorrel Island, but since he's proved himself to be a lying snake, I searched him up online before I started making any plans. It turns out he's got some type of boating business out there, and he seems to be doing okay if the company website's anything to go by. And before you say you can't trust what's on the internet, I rang the number on the contact page and asked to speak to him.'

Griffin raised an eyebrow and Ruby dropped her gaze. 'Okay, so I lost my nerve and hung up before he came on the line, but, yes, he's definitely still there. I tried again a bit later, but it went to answerphone, so I left a message for him and said I'd be in touch once we arrived on the island.'

'Fair enough, but what about the plane tickets and stuff? Do you need any money for—?'

'I'm good, thanks,' Ruby cut in. 'I have enough in my savings to take care of flights and a hotel. There wasn't much information on the internet about accommodation on the island, but it's not exactly a massive tourist destination so I can't imagine it'll cost a fortune to find somewhere clean and safe for a few weeks.'

'Rubes, you know you only need to ask if—'

She cut him off again. 'Look, maybe I'm not a wealthy playboy like someone I could mention, but I'm perfectly capable of taking care of myself and Jake.'

Griffin winced. 'I hate it when you call me that.'

'Well, what else do you call someone who insists on doing nothing with their money and their life – except messing women around?'

She looked meaningfully at the waitress, who, having left the order of chips on their table, was openly ogling Griffin from behind the bar.

'I've told you a hundred times that I'm sorry about Shirlee coming over to yours,' Griffin protested, his face the picture of injured innocence. 'I even went round to apologise to Auntie Pearl.'

'Did you? She didn't mention it. What did she say?'

'What do *you* think?' Griffin pursed his lips into a rueful grimace. 'After I'd said my piece, she gave me that disappointed look I swear she saves especially for me and then launched into "Now you know I'm not one to say I told you so, but . . ."'

Ruby snorted with laughter, and Griffin gave a reluctant chuckle. 'Yeah, well, you can imagine the rest. Basically, she gave me a full-blown lecture on why I should be settling down and making babies instead of sowing my wild oats like there's a famine on the way.'

'That's Auntie Pearl for you,' Ruby giggled. 'She's got a point, though. We're in our thirties now, and I'm sorry, but you're still basically drifting through life.' She ignored Griffin's scowl. 'You know what I mean – it's not like you go into an office every day like the rest of us. Playing occasional gigs with a band and jetting off here and there at a moment's notice doesn't exactly scream "focused adult".' She crooked her fingers in the air to make her point. 'Seriously, Griff, just because you don't need the money shouldn't stop you having a purpose in life.'

'Maybe you and Jake are my purpose,' he said lightly.

Ruby shook her head in exasperation and reached for a chip from his plate. 'Don't use us as an excuse. You need to find something that makes you feel good about yourself. You know your mum would—'

Griffin held up a hand to cut her off. 'Yeah, okay, you don't need to remind me that Mum would be pissed off at me. Trust me, I already feel like crap, knowing I don't have a clue how to make good use of the money.'

'Well, you love helping people and you're really passionate about music, so maybe you could think of something worthwhile that brings it all together. You can't coast along for ever jumping from one Shirley – sorry, Shir*lee* – to another.' Ruby smiled to cushion the impact of her words. 'Don't you get tired of the drama?'

He grimaced. 'Trust me, I don't go looking for it. These women are all *so* sweet – until they turn on me! You *know* me, I'm always upfront about not looking to settle down, and I honestly don't lead anyone on. But then after a few weeks, it's like they forget the ground rules—'

'Ground rules . . . *Really?*' Ruby glared at him with exasperation. 'These are people, Griffin, not a football game! I don't know what you do to these poor women to turn their heads so badly, but whatever it is, it's on you! So, in future, just leave me out of it.'

'It wasn't my fault Shirlee decided to come over to yours!' he objected.

'Fine. Then what about the time you begged me to come over and talk down that girl who was threatening to cut all the sleeves off your suit jackets because you cared more about your clothes than about her?'

When he struggled to produce a response, Ruby gave a satisfied 'Ha!' followed by, 'You need to sort your life out, my friend. Jake looks up to you, and I don't want him led astray by your dodgy lifestyle choices.'

'Don't stress, I'll figure it out. Besides, what else would you do with your life if you didn't have me to worry about?' He leaned forward and cuffed her gently under the chin, his eyes alight with mischief.

'Quite a lot, probably,' said Ruby dryly.

'Yeah, and maybe that's what I'm afraid of,' he laughed, gesturing to the waitress to bring their bill.

7

With the bar packed three people deep, it was hard to tell if Priya was any closer to placing their order. Although Ruby was tempted to help her assistant get in the next round of drinks, with so many after-hours City workers circling and ready to pounce on an empty chair, she didn't dare leave her seat.

'Relax, Rubes, she'll be fine. If, as you say, Priya can handle our bolshie account managers, then she's not going to be fazed by a few leery blokes at the bar.'

Ruby turned to argue with Fi and then thought better of it. Behaving like a protective mother hen wasn't the best way to instil her boss with confidence in Priya's people management skills.

'You're looking rather hot for a casual after-work drink,' Ruby observed. 'I don't remember seeing you in that dress in the office.'

The low-cut, tight-fitting wrap dress emphasised Fi's generous bust and tiny waist, and she patted the blonde curls piled high on to her head with a gratified smirk. 'Why on earth would I waste this on my staff? I always have a couple of outfits in the office in case I don't have time to go home and change before going out in the evening. Tut all you want, but it never hurts to look your best. Like I always say, if you've got it—'

'Well, you're definitely flaunting your puppies in that dress,' Ruby said darkly. 'Let's hope it doesn't land you in trouble.' She drained the rest of her vodka and lemonade and turned to scour the bar area again. 'I know it's busy tonight, but how long does it take to get a few drinks?'

'Go easy there, friend,' Fi murmured, sipping delicately on the straw sticking out of her cocktail. 'Just remember I'm not carrying you home tonight.'

'You're hardly big enough to carry a cat, let alone me,' Ruby scoffed. 'Oh, good, here she is!'

Clutching three brimming glasses, Priya nudged her chair out from under the table with her knee and carefully set the drinks down. Ruby removed the coats piled on to Priya's chair and her assistant sank on to the seat and exhaled loudly. 'I hope these last longer than the last round. It's like a circus up there.'

'You took long enough,' Fi remarked. 'We were beginning to wonder if you'd been kidnapped.'

Priya took a sip of her drink and shook her head, crinkling her nose in irritation. 'Some posh-sounding idiot kept trying to push in front of me and I had to stick my elbow in his beer gut to get my order in first.'

Ruby shot Fi a knowing glance and turned back to Priya. 'Okay, now you're back, can you watch my chair while I dash to the loo, please? If anyone tries to nick it, do your elbow trick again – or get Fi to bite them on the ankles if you need back-up.'

'*Oi!*' Fi spluttered indignantly, almost spitting out her drink.

With a grin, Ruby picked up her handbag and made her way through the crowded wine bar in search of the toilets. After a ten-minute wait to use one of two small cubicles, she washed her hands, crouching to use the tiny square of mirror provided to smooth back her hair and touch up her lip gloss. When she emerged, the wine bar looked even busier, and she strode across the room with her freshly braided hair swinging freely down to her waist. Conscious of several pairs of eyes following her, she tried to shrug off the nagging feeling of never quite belonging. While she accepted that a six-foot-tall Black woman in black jeans, a black leather jacket and dizzyingly high-heeled boots would probably stand out in a wine bar in the heart of the financial district, it would also have been nice to just occasionally blend in with the crowd.

'I wish I had your legs,' Priya said enviously as Ruby walked up to their table. She shook back her long dark hair with a pout. 'Mine are way too skinny to look sexy in tight jeans, and I'd probably break my neck if I wore heels like yours.'

'I definitely wouldn't advise it, love,' Fi cautioned, taking a long sip of the blue liquid in her glass. 'Ruby's been wearing dominatrix heels for years, and she can probably turn cartwheels in those. Makes me feel like a bleeding munchkin, standing next to her!'

'You are kidding me, right?' Ruby quipped, settling back into her seat. 'If I were a curvy little pocket Venus like you, I'd be on my knees thanking every god I'd ever heard of.'

Priya shook her head. 'I can't imagine you as petite, Ruby. You're such a big, you know—'

'—girl?' Ruby interrupted.

Priya frowned. 'No, I was going to say such a big *personality*. You're amazing!' She paused. 'A bit stern, sometimes, but still amazing.'

Ruby gave a non-committal shrug. Had the praise come from anyone else, she might have been more impressed, but in Priya's world anyone who wasn't a tosser – their account managers being her point of reference – was amazing.

'Stern suits me just fine. Now can we please stop dissecting me and talk about something else?'

She had barely finished speaking when a harried-looking waiter came up to their table and set down glasses and an ice bucket containing a bottle and a smattering of ice cubes.

'Sorry to interrupt, ladies, but the gentleman over there sent over this bottle of wine with his compliments.'

He nodded in the direction of an attractive dark-haired man in a suit sitting by himself a few tables away and, as one, the three women turned to stare at the man, who returned their scrutiny with a friendly smile.

'Blimey, Fi,' said Ruby, arching an eyebrow. 'That's impressive! I warned you about that dress, didn't I?'

'Actually, miss, the gentleman said to bring the wine to you,' the waiter said, looking directly at Ruby.

Ruby's eyes widened, and she looked so shocked that Fi and Priya dissolved into hysterical giggles. Without so much as a second glance at the man in the suit, Ruby scowled at the waiter and shook her head. 'Take it away, please, and tell him I can get my own drinks.'

'*Ruby!*' Fi and Priya protested in unison.

'Hold on just a sec, love, and put that back down, please,' Fi demanded, motioning to the waiter, who had picked up the bucket as instructed. He glanced at Ruby's set expression and hesitated before setting it down again.

'Now listen here, Rubes,' Fi hissed, 'the man is not proposing marriage, for God's sake! It's just a drink!'

'It's never just a drink,' said Ruby grimly. 'That's how it starts, and if you don't nip this kind of thing in the bud, before you know it, they're reeling you in like a fish and setting you up for a world of pain.' She glowered at the waiter and her voice brooked no argument. 'Like I said, tell him thanks, but no thanks.'

The waiter's gaze moved from Ruby's stubborn expression to Fi's exasperated one and then back to Ruby's. With a shrug, he picked up the ice bucket and walked away.

Fi sighed. 'You really *do* need to go away and sort your head out. That bloke is a real looker and he's probably loaded if the label on the wine he ordered is anything to go by.'

Ruby picked up her drink without comment and it was left to Priya to break the awkward silence. 'We're really going to miss you while you're away, Rubes. But then you're going to be on a lovely island in the sun! I'm sure you'll have an amazing time.'

Ruby took a sip of her drink and pulled a face. 'I seriously doubt it. It's not like I'm going on a proper holiday now, is it?'

Before Priya could reply, Griffin appeared out of the crowd and strolled over to their table. Dressed in a grey suit with a white shirt open at the neck, his hazel eyes twinkled in merriment.

'Hello, ladies! Sorry I'm late for the leaving drinks, but my meeting overran.' He raised an eyebrow at the empty glasses on the table. 'Although, from the looks of things, you've started without me.'

'She's *not* leaving,' Fi growled. 'We're just wishing her *bon voyage* for her extended – er . . . trip.' Her face cleared, and she beamed and opened her arms wide. 'Come here and give me a kiss, you handsome devil! It's been far too long.'

Griffin chuckled and bent to kiss the proffered cheek, following suit with Ruby, and then a fiercely blushing Priya.

Ruby cast her eye around the packed wine bar and looked up in apology. 'I'm really sorry, Griff. We reserved this table, but it was so busy when we got here that we were lucky the chairs hadn't been nicked . . .' She tailed off and looked around again. 'I can't see a spare chair anywhere.'

Griffin scanned the room quickly and then walked over to a booth where a few women were clustered around a table. While Ruby couldn't make out Griffin's words over the hubbub in the bar, she didn't miss the flirtatious smile he flashed at the group. After a couple of minutes of conversation, the woman sitting on a chair at the end of the table stood up. Her friends shuffled together to make space for her on the cushioned banquette and, giggling helplessly, she gestured to Griffin to take the chair she'd just vacated.

Griffin walked back with his newly acquired chair and placed it next to Fi, giving her a cheeky wink as he sat down. He unbuttoned his suit jacket and crossed his legs, resting an ankle on his knee and looking supremely relaxed.

Fi's blue eyes were alight with laughter. 'You're such a charmer! How the hell did you manage that, then?'

'He is so annoying,' Ruby huffed. 'I bet that woman wouldn't have offered me her chair if I'd begged on bended knee.'

'Let's just say I made her an offer she couldn't refuse,' Griffin said, dropping his voice to sound sinister. When Ruby simply looked sceptical, he reverted to his normal tones. 'Okay, I might have mentioned that I suffer terribly with a dodgy back and that standing for too long could cause me irreparable damage.'

'And she actually fell for that load of rubbish?' Ruby snorted.

'Well, that and the bottle of champagne I offered in exchange for the chair.' He grinned, and then, gesturing to a passing waiter, mouthed some instructions in his ear with a nod towards the women at the table. Pulling out his wallet, he slipped a couple of notes into the waiter's hand, adding, 'And keep the change.'

'Do you really have back problems, Griffin?' Fi asked curiously. 'You know I trained as a masseuse before setting up the business.'

'Truthfully, my back is fine, but please don't let that stop you from giving me a massage any time you feel like it,' he teased.

Fi roared with laughter and slapped his shoulder. 'If I was twenty years younger, you might have tempted me to consider marriage number three.'

Griffin snorted and Ruby looked from one to the other, unable to decide which of them was worse. 'Fi, if you were ever daft enough to marry him, I'd lay bets on you being back in the divorce courts within six months.'

'As you can see, ladies,' Griffin said sorrowfully, 'Rubes has absolutely no faith in me when it comes to women.'

'Can you blame me? I'm only pointing out what half the female population of London has learned the hard way.'

Priya had scarcely taken her eyes off Griffin since his appearance, and two strong cocktails had loosened her tongue. Without warning, she burst out, 'Oh my God, Ruby, your boyfriend is *soo* amazing!'

'I don't know how many times I have to tell you he is *not* my boyfriend!' Ruby said testily.

'Can't say I blame you, Priya, love,' Fi remarked. 'I've been watching The Ruby and Griffin Show for years, and quite frankly they make it awfully hard for us to tell the difference.'

Ruby looked visibly irritated, while Griffin's lips twitched in amusement. After a moment of silence he said, 'I'm sensing this might be a good time to get another round in. What's everyone drinking?'

After taking their orders, he twinkled at Priya. 'And now we've established that I'm blissfully single, why don't you come and, er, give me a hand with the drinks?'

Blushing a deep crimson beneath her dusky complexion, Priya didn't need to be asked twice. Jumping out of her chair, she led the way to the bar, elbowing aside anyone in her way.

The moment they were out of earshot, Ruby groaned. 'He'd better not mess her around. She's a great employee, and I'd like to keep her.'

'Ah, give it a rest. Priya's a big girl.' Fi swallowed the last drops in her glass and delicately licked the corners of her lips. Following Ruby's gaze to where Griffin and Priya stood chatting in the queue for drinks, Fi's eyes crinkled in amusement.

'You always insist Griffin's just a friend, so why do you even care what he does?' She cackled wickedly. 'Or who?'

Ruby shrugged and turned away from the couple at the bar. 'I don't. What Griffin gets up to doesn't matter to me in the slightest.'

Fi's grin widened, and she placed her empty glass on the table with a murmured, 'If you say so, Ruby.'

PART TWO

Paradise

8

The small plane circled the island below and then dipped sharply, sending Ruby's clenched stomach muscles into spasm. *What the hell possessed me to do this?* Taking deep breaths, she gripped the arm of her seat and tried not to imagine the aircraft plummeting nose first into the dark green forests visible through the windows. The first leg of their journey on the modern long-haul commercial jet from London to Jamaica had been fine, notwithstanding the occasional patch of turbulence. It was only when she spotted the small plane taking them from Montego Bay to Sorrel Island that Ruby's nerves had kicked in, intensified by the restricted leg room on the plane and seats scarcely bigger than those in Fi's office.

Jake, on the other hand, had spent most of the almost two-hour flight with his nose glued to the window. Bubbling with excitement, he would have leaped from his seat when the captain announced they were twenty minutes from landing if he hadn't been restrained by his seatbelt.

'Mum, *look*! There's Sorrel Island! It's shaped just like a heart – isn't that so *cool*?' His high-pitched voice carried above the sound of the engines, and as Ruby glanced around the cabin to check he wasn't disturbing the other passengers, her eyes met those of an elderly Black woman sitting across the aisle. Something about the woman's smile reminded her of Auntie Pearl, and Ruby felt a pang of sadness at the thought of not seeing her beloved aunt for the next couple of weeks – or longer, depending on how things went with Kenny.

With their destination literally in sight, Ruby's apprehension at how Kenny would react to the appearance of his ex-girlfriend and their son was increasing by the minute. Griffin and Fi had been right to question the wisdom of just showing up on Sorrel Island with Jake, she thought, mentally kicking herself for losing her nerve and hanging up the phone after calling Kenny's workplace. On one hand, the fact he hadn't been in touch to tell her not to come was reassuring, in so far as she knew Jake wouldn't be rejected by his father. But, on the other hand, if she hadn't bottled it, she would at least have come better prepared. Leaving the message on his office phone would have given Kenny time to prep whoever needed to know – for all she knew, the man was happily married with a family who knew nothing about his past – but it didn't give *her* any information about his circumstances to help her deal with what was undoubtedly going to be a very awkward reunion.

Momentarily distracted by the unnerving sensation of the aircraft rapidly losing altitude, Ruby gripped the seat rest between her and Jake so tightly that her knuckles turned white. When the plane righted itself, she slowly released the breath trapped in her chest and reminded herself she wasn't the one in the wrong. If Kenny hadn't walked out on them, Jake wouldn't be going through a crisis, and she wouldn't be on a plane that looked more suited to spraying crops in a field than carrying passengers.

The captain's voice announcing their imminent landing was barely audible above the roar of the plane's engines, and Ruby reached for Jake's hand, more for her own reassurance than his. Glancing at his mother's fixed expression, Jake gave her a sweet smile before returning his attention to the thick forests and sandy beaches coming into sharp focus.

The plane swooped ever lower before finally landing with a gentle bump and screeching unsteadily down the runway. As soon as the aircraft came to a standstill and the engines were switched off, the aircraft doors swung open. Eager to escape the confined space, Ruby unbuckled her seatbelt and stood up to retrieve their backpacks from the small overhead locker.

A few minutes later, they were outside the plane and bathed in brilliant sunshine streaming from cloudless, deep blue skies. Standing at the top of the aircraft steps, Ruby looked around curiously, not altogether surprised to find Sorrel Island's airport a far cry from the bustling international hub they had passed through in Jamaica. Jake's impatient nudge in the small of her back galvanised her into motion and she descended the metal steps, wondering afresh just what had possessed her to take Auntie Pearl's advice.

Trailing behind the other passengers, they arrived at a whitewashed building marked 'Arrivals', where an official in a short-sleeved khaki green jacket and matching shorts held open the door, greeting each passenger with a smile and a tip of his brocade-embroidered cap. The air-conditioned building was a welcome relief from the intense sunshine and, along with the other passengers, Ruby and Jake continued down a long, wide corridor with whitewashed walls displaying colourful posters of beaches, coral reefs, tropical forests, and clear natural springs. Joining a short queue, they passed through passport control, where a sleepy-eyed man behind a glass booth gave their passports little more than a passing glance before stamping them with a flourish.

Why Kenny had chosen this tiny, out-of-the-way island was a mystery. In the past, their holidays together had been spent in cosmopolitan cities that provided the bustling nightlife, slick entertainment and five-star restaurants Kenny favoured. Notwithstanding the posters showing off the island's stunning biodiversity, nothing Ruby had seen so far suggested Sorrel Island was anyone's idea of a sophisticated tourist destination.

By the time Ruby and Jake arrived at the solitary luggage carousel, only a few of their fellow passengers were there waiting for baggage. Ruby felt the first stirrings of unease, acutely conscious that this was where her itinerary planning ended. According to the travel agent, there was an official tourist office in the airport where she could book accommodation, but as the remaining passengers disappeared after collecting their cases, her misgivings about relying on travel advice from someone thousands of miles away in London were growing stronger.

Ruby loaded their luggage on to a trolley, trying to hide her disquiet from Jake, who was too excited by their new surroundings to notice they were the only people left in the hall. The wheels of the trolley seemed to have a mind of their own and it took all her strength to steer it past an unattended desk marked 'Customs' and towards the exit. When they emerged into a quiet airport terminal, Ruby was relieved to see a large signboard with the words 'Tourist Office' above an arrow and she turned the uncooperative trolley in the direction indicated. However, her relief was short-lived when she found herself in front of the tourist office itself. The glass-fronted unit was in darkness, and when she reached for the handle in the hope someone might be inside, the door was locked. Squeezing her eyes shut, Ruby leaned her forehead on the cold glass, unable to hold back an involuntary groan. Why, why, *why* had she been such a coward about speaking to the only person she knew on Sorrel Island?!

'Need a taxi, miss?'

Ruby opened her eyes and spun around to see a wiry, dark-skinned man watching her with interest, his jaw working rhythmically as he chewed what she presumed was gum. Ruby frowned as she scanned the stranger's face – or what she could see of it under his rather battered straw boater. Although his expression seemed kindly, she was stranded in an almost deserted airport on a remote island, and it was hard to know who to trust.

'Yes, I'm sure we will, but I need to find a hotel first.' Not wanting Jake to sense her apprehension, Ruby tried to sound calm.

'Don't you worry none 'bout that, miss,' the man said cheerfully. His accent held a pleasant musical lilt, and his smile was so infectious that Ruby couldn't help responding. Briefly lifting his hat to scratch a balding pate, he added, 'I can drive you and your boy over to Paradise Inn. Miss Ida's always got room for guests.'

Paradise Inn! Ruby looked at him uncertainly. The name sounded lovely but what if it turned out to be a dump?

'Erm, that's very kind of you but . . . is there anyone actually working in the tourist office?'

The man burst into laughter. 'Not since old Marvin passed on last year. I hear they're looking for someone else to run it, but you'll be waitin' a while.'

Clearly tired of all the chit-chat, Jake nudged his mother. 'C'mon, Mum, let's *go!*'

'Okay, then I guess Paradise Inn it is,' Ruby conceded with a mental shrug. Given the circumstances, it wasn't as if she had much choice, and if the place proved awful, Kenny would surely be able to recommend somewhere else for them to stay. Once they found him.

'I'm Ruby, by the way, and this is my son, Jake.' She smiled at the man, hoping he hadn't been offended by her earlier brusqueness.

'My name's Hezekiah, but everyone calls me Zeke.' He held out a hand in greeting and when she returned his firm handshake, Zeke's gaze ran up and down the length of Ruby's lean frame with a raised eyebrow.

'My, you're a tall one,' he observed.

'All my life,' Ruby quipped. Being part of an African-Caribbean community made her no stranger to unsolicited personal comments, and besides, Zeke's expression was so obviously one of admiration that it was impossible to take offence.

With an appreciative chuckle, Zeke reached for the trolley, spinning it around easily despite the heavy suitcases. 'My taxi's outside, folks. Jus' follow me.'

◆ ◆ ◆

The yellow taxi wound its way along a single-lane road lined by tall trees with thick branches shrouded in green foliage. Although it was late in the afternoon, the sun remained bright in the clear blue sky and Ruby relaxed in the back seat, admiring the passing scenery and enjoying the breeze coming through the open windows of Zeke's roomy vehicle. The colourful landscape and occasional glimpse through the trees of brightly painted bungalows set on stilts were a world away from the brick buildings and choked traffic of London's streets.

Jake had insisted on sitting in front next to Zeke and, since leaving the airport, he had lobbed a non-stop barrage of questions in his high-pitched voice at their driver. Ruby caught Zeke's eye in his rear-view mirror, and he returned her wry smile with an easy grin, clearly enjoying Jake's excitement at his new surroundings.

'*Look*, Mum, it's the sea!' Jake jabbed his finger against the glass of his window.

Ruby followed his instruction and caught her breath at the picture-postcard scenery. The curtain of trees had thinned out to reveal turquoise waters and bleached-white sandy beaches fringed with swaying palm trees. The faint scent of salty sea wafted in through the open windows and Ruby inhaled deeply, slowly feeling the tension from the flight and their arrival drain away. *Sorrel Island must be casting a spell on me*, she thought dreamily, as suddenly even the looming hurdle of confronting Kenny felt less daunting.

'Y'all picked a good day to arrive,' Zeke remarked during a brief lull between Jake's questions. 'Yesterday, it rained so hard I had to go round and fix a leak at Miss Ida's place – and that roof is sealed tighter than a tin can.'

'Do you think there'll be a hurricane while we're here?' Jake asked, sounding unusually subdued.

'No, son,' Zeke chuckled, his tone reassuring. 'There hasn't been a hurricane on Sorrel Island as long as I've been alive. We get the odd monsoon rain this time of year but that's all you need to worry 'bout.'

'There weren't that many people on our plane, Zeke. Do you keep busy driving a cab here?' Ruby asked. If the island's sleepy airport was anything to go by, it was hard to see how the man sustained a taxi business.

'Well, I can't say we've had too many tourists lately, but the plane comes in four times a week and I'm always right there to meet it. Other days, I get some work downtown or I pick up folks from where they're staying and drive them around the island. If things get real quiet, I keep myself busy doing odd jobs here and there, and helping Miss Ida out at Paradise Inn.'

'It's a shame you don't get more tourists,' said Ruby. 'The island is beautiful.'

'We're a long way out, Miss Ruby, and most folks visit the islands with big tourist resorts. But when people come to Sorrel Island, they fall in love and never want to leave.'

Ruby fought the temptation to ask Zeke if he knew Kenny, but conscious that Jake was listening to the conversation, she held her tongue. She had the name and telephone number of Kenny's business, and that would have to do for now.

Settle in first, Ruby, and worry about Kenny later.

9

Zeke turned into a side road, and the deep fissures in its untarred surface came as a rude shock after the smooth highway. Ruby clutched her seatbelt as the car's tyres bounced along the dirt road. Just as she began to question Zeke's assurances about Paradise Inn, he turned into a gravelled road that led to a wide circular driveway and pulled up in front of a whitewashed plantation-style mansion that could have come straight out of *Gone With The Wind*. Blooming vines of flowering wisteria climbed its graceful columns, winding around the sides of the house and framing the roof of a wide, shaded porch filled with colourful potted plants.

'Here we are, Miss Ruby,' Zeke announced. 'This is Paradise Inn. I know Miss Ida will take good care of you and young Jake.'

Jake flung open his door and was out of the car in seconds, and Ruby quickly followed his lead. While Zeke went to fetch their suitcases from the boot, she stared in wonder at the elegant house, which, even at first sight, was more than worthy of its name. She spun around in delight to take in the beautifully maintained green lawns surrounded by tall trees with widely spread branches. Birds with bright plumage chirruped in the quiet as they darted between the lush flowering shrubs planted around the house, adding to the serene tranquillity of the setting. *This place is absolute heaven!*

Lost in her surroundings, it took Ruby a few moments to register the small, slightly built woman in a coral-pink dress and an orange sun hat emerging from behind the house. After exchanging a few words with Zeke, the woman walked over to Ruby, pulling off a well-worn gardening glove and extending a slender hand in greeting.

'Welcome to Paradise Inn. I'm Ida Hastings, and this is my home.' She beamed as her gaze darted from Ruby to Jake, who had wandered further down the drive. 'Zeke tells me you and your boy need a place to stay?'

The broad brim of her hat shaded dark, twinkling eyes in a honey-brown face adorned with a sprinkling of darker freckles. Instantly drawn to her warmth, Ruby returned the woman's smile and shook the outstretched hand.

'Hello, Ms Hastings. It's a pleasure to meet you. I'm Ruby Lamont and' – she broke off and gestured impatiently to Jake, who ran over to stand beside her – 'and this is my son, Jake. Your house is – it's simply *exquisite*! We'd love to stay here if you'll have us.'

'That's no problem, sweetheart,' she replied, chuckling at the naked plea in Ruby's voice. 'And just so you know, I'm plain Miss Ida to everyone.' She gave Jake's shoulder a gentle pat before adding, 'Zeke will bring in your bags. Let's get inside and I'll fetch you something to drink while we fix up a room for you real quick.'

Ruby tried to place the twang of Miss Ida's accent, but before she could give it much thought, the woman shooed them up the short flight of steps leading to the porch and ushered them through tall double front doors into a large hallway lined with indoor plants. Despite its grandeur, the house felt instantly welcoming, the gently whirring fans suspended from the high ceiling creating a pleasantly cool contrast to the tropical heat. The creamy white walls displayed an eclectic mix of vividly colourful contemporary art while the black-and-white tiled floor was spotless.

Miss Ida excused herself, and Jake ran over to the reception desk close to a sweeping staircase where Zeke stood waiting by their suitcases, his jaw working the ever-present gum in his mouth.

Ruby was so relieved Zeke had found them such a beautiful place to stay that she almost hugged him. Instead, she scrabbled in her bag for the envelope of crisp dollar notes she had exchanged before leaving London.

'Honestly, Zeke, I can't thank you enough for bringing us here! Paradise Inn is gorgeous, and Miss Ida seems lovely. How much do I owe you for the ride?'

Zeke named his price and Ruby counted out the dollars and handed them over with a generous tip. Folding the notes, he thrust them into the front pocket of his shirt and tipped his hat in thanks.

Miss Ida returned soon afterwards. She had removed her hat and gloves, and was carrying a tray bearing glasses and a full jug. 'You folks must be thirsty after your trip. Come on into the parlour and have a glass of my special sorrel drink while I fix your room.'

She paused to eye the suitcases by the front desk. 'Zeke, take those bags up to the Cloud Room and then come get a drink before you go.'

Zeke picked up one of the suitcases and headed for the stairs while Ruby and Jake followed Miss Ida through a door leading from the hallway into a room with high ceilings and polished dark wood floors. Ruby's first impression was of a riot of colour; from the brightly woven rugs covering the floorboards to the rich, jewel-toned, overstuffed sofas and armchairs, and multicoloured lampshades. The tall bookcases filled with books immediately gave the large room a warm, homely feel. Amidst all the colour, Ruby's eyes were instantly drawn to a gallery of framed black-and-white photographs mounted on a wall, and while Miss Ida set the contents of the tray on to a side table, she wandered over for a closer look.

'I'm no expert, but these photographs are stunning!' she exclaimed.

Miss Ida came over to join her and scrutinised the images with a pensive expression as if seeing them for the first time. 'Marty, my late husband, took these before we left Louisiana almost forty years ago.'

That explains the accent, thought Ruby, immediately wondering why Marty and Miss Ida had decamped to this faraway island.

'What brought you to Sorrel Island?' The words spilled out before Ruby could help herself, and she flushed with embarrassment. 'I'm so sorry! It's none of my business and I'm just being nosey.'

Clearly not offended, Miss Ida smiled and patted Ruby's arm reassuringly. 'Marty took his camera everywhere and he loved taking shots of people when they didn't know he was doing it. He always said people were more themselves when they didn't think anyone was watching.'

She pointed to a close-up of a muscular man with a blond crew cut smiling into the eyes of a young woman who was clearly Miss Ida. 'That's the only picture Marty didn't take himself.'

'He's gorgeous,' Ruby observed with an approving smile. 'No wonder you fell in love with him.'

Miss Ida chuckled. 'I adored him, but Louisiana in the late sixties wasn't a safe place for couples like us. After Marty quit the army and we had Martin Junior, things got even worse, and we knew we had to get out of the States. One of Marty's army buddies had told him about Sorrel Island while he was overseas on tour and later Jimmy helped us come out here for a visit. Sorrel Island is a magic place, Ruby, and the first day we got here, we knew this was where we wanted to stay and make a fresh start for our family. We sold everything we had in Louisiana and used Marty's inheritance from his late uncle to buy the land and build Paradise House. It took us a while, but this house has been my home ever since. When

Marty died, I changed the name to Paradise Inn and now it's also my business.'

Jake, who had been listening intently to the conversation, piped up curiously, 'Where's Martin Junior?'

Miss Ida's bright smile dimmed. 'Sweet child, we lost Martin Junior just five years after we came to Sorrel Island. But Marty's in Heaven with him now, so our baby has someone up there taking care of him.'

Jake absorbed Miss Ida's words and then, to Ruby's astonishment, he went over to her and wrapped his arms around her waist, making no protest when she gently stroked his hair.

Miss Ida blinked rapidly, and hugged Jake to her for a moment before gently disengaging herself. 'Well, now, it's getting late, and I should get your room made up before I start on dinner. The two of you must be worn out from all that travelling.'

She bustled across the room and flung open a set of French doors which led out to a stone terrace. 'It's getting cooler and you have the place to yourselves until the other guests get back. Take a walk on the terrace and visit the gardens while you're waitin' on me, and I'll come fetch you when I'm done.'

With that, she left the room, and Ruby filled a glass from the red juice in the jug, handing it to Jake before pouring her own. The ice-cold drink was delicious and tasted like a blend of sweet berries, ginger, and sugar, with a hint of spice.

Zeke appeared, his straw boater tucked under his arm, and Ruby poured him a glass, which he swallowed in a few gulps before jamming his hat on his head with a satisfied smile.

'Y'all have a good visit, now, and I'll be seeing you soon.'

Touching the brim of his hat respectfully, he gave them a nod of farewell and left.

10

By the time Ruby had finished unpacking, Jake was visibly flagging. Pushing the empty suitcases into one of the roomy wardrobes in their bedroom, she gave him a bracing smile.

'I know you're tired, buddy, but dinner will be ready at seven, so hang in there until we've had something to eat and then we can both get some sleep.'

Jake yawned and then nodded. 'Okay, but aren't we going to look for my dad?'

'We've got plenty of time for that tomorrow. It's been a long day and all we're going to do now is have dinner and an early night. Tell you what, why don't you take a shower? It'll help you stay awake, and after I've had mine, we can go downstairs and look around the inn before dinner.'

Ruby shooed him into the adjoining bathroom before he could protest, and, closing the door behind him, looked around with a sigh of pleasure. The Cloud Room Miss Ida had offered them boasted a stunning feature wall painted a deep shade of blue with puffs of white clouds that ran along the length of the room. Two double beds, draped in blue floral bedspreads and matching pillowcases, were separated by an ornate wooden screen with diamond cut-outs, while large fans circulated a cool breeze around the room. On one side of the room, an archway framed an alcove with a sofa and a large desk and chair, perfect for Jake to work on the school assignments she had promised Mr Hinton would be submitted at the end of each week. At the other end of the room, floor-to-ceiling glass doors opened to a covered balcony overlooking the gardens.

Eager to explore the balcony, Ruby slid open the glass doors and stepped out on to sun-warmed white tiles. Leaning against the wrought-iron balustrades to take in the view of the landscaped grounds, she sniffed appreciatively as the warm breeze carried over spicy aromas from the kitchen. Knowing Jake could spend hours in a shower if left to himself, Ruby moved to sit on one of the sun loungers set out on the balcony and stretched out, flexing her toes to ease her tired leg muscles. Within moments, she had drifted off, only waking when she felt Jake's damp fingers shaking her by the shoulder.

'You said we couldn't sleep until *after* dinner,' he said accusingly.

'Sorry, buddy.' Smiling sheepishly, Ruby scrambled to her feet. 'I must have dozed off. Give me a few minutes to take a shower and then we'll go downstairs.'

When Ruby and Jake walked into the spacious dining room adjoining the parlour, it was still early. Tables of varying sizes covered with pristine white cloths had been set up for dinner with gleaming cutlery and polished glasses, but the only diners present were two elderly women seated together at a table and a young couple with a small boy and a little girl in a highchair at another. Saloon doors on one side of the room led to the kitchen, while, at the back, two sets of sliding glass doors opened on to a floodlit stone terrace that stretched the width of the room and overlooked the sea.

Ruby's gaze lingered on the young family as she walked past. Seeing the father attempt to persuade the little girl in the highchair to swallow the food he was spooning into her mouth reminded her of the tactics Griffin had used in the past to coax a fussy Jake to eat. Not for the first time, she wished her best friend was there with them. Griffin really *did* make everything fun, she thought wistfully, as she steered Jake towards an empty table by the window.

The aroma of spicy food emerging from the kitchen set Ruby's stomach growling with hunger. It had been hours since their meal on the plane, and Jake had long since devoured the snacks she had stuffed into their backpacks. Right on cue, a pretty dark-skinned girl in a white shift dress that emphasised her slender figure approached their table.

'Good evening, folks. I'm Narita,' she announced with a sunny smile. 'I'll be serving you this evening. I hope you found everything in your room to your liking?' Her soft, lilting accent instantly reminded Ruby of Zeke.

'The room is lovely, thanks.' Ruby smiled. 'In fact, everything is simply perfect.'

'I'll let Miss Ida know, for sure. She's in the kitchen and says if you need anything, you must be sure to let her know. May I inform you of tonight's menu?' Without waiting for an answer, Narita reeled off a list of dishes so quickly that Ruby struggled to keep up.

'I'd like the chicken and spicy rice, please,' Jake announced as soon as the waitress paused for breath, and Ruby raised a surprised eyebrow. Her son was notoriously picky about food, and she bit back a smile. Clearly, she wasn't the only one the island was working its magic on.

'I'll have the Paradise grilled fish with the spicy rice, Narita,' Ruby said. 'It sounds yummy.'

When their food arrived, Jake wolfed down his meal, scarcely pausing long enough to respond to Ruby's questions. After gulping a glass of iced water, he slumped into his chair while Ruby finished her meal at a more sedate pace.

'What do you think my dad's house will be like?' Jake demanded suddenly. 'I bet it's just as big as Miss Ida's.'

'I have no idea, but hopefully we'll get some more information tomorrow. It's a small island and I'm sure it won't be that hard to find him.'

Ruby took another mouthful of the deliciously flavoured fish and suppressed a sigh. The sooner she got Jake in front of Kenny and put an end to the boy's grandiose fantasies, the better.

By the time Ruby finished eating, a few more people had arrived, but with more than half of the tables still unoccupied, she couldn't help wondering once again why so few people appeared to know about the place. Had it not been for Kenny, she mused, she would never have heard of Sorrel Island. It was easy to imagine how popular this gem of an island could be – although perhaps the fact that it wasn't crowded with tourists also added to its magic.

Jake's head was nodding, and he looked ready to fall asleep at the table. Quickly finishing the water in her glass, Ruby wiped her lips with the white linen napkin and pushed back her chair. 'Come on, buddy, let's get you to bed. You look shattered.'

With a wave to Narita, Ruby steered Jake out of the dining room and up the stairs. She stood by the bathroom door as he sleepily brushed his teeth and then watched him climb into the bed nearest the balcony that he had chosen. In the short time it took for Ruby to drape the blue coverlet over his small frame and kiss him lightly on the cheek, Jake was fast asleep.

Switching off the overhead lights and leaving on a table lamp in case he woke up in the night, Ruby crept to the bathroom. After brushing her teeth, she came back into the room and quickly undressed, pulling on the faded, oversized '*I* ♥ *Nairobi*' t-shirt she had borrowed from Griffin – and refused to return – before slipping beneath the bed covers.

The bed accommodated her height comfortably, and as Ruby lay back against the plump pillows, she couldn't help smiling. This place was truly a paradise – with Kenny being the only fly in the proverbial ointment.

I'll worry about that tomorrow, she decided, and, pushing aside all thoughts of her ex, Ruby rolled on to her side and closed her eyes.

11

Finishing the last delicious mouthful of fluffy pancake, Ruby sighed with contentment. As she relaxed in her chair watching a green dragonfly with shimmering translucent wings hover over a striking purple bougainvillea bush, the chill of a London winter felt a world away.

They had awoken that morning to a cloudless blue sky, and even at ten o'clock in the morning, the sun-drenched terrace off the dining room was more than warm enough for the silky teal vest Ruby had paired with white shorts and high-heeled wedged sandals. Miss Ida's breakfast of pancakes served with sweet sorrel jam and accompanied by fresh juice and surprisingly good coffee had been both tasty and filling. Ruby took another sip of the cool blend of orange and pineapple juice and watched in amusement as Jake carefully wrapped the last bit of sausage on his plate with a jam-soaked piece of pancake before cramming the whole thing into his mouth.

The family she had spotted in the dining room the night before strolled past their table with a cheery 'Good morning!' which Ruby echoed with a smile. Greeting total strangers was confirmation – if she needed it – that this was not keep-your-head-down-and-mind-your-own-business London, she thought wryly, her eyes following the family's progress down the terracotta tiled steps at the end of the terrace that led to the pathway for the beach.

Her attention was diverted by Miss Ida arriving at their table bearing a heaped platter of steaming hot pancakes. Her cornflower-blue dress sat loosely against her tiny frame and the matching headscarf highlighted the rich sheen of her dark skin. Without prompting, she speared two pancakes and deposited them on Jake's plate.

'Miss Ida!' Ruby exclaimed. 'He's already had three of them!'

'He's a growing boy. If he wants to be tall like his mama, he's gonna need more meat on his bones.'

Ruby opened her mouth to protest and then closed it again. Jake was already spooning sorrel jam on to the pancakes and there was no point arguing with the woman's distinctly Auntie Pearl-esque tone.

Miss Ida beamed as she watched Jake tucking in. 'So, sweet child, are you excited to see around the island?'

Jake's mouth was crammed with pancake, and he settled for nodding vigorously until he'd swallowed. 'Yeah, cos we came here to find my dad!' he divulged happily.

Ruby groaned under her breath, but Miss Ida maintained a diplomatic silence, topping up Jake's glass with juice before leaving him to enjoy his breakfast.

Ruby gazed out at the flowerbeds below the terrace, but the reference to Kenny had destroyed her mood. Paradise Inn might be a gorgeous oasis but there was no putting off what they had come here to do, she thought gloomily, trying to ignore the spasm in her stomach at the prospect of facing her ex. She glanced across the table at Jake and frowned at his suddenly forlorn expression. His head resting on one hand, he had abandoned his food and was trailing the handle of his fork across the white tablecloth.

'Hey, what's wrong?' Ruby leaned in closer. 'You okay, buddy?'

'You left Jellybean at home, Mum,' he said quietly.

Ruby slumped into her chair and cursed silently. In her rush to finish packing, she had forgotten Jake's beloved toy rabbit.

'I am *so* sorry! I put him on the desk when I was packing your clothes just so I'd remember, but I must have left him there when I brought your suitcase to my room.' She hesitated, and then in a bid to cajole him out of his despondency, added, 'You're a big boy now. Don't you think you can do without Jellybean just for the time we're here?'

The accusatory look Jake turned on her and the stubborn set of his jaw were answer enough. With enough battles looming, Ruby really didn't need another.

'Okay, then, here's what we'll do. Finish your breakfast while I go and find Miss Ida and ask her advice about the best way to make calls from here. The wifi's patchy and I need to phone Grandma Pearl and Uncle Griffin to let them know we've arrived safely. I'll ask Uncle Griffin to pick up Jellybean from the house and courier him over to us. But, Jake, it'll take days for a parcel to get here,' she warned. 'Is that alright with you?'

The cost of a courier from London was far more than Jellybean was worth, but she couldn't take the chance of him being lost in the post. Jake would be dealing with enough turmoil on this trip, and if his childhood toy would be a comfort, she didn't have much of a choice. Jake nodded in agreement and, leaving him to finish his breakfast, Ruby left the table and walked through the empty dining room and out into the hallway in search of their host.

Miss Ida was standing at the front door waving off some guests and as Ruby approached, she turned with a bright smile.

'Were you looking for me?'

'Yes, Miss Ida. I was hoping you could tell me where I can buy some phone data. I'm not sure what—'

'That's no problem, sweetheart,' Miss Ida cut her off gently. 'I keep a few phone cards in my office for guests. We have wifi here but the connectivity isn't the best and cards are cheaper for calling overseas when you can't get on the internet. Come with me.'

Ruby followed the older woman back into the hallway and through a door next to the dining room. Inside the office, a huge desk was topped with piles of receipts and an in-tray weighed down by papers threatening to spill on to an old-fashioned wired telephone. It was clear from Miss Ida's clothes and the decor of Paradise Inn that the woman loved colour, Ruby thought, as she followed behind her and shut the door, and Miss Ida's office was no exception.

Against the wall was a plump sofa in a sea-green paisley fabric with emerald cushions propped at each end. Irregularly shaped and colourfully blended rugs and woven mats were scattered over the wood flooring, and at the far end of the room, a tall lamp with a black-and-white harlequin shade stood close to glass doors leading out to a private terrace. While Miss Ida rummaged through the drawer of one of several steel-blue filing cabinets, Ruby's attention was caught by a large poster on the wall. The aerial view of Sorrel Island brought its perfectly heart-shaped outline into such stark relief against the surrounding blue sea that Ruby couldn't help the tiny gasp that escaped her.

Miss Ida glanced up from her search and smiled at Ruby's open-mouthed astonishment.

'It's real pretty, don't you think?'

'It's incredible! We saw the island from the plane, but I thought it was just a trick of the eye.'

Miss Ida paused her search and eyed her thoughtfully. 'Have you heard the legend of Sorrel Island and why it's shaped like a heart?'

What Ruby *had* heard was enough folklore from Auntie Pearl's Caribbean and African friends to anticipate what was coming, and she shook her head with a smile. 'Let me guess. It involves magic of some kind, am I right?'

'Most definitely, Ruby.' Miss Ida nodded, studying the poster thoughtfully with her head tilted to one side. 'Sorrel Island is a place of love and healing. You might even call it an enchanted island.'

'Well, it's a beautiful island, no question, but *enchanted*? Really?' Ruby didn't even try to hide her scepticism.

'Oh yes,' Miss Ida assured her. 'The legend of Sorrel Island has passed down through generations of islanders and it goes right back to the days of the slave trade, when people were forced on to ships and brought over from Africa to labour on sugar cane and cotton plantations. The story goes that two enslaved young people sent to work in a sugar cane plantation on a Caribbean island fell deeply in love. The girl was beautiful, and soon caught the attention of the plantation master. In those times, you couldn't even look up at plantation owners, and an enslaved man could get whipped to death or lynched just for showing interest in a woman a white planter had earmarked for himself. So, knowing they faced certain death unless they ran away, the couple planned their escape, and one night they made it to the coastline without being recaptured. According to the legend, they found a small boat and sailed out to sea, preferring to die together in the ocean rather than accept the fate that awaited them back on the plantation. They drifted for days with no food and only the water they had brought with them, and with no land in sight, they had all but given up when an island magically appeared out of the sea. When they washed up on to the beach, they found a paradise of freshwater streams, fruits, and berries. Sorrel trees grow in abundance around the island and are known for their natural healing power, and so with everything they needed to survive, the young couple lived as free people for the rest of their lives. So, you see, Ruby, Sorrel Island was created as an enchanted refuge for lovers and that is why it's shaped in the symbol of love.'

As Miss Ida recounted the story, her voice grew dreamier, and the years appeared to fall away. Observing the woman's shining eyes and delicate features, it was easy for Ruby to see why Marty had fallen so hard for his wife. But while Ruby didn't buy Miss Ida's fanciful explanation for the island's curious quirk of geology, there was no denying Sorrel Island had provided a refuge for the young couple fleeing deep racism in the American South.

Almost as if her thoughts had drifted in the same direction as Ruby's, Miss Ida said softly, 'When I met Marty, my heart knew right away that he was the one for me, and it was just the same for him. You know, Ruby, every heart has its twin, and hundreds of years ago, those two young lovers knew they had found the other half of theirs and were prepared to die if they couldn't be together.'

'Well, it's certainly a charming story – *if* you believe in magic,' Ruby conceded, trying to be diplomatic.

'Are you in love, Ruby?'

Caught off-guard by the unexpected question, Ruby spluttered, 'Er . . . I don't think so . . . I mean, *no*, definitely not!'

'Then you're going to find love here,' Miss Ida stated, her Auntie Pearl-like conviction putting paid to further argument. She extracted a small cellophane-wrapped card from the cabinet and handed it over.

'The instructions are in the leaflet, sweetheart, and you can use the code to call wherever you like without paying a fortune. Stay here if you need some privacy to make your calls, and I'll go and watch young Jake.'

Miss Ida headed for the door and as she went to open it, Ruby blurted out, 'Miss Ida, I know it's a bit of a long shot, but – would you happen to know someone called Kendrick – or Kenny – Baptiste?'

Miss Ida turned around, her eyes wide with surprise. 'Sure, I know Kenny. He stayed here for a while when he first came to the island. Is he a friend of yours?'

'We-ell, in a manner of speaking, although I haven't seen him for quite some time,' Ruby admitted after a momentary hesitation.

It was obvious from Miss Ida's shrewd look that she wasn't fooled by Ruby's artless expression. '*Now* I see the resemblance. That sweet boy is Kenny's son, ain't he?' she asked softly.

Ruby hesitated and then nodded. 'The thing is, Kenny doesn't know we've arrived, and I've only got his work phone number. I-I thought maybe I should call him first to let him know we're on the island?'

Miss Ida pursed her lips and then shook her head decisively. 'I don't see what good a phone call's gonna do when Kenny's only twenty minutes away. He's usually down at the marina in Sugar Bay unless he's taking folks cruising around the island. Zeke'll be over shortly to fix a fence round the back for me; he can drive you down to Kenny's before he gets started.'

'Oh . . . er, thank you,' said Ruby, dazed by the speed with which things were moving. She had been secretly hoping to buy more time before confronting Kenny but that was evidently not going to happen.

'I'll tell Zeke to come find you when he gets here, sweetheart.' With an encouraging smile, Miss Ida walked out of the room and closed the door behind her.

Left alone with a chest that suddenly felt constricted, Ruby took her phone out of her shorts pocket, her fingers fumbling clumsily as she ripped open the cellophane packet. *Keep it together, Rubes!* Having travelled this far, she reminded herself, it was time to get the job done.

12

Within an hour, Ruby and Jake were in Zeke's yellow taxi, speeding along the coastal road towards Sugar Bay. A subdued Jake had opted to sit in the back with his mother and as soon as they left Paradise Inn, his hand crept into Ruby's. Zeke's initial attempts to draw Jake into conversation had fallen flat, and eventually the three of them lapsed into silence.

Ruby stared blindly out of the window at the passing scenery, her pulse picking up speed with every mile. Knowing she was minutes away from confronting a man she had once loved but hadn't seen in years felt surreal. There was a time when she had been consumed by the idea of bumping into Kenny, imagining what she would say when their paths eventually crossed. She had rehearsed lines that would be both cutting and witty; each word painstakingly selected to wound, while also showing how well they had managed without him. She had even practised in front of a mirror to perfect the look of disdain that would convey her unspeakable contempt for his cowardice in disappearing without a word of explanation.

But that was then.

This trip is about Jake, and not about you, Ruby told herself sternly in a bid to get her racing heartbeat under control. Her son would be present when she found herself in front of Kenny, and however tempting it might be to launch into a blistering tirade or even, God forbid, smack the man around his gutless face, she had to put Jake's feelings first.

Oh God, I wish Griffin was here! In that moment, all Ruby wanted was her best friend by her side to talk her down from the ledge of her rising panic. But Griffin wasn't here, and Kenny was her problem to handle alone. Which was only right since she was the one who had blithely ignored Griffin's and her parents' words of caution against rushing into a serious relationship with a man she had known for a matter of months. She was the one who had used Kenny's seductive charm and passionate declarations to soothe the hurt of childhood taunts about her appearance and the resultant lack of romantic interest in her from the boys she had grown up around. It was she who had let Kenny coax her into trying for a baby to reassure him of her commitment, feeling so gratified that a handsome and successful man had fallen head over heels in love with her that she had questioned nothing else. Now, she was the one who had to deal with the consequences of that choice.

Zeke turned off the main highway to drive down a steep road and Ruby smelled the salty sea air before she caught her first glimpse of the marina. Under different circumstances, she would have found the sight of scores of white boats bobbing on crystal-blue waters in bright sunshine a delight. As it was, the only sensation Ruby felt – aside from her mounting dread – was the grip of Jake's hand.

Zeke turned into a gravelled clearing where cars and trailers were parked in neat rows, slowing to avoid people unloading items from vehicles and carrying ice coolers and equipment up and down a path that traced the curve of the marina.

'This is Sugar Bay,' Zeke announced, pulling up near the footpath and switching off the engine. He pointed towards the far side of the marina. 'If you're looking for Kenny, you'll find his boats moored over that way. Jus' follow those folks on the pathway and keep going round till you see the sign for Sugar Bay Tours.'

He restarted the engine and Ruby opened the car door and waited for Jake to scramble out behind her. She handed some notes to Zeke through the open window, and he tipped his hat cheerily and drove off. Now they were left to their own devices, Ruby was hit by the enormity of her decision to bring Jake here, and her legs suddenly felt like they had lost their strength. She should have begged Griffin to come with them; *he* would have known what to do! As if sensing his mother's unspoken panic, Jake took Ruby's hand in a firm grip and urged her forward.

They set off down the walkway and Ruby shortened her stride to keep pace with Jake, drawing strength from the hand so trustfully holding hers. From the hum of activity all around, it was clear the marina was a working community, and continuing along the path, they went past a huge yard with rows of boats propped up on wooden structures for repair. Seeing them pass, a couple of men in khaki overalls paused from their task of hammering the hull of a large boat to shout a cheerful good morning.

'Mum! We've been walking for ages! Are you sure we're going the right way?' Jake tugged on Ruby's hand, the hint of a tremble in his impatient tone.

'Zeke said to follow the path and, as far as I can tell, this is the only one,' Ruby said reasonably. She could hear the tension in Jake's voice, and she tried to sound reassuring. 'Look, there's a café over there. Maybe someone inside can tell us if we're on the right track.'

As they walked into the café, Ruby was hit by the strong aroma of freshly brewed coffee, and she would have loved nothing better than to sit down outside with a mug of black coffee and enjoy the view of the stunning marina. Anything would have been preferable to the impending meeting that had her stomach tied up in knots. Mindful of Jake watching, she tried to stay calm as she waited for the woman behind the counter to finish serving coffee to the man in front of her.

The woman placed some change on the counter for the man and then turned to Ruby with a pleasant smile. 'Good morning, miss. How are you today?'

'Good morning. I'm fine, thanks, and how are you?' Ruby responded, having quickly picked up on the local social niceties.

'I'm doing great, thank you. Can I get you a snack or something to drink?'

Ruby shook her head. 'I wonder if you can help me. I'm trying to find Sugar Bay Tours and I'm not sure if we're going in the right—'

'You lookin' for Kenny?' The man who had just paid for his coffee cut in, and Ruby nodded, wondering if there was anyone on the island who didn't know her ex.

The man pocketed his change and picked up his drink, gesturing to Ruby to follow him. Once outside the café, he pointed towards a docking bay about a hundred metres away where a row of boats was anchored to concrete posts.

'I've seen him this morning and his boats are all moored, so he hasn't taken anyone out. Go on over there and holler for him – he's more than likely up on one of the boats. You folks have yourselves a good day, now.'

The man ambled off in the other direction and Ruby looked down at Jake and pretended to adjust his cap, while breathing in deeply to pull herself together. Jake looked up at her, his face solemn, and once again reached for her hand as they set off in the direction the man had indicated. Just as Zeke had said, there was a large blue signboard with the words 'Sugar Bay Tours' emblazoned in bold white letters.

As they drew closer, Ruby raised a hand to shield her eyes from the sun and scanned the decks of the tethered boats. There was no sign of anyone on board, but she would have died before announcing their presence by shouting for Kenny, as the man from the café had instructed. She looked around and spotted a building a short distance away with a smaller version of the blue signboard on its frontage.

Suddenly, Jake nudged her sharply with his elbow. '*Mum!*' he hissed urgently.

Turning back, Ruby followed his gaze and froze. A tall figure in jeans and a baseball cap had emerged from below the deck of the boat nearest to them and was clearly about to disembark. Her pulse racing, she stared as the man bounded lithely from the boat on to the docking walkway and headed straight towards them, whistling cheerfully. As he approached, he glanced their way and tipped his cap with a muttered greeting before continuing past them towards the building.

Ruby's heart was thudding with the frenzy of an unleashed jackhammer as she watched him stop abruptly in his tracks. Clinging on to her son with the desperation of a drowning swimmer, she watched the man slowly turn around.

13

Ruby stared dumbly at the man returning her scrutiny, barely registering the pressure of Jake's equally desperate grip of her hand. Every nerve in her body was on high alert as she watched the man's eyes widen and his mouth fall slightly open, and she hardly dared blink as he retraced his steps until he was within touching distance. He was tall – one of the first things that had drawn her to him – and even in her high wedged sandals, he topped her by a couple of inches. His white polo shirt clung to broad shoulders and muscular arms, and through the open-necked top she could see the glint of a thin gold chain against his dark brown skin. All the imagined scenarios and well-rehearsed speeches vanished as her eyes drank in the familiar face with its strong jaw and deep-set dark eyes identical to Jake's.

'*Ruby?*' He sounded so incredulous that she couldn't help the wry smile that tugged at her lips.

'Kenny,' she echoed faintly.

Kenny lowered his gaze to Jake. He drew in a long, shuddering breath and pressed his fist hard against his lips. The sound of a suppressed sob escaped as, slowly shaking his head, Kenny dropped on to one knee to come face to face with the boy.

'Jake?' he whispered.

Jake's eyes were enormous in his face as he nodded dumbly. For a long moment, the three of them remained frozen in a tableau, and then Kenny held out his arms. Without hesitation, Jake let go of Ruby's hand and walked into his father's embrace.

Ruby felt her breath leave her chest in jagged bursts as she watched her son wind his arms around his father's neck, and it took every bit of her strength not to burst into tears.

Kenny held on to the child for a long moment before releasing him. '*Jake!* I-I don't even— You're so big now . . . My God, look at you!' he stammered, shaking his head as if trapped in a dream and willing himself to wake up. 'I can't believe you're actually here . . .'

Kenny's voice tailed off as he visibly tried to regain control. He stood up unsteadily and ruffled Jake's hair gently before turning to Ruby.

'Why didn't you call or write to say you were coming?' The lilt in his Trinidadian accent sounded stronger than she remembered, and Ruby shrugged defensively. He clearly hadn't picked up the message she'd left on the answerphone and now she felt like a prize idiot for hanging up on him and then turning up unannounced.

'It was a sudden decision, and there wasn't time to . . . well, you know . . .'

She nodded towards Jake, who was staring, transfixed, at his father, and Kenny appeared to pick up on her signal. He glanced back in the direction of the boats and beckoned over a stocky man in denim cut-offs and a black t-shirt making his way down the walkway with a mop and a large metal pail. The man obligingly set down the bucket, dropped the mop inside it, and came over, wiping his hands on the back of his shorts.

'Yes, boss?' He flashed Ruby a curious glance before turning his attention to Kenny.

Kenny smiled and patted him on the shoulder. 'Sam here oversees the maintenance of our boats. He's worked with me for years and he knows everything there is to know about this island. Sam, this here is my son, Jake, and his mother, Ruby.'

Sam's eyebrows shot up and Ruby winced at the stunned expression he quickly tried to disguise. Not that she could blame him; if he'd known Kenny for years, of course he'd be shocked to suddenly discover his boss had an apparently ready-made family.

Kenny made no attempt to elaborate further. 'Sam, do me a favour. Can you show Jake around while Ruby and I have a chat in the office? I'm sure he'd like to see the boats, but take him over to the café for an ice-cream first.' He hesitated and glanced at Ruby. 'If that's alright?'

When Ruby nodded without comment, Kenny crouched in front of Jake and cuffed him gently on the chin. 'Sam will take good care of you, son, and you know what? The marina café sells the *best* ice-cream! Make sure you ask for two big scoops, okay?'

Jake gave him a shy smile and nodded, and Kenny pointed towards the moorings. 'You see that big boat over there? It's our newest one, and it has the coolest dashboard and controls. Sam's going to take you on board after you get your ice-cream, and your mum and I will be in my office, which is in this building right here.'

Jake looked up at Ruby and she gave him a reassuring smile. 'Go ahead, buddy. It sounds exciting and you can tell me all about it when you get back.'

Kenny peeled a few notes from a wad in his back pocket and handed them to Sam, who glanced from Kenny to Ruby and then back again, clearly trying to make sense of what was happening. Then, with a shrug, he turned to Jake.

'Come with me, kid. Since your old man's paying, let's go buy you the biggest ice-cream in the shop.' He lowered his voice into a deep growl. 'Then we'll go up on to the boats and pretend to be pirates.'

With that, Sam held up his palm and a giggling Jake slapped his small hand against it in a triumphant high-five before skipping off without a backward glance. Watching their receding figures for a few moments, Ruby was the first to break the tense silence.

'So, you're the boss, then?' She cringed at the lameness of her question, but it felt so weird to be talking to Kenny that she was amazed she could string together a coherent sentence.

Kenny scratched his low-cut beard – another thing to add to the list of surprises; the Kenny she knew had always been clean-shaven – and took a step towards her. She instinctively moved back to create more space between them.

'Why do you sound so shocked that I run a business?' he asked, his voice laced with humour. 'Were you expecting me to have turned into a beach bum or a drug lord or something? You always did have a vivid imagination.'

Ruby flushed. 'Don't be daft! Besides, I didn't just come out here on a whim. I'd already searched up on the internet and found out where you work.' She turned and gestured towards the boats moored behind them. 'It looks like your business is doing well. I'm counting, what, four boats over there?'

'I'm doing okay,' Kenny conceded, and she turned back to find his eyes looking straight into hers. His probing gaze was unnerving, leaving her cursing herself for leaving her sunglasses back in her room, and wondering why she felt flustered and confused instead of the uncontrolled fury she had feared.

Fighting to keep the unexpected butterflies in check, Ruby directed her focus on to their surroundings. There were more people milling about the area than when they had arrived, and the activity around the marina was growing busier – and louder – with the piercing squawks of sea birds weaving between the masts of the berthed vessels competing with the noise of workers and crew shouting across boats to each other.

Ruby shook her head in wonderment. 'I'm really struggling to believe this place is you. You were always such a *city* boy. I mean, you love – or should I say, loved – clubbing and eating out at the best restaurants. This is so . . . well, you know . . .' She tailed off with a shrug.

'What can I tell you, Rubes? People change,' Kenny said lightly, pulling a handkerchief out of the pocket of his jeans to wipe the back of his neck. 'Don't forget I come from an island, and, besides, this place is so beautiful that living here isn't exactly a hardship. We have some great restaurants downtown, as you'll find out while you're here, so I'm certainly not missing out on gourmet cuisine.'

Then, as if struck by a thought, he glanced around. 'Are you here on your own? I mean, just you and Jake?'

'Yeah. Why?'

Kenny shrugged. 'I don't know. I thought maybe Griffin would have come with you.'

'Why would he?' She frowned and squinted up at Kenny, using her hand to shade her eyes from the bright sunshine.

'Oh, come *on*. Even when we were together, the two of you were inseparable. After I left London, I assumed—'

She shook her head in irritation, ignoring the fact she had been wishing for her friend only minutes earlier.

'You know perfectly well that Griffin and I are just friends, so no, he didn't come with us. Although it wasn't for want of Jake begging him to. Jake adores him – and Griffin's been like a father to him.'

As Kenny inhaled sharply and his jaw tightened, Ruby felt a flash of satisfaction that the barb had hit home.

'Let's go inside, shall we?' He mopped his forehead with his handkerchief, and gestured towards the nearby office. 'It's more private than standing out here, and a hell of a lot cooler.'

Clutching on to her tiny, silent victory, Ruby nodded and followed him into the building.

14

Sitting opposite Kenny in the compact, air-conditioned room, Ruby toyed with the unopened bottle of chilled water he had handed her from the mini fridge in the corner and looked around. The room was tidy, with serviceable furnishings, steel filing cabinets, and nautical maps pinned on to plain white walls. A half-open door on one side of the office led to a storage room, judging from the piles of coiled rope on the floor and other equipment she could see stacked against the wall. The hum of the air-conditioner muffled the sounds of the busy marina, creating an uncomfortable intimacy in the stillness of the room.

The visitor's chair Kenny had offered her was comfortable, unlike Fi's Lilliputian furniture, Ruby noted abstractedly, acutely aware of Kenny quietly observing her from behind his desk. He had removed his baseball cap and, despite a thinning hairline and a sprinkling of grey throughout his closely cropped hair, he was – much to Ruby's irritation – just as attractive as she remembered. From under her lashes, she watched him effortlessly twist the cap off the small plastic bottle in his hands, unable to tear her eyes away when his full lips closed around the rim. Like a rabbit hypnotised by a rearing snake, her eyes were riveted to the bobbing Adam's apple in his throat as he took a long, slow swallow of water.

Appalled by the direction her thoughts were taking, Ruby frowned ferociously and sat bolt upright. She hadn't travelled God knows how many bloody miles to watch Kenny drink water, however sexy he made it look. If this was the showdown she had long been waiting for, then she was more than ready to shoot.

Kenny screwed the cap back into place with a satisfied sigh before placing the bottle on the desk.

'I wish you had told me you were coming.' He looked her right in the eye and she laughed mirthlessly as the fog in her brain slowly cleared.

'Why? To give you a heads-up so you could disappear again?' The scorn in her voice underlined the sarcasm.

'I guess I deserve that,' Kenny said quietly. 'But what I meant was that it would have been nice to welcome you to the island myself.'

'I did call, as it happens,' she said, wrestling with the temptation to ask why he would have wanted to welcome the family he had gone to so much trouble to leave. 'Only no-one answered' – *the second time*, she silently added – 'and so I left a message.'

He grimaced. 'Sam's the best when it comes to boat maintenance, but he has an unfortunate habit of erasing messages as he's trying to play them back. I'm very sorry about that. Where are you guys staying?'

'Paradise Inn,' she said shortly.

Kenny's lips curved into a slight smile. 'Ah, yes, Miss Ida. She's a lovely woman. She took good care of me when I first came here.'

Curiosity got the better of Ruby's antagonism. 'How did you even know about this place? I'd never heard of Sorrel Island until you wrote to say you were living here.'

'We have a saying here that you don't find Sorrel Island, Sorrel Island finds you. When I left London, I went back to Trinidad to stay with family, but I just couldn't settle. I was going through the

100

motions, but it was a struggle after everything that had happened, and it was obvious I wasn't happy.'

Ruby resisted the sarcastic retort aching to escape her lips and allowed him to continue.

'My uncle pulled me aside one day and suggested I take some time away to figure things out. He suggested Sorrel Island, said it was a healing place. I needed a fresh start, and I knew I didn't want to stay in Trinidad, so I came here and hung around for a while.'

'So, you *were* a beach bum, then?' said Ruby, unable to resist the dig.

Kenny scratched his jaw and smiled faintly. 'I suppose. For a little while, anyway. Those first few weeks, I just spent time around the beach and did some diving and snorkelling on the tour boats. That's how I met Vic. He owned Sugar Bay Tours at the time, and I started helping him out at the marina. I learned my way round boats and after a while he let me take tourists around the island. But once Vic found out I had a business degree and a background in finance, he would ask my advice about how he could grow the business and improve the marketing. That's when we created the website and began adding on services like hiring out snorkelling and diving gear to other operators. While this place isn't a tourist hotspot like some of the bigger islands, we've still got spectacular coral reefs and marine life, and we did good business. Vic took my advice and invested in buying more boats, and within a couple of years we had doubled the income from tours. After the pandemic slowed down travel for a while and the takings dipped, Vic decided to call it a day and retire. By then Sorrel Island had worked its own peculiar alchemy on me and it felt like a place where I belonged, so I bought him out. Vic moved to Miami two years ago, and I own the company. That – in a nutshell – is my story.'

Kenny swallowed another gulp of water and tilted his head to one side, taking in her set expression. 'I know you're pissed off with me, Ruby, and you have every right to be. But to be honest, right now, I'm still trying to process that you're actually here and sitting in front of me. You look incredible, and I can't get over how beautiful my son has grown. I'm so thankful to you for taking such good care of him.'

Ruby swatted away the praise like a pesky fly. She wasn't the same gullible young woman hungry for compliments that he had left behind. Every word of admiration, every endearment, every declaration of love Kenny had ever made had been proved by his behaviour to be nothing more than empty flattery and lies. She had been forced to learn the hard way that words of appreciation from Kenny were meaningless, but she had learned her lesson nonetheless, and his words only served to stir her dormant anger.

'You're right, I *am* pissed off with you, and I have a lot of questions about . . . about . . . *everything*! I need answers, Kenny – and Jake does too,' she added belatedly.

'I understand, but . . . why *now*?' he probed, his eyes narrowing into slits. 'You've always known where I was. God knows you returned every damned cheque I sent you.'

'A post office box number on some island no-one's ever heard of is *not* the same as knowing where you are,' she said acidly. 'Our son needed his father, and *I* needed an explanation, not your bloody money!'

To her further annoyance, Kenny didn't seem put off by her hostility. On the contrary, his face relaxed into a half-smile as he held her gaze.

'So, what made you decide you want to see me now?'

For his own sake, Ruby prayed she was only imagining the hopeful note in Kenny's voice.

'Let's get one thing straight,' she said flatly. 'I'm here solely because of Jake. I couldn't care less about you or your new life, but it seems my son has inherited my – what did you call it? – vivid

102

imagination and has been making up all sorts of fantastical stories about his father. It's been getting out of hand and Jake has found himself in trouble at school for not telling the truth and generally playing up. He almost got excluded recently, and Auntie Pearl and I thought it was best that I bring him here so he could meet you and—'

She broke off abruptly and Kenny gave a short, humourless laugh.

'And what? See for himself that the real thing is nothing to get excited about?'

Ruby shrugged, and they sat in silence for a moment.

'So now, what?' Kenny asked quietly.

'What do you mean?'

'What was your plan after bringing me and Jake together?'

Ruby's blank expression was answer enough, and Kenny shook his head resignedly. 'Christ, you really don't think much of me, do you? You hadn't even considered the possibility that I might not be the monster you clearly think I am?'

'*You're* the one who left us,' Ruby said defensively. 'I don't know why you did, and I had no reason to assume you'd want to play an active role in Jake's life going forward.'

Kenny exhaled and nodded slowly. 'You're right, and I'm sorry. Look, me leaving wasn't your fault . . . it's just that—' He paused and looked straight at her, his eyes probing her tense features.

'Just that what, Kenny? Please don't give me any of that "It wasn't you; it was me" crap because *I'm* the one you left. I thought we were happy, so what changed?'

'Rubes, nothing's changed for me.' Kenny took a deep breath. 'I love you. I always have. Believe me, it was never my plan to leave for ever. I don't know, my head was all over the place and somewhere in my warped thinking I even hoped it would push you to come to me. But a year passed, and then another year, and by then I'd heard about your parents and knew you would hate me, and so I kept putting it off. When you feel so much shame that you don't know how you can ever face your own child again, it's easy to convince yourself that he's better off without you and that one day, if you're lucky, you'll get a chance to see him and try to make amends.'

Shocked, Ruby stared at him in disbelief. Kenny *loved* her. If that were true, then what the *hell* had the last six years been about? '*My head was all over the place*'? What did that even *mean*? Kenny claimed to love her and yet he had broken up their family and stayed away for reasons he couldn't even properly articulate. Stunned, she stared at the floor, trying to process his words. She couldn't understand what had triggered his actions, but Jake was the reason she was here, and she had to keep that as her focus.

After a few moments, Kenny broke the silence. 'So how long are you staying?'

It was a question to which Ruby still didn't have an answer. 'I'm not sure,' she hedged, still jolted by his confession. 'We have enough assignments from Jake's school to cover the next three or four weeks, so I guess it depends on how things go with you and Jake, and what's best for everyone.'

Suddenly feeling parched, she twisted the bottle open and took a long sip of water. Looking around the office, she was struck by the spartan decor. There was nothing remotely decorative in sight, and she couldn't help wondering what, if any, female influences were part of Kenny's new life.

'Soo . . . are you married or – or anything?' The words burst out before Ruby could restrain them and she could cheerfully have bitten off her tongue. *Didn't you just tell him you were only here because of Jake?*

Kenny looked her straight in the eye. 'No, I'm not married – or anything.'

She flushed at his quizzical, almost amused, expression and dropped her gaze, furious at the turn the conversation had taken – even if she had initiated it. She wasn't here to find out about Kenny's love life. *That* was none of her business. The only connection she had to him was Jake, and however much he claimed to still love her, nothing else about Kenny's situation mattered. Steering the topic away from dangerous territory, Ruby glanced at her watch.

'Look, Jake will be back at any moment, and clearly there's a lot we have to talk about. I've certainly got things I need to get off my chest, but this isn't the right time or place, so let's park this until we can talk properly.'

Kenny nodded, and Ruby, quietly relieved at the temporary reprieve from revisiting old wounds, kept the chat on neutral ground until Jake and Sam returned shortly afterwards and put an end to the conversation.

15

Ruby tucked her braids into the plastic cap and stepped into the white marble-tiled shower stall. After the emotional rollercoaster of a day, she was desperate for time alone to take stock. Adjusting the direction of the spray, she tipped her head back to let the lukewarm water cascade over her and cool her heated skin. After a few minutes, she poured some of the creamy shower gel provided with the room into the palm of her hand and smoothed it over her body, breathing in the sweet fragrance of coconut and lemongrass. Eventually, as the water flowed over her, Ruby felt the tension slowly ease from her neck and shoulders and drain away with the scented water.

The trip to the marina had ended with Jake's return, although Kenny's insistence on taking them to lunch at a charming, family-owned restaurant a short drive away had further prolonged Ruby's misery. Jake's outing on the boat with Sam had broken the ice and helped him overcome his initial shyness, and he had sat in the front seat chatting happily with Kenny on the drive to the restaurant and on the way back to Paradise Inn. Ruby, meanwhile, had maintained a brooding silence in the back seat, disconcerted by how swiftly her son had been drawn in by the father he hadn't seen for years. Unlike Jake, she was not prepared to reward Kenny with a welcome he didn't deserve.

People change, Kenny had said, but did people really change that much? she wondered. If she were honest, Ruby conceded, it was a struggle to reconcile the charming, party-loving, and occasionally overbearing man with whom she had once shared a life to the affectionate father and thoughtful business owner she had met that morning. Was the real Kenny – the one who could walk away from his responsibilities without a second thought – still lurking within this new mature version, and could she trust him with her son's emotions . . . or her own?

Aghast at the disturbing turn of her thoughts, Ruby switched off the shower and grabbed a towel. Drying herself briskly to shake off the unwelcome direction her mind had taken, she tied her bathrobe around her and padded out of the steamily fragrant bathroom in her bare feet.

The combination of jet lag, larking around with Sam, and a huge lunch had taken its toll, and Jake lay across his bed sound asleep. Ruby slipped on a short summer dress and twisted her long braids up into a bun, and – leaving Jake to nap – she wandered downstairs and into the parlour. There were no guests to be seen and she walked over to the patio doors and stepped out on to the terrace. Enjoying the feel of the warm breeze caressing her neck and bare legs, Ruby leaned against the stone balustrade, admiring the simple beauty of the garden, and breathing in the sweet scents from the flowering shrubs. Once again, her thoughts returned to the reunion with Kenny. Briefly toying with the idea of phoning Griffin, she sighed. This time, she doubted if even the man who knew her best could help make sense of her tangled emotions.

'How did it go with Kenny, sweetheart?' Miss Ida's soft voice interrupted her reflections, and Ruby turned to find her host standing in the doorway, an anxious expression in place of her usual bright smile. Under normal circumstances, Ruby would have recoiled at the idea of discussing her personal life, particularly with someone she had known for all of two days, but she had felt an instant bond with Miss Ida, and seeing the concern in the woman's eyes, Ruby instinctively knew she could trust her.

'I don't know, to be honest. I'm still trying to figure it out,' Ruby confessed with a helpless gesture. 'Seeing him after all this time was so weird. I mean, he hasn't changed much physically – although he does look a bit older – but he seems different somehow. I can't—'

She broke off and took a deep breath to stem her babbling. 'I suppose it went better than I expected. Jake was a bit shy around him at first, but by the time we'd finished lunch, he was chatting away as if he'd known him for ever.'

Miss Ida came out on to the terrace to join Ruby. 'And you? Were *you* happy to see him again?'

Ruby gnawed at her lip in silence for a few moments and then shook her head. 'To tell the truth, my emotions were – are – all over the place.' She hesitated and then said baldly, 'Miss Ida, I should probably tell you that Kenny walked out on us when Jake was only two years old, and we haven't seen him since – until today.'

Miss Ida squeezed her eyes shut as if physically pained by Ruby's words. Then she opened them and searched Ruby's face with an expression of utter bewilderment. 'But why in the world would he do such a thing to you and that sweet, darling boy?'

Ruby shook her head. 'I don't know. He's never had the decency to explain why he disappeared. He wrote to me many weeks later to say he was here on Sorrel Island, and that he'd let me know if he moved on. I don't know if he expected me to follow him out here or what, but I was too hurt and upset that he'd abandoned us to write back.' She took a deep breath before continuing. 'And then my parents died suddenly, and after that all I cared about was making sure Jake and I were okay.'

Miss Ida's dark eyes were warm with compassion as she gently stroked Ruby's arm where it rested on the balustrade. 'I'm so sorry to hear that, sweetheart. Relationships ain't easy, but you're here now, so you take all the time you need to work things out with Kenny. How did you leave things with him?'

Ruby sighed. 'He suggested we take a couple of days to settle in and find our feet and then we'll meet up again and see how to make the trip work for Jake.'

Miss Ida looked around. 'Where is my sweet boy?'

'Fast asleep.' Ruby summoned up a weak smile. 'Between jet lag and eating his entire body weight in food today, he crashed out, and I've left him to rest for a bit.'

'Well, I sure hope he's hungry when he wakes up because I've got Southern-fried chicken on the menu tonight. It always goes down well with my guests – not that I'm getting so many these days,' Miss Ida added wistfully.

'It does seem pretty quiet. Is it because of the time of year?' asked Ruby.

'This used to be part of our busy season, but business slowed down some when folks stopped travelling for a while. Even though things are back to normal, we're still not getting the tourist trade we need here.'

For a moment, the two women contemplated the garden in silence and then Miss Ida sighed. 'I don't mind telling you, Ruby, that if I don't start getting in more paying guests, I might have to sell up.'

'Oh no!' Ruby stared at her in horror. 'But Paradise Inn is your home, Miss Ida.'

'I know, sweetheart, but it's also a business, and right now there just ain't a lot of it. This is a big house with land that needs tending, and even though I do as much as I can myself, it takes money coming in to keep the place in good shape. But I'm gonna keep praying the island gods will work a miracle and things will pick up.'

She patted Ruby's arm affectionately. 'I'd better go see if Narita's here to help me set up for dinner. She's Zeke's granddaughter, you know, and she helps out a few evenings a week.'

As Miss Ida made to leave, she turned back with a mischievous twinkle in her eye.

'Don't forget, Ruby, you're on Sorrel Island, and I know you and Kenny will work things out just fine. He's made mistakes, but the Kenny I know is a good man. There's no shortage of pretty girls on the island and if the man is still single after all these years, who knows? Maybe *his* heart already found its twin.'

Ruby stared at Miss Ida in frustration. The woman was a completely *hopeless* romantic! Had she even *heard* a single word of Ruby's explanation?

'Miss—'

Miss Ida cut her off with an easy chuckle. 'I need to get on, sweetheart. My Southern-fried chicken ain't gonna cook itself!'

16

'Come *on*, Jake, you've been stuck on that page for ever! Look, if you focus on your reading and get through the chapter, I promise we'll go down to the beach.'

Speaking from her vantage point on the sofa, from where she had been monitoring her son's less than stellar performance that morning, Ruby returned Jake's obdurate stare with an unyielding one of her own. After three days of leisure to recover from jet lag, Jake's grace period was over, and it was time to start work on his school assignments. Mr Hinton had proved surprisingly cooperative about allowing the boy out of school for an extended period, and Ruby had no intention of abusing his trust.

Jake sighed and kicked his legs into the space under the desk. 'But, Mum, it's *boring*! Can't we go to the beach now? I'll read this later, I *promise*!'

'We agreed that mornings are going to be for your schoolwork, and I'm not budging.' Ruby frowned, her tone non-negotiable. 'I promised Mr Hinton you would keep up with your work, and the last thing I want is for you to fall behind in class because I brought you out here. This week is half-term, so you've only got the book report to do, but you still need to *read* the book before you can write about it! Please, buddy, the sooner you finish that chapter, the sooner we can get on with the rest of our day.'

Jake grumbled under his breath but returned his attention to the open book in front of him. Ruby picked up the chunky novel she had brought with her, only to toss the book aside a few minutes later. Jake wasn't the only one struggling to concentrate, and it was proving a challenge to focus on the seventeenth-century English love story while Ruby was on a tropical island dealing with her own twenty-first-century relationship. With Jake now engrossed in his book and Ruby not wanting to distract him, she quietly slipped off the sofa and stepped out on to the balcony.

It was another bright day with beautiful blue skies, and Ruby ran her hands through her braids and lifted her face to the sun. In the short time they'd been on the island, the strong Caribbean sun had already darkened her skin tone and she stretched luxuriously, loving the sensation of heat on her bare arms.

Now they were past the initial thorny meeting with Kenny, not only did Ruby feel more relaxed, but Jake also seemed to have adapted well, and the speed with which he had accepted Kenny back into his life had been remarkable. Other than his dogged insistence that she send for Jellybean, her son was displaying none of the anxiety that usually accompanied changes to his routine.

Ruby slipped her phone out of her pocket to remind Griffin of his promise to courier the toy rabbit and then remembered the time difference. He was unlikely to welcome a phone call so early in the morning, but if she didn't do it now, she risked them both forgetting. She tapped out his number and huffed when the call went straight to voicemail. *He's probably shacked up with Shirlee's successor*, Ruby thought irritably, typing out a short text instead.

There was one person Ruby knew would be awake, and that was Fi, who rarely slept for more than four or five hours a night. She dialled the number and, right on cue, her call was answered on the second ring.

'Hi, Rubes!' Fi's voice sounded even deeper across the phone line.

'How did you know it was me?' Ruby asked in surprise. 'I'm using a local routing number.'

'Because it's an unknown foreign number I haven't yet blocked *and* it's about time I heard from you! Besides, you're the only one I know who'd have the nerve to call this early in the morning and expect me to answer. Anyway, how's it going out there? Have you found him yet?'

Ruby glanced in the direction of the open balcony door and lowered her voice. 'Yes, we saw him a couple of days ago, but I haven't had a chance to call you. It was all very emotional between him and Jake, and incredibly weird for me, if I'm honest! He hasn't changed much – to look at, at least.'

'I'll bet he was shocked to see the two of you. Have you killed him and buried the body?' Fi asked cheerfully.

Ruby laughed. 'I'm still in shock, but it could yet happen. He's called twice every day since and spoken to Jake for ages. He's taking us out to dinner tonight, so he's certainly putting in the work, even if he's six years too late! I can't say much now cos Jake's nearby, but I'll call you another time for a proper chat. I just wanted to say hello and let you know we're still in one piece.'

'Hold on a sec, how's the divine Griffin coping without you? I bet he's like a lost puppy. Tell him to call me if he needs comforting.'

Ruby rolled her eyes. 'I honestly can't deal with the two of you. I just rang him, actually, and got his voicemail, which means he's either not up yet or he's with some chick and too – erm . . . busy to answer the phone.'

'The man is gorgeous, and you can't blame any girl for falling, Rubes. I certainly wouldn't kick him out of my bed.'

'Fi . . .' Ruby warned.

'Okay, okay, I'll change the subject! What's the weather like where you are? It's dark, pouring with rain and bloody miserable here.'

'Honestly, Fi, this place is absolutely beautiful! It's hot and sunny, but not oppressive. Can you believe I've got a tan already? We're staying at a family-owned place called Paradise Inn which is literally heaven! I'm standing on the balcony looking at some stunning gardens as we speak.'

Fi grunted. 'Well, don't go getting too attached to the place. Priya's doing okay so far, but it's only been a couple of days. Remember what I said before you left – I need you back here.'

'Erm . . . talking of work, I need to ask a favour,' Ruby began.

'What favour?' The panic in Fi's voice was audible. 'Please don't tell me you want to stay out there for another six months or anything?'

'No, of course not, although now you mention it— Okay, calm down, I'm kidding!' Ruby laughed in response to Fi's squawk of protest. 'No, it's just an idea I've been thinking about, and I haven't even asked her yet but—'

'Rubes, for crying out loud, will you get to the point already!'

'*Okay!* So, the lady who owns Paradise Inn is a real sweetheart and she's practically adopted me and Jake since we got here. She's American – from Louisiana – and she has the loveliest accent.'

Fi growled impatiently, and Ruby quickly continued, 'Anyway, she and her husband came out to the island almost forty years ago to start a new life together because of all the racial tension in the States. He died a few years ago and she's struggling to get enough visitors to keep the business going.'

'Rubes, that's a real shame but I need to finish getting dressed and I have no idea what this has to do with work.'

Ruby continued doggedly, undaunted by Fi's exasperated tone. 'I will tell you if you let me finish! The thing is, Paradise Inn is *divine*, and I think that with a great website and some digital marketing, it could attract heaps of customers. Now, I can take pictures and put some copy together, but—'

'—but you haven't got the first idea about the mechanics of setting up a website, and you want us to do it,' Fi finished dryly.

'*Please*, Fi,' Ruby wheedled. 'Nick could knock up a basic website in a matter of hours and I could email him some images and text to use. I'm going to be working with him on stuff like this in my new role and this will boost my digital skills no end. If it helps, think of it as our corporate social responsibility project for the year. Poor Miss Ida might lose her home and her business if things don't improve.'

'*Miss Ida?* She really is from the South, isn't she?' Her boss sounded amused rather than annoyed, and Ruby exhaled with relief. Fi was unpredictable at the best of times and asking her for a favour before she'd had her morning coffee was a bit of a gamble, although well worth it if she agreed to Ruby's suggestion.

After a short pause Fi said briskly, 'Fine. If helping your old lady means you won't follow in Kenny's footsteps and take up residence on Sorrel Island, then I'm on board. I'll brief Nick when I get into the office, but you'll have to call him yourself and explain what you need. And keep it simple, d'you hear? He already has a ton of *paying* projects on his plate.'

'I will,' Ruby promised, grinning happily. 'Thanks *so* much, Fi. Miss Ida's going to be *stoked*!'

'Okay, I've got to go. Give the munchkin a kiss from me and call me when you can talk properly cos I want *all* the details. Oh, and Rubes . . . ?'

'Yes?'

'Make sure you ring me at a civilised time in future.'

The line clicked off, and Ruby groaned aloud. Pigs would fly the day Fi failed to get in the last word.

Then, remembering the marketing coup she had just scored for Miss Ida, Ruby burst into a spontaneous happy dance. *I can't wait to tell Miss Ida how we're going to save her business.*

'MUM! I've finished the chapter. *Please* can we go to the beach now?' Jake's plaintive voice wafted out on to the balcony.

'Coming, buddy!' Ruby grinned, skipping back into the room.

17

Armed with towels, sun hats, and water, Ruby and Jake walked down the tiled steps from the terrace on to the pathway that led to the beach. Unlike their brief peek around the private cove the day before, this afternoon they had come prepared. Ruby had optimistically packed her novel and Jake's half-term reading in her beach bag, but one look at the azure-blue water glittering in the sunlight immediately dispelled any thought of reading.

'Mum! It's *awesome!*' Jake raced across the white sands, whirling his small body around and waving his arms so energetically that his baseball cap flew off his head.

Ruby smiled as she watched him pick it up and then run to paddle in the shallows where the waves lapped on to the sand. It was a joy to see Jake looking so carefree, and for the first time she silently thanked Auntie Pearl for badgering her into making the trip. She could only pray that Kenny played his part and did nothing to threaten their son's happiness while they were here.

She spotted a pair of beach loungers under the shelter of a large umbrella and trudged over to claim the spot. Dumping her bag on the table supporting the umbrella, she shook the grains of sun-warmed sand from her flip-flops and dropped on to a lounger. She took off her wide-brimmed straw hat and shook her braids free before untying the colourful sarong she had bought to go with her new one-piece black swimsuit, and reclining along the length of the lounger.

The stretch of beach behind Paradise Inn was quiet, and other than the young couple who were splashing around the water's edge with their children, the other loungers around the cove were unoccupied. Ruby lay back and gazed out to sea through her oversized sunglasses as she reflected on Miss Ida's predicament. Paradise Inn was much too beautiful a house for anyone to have to relinquish, let alone someone as lovely as their hostess. Miss Ida had been too busy at lunchtime for a chat, but Ruby couldn't wait to see the older woman's face when she broke the news about the plan to save her home.

'*Mum!* Come into the water with me,' Jake shrieked, rushing up to the lounger and tugging on Ruby's arm. 'You can't nap now we're on the beach.'

'I just wanted to relax for a few minutes,' Ruby laughed, but when Jake refused to take no for an answer, she shook her head in resignation.

'*Okay!* Come on, I'll race you to the water!'

Two hours later, even Jake had tired of splashing around in the sea, and he and Ruby lay on their loungers sipping water from the flasks they had brought along.

'I love Sorrel Island!' Jake enthused. 'Can we come here again?'

Ruby hesitated, not sure of how to respond when there was still so much to be resolved with Kenny.

'I hope so,' she hedged. 'It would be lovely to visit another time, but let's see how things go, hmm?'

Jake lapsed into silence for a few minutes. 'Next time we come, I want Uncle Griffin to come with us so we can play our pebble game. I bet I'd win!'

Trying to manage Jake's expectations about a future trip was plainly an exercise in futility.

'As long as you and your godfather leave me out of your pebble-skimming contests, that's fine with me,' she murmured, reclining against the lounger, and closing her eyes.

It wasn't long before Jake grew restless. 'Can we go and see what's up there?'

Ruby opened one eye to see Jake pointing upwards to an outcrop of trees and flowering bushes further along the cliffs overlooking the sea. There was no access to the patch of pretty woodland from their cove, which meant walking along the shore and past the rocks forming the cove to find a way up.

'Jake, can't you just let me lie here for a bit?' Ruby groaned.

He giggled and prodded her thigh. 'Come on, Mum, don't be a spoilsport.'

Knowing she would get no peace until she agreed, Ruby sat up and tied her sarong around her waist. 'Fine but pass me the sunscreen first and hold out your arms,' she instructed. 'And put your cap back on – I don't want you getting sunstroke.'

By the time she'd retrieved her straw hat, fished around for her flip-flops, and slid on her sunglasses, Jake had already taken off, and Ruby trudged after him unenthusiastically.

'Hey, wait for me!' she called, picking up her pace as Jake vanished around the bend of the cove. Turning the corner, she came to an abrupt halt and stared in wonder. Before her was a perfectly formed sandy inlet set back from the sea and fringed with palm trees. The beach was deserted, with only the squawking of seabirds and gentle waves breaking on to the shore disturbing its tranquillity.

This island is truly a paradise!

Ruby picked her way over the rocky outcrop and walked up on to the sand, where a cool breeze blew in from the water and rustled through the fronds of the swaying palm trees lining the cove.

'*Mum!*'

At the sound of Jake's voice, Ruby craned her neck to find her son halfway up a steep, sandy pathway that appeared to lead to the wooded area he had pointed out. How the hell did he get there so fast? she wondered grumpily as she plodded towards the path.

Struggling to navigate the uneven track in her flip-flops, Ruby longed to return to her lounger. What was the point of a private beach if you weren't allowed a moment to sunbathe? she muttered under her breath. By the time she caught up with Jake, he was standing at the top of the path, staring out to sea.

'Mum, look! Do you think that boat out there is one of my dad's?' he asked excitedly, his eyes fixed on a large white boat with billowing sails in the distance.

Puffing from the unaccustomed exercise, Ruby followed his gaze and took a moment to catch her breath before answering. 'I don't know, buddy. Don't forget we saw an awful lot of boats down at the marina.'

Clearly keen to explore, Jake skipped along a well-trodden sandy path running through a carpet of thick grass and surrounded by leafy trees and wildflowers while Ruby did her best to keep up. Just as she opened her mouth to plead with him to slow down, he suddenly stopped in front of a small clearing. He turned to his mother with wide eyes and beckoned silently. When she reached his side, Ruby stared in surprise at the sight of a man seated on a folding chair in the middle of the clearing. He had his back to them while staring at a large square of blank canvas propped on an easel. On the grass at his feet lay a pile of sketch pads and a pack of coloured pencils.

Glancing at Ruby, Jake hissed in a not-so-quiet whisper, 'I think he's an artist!'

The man spun around on his chair, and Ruby's jaw dropped as she gaped at the stranger in shock.

What the hell was George Clooney doing on Sorrel Island?

18

The man stared at Ruby, his expression mirroring her shock. Then, recovering quickly, he jumped from his chair and strode purposefully towards her. She stepped in front of Jake, holding out her arms protectively as the man circled them without a word. Taking a half-step forward, he examined Ruby's face intently through narrowed bright blue eyes that showed not a hint of embarrassment. Up close, although with his salt-and-pepper hair and beard he was still a dead ringer for George Clooney, this man was much taller and at least twenty years younger.

'The gods have done it again! *Magnificent!* Absolutely superb!' When he finally spoke, his voice had an unmistakeable American twang.

Ruby stared at him blankly, far too shocked by the brazen scrutiny to protest the man's bizarre behaviour.

'You've just gotta love this island, am I right?' He flashed a brilliant smile that showed off perfect white teeth. 'Lady, I don't know who the heck you are, but what I do know is that you are *exactly* what I was praying for!'

George Clooney – or not – what the actual hell?! The sheer effrontery of the stranger snapped Ruby out of her trance, and she exploded.

'Now you hold on just a minute! Are you taking the pi—?'

'*Mum!*' Jake nudged an elbow into her side in warning.

The man blinked, clearly taken aback by her reaction. Then, looking her straight in the eye, he surprised her with a smile so radiant she was shocked to feel her pulse quicken.

'I mean it, lady. Trust me, you really are the answer to my prayers.'

Ruby frowned and scrambled to gather her wits. The man might be good-looking, but he was also a complete nutter. She backed away from him slowly, reaching for Jake's hand and casting a furtive glance around for an escape route.

'Look, lady, I promise you I'm not crazy,' he chuckled, looking more amused than offended. 'My name's Mac. I'm guessing you're also staying at Paradise Inn, is that right?'

When she nodded cautiously, he waved a hand as if swatting away her misgivings. 'Well then, Miss Ida will vouch for me. I've been visiting for the past five years.'

It was Ruby's turn to narrow her eyes. She was familiar with the few guests staying at the inn, but she had never seen Mac, either at mealtimes or on the grounds.

'We've been here for three days, and I've never laid eyes on you.' *Believe me, I would have noticed.*

'I'm an artist, and I keep my own hours,' said George Clooney/ Mac, his tone so dismissive that Ruby bristled.

Jake's nudge in her side reminded her of the need for manners, even when dealing with deranged strangers, and she shrugged.

'Fine. Well, I'm Ruby and this is my son, Jake.'

Mac stared at Jake and held up a hand, stooping so Jake could obligingly slap it with his own. Evidently done with the pleasantries, Mac turned back to Ruby. 'So, here's the thing, Ruby.'

She remained silent while he scratched his beard thoughtfully. 'Okay, I realise this might sound absurd since you don't know me from Adam, but here's the thing.'

He paused and leaned forward to peer once again at her profile, and Ruby bit her lip to stop herself from screaming. *Will the man ever get to the point?*

'Perhaps I should introduce myself properly. Mackenzie Castro, at your service,' he announced grandly. He raised an eyebrow and looked at her expectantly, but Ruby just looked blank.

'I am a *very* well-known figurative artist,' he elaborated, looking somewhat pained. When Ruby still looked clueless, he sighed and added slowly, as if speaking to a child, 'I paint portraits.'

'*Oh!*' Her brow cleared as she finally understood what he was talking about. Although she still didn't see what that had to do with her or why he was behaving so strangely. Admittedly, it was also hard to concentrate on his words when she was so distracted by his looks.

'I've been invited to submit a portrait for an exclusive exhibition in New York next year. It's a high-profile, prestigious event, involving only the *best* figurative artists,' he added pointedly.

'Oka-ay,' Ruby said, still baffled as to where all this was going.

'So, the thing is, I've been trying to come up with a concept I can get excited about. Now, I visit Sorrel Island every year because it's always been a real creative place for me. But I've been here almost two damned weeks and, so far, nothing! Then, just as I'm about to lose it, the island gods sent *you!*' He threw his arms into the air with all the energy of an orchestra conductor at the finale of a symphony.

'*Me?*' Ruby exclaimed, not sure whether to laugh or simply grab Jake and run.

'Yes, *you!*' he repeated impatiently. 'So, will you let me paint you?'

'*Paint* me! Why me, for God's sake? I'm hardly your model type!'

'You don't know my type,' Mac pointed out. 'Besides, everything about you is *magnificent*! Everything . . . your height, your colouring, your body – it's all perfect for the Caribbean-island-goddess idea I've been playing with!'

Despite his over-the-top effusiveness, Mac sounded sincere, but Ruby's first instinct was to flatly refuse his request. Although her schooldays were far behind her, the years of being taunted about her height had left her deeply insecure about her appearance. The idea that she could model for a portrait destined for a prestigious exhibition sounded patently ridiculous.

She opened her mouth to turn down Mac's offer, but Jake tugged hard on her hand and when she looked down, his eyes shone with excitement.

'Do it, Mum! You'd be a brilliant model and I'd get to watch him while he draws you.' As if sensing her hesitation, he looked at her with pleading eyes. '*Pleeeease?*'

Mac looked at the boy quizzically and then knelt on the grass, bringing himself to eye level with Jake. 'Are you interested in art, son?'

When Jake nodded vigorously, Mac looked up at Ruby, who shrugged in agreement. 'He loves drawing and he's very talented.'

Mac's gaze moved speculatively from Ruby to Jake and then he stood up and brushed the grass off his trousers before facing Ruby squarely.

'Well, then, how about we make a deal? You sit for me, and I'll let Jake watch *and* I'll give him some free art lessons while you're here. What do you say?'

'That's pure bribery!' she protested. 'Besides, why would I let a perfect stranger hang around my son?'

'That's a fair point. Look, Ruby, all I'm suggesting is that we help each other out here. I know I'm a stranger, but I swear Miss Ida will give me a great character reference.'

'*Please*, Mum?' Jake begged in a voice thick with longing. 'I'm already missing Art Club, and Mac's a *real* artist. I want him to teach me.'

Ruby sighed, wishing Griffin was there to help her work out what was best. The only reason she had come to the island was to sort things out with Kenny so Jake could move on with his life. She certainly hadn't counted on this – this ridiculously handsome stranger who seemed bent on digging into and exposing her deepest insecurity. She looked at the naked entreaty on the faces of both Mac and Jake and allowed herself to consider the possibility of being a real, live model. Clearly, George Clooney – okay, Mac – didn't see her as an unattractive, intimidating hulk. He actually *wanted* to paint her! Furthermore, if the man was as renowned an artist as he claimed to be, this would be an incredible opportunity for Jake to learn from the best. Moreover, she'd be right there to keep an eye on his interaction with her son, so what could it hurt?

Mac had been watching the changing expressions chasing across Ruby's face as she wrestled with her decision. 'I promise I won't interfere too much with your holiday,' he pleaded. 'I'm talking about a couple of hours a day for a week or so, tops. I just need to get the preliminary sketches down and I can take it from there.'

Mac's dimpled smile and wheedling tone were so at odds with his earlier hauteur that Ruby couldn't help laughing.

'I still don't get why you'd want to paint me, but if it helps Jake, then okay.' She shook her head resignedly as Jake cheered loudly and Mac joined in.

'So, can we start tomorrow morning?' Mac asked, rubbing his hands together and skewering her with another dazzling smile.

Mesmerised, Ruby bit her lower lip and stared at him wordlessly. Once again, Jake nudged her, and she blinked and cleared her throat.

'Um . . . sure. Jake does his schoolwork in the mornings, so it would need to be after that.'

'Whatever's good for you guys works for me,' said Mac, 'but I like to start as early as possible to get the best light. That okay?'

Ruby nodded, already regretting her decision. Just being around Mac left her feeling flustered, and the idea of spending hours with him every day suddenly seemed fraught with challenge.

Whichever way she looked at it, her straightforward mission to set her son straight about his father was becoming more complicated by the day.

19

'After you,' Kenny said, stepping aside and gesturing towards the open front door.

Ruby hesitated, troubled by even the symbolism of crossing the threshold into Kenny's home. She had assumed dinner would be at a restaurant until he had casually remarked in the car how much he was looking forward to cooking for her again. Before she had time to object, he had turned the car into a driveway and was pulling up in front of a white two-storey building. Despite Jake's wishful thinking, his father's house in no way rivalled Paradise Inn for size and, unlike Miss Ida's plantation-era mansion, was built in a contemporary style with clean lines and solar panels in one side of the roof. In the falling dusk, spotlights in the front garden illuminated a profusion of colourful flowers tamed into neatly fashioned beds.

While Ruby wavered on the doorstep, Jake slipped past her with an impatient tut and dashed in. Torn between her son's obvious excitement at seeing his father's home and her desire to avoid getting pulled any further into Kenny's life than she had to, Ruby reluctantly followed suit. Inside, the layout was open plan with high ceilings and large glass windows. On one side, the hall flowed into a spacious living area with a huge sofa and furnishings in shades of grey and white. To the right and through an archway was a formal dining room with a polished mahogany table and matching chairs upholstered in grey. If Miss Ida's house spoke of warmth and colour, Kenny's was sleek and modern with an elegant simplicity. Despite the openness and monochromatic decor, there was nevertheless a welcoming feel to the place and an even more welcoming aroma wafting across from the other side of the dining room.

'Why don't you take a seat in the living room while I check on dinner,' Kenny suggested. 'I'll show you around the house in a moment.'

Ruby nodded without comment, trying not to let him see just how thrown off balance she was feeling.

Whistling cheerfully, Kenny strode through the dining room towards a door leading into what Ruby presumed was the kitchen. She turned and followed Jake into the living area and perched gingerly on the edge of a stylish corner sofa while her son roamed around the room inspecting the large television screen with satellite box and a very expensive-looking music system. Kenny clearly didn't do fluffy throw pillows or fussy ornaments, Ruby noted. The minimalist design was functional and uncluttered, with no sign of softer feminine touches. All in all, a veritable man cave, she concluded, recalling his earlier assertion that there was no woman in his life.

When Kenny returned a few minutes later, Jake accepted the invitation to tour the house with alacrity and, too curious to refuse, Ruby followed them up the wide flight of stairs. Upstairs, the bedrooms were spacious and airy, with large windows contributing to a loft-like feel.

As Jake wandered around one of the rooms, exploring the deep wardrobes and adjoining bathroom, Kenny announced with a grin, 'Son, this room is yours now and it's here for you whenever you come to visit.'

Jake's eyes widened with delight. '*Cool!* Look, Mum, the bed is massive!'

Ruby smiled at his enthusiasm, although she couldn't help feeling things were progressing at breakneck speed. They hadn't even discussed how Kenny would feature in his son's life going forward, and she silently prayed the man would keep his word and not break their son's heart again.

Kenny walked further along the corridor and opened a door that Ruby instinctively knew led to his bedroom. With Jake pulling her along, she hovered in the doorway while the boy went in. Obviously the master bedroom, the room was huge, with an en-suite bathroom. There were a couple of paintings on the walls, a full bookcase and a smoke-grey sofa with a matching footstool. Ruby's gaze landed on the king-sized bed dominating the room and her mind flashed back to the bed she and Kenny had once shared. She felt a deep flush rising into her cheeks and looked up to find him eyeing her with a quizzical expression, almost as if he could read her thoughts.

'I'll go and set the table. The food should be ready but take your time exploring and come down when you're done.' Although Kenny directed his remark to Jake, his eyes remained on Ruby and, disconcerted, she turned away.

By the time Ruby finally dragged Jake out of his newly acquired room and followed him downstairs and into the dining room, plates, cutlery, and glasses had been laid out on the table. Kenny walked out of the kitchen holding a jug of water and set it down.

'It's nice to have company,' he said with a smile. 'It can get pretty lonely sometimes.'

Am I supposed to feel sorry for him? Ruby thought sourly. Then, remembering she was here for Jake, she fixed a smile on her face. 'It's very kind of you to have us over. I hope you didn't go to too much trouble.'

'I'm just happy for the chance to have you both here. Take a seat and I'll bring the food through.'

Moments later, he returned carrying two large serving bowls, which he set down on the table. 'I'll fetch the salad and then we can tuck in.'

Ruby eyed the large bowls filled with mouth-watering steaming white rice and what looked like a stew with fish and seafood and sniffed appreciatively. She might be pissed off with Kenny, but he had always been a fantastic cook and she had no doubt the food would be good.

Taking the seat they had left for him at the top of the table, Kenny passed around the dishes and they all filled their plates. Jake brushed aside his mother's attempt to help him and spooned rice on to his plate before ladling a generous portion of stew alongside it.

'I think I managed to take out all the fish bones, but just be careful in case there are still a few small ones,' Kenny cautioned as he filled their glasses with water.

Watching Jake dive into his meal, Ruby followed his lead, and for a while the only sounds came from the chink of cutlery against plates as they concentrated on the food. After several mouthfuls of the tender, flaky fillets of fish and flavourful sauce, Ruby paused with a sigh of pleasure.

'Do you like it?' Kenny looked at her expectantly, and she nodded.

'It's delicious,' she said sincerely. She reached for the bowl filled with salad and piled some on to her plate. The man might be a bastard, but there was no denying he could cook.

After a dessert of fruit salad in a tangy dressing accompanied by vanilla ice-cream, Kenny stacked their empty bowls and carried them to the kitchen, waving aside Ruby's offer of help.

Ruby returned with Jake to the living room and, settling herself on to the sofa, tucked a leg under her, feeling more relaxed. Until she looked up to find Kenny standing close by and watching her once again, his expression inscrutable.

'You have a lovely house,' she remarked, trying to ignore the unexpected heat in her cheeks.

'Thank you. Were you hoping I'd be living in a hovel?' He grinned, moving to sit in the large armchair opposite her.

'No,' she lied. It would have been a whole lot easier to keep him out of Jake's life if he had been. 'You're obviously doing well out here.' She looked around the room and then back at him. 'This place suits you. It's very modern and has that "everything in its place" look.'

Kenny shrugged. 'I bought it a couple of years ago from a Brazilian architect who decided to sell up and return home. I liked the fact he'd built it to be environmentally friendly and had sourced eco-friendly woods and materials for the construction. It's a great space to come home to after a long day at the marina.'

Then he turned to Jake with a mischievous grin. 'Hey, son, what do you say we play some records and do some dancing?'

Jake giggled, and Kenny stood up and walked over to a nut-brown wooden cabinet. He pressed one side and a concealed door swung open to reveal an extensive collection of vinyl records. Choosing one, he slipped it out of the cover and, after placing it carefully on the slim record player at the top of the music system, the room was instantly filled with the rhythmic sounds of calypso.

'Come on, my boy, move those hips!' Kenny's Trinidadian lilt was even more pronounced as he sang the lyrics to the song while taking Jake by both hands and dancing around the room. Ruby giggled helplessly at the sight of her son wiggling his slight hips in time to the fast drums, bass, and horns of the steel band. Watching them, she couldn't help remembering how often Kenny had held Jake's hands when he was a toddler and danced with him around the living room to his favourite calypso and soca.

When the song ended, Kenny returned to the cabinet and rummaged through his collection, pulling out an album with a triumphant smile. Placing the disc inside on the record player, he said to Jake, 'Your mum and I used to dance to this one all the time.'

The familiar sound of the calypso tune Kenny had always called 'their song' instantly brought long-buried memories flooding back, almost destroying Ruby's composure. While Jake carried on dancing, blithely unaware of the sudden tension in the room, Kenny's gaze sought Ruby's. When their eyes met, she shivered at the intensity she saw there and, for just a moment, all her bitterness and anger was suspended.

'Dance with me?' he asked, holding out his arms.

Jake gleefully tried to pull Ruby off the sofa, but she shook her head with a laugh that even to her own ears sounded strained. 'Thanks, but I'm way too full after that lovely dinner to move.'

'Another time, then?' Kenny's eyes were hooded as he took in her flustered expression, and Ruby dropped her gaze. *He's not exactly making this easy*, she thought, trying to corral her wayward emotions. First a delicious meal, and now dancing. But although Kenny was making it obvious that he still had feelings for her, how could she even *contemplate* turning back the clock to the way things had once been?

When she didn't answer, he said softly, 'I meant what I said, Rubes. Nothing's changed.'

◆ ◆ ◆

'Griff, can you hear me?' Ruby demanded as the connection dropped again. She lowered her voice, not wanting to wake up Jake, who had fallen asleep within seconds of his head hitting the pillow.

Other than the awkward moment when Jake had tried to cajole her into Kenny's arms, dinner with her ex had gone better than she expected. But now, far too restless to go to bed after an evening that still felt surreal, and with Jake out for the count, Ruby had slipped on to the balcony to call Griffin. With her son constantly within earshot, she hadn't yet had a chance to give her best friend more than a basic recounting of their first meeting with Kenny. After the emotional havoc wreaked by this latest encounter, she desperately needed Griffin to help her analyse her feelings. So far, to her utter frustration, her efforts had been sabotaged by the poor phone connection.

'Can you hear me now?' Griffin's deep voice sounded crystal clear, and Ruby dived in before the signal disappeared again.

'As I was saying . . . when I asked him why he'd left, he apologised and then said he's still single and nothing's changed about his feelings for me and that he still loves me.'

'And what did you say?' There was an odd note in Griffin's voice she couldn't quite identify, and she frowned even though he couldn't see her.

'What do you *think* I said? Nothing! I was in total shock! I don't get what all this drama has been about if he still loves me.'

For a moment there was silence, and then she continued. 'So, anyway, we went to his house for dinner this evening. I thought we were going to a restaurant, but he'd cooked and everything. To be honest, the food was incredible – he's still brilliant in *that* department, at least. His house is lovely and very modern, and he showed us this huge room which he says is Jake's from now on. So, of course, the boy's all excited about the idea of actually living with his father! Kenny's made it clear he wants to co-parent in some way going forward, but it's early days and we couldn't exactly discuss Jake's future while he was sitting with us.'

'So, when are you seeing Kenny again?'

'He's picking us up to go out tomorrow. Like I said, he genuinely seems keen to make amends and to spend time with us – I mean, with Jake—'

'Are you catching feelings for the man?'

Ruby winced at Griffin's incredulous tone. 'I wouldn't go that far, although I won't lie, he's not the same Kenny that I remember. He seems . . . I don't know, gentler, somehow. More fun and relaxed, and it's not as awkward talking to him as I thought it would be.'

'I thought you said this trip was about Jake and not about you.' Griffin sounded grim.

'It *is*,' she protested. 'I'm just feeling a bit – I don't know – overwhelmed by everything. It's not that I believe him, exactly, but you should have seen Jake tonight. He was dancing and laughing, and he looked so happy! I'm not saying I'm ready to forgive and forget just like that, but . . . honestly, Griff, I don't know what to do for the best and it is *such* hard work trying to explain things to people who don't understand the history. Miss Ida says Kenny is a good man and I should give him a chance to redeem himself. I love the woman, but, honestly, she's such a hopeless romantic.'

'*Romantic?* What, she actually thinks you should get back together with him?' Griffin sounded outraged, and Ruby grimaced.

'Who knows *what* she thinks! That lady is determined I'm going to fall in love with someone while I'm here because, you know, this place is the original love island . . . Griff? Are you still there? *Dammit*, have I lost you again?'

Ruby groaned with frustration as the line went dead. Muttering under her breath, she punched out his number and redialled, only to hear a long, continuous beep. After a few more abortive attempts to resume the conversation, she gave up and went to bed.

20

The door to Miss Ida's office was ajar, and Ruby knocked softly before poking her head around.

Miss Ida was seated behind her desk, and she whipped off her tortoiseshell glasses and beckoned Ruby inside with a smile and a nod towards the visitor's chair.

'Have a seat, Ruby. How are you this morning? Everything good with you and my sweet boy?'

'Everything's fine, thank you.' Ruby paused to admire the deep magenta upholstery of the chair before sitting down and crossing her legs. 'Jake's upstairs finishing his book report – at least I hope he is – and I thought I'd come down for a quick chat.'

'Is that right?' Miss Ida's face lit up with a knowing smile and her eyes twinkled with merriment. 'I hear you met Mac yesterday. He says he bumped into you by the beach, and he seemed pretty smitten.'

Ruby felt her face burn with embarrassment, and she uncrossed her legs and tried to look unconcerned. Miss Ida was an out-and-out romantic of the worst kind and clearly prone to reading things into the most innocent of interactions. There was absolutely no way that Mac fancied her.

'I think you've got the wrong end of the stick,' she said firmly. 'He was simply grateful to find someone daft enough to pose for him.'

Miss Ida looked sceptical. 'I don't know, sugar. He looked plenty excited to me, saying you were the answer to his prayers and all. I told you this island brings out love, didn't I?'

She chuckled at Ruby's obvious discomfort and then said kindly, 'So if you're not here to talk about Mac, sweetheart, how can I help you?'

Ruby was more than ready to change the subject and she leaned forward, her voice quickening with excitement. 'Well, actually, it's more like how I can help *you*!'

Miss Ida looked bewildered, and Ruby quickly outlined her idea for a website for Paradise Inn, relaying the gist of her conversation with Fi the previous day. 'I've just got off the phone with Nick – he's our guru for all things digital – and he's totally on board to design the site. He's also going to incorporate a room booking system and design an app and everything!'

Ruby's triumphant smile faded as Miss Ida's face clouded over. This was definitely not the response she had anticipated.

'What's the matter, Miss Ida? I thought you'd be pleased,' she asked hesitantly. 'It will be a lot easier to attract more visitors if you have your own website.'

'It's so kind of you to want to help me, darlin', but . . .' Miss Ida tailed off and, instantly remorseful, Ruby jumped in.

'I'm so sorry! It was presumptuous of me, and I've overstepped, haven't I? I didn't mean to offend you. I honestly just wanted to help you keep your home and—'

Miss Ida raised her hand to cut her off. 'No, *no*, Ruby! I'm not offended at all! It's just that I don't have the kind of money to spend on everything you've just described. I'm just about getting by as it is. Although I do thank you for trying to—'

'But wait, there's absolutely no charge for doing this!' Ruby interrupted, mentally kicking herself for not leading with this crucial piece of information.

When Miss Ida still looked dubious, Ruby took a deep breath and continued more calmly. 'I'm so sorry, Miss Ida, I should have made myself clearer. The thing is, I told Fi – my boss – about how you've been taking such good care of us and about your beautiful home. I also shared your concerns about needing more guests so you didn't have to sell Paradise Inn, and she agreed to my idea straightaway. The thing is, we *want* to do this for you, and you don't have to pay a penny! If you're happy about it, we can share a little bit about you and Marty's story on the website to add a more personal touch, and we can even write about the Sorrel Island love-magic legend stuff you talked about. It's the sort of thing that will have guests flocking over here.'

'Now, I don't want too many folks all coming at one time.' Miss Ida frowned, looking alarmed at the prospect of visiting hordes.

'Don't worry about that,' Ruby said firmly. 'Nick will set up the site so you can control the availability of bookings and decide the number of guests you want to accommodate at any one time.'

As Miss Ida absorbed Ruby's words, her frown disappeared, and her eyes sparkled. 'Oh *my*! Why, Ruby, that's the *nicest* thing anyone has ever done for me! I don't know much about the internet, but Narita's always on the computer and she can help me.'

Suddenly energised, she jumped up from her chair and clapped her hands in delight. 'If we get more guests, I can afford to give her a full-time job so she doesn't have to leave the island and break Zeke's heart. Goodness, Ruby, if this works, it will make *such* a difference!'

Ruby grinned, only just restraining herself from breaking into her happy dance. Miss Ida's face was glowing, and Ruby felt an unexpected lump in her throat. She swallowed hard, finding it hard to believe she had only known their lovely hostess for a few days.

Ruby cleared her throat and stood up. 'I'd better go upstairs and check on Jake. Kenny's taking us out this afternoon and I promised Mac I'd sit for him for a bit first. Is it okay if I come and find you later and share some of my ideas for the website?'

Miss Ida stood and came around her desk with her arms outstretched. When Ruby obligingly bent to embrace her, Miss Ida kissed her gently on the cheek.

'Mac was right,' Miss Ida said softly as she gazed up at Ruby with suddenly moist eyes. 'The gods really *did* bring you to Sorrel Island.'

21

Mac's eyes remained fixed on Ruby's face, with only the occasional glance down at the sketch pad in his hand. Every so often, he would flip over a page and his pencil would once again fly back and forth over the paper. They were in the same patch of clearing high above the inlet where Ruby and Jake had stumbled across him the previous day, and while Mac sat on his folding chair, Ruby reclined on a grass-covered mound, enjoying the cool breeze wafting through the light fabric of her long, floaty skirt. Her initial anxiety about posing had long since been replaced by the tedium of sitting in one place under stern instructions not to move. Even Jake had eventually grown bored of watching the artist at work and wandered off to explore their surroundings, leaving Ruby alone with Mac.

'So, tell me about yourself, Ruby.'

'Why?' she demanded, and then, realising she sounded rude, added in a more conciliatory tone, 'I mean, what do you want to know? I'm not particularly interesting.'

'On the contrary,' Mac chided. 'Here you are with your kid, thousands of miles away from home on an island most people have never heard of. You don't seem like a regular tourist, so what's your story? And just so you know, I'm not trying to butt into your business, but the more I know about you, the better I can capture your spirit and the essence of your personality in the portrait.'

Her sceptical expression was met with one of wide-eyed innocence. 'C'mon, Ruby,' Mac murmured persuasively. 'Think of me as your priest – or your shrink, if you prefer. Look, if you're on the run after pulling off a bank heist or whatever, you can tell me. I promise your secret will stay safe.'

He winked at her, and Ruby rolled her eyes, trying not to laugh. Much to her surprise, she felt far more relaxed in Mac's company than she had expected, although she still found herself taking the odd surreptitious peep to confirm he really wasn't George Clooney.

'Why do you need to make so many sketches?' Ruby queried after a few minutes of silence. Mac's process was confounding her vague assumption that he would draw an outline on the untouched canvas and then colour it in.

Mac pursed his lips as his hand moved swiftly over the page. 'I want to test different angles of your face. It'll help me figure out the best approach and a pose that captures you the way I see you.'

'And how do you see me?' The words spilled out before she could check them, and she felt a flush of heat rise into her face.

Mac paused and looked at her for a long moment. This time the scrutiny felt different from the earlier, impersonal glances, and instead of dropping her eyes, she returned his gaze boldly, feeling her heart suddenly beat faster.

'I'm not sure yet,' he said slowly. 'On the outside you're this stunning, statuesque woman with an amazing physique and incredible facial bones. You look like a strong woman who doesn't take any crap, but . . . I also get the sense that behind this magnificent brick wall is another Ruby you're hiding who isn't quite so tough.'

The heat in her face coursed throughout her body, and she deeply regretted having opened the door to this line of conversation.

She clenched her jaw as she fought the overwhelming temptation to get up and run away. She had agreed to pose for Mac, not to share her life story or subject herself to his amateur psychology.

But Mac wasn't finished. 'I've told you why I'm here. Tell me what brought you to Sorrel Island.'

Ruby took a deep breath to restore her equilibrium. It was obvious Mac wasn't going to stop probing, and given that she was stuck with him for the next few days, she might as well get this over with. Keeping it brief, she explained the reasons for their trip while Mac listened without interruption, occasionally moving his chair to capture a different angle. It was easier confiding to this near-stranger than she'd expected, and she saw no judgement in Mac's expression.

'So, Jake's met up with his father now?' he asked when she finished.

'Yep. We even had dinner at his house last night. It seems to be going well so far and Jake is really happy.'

Well, at least one of us is, she mused. Kenny's attempts the night before to slip back into old times still felt utterly surreal, and after a restless night, she was no closer to reconciling the resentment she still harboured against him with her desire to make her son happy. What was best for Jake was one thing, but what about what was best for her?

'And how about you, Ruby?' Mac's drawl broke into her mental tussle. 'You got anyone special waiting for you back home?'

She hesitated, and then she shook her head. 'Nope. Totally single. I seem to scare men – which is perfectly fine by me,' she added, in case he thought otherwise.

'Well, I don't scare easy.' Mac looked up and his bright blue eyes fixed her with a challenging stare that caused her to blush again. Feeling like a confused deer in the face of brilliant headlights, Ruby was desperate to change the subject.

141

'What about you, then, Mac? What's *your* story?'

'Me? I'm just an ageing New Yorker trying to keep body and soul together,' he drawled. 'I've been drawing and painting since I was about Jake's age. I quit school as soon as I could and then spent a bunch of years working odd jobs until I could make my art pay. Sometimes, I'd sit on the sidewalk and draw quick sketches of people for a few bucks. One day I got lucky and sketched a rich Wall Street guy who asked if I did formal portraits and, of course, I said yes. He paid upfront so I could buy the materials and, lucky for me, he loved the portrait and showed it off to his friends. Those guys all live to outdo each other so next thing I know, a bunch of rich guys are beating down my door wanting to book me to paint them. I guess things took off from there.'

'What does your family think about what you do?' Ruby asked curiously.

Mac shrugged. 'My mom took off when I was ten and my old man spent too much time looking down a whisky bottle to tell me what he thought about anything. I spent most of my teens being moved around the city's juvenile care system.'

Ruby couldn't help her exclamation of dismay at what sounded like a horrific childhood, but Mac seemed unperturbed. 'It could have been worse. I was always tall for my age and pretty scrappy, so I could take care of myself. That's not true for a lot of kids. See that house way over there?'

He pointed towards a tall building in the distance almost completely shrouded by trees and with only a portion of the roof visible. Puzzled, Ruby followed his gaze and nodded.

'It's called Ocean House. It's Sorrel Island's orphanage – or at least, one of 'em.'

Ruby looked stunned, and Mac nodded. 'I know, right? This place looks like paradise on steroids, but there's an ugly side to everything.'

'But – but I thought communities out here took care of their own.'

Mac returned his attention to his sketch pad. 'One downside of this place is there aren't enough businesses on the island to provide the jobs needed, and Sorrel Island doesn't yet have a tourist industry big enough to support its population. So, islanders – especially the young ones – often go away to find work and leave their kids with their extended family while they head for the bigger islands or even further afield. If the relatives here can't cope or they die, the authorities put the kids into places like Ocean House. Sadly, some youngsters go through a hell of a lot before they ever get to an Ocean House.'

Jake suddenly reappeared, crashing noisily through a nearby bush into the tree-shaded clearing, and Mac beckoned him over.

'Hey, kiddo, I've done enough sketches of your mom for today. Are you ready for your first lesson with me?'

Jake didn't need to be asked twice, and he raced over to Mac's side while Ruby stretched her arms above her head to loosen the tightness in her shoulders.

Mac's easy, direct manner and Miss Ida's reassurance had erased any qualms Ruby had about letting Jake spend time with the artist. Ten minutes later, with her son absorbed in practising pencil strokes under the direction of his new tutor, Ruby grabbed her straw hat and left them to it. Taking a long, leisurely stroll inland over the grassy dunes to stretch her cramped muscles, she thought about the grim side to life on Sorrel Island that Mac had described. She could see Ocean House clearly through the trees and felt a pang of sadness for the abandoned children living within its walls. Was anything – or anyone – ever really as it appeared? she wondered. Even this beautiful paradise hid a darker underbelly. Shaking off her bleak thoughts, she checked her watch and retraced her footsteps to fetch Jake before heading back to wait for Kenny.

22

By the end of their first week, life on Sorrel Island had settled into a pleasant routine for both Ruby and Jake. Weekday mornings were largely devoted to Jake's schoolwork, and now knowing he had plenty to look forward to later, his concentration had improved by leaps and bounds. Lessons were followed by phone calls to Griffin and Auntie Pearl, as well as the occasional check-in with Fi, before heading down to the beach to meet Mac.

Kenny was becoming a regular visitor and had taken to stopping by unannounced, driving them sightseeing around the island, often followed by a meal at one of many family-owned restaurants. The cuisine – almost uniformly local dishes featuring large portions of spiced grilled fish, lobster, and seafood as well as rice, beans, and plantains – was unfailingly delicious.

The rest of the time was spent swimming and lounging on the beach, where, to Ruby's delight, Jake had befriended the family on holiday at Paradise Inn. While her son played sandcastles and splashed in the shallows with young Miles and baby Carrie under the watchful eye of their parents, Derek and Michelle, Ruby would work on content for Miss Ida's website on her laptop, while taking scenic shots of the beach and its surroundings to send to Nick.

But, for Ruby, there was still one very large elephant in the room, and that was Kenny. With Jake ever present, there had been no opportunity to continue the conversation she and Kenny had started in his office, and the emotional see-saw she experienced after each outing with her ex-partner left her feeling drained. Although overjoyed to see her son so happy, the pain of the past continued to bubble up to the surface and the effort required to keep her personal feelings in check when she was around Kenny was increasingly challenging. There was no denying his efforts to forge a relationship with Jake, but while Jake had wholeheartedly embraced his newly rediscovered father, Ruby's continuing distrust of Kenny left her constantly on edge. She was still unconvinced by his explanation for abandoning them and remained fearful that he could let them down again. Sharing her misgivings with Griffin was impossible as any meaningful conversation was stymied either by Jake's presence or the patchy phone connections.

Without Griffin to talk to, and having committed to spend time with Mac, Ruby was finding the artist a sympathetic outlet for her conflicted emotions. Mac's shrewd intellect and straight talk, combined with a surprising degree of sensitivity and insight, made it surprisingly easy for Ruby to confide in him.

After several days and two pads filled with sketches, Mac had finally decided on the pose he wanted Ruby to adopt for the portrait and pronounced himself ready to start work on the canvas. As it was Sunday and Jake was spared lessons, Mac had persuaded an aggrieved Ruby to leave Jake in the care of Derek and his family and join him at the clearing for an early sitting.

'I was hoping to have a lie-in today,' Ruby grumbled, grudgingly shifting her left leg forward as directed. 'At the very least, I should be down on the beach lounging in the sun instead of getting cramp from sitting on this lump of grass. Do you really expect me to hold this position for two hours?'

'I need you to look back at me over your shoulder . . . like this,' Mac said patiently. Ignoring her grouching, he angled her head gently towards him. 'Don't worry, I'll give you a break every ten minutes. It feels annoying now, but trust me, you won't even notice in a week or two.'

'If I remember rightly, you said you only needed me to sit for a few days, tops,' Ruby reminded him sourly. 'You do know I'm supposed to be on holiday, don't you?'

'I thought you were on a mission, not a holiday,' Mac retorted, returning to sit behind his easel. 'Besides, you wouldn't want to deprive Jake of his art lessons, would you?'

'Oh, so now you're *blackmailing* me?'

'Blackmail is such an ugly word, Ruby, and don't frown – you're ruining my profile.' He creased his brow in concentration as his pencil swept across the canvas and she subsided into silence.

'You know, I thought you were just doing the whole mom cheerleader thing when you said Jake was good, but the kid has real talent,' Mac observed.

Ruby nodded, forgetting Mac's instruction to keep her head still. 'That's partly why I was so desperate to bring him here. Jake's school has a fantastic art club and if the school had made him leave, it would have been a disaster in more ways than one.'

Mac made no comment, and all Ruby could see were his pursed lips and his arm moving across the canvas.

'After all the torture you're putting me through, I'd better get to see this piece of art when it's finished,' she ventured, after the silence had stretched into minutes.

Mac's lips curved into a smile, and he scratched his beard in the now familiar gesture. 'Don't worry, you'll definitely get an invite to the exhibition. You'll have to do some press interviews nearer the time, anyway, but my PR team will sort that out.'

Ruby's eyes widened. '*Wow!* Are you *really* that well known?'

'Yes, I really am,' he assured her without a hint of modesty.

'In that case, I'll stop moaning.' Ruby grinned. 'This might all be worth it if I end up becoming a celebrity. Next thing you know, I'll be on some reality TV show climbing into snake pits and eating live bugs.'

'Keep your head still,' Mac ordered, 'and that sounds gross, by the way.'

Ruby giggled, delighting in their easy rapport. Posing for Mac and spending time with him was slowly drawing her out of the protective shell she had grown as a safeguard against men. Unlike Kenny, with Mac there was no emotional baggage and unspoken resentment from the past or unsettling questions about the future. Despite her grumbling, she enjoyed their time together and even his extravagant compliments had become less disconcerting. His lifestyle, as far as she could tell, consisted of a few months a year in his native New York, with the rest of the time spent travelling around the world painting portraits commissioned by wealthy individuals, private organisations, and even governments. His endless supply of anecdotes enlivened the long periods of posing, although once she had been so hysterical with laughter after he recounted an unfortunate incident during a sitting by an unnamed prime minister, that Mac had been forced to let her go for the day.

'We'll need to finish soon,' Ruby warned. 'Kenny's picking us up in half an hour. He's promised to take Jake horseback riding on the beach near Sugar Bay.'

'Sounds like Kenny's really trying to make up for lost time with the kid,' Mac remarked.

'It looks that way,' Ruby admitted, 'but I still have my doubts about the man's staying power when it comes to family. As they say, "Once bitten, twice shy" or, in my case, forever shy.'

A faint smile played at the corner of Mac's lips. His eyes still on the canvas, he asked, 'It's great that he's trying so hard with Jake, but is he also trying to make it up to you?'

◆ ◆ ◆

Sitting across the table from Kenny in a café later that day, Ruby was no closer to finding an answer to Mac's question. After a pleasant drive around the island, Kenny had taken them past the marina to a long stretch of white sandy beach where Jake had gone riding, shrieking happily as his horse picked up speed, and displaying not one shred of anxiety. To see her son looking so carefree was worth every heart-stopping moment Ruby spent watching him canter alongside the experienced riding instructor holding the horse on a leading rein.

'Dad says I can go riding again next weekend!' Jake's voice cut through Ruby's thoughts, and she smiled absently at her son. His face was smeared with cream from the chocolate sundae he had just ploughed through, and she automatically picked up her napkin and leaned forward to wipe his face.

'*Mu-um!*' He jerked his head away with reproachful eyes. 'I'm not a baby!'

Kenny dribbled some water from the jug on to Jake's napkin and handed it to him without comment. Watching Jake swipe the damp napkin across his mouth, Ruby felt a pang of sadness. When had her baby disappeared? But then, she remembered, not all his childish habits had vanished.

'Just so you know, Jake, I tried calling Uncle Griffin this morning to find out when Jellybean will be delivered, but I couldn't reach him, and he hasn't called me back yet.'

'Can't you text him, Mum?' Jake pleaded.

Ruby nodded and reached for her bag. After dashing off a quick text, she placed the phone on the table and, as she looked up, caught an expression she couldn't decipher on Kenny's face.

'What?' she demanded.

'It's nothing,' he said shortly.

148

'It didn't look like nothing,' she insisted.

Kenny sighed. 'Leave it, Ruby. You're just imagining things.'

She stared at him in irritation, remembering afresh how maddening Kenny could be when he clammed up. Conscious of Jake observing the interaction between his parents, Ruby bit back her response and sipped her fruit juice in silence.

Mac's question popped into her mind again, and this time Ruby knew the answer. Despite his commendable efforts towards Jake, Kenny wasn't even close to making things better with her. They needed to speak without Jake present, and soon. It wasn't just Jake's future that had to be discussed; it was now painfully clear that until she properly understood Kenny's past actions, she couldn't forgive him or, much more importantly, move forward with her own life.

With Priya holding the fort at the office even more effectively than expected, Ruby felt under no immediate pressure to rush back, despite Fi's hopeful noises. Having come all this way, she wanted to give Jake as much time as possible with his father, but for her own peace of mind, she had to have things out with Kenny. Miss Ida had offered to babysit Jake whenever Ruby needed, and it was time to take her up on her offer.

Relieved to have reached a decision, Ruby relaxed and tuned back into the conversation between Kenny and Jake.

'So you see, son, I had to start by learning my way around a boat first. That way, I can fix any engine problems that might happen when I'm out on the water.'

'That's so cool! Sam says you take people deep sea diving and that you're the captain of the boat.'

Kenny chuckled at the awe in Jake's voice. 'Sorrel Island might be small, but it's very eco-friendly with lots of untouched natural habitat to explore, and we always try to give tourists a memorable experience.'

'Can I come on the boat with you and Sam when you take people out?'

'If your mum's okay with it, I'd love to take you with me.' He looked at Ruby with a silent question, and when she responded with an almost imperceptible nod, Kenny flashed a grateful smile and turned back to Jake.

'You know what? I'll take you on a couple of tour bookings next Saturday. Your mum can come too, unless she still gets seasick. Did she ever tell you about the time I took her to the Isle of Wight and how she spent half the weekend throwing up after we went sailing?'

As Jake hooted with laughter, Ruby smiled weakly at the unwelcome memory. Jake looked so cheerful that it would be churlish to ruin the mood by pointing out that she hadn't felt the need to share any memories of a man who had callously abandoned them. There would be a time to speak her mind and demand proper answers, Ruby reminded herself. Right now, she had to put Jake first, and seeing the joy on her son's face, her heart swelled in her chest.

You made the right decision, Rubes. Whatever happens.

'Thanks for the offer,' she said lightly, 'but I think the two of you can manage without me. I get sick on a cross-Channel ferry, never mind a small boat.'

'So, Jake, that's a date then,' Kenny said decisively. 'We'll do the boat trips in the morning and if you're still up for it after lunch, you can go horse riding again.'

Jake squirmed in his seat with excitement and was barely able to contain himself when Kenny added, 'And when you're a bit older, I'll teach you how to snorkel. You'll love the coral reefs and seeing the tropical fish and sea turtles up close. Most of the bays around the island are pretty calm, so it's ideal for first-timers.'

Trying not to overthink the 'when you're a bit older' part, Ruby covertly observed Kenny from under her lashes. *This is the man I remember*, she thought sadly. *Smiling, upbeat, enthusiastic, and fun . . . What went wrong with us?*

A little later, as they walked into Paradise Inn with Jake between them, holding both his parents' hands, Ruby couldn't help the wistful thought that anyone who didn't know better would imagine they were a happy family returning from a day out. *Would it be so impossible to—?*

The burgeoning thought died in her mind as her eyes focused on a tall figure in a t-shirt and baseball cap standing by the reception desk chatting to Miss Ida. He had his back to Ruby and, for a second, she assumed it was Mac. But Mac's shoulders were not that broad . . . nor were his arms brown!

As if sensing the scrutiny, the man turned around, and his face broke into a smile. 'Hi, Rubes.'

Ruby's eyes widened in shock. '*Griffin!* What on earth are you doing here?'

'*Uncle Griffin!*' Jake screeched, pulling his hands away to rush over to Griffin, who scooped him up into a tight bear hug, almost knocking over a battered guitar case propped against the counter. Placing Jake back on his feet, Griffin reached into a rucksack on the floor and pulled out a threadbare knitted blue rabbit. Holding it up with a cheery grin, he shook the toy gently.

'You said you needed Jellybean, so I thought I'd better bring him myself!'

23

Ruby rapped on the closed door and strained to hear a reply. There had been no sign of Griffin in the dining room at breakfast and after waving Jake off to play on the beach with Derek and the children, she had checked with Miss Ida to find out which room she had allocated to her newest guest.

Hearing nothing, Ruby knocked harder. After a few moments, the door opened a crack and Griffin peered through the gap with bleary eyes.

'Bloody hell, Rubes! Do you know what time it is?' he mumbled, stepping back to let her in. Wearing nothing but a pair of boxers, he scratched his head, yawned widely, and retraced his footsteps back to bed.

Ignoring the plaintive note in his voice, Ruby marched over to the window and pulled back the thin muslin curtains, letting bright sunlight flood the room. Griffin's room was smaller than hers, and his balcony faced the side of the house, overlooking Miss Ida's immaculately maintained vegetable garden. Taking care not to trip on the rucksack and the open sports bag on the floor, Ruby went over to where Griffin lay prone on the bed.

'Are you planning to get out of bed today?' she demanded, ignoring the muffled groan that emerged from his pillow. She sat on the corner of the bed and kicked off her wedges, tucking a leg under her. 'We've been up for hours, and Jake raced through his schoolwork just so he could spend time with you. He got bored of waiting and went down to the beach, so I thought I'd better come and check you were still alive.'

Griffin grunted and rolled over to face her, bunching up a pillow under his head. Even first thing in the morning and suffering from jet lag, the man still managed to look good, Ruby thought enviously.

'Only just,' he muttered. 'You should have warned me that coming here meant getting on to a tiny plane. I would rather chew on broken glass than do it again.'

'Are you still moaning about that?' she said impatiently. 'You got here in one piece, didn't you? Besides, how was I supposed to warn you when I didn't have the first idea that you'd follow us out here!'

'Yeah, well, I didn't exactly think that through,' Griffin admitted, scratching the stubble on his chin. 'I *was* going to courier the bunny like you asked, but it's been a nightmare trying to have a decent conversation with you on the phone. London's so bloody cold and miserable that it was either go to Nairobi and visit Granny Sarah or . . .' He tailed off with a shrug.

'So, just like that, you decided to jump on a flight out here. Mate, we've only been gone a week!' She shook her head, torn between her joy at seeing him and exasperation at his impulsiveness.

'It's your own fault for going on about how incredible this place is. I phoned Miss Ida to book a room and told her I wanted to surprise you. She was well up for it, and she even arranged for Zeke to pick me up from the airport.'

'Well, if it helps, I wasn't surprised.' Ruby grinned. 'I was *shocked*! I couldn't believe it was really you in the hallway. Jake's over the moon – although I have to say he's even happier about getting Jellybean back,' she laughed.

Griffin propped himself up on one elbow and studied her critically. 'There's something different about you. Maybe the island magic you talked about is working its spell because you look – I don't know . . . I can't quite put my finger on it. I'm loving the tan, by the way.'

Ruby stretched her legs out in front of her, smiling at the contrast between her white shorts and the glowing dark bronze of her skin. 'I know, right? We spend so much time outdoors here. Have you seen how much Jake has changed? He's been like a different child since we arrived. He eats anything he's offered and he's nowhere near as shy as he is at home. He's even made friends with another family staying here and he's with them now.'

Griffin gave a brief smile. 'I'm glad he's okay. I was worried when you said he was insisting on Jellybean, which is partly why I wanted to come.' He hesitated. 'You and Kenny looked pretty loved up when you came in last night. I noticed you holding hands . . . So, what gives?'

'First of all, *we* were not holding hands, Jake was,' she corrected. 'Secondly, the real question is what gives between you and Kenny?'

The frostiness between the two men the previous evening had been palpable, with little more than a courteous nod on both sides before Kenny abruptly took his leave.

When Griffin didn't answer, Ruby sighed. 'I know you hate him for leaving me and Jake in the lurch, but you've got to try to get on with him while you're here – for your godson's sake, if not mine.'

'Oh, so we like him now, do we?'

Ruby ignored the sarcastic tone. 'I wouldn't say that exactly, although he does appear more mature and grounded than before. He seems very happy living on a small island, and he's making a real effort with Jake.'

'It shouldn't be an effort to spend time with your own kid,' Griffin scoffed.

'I know – and believe me, I'm worried about how long it will last, and whether things will blow up in my face if I trust him again.' She stopped and beamed at him. 'I'm *so* glad you're here! I need reinforcements to keep Miss Ida at bay. First the woman badgers me to give Kenny a chance, and *now* she thinks Mac has a thing for me and— *Oh, crap!* I totally forgot about Mac! I'd better go, or I'll be late for my sitting.'

She shuffled to the edge of the bed to fish for her shoes, and Griffin sat up, his eyes suddenly alert.

'Hold on, is Mac the George Clooney lookalike you've been getting all googly-eyed about? Now *him* I want to meet! Give me ten minutes to have a quick shower and put some clothes on, and I'll come with you.'

About to protest that he would make her late, Ruby bit back the words and nodded happily. It felt so good to have Griffin back at her side, and it wouldn't kill Mac to wait a few minutes longer.

'Okay, I'll be downstairs. But hurry up!'

24

Ruby was on the dining-room terrace chatting to Miss Ida when Griffin finally appeared almost half an hour later. Dressed in a slightly crumpled pair of long shorts, a white t-shirt, and leather sandals, he had his guitar strapped across his back, and held a glass of what looked like fruit juice.

'Good morning, Miss Ida!' His hazel eyes sparkled as he approached. 'You're looking particularly lovely today.'

Miss Ida tittered like a schoolgirl and smoothed her powder-blue cotton dress. 'Well now, that's mighty charming of you. Did you have a good night?'

'I slept like a baby, ma'am,' Griffin assured her. 'Until this one here came banging on my door this morning.'

Unimpressed, Ruby held out her wrist and pointed at her watch. 'I am officially late for my sitting, so can we go?'

'But, Ruby, Griffin hasn't had his breakfast yet!' Miss Ida exclaimed with a reproachful frown. She looked up at Griffin. 'Can I fix you a plate of eggs or some pancakes, sugar? That juice isn't going to take you far.'

Knowing Mac was waiting – and probably tearing his hair out – Ruby glared at Griffin, silently willing him to turn down the offer. To her relief, he tossed down the rest of the juice and handed the empty glass to Miss Ida with a grateful smile.

'That's very kind of you, but I'll save my appetite for lunch. Ruby tells me your food is incredible.'

Miss Ida's face creased into a bright smile. She patted Griffin's arm and then headed back inside while Ruby took the lead down the steps from the terrace and on to the pathway.

'Sorrel Island definitely hasn't changed *you* from being such a shameless flirt,' Ruby remarked, picking up the pace as they strode towards the beach. Mac was going to kill her!

'Miss Ida's a total babe,' said Griffin. 'Now, if she were thirty years younger—'

Ruby laughed and punched his arm in mock outrage, and he threw an affectionate arm around her shoulder. When they arrived at the beach, Griffin stopped to take in the idyllic scenery, but Ruby gave him no time to linger, propelling him along the beach, around the cove, and up the sandy slope.

By the time they reached the clearing, they were both out of breath. Mac, absorbed in studying the sketch on the canvas, turned as Ruby crashed into the secluded clearing. His eyes fell on Griffin behind her, and he looked at Ruby in silent enquiry.

'I'm *so* sorry I'm late,' Ruby wheezed, trying to catch her breath after their mad dash. 'This is my friend, Griffin. He arrived last night from London, and we were so busy catching up that I lost track of time.'

For a moment, the two men appraised each other silently. Then Griffin slipped the guitar off his back and walked up to Mac with his hand outstretched, and Mac stood up and shook it without hesitation.

'Welcome to the island, man. I've heard a lot about you,' he drawled.

'She's spoken about you quite a bit too,' Griffin conceded. 'Sorry I made her late and kept you waiting.'

Ruby stared, bewildered, as the men continued to size each other up. It felt like watching two wary tigers circling. *What the hell kind of bizarre male ritual is this?*

Mac's gaze shifted to Griffin's guitar, and he blinked. 'Is that a *Lowden?*'

Griffin nodded and handed it over to Mac, who looked at it in awe, and then examined it carefully for a few minutes before passing it back.

'*Very* nice. I played with an amateur band a few years back, and one of the guys owned a Lowden. It cost a fortune, but I still remember the quality of the sound.'

While Mac and Griffin discussed the merits of the instrument, Ruby walked over to her usual spot and arranged herself into her pose. After a couple of minutes, she cleared her throat loudly, startling both men into silence.

Mac took one look at her expression and went back to his stool, while Griffin perched on a grass mound a little distance away.

'So, what brings you out here to the island, Griffin?' asked Mac, his eyes darting between Ruby and the canvas he was drawing on.

Griffin, who was craning his neck, trying to see what Mac was doing without being too obvious, replied absently, 'Rubes asked me to send Jake the toy rabbit I got him when he was three. I didn't want to risk it getting lost in transit, so I brought it myself.'

Mac paused mid-stroke, his expression so incredulous that Ruby couldn't help laughing.

'I know it sounds ridiculous and I wish I could tell you Griffin's kidding, Mac, but honestly, that's how he is. He takes his responsibility as Jake's godfather very seriously. He taught him to play the guitar when he was barely big enough to hold one, and he was the one who encouraged him with his art when the rest of us thought Jake was just going through another phase.'

'Well, this is a whole other level of friendship,' Mac said. 'Can't think of any of *my* friends who'd travel halfway round the world to hand-deliver a toy.'

Griffin's attention was on the canvas. 'Ruby says you do this for a living?'

Mac ignored the slight hint of scepticism hovering beneath Griffin's words. 'I do, indeed! The great Mackenzie Castro has been in this business for over twenty years.'

'*Mackenzie Castro!*' Griffin echoed, visibly shocked. 'Hang on, you mean Mackenzie Castro as in *Portrait of the Widow* – the painting hanging in the New York Metropolitan Museum of Art?'

'That would be me,' Mac confirmed.

'But that's an *incredible* piece of work!'

'Indeed it is,' Mac agreed.

Ruby dropped her pose to stare in surprise at Griffin. 'How come *you've* heard of him? I didn't know you knew the first thing about modern art.'

'Which just goes to show you don't know everything about me, even if you think you do.'

'What*ever*! Well, I suppose it's reassuring to know you have other interests beyond making half the women in London fall in love with you before torturing them,' Ruby sniffed. 'By the way, how *is* broken-hearted Shirlee these days?'

'You two sure sound like an old married couple. Are you really just friends?' Despite Mac's casual tone, the look he trained on Ruby was anything but. The unexpected intensity in his piercing blue eyes sent her stomach into freefall and, desperate for a distraction, Ruby launched straight into her awful-kiss-and-of-course-we're-just-friends story.

While Mac's expression relaxed into laughter at Ruby's description of the fumbled drunken teenage kiss, Griffin's face remained impassive.

'It really didn't go well!' Ruby snorted with laughter. 'Between the booze and my braces, the whole thing was a mess. It was *such* a bad kiss, wasn't it, Griff?'

'It was indeed a bad kiss,' he acknowledged solemnly.

'And that's when we knew that we'd make great mates, but we could never be lovers!'

'You must be pretty close, though, if he's crossing oceans for you – so what's the deal?' Mac persisted. 'Is he, what, like a brother to you?'

'Well . . .' Ruby hesitated, finding it a struggle, as always, to define her relationship with her oldest friend. Although 'best friend' was the term she used most often, that didn't really cover it. Griffin had been an integral part of her life for as long as she cared to remember; they had laughed together and cried together, shared key moments in their lives and knew secrets about each other they would carry to their graves. Trying to label their relationship into something other people would understand or feel comfortable with had always been difficult, but from the way Mac was looking at her, Ruby intuitively knew what he was really asking.

Griffin yawned and rose to his feet, brushing the sand off his shorts. 'The brother you've never had is going to leave you to it. Good to meet you, Mac, and I'm sure I'll see you again soon. Rubes, I'm going to find Jake and get him to show me around before I end up falling asleep. Looks like there's a whole magic island waiting for me to explore.'

Slinging his guitar over his shoulder, Griffin slipped on his sunglasses and resettled his baseball cap, tipping Mac a nod of farewell before striding out of the clearing.

25

'*Mum!* You'll never guess what happened today!'

Jake glanced over at Griffin, who was seated next to him at the dining table, clearly itching for the go-ahead to spill the beans. Earlier that afternoon, busy exchanging emails with Nick and researching information for the Paradise Inn website, Ruby had paid little attention when Griffin and Jake had headed out to 'explore'. But since returning shortly before dinner, Jake had been unusually fidgety, and once Narita had taken their food orders, he could no longer restrain himself.

'Go ahead, buddy, tell her. She's going to love this,' said Griffin.

'Am I?' Ruby laughed. 'What have you two been up to?'

'I made a new friend. His name's Drew, and he's ten.'

'Oh, okay.' Expecting a rather more dramatic announcement, Ruby was slightly taken aback. 'What's he like, then?'

'He doesn't speak,' Jake pronounced, reaching for one of the freshly baked bread rolls Narita had placed on their table. 'He's an orphan and he's always running away.'

Confused, Ruby turned to Griffin for clarification.

'I think I'd better tell her, buddy, what do you say?' Griffin's broad smile was a world away from his earlier grumpiness, and when Jake nodded, Griffin picked up the story.

'Jake and I went exploring further inland from the clearing where Mac does his painting. So, we'd stopped for a bit of a rest and I'm playing Jake a couple of tracks on my guitar when this kid suddenly appears out of nowhere. He doesn't look lost or anything, but he just comes to sit on the grass next to Jake without saying a word.'

'That's cos he can't speak,' Jake interjected.

Griffin hesitated. 'Well, he *can*, Jake, he just chooses not to. Anyway, we kept asking him questions, trying to find out his name and where he lived, but all he did was shrug and shake his head.'

Ruby's eyes widened. 'So, what did you do?'

'Nothing – for a while. As I said, he didn't look like he was lost or in any distress. The opposite, if anything. He was smiling and seemed happy enough, so I assumed he lived nearby and just carried on playing the guitar.'

'Uncle Griffin gave him his hat so he didn't catch sunstroke,' Jake threw in helpfully.

'Hey, I thought *I* was telling the story,' Griffin laughed. 'Anyway, after a bit, I suggested we take him home before his family got worried. So then the kid stands up, grabs my hand, and pulls me along with him. To cut a long story short, we ended up at this mansion, which, as it turns out, is—'

'Ocean House,' Ruby interrupted, her mind racing to join the dots.

Griffin looked at her in surprise. 'Do you know about the orphanage?'

'Mac mentioned it the other day. But go on, what happened next?'

'Well, the man who answered the door told us that the kid – Drew – has been with them for a couple of weeks and he's already run off three times. They had just realised he was missing again and were about to start a search when we showed up.'

Ruby's face clouded over. 'The poor child! Did they tell you why he was placed in the orphanage?'

'His house caught on fire and his grandpa died,' Jake pronounced. 'But Drew escaped, so he wasn't hurt.'

'Oh my God, that's *horrific*!' Ruby felt a shiver run through her body. 'That poor, poor boy! Is that why he doesn't speak?'

Griffin's smile faded. 'The director said the whole experience was hugely traumatic for Drew and he gets anxious if he stays inside for long. His parents left the island a couple of years ago and he was living alone with his grandfather. Apparently, the authorities are trying to trace them, but everything in the house was destroyed and there's no record of where they went.'

'The child must be going through hell after such an awful experience. Mac said a lot of younger people migrate from the island to find work. God, I really hope they're able to track down Drew's parents, but they could be anywhere,' said Ruby, automatically reaching out to touch Jake's hand. Hearing about disadvantaged children always made her incredibly grateful that her own child was safe.

Griffin nodded. 'We have some good news, though. The director said it was the first time they'd seen Drew smile since he came to Ocean House, and he asked what we'd done to cheer him up. So— Go on, kid, you can take it from here.'

'I said Uncle Griffin's music had made Drew feel better, and the man asked if he could come and play for the other orphans.' Jake beamed, jumping in to finish the story.

'What a lovely idea!' Ruby exclaimed. She turned to Griffin expectantly. 'Will you?'

'Yes, of course! Those children have had a tough time and if anyone knows how therapeutic music can be . . .'

Griffin tailed off for a moment, and then his face brightened. 'Anyway, I've offered to spend some time with the kids while I'm here and run some music sessions and singalongs.' He reached out to ruffle Jake's hair. 'And this one here has volunteered to help.'

Narita arrived with their food, setting the dishes carefully on the table before topping up the water in Jake's glass.

'Would you like some water, sir?' Narita smiled at Griffin with an expression Ruby could only describe as starstruck.

Dear God, not another one! she groaned silently, noting the slight tremor in the girl's hand as she filled his glass, although Griffin, preoccupied with helping Jake cut the steak he had ordered, didn't seem to notice.

Watching Jake tuck into his meal, it wasn't lost on Ruby that today was the first time Kenny hadn't been over to Paradise Inn, or even phoned. While she appreciated that he might feel uncomfortable about facing Griffin, Kenny's personal embarrassment over his past actions was no excuse for avoiding his son. Remembering the promises he had made to Jake, she could only hope the man wasn't about to let their son down again.

Pushing away the disquieting thoughts, Ruby eyed the grilled lobster on her plate and picked up her fork. Spearing a tender piece of white meat, she chewed slowly, savouring the spicy, buttery flavour.

'I am *so* going to miss eating like this once we're back in London. You have got to try this lobster, Griff, it's beyond yummy.'

Griffin obligingly swallowed a mouthful of lobster and then glanced at her. 'What did you get up to this afternoon?'

Ruby took another bite before answering. 'I was pretty busy. Nick has designed a lovely template for Miss Ida's website and he's working on the app, so we were playing around with the content. He's really excited about doing this and it's a nice change for him from his usual work, although Fi's grousing about the time it's taking. Still, I'm glad I brought my camera because I've taken some gorgeous pictures of the house and around the beach. I still need shots of the bedrooms and I want to include a few more images from around the island. The great thing is all the guests I've approached are super keen to help Miss Ida save Paradise Inn and they've agreed to write testimonials for the site. I've even got Mac to do a video endorsement since he's the closest we've got to a celebrity.'

Griffin raised an eyebrow. '*Very* impressive. Who is this woman and what have you done with my friend? I can't quite get my head around this. The Ruby I know would have balked at the very idea of approaching strangers and growled at anyone with the temerity to approach her.'

Although slightly stung by Griffin's less than complimentary description, Ruby was enjoying her lobster too much to argue, and she concentrated on scraping the last slivers from the shell. She had never suffered fools gladly, preferring to be direct rather than pussyfooting around an issue, but while some people might find that challenging, it didn't mean she was insensitive to other people's situations or couldn't be kind. Indeed, helping Miss Ida was something Ruby had instinctively sought to do.

At the next table, Derek was struggling to spoon food into Carrie's stubbornly closed mouth. When Carrie finally opened her mouth and swallowed a mouthful, Ruby watched with a wistful smile as the other family members cheered. Something *had* shifted for her since coming here, she acknowledged, and, lately, being determinedly single didn't feel quite such a triumphant statement of independence. Her confidence issues, compounded by Kenny's abandonment, had left her deeply suspicious of men and convinced she was happier on her own, but that conviction was slowly crumbling. Living a cautious life to avoid rejection might be safe, but was it really living? Was Griffin right? Ruby wondered. Having pooh-poohed Miss Ida's predictions, was Sorrel Island changing Ruby from the no-nonsense love cynic she had been when she arrived? As a picture of Mac's vivid blue eyes flashed through her mind, change suddenly didn't seem like such a bad thing.

Whether her stirring desire for something more stemmed from leaving the routine of her life in London, the magic of Sorrel Island, or even the pulse-quickening, stomach-flipping effects of Mac's obvious interest in her, Ruby didn't know. What she *did* know was that after years of being stuck in limbo, it was time to move forward.

26

Miss Ida's eyes were glued to the laptop as Ruby scrolled through the draft pages of the Paradise Inn website, and she listened intently while Ruby explained the rationale behind Nick's design and the features for the app currently in development.

'What do you think so far?' Ruby asked, closing the laptop. 'We still need to upload the pictures and I want to include a page about the island's history and, of course, the story of you and Marty.'

Relinquishing Miss Ida's chair, Ruby returned to the visitor's chair on the other side of the desk, hoping Miss Ida didn't hate what she'd seen so far. But Miss Ida didn't reply, and as the silence stretched out, her eyes suddenly filled with tears.

'Miss Ida!' Caught off-guard, Ruby gasped in dismay. 'What's the matter? If you don't like it, we can change the colour scheme or even the whole layout. Honestly, whatever you want—'

'No, no, sweetheart!' Miss Ida said shakily. 'Don't pay me no mind, I'm just being foolish. It's beautiful just as it is. I'm just so – so overwhelmed and – and *grateful* for what you folks are doing for me. It's hard to imagine that people all over the world will be reading about our home. Oh, *Ruby*!'

Miss Ida clasped her hands together and shook her head slowly, and Ruby blinked back her own unexpected tears.

'I'm so glad you like it, and I know Nick will be over the moon when I tell him. Your love story is incredibly inspiring – even to grouchy non-romantics like me.'

Keen to lighten the mood, Ruby lightly tapped the computer on her lap. 'Once I've finished with the pictures and sent everything to Nick, he'll finish the site in no time. Just promise that when you and Paradise Inn become world-famous, you'll find space for Jake and me when we visit.'

'There'll *always* be a room here for you and my sweet boy!' Miss Ida rested her arms on the desk with an amused twinkle in her eyes. 'So, you do plan on coming back, then? See, a few days ago, I'd have bet it was because of Kenny – or even Mac, since he comes every year. But now your beautiful man-friend has shown up, I'm not sure what to think.'

Ruby shook her head. 'You really are a hopeless romantic, Miss Ida! Well, I'm sorry to disappoint you but Griffin and I have been best friends since we were kids.'

'Can't say as I know many friends who'd pick up and travel all this way just to surprise you. Calling me up to book a room and all.'

'It does sound hard to believe when you put it like that,' Ruby giggled, 'but that's typical Griffin. We have a bond that is hard to explain to people. Neither of us has siblings, and growing up we were in and out of each other's house all the time. I was really close to his mum and, after she died, Griff was a mess for ages.' Ruby paused. 'In some ways, he's still a bit lost.'

'And you're the one he turns to?'

Ruby drew in a sharp breath, unsure of how much to reveal. But Miss Ida was someone Ruby instinctively knew she could trust.

'Yes, I am,' she said. 'When his mum got sick, she made me promise that I'd always be there for him because – well, Griffin's mum was rich. Like, properly, *seriously* rich. But the thing is, no-one, including Griffin, knew about the money. Marilyn's father built a massive international property portfolio, but he was also an out-and-out racist. Marilyn was his only child, but when she went against his wishes and married Griffin's dad, who was from Kenya, her old man cut her out of his life and never spoke to her again. But, as it turned out, he never actually carried out his threat to disown her and he left her everything when he died.'

Miss Ida's brown eyes were as wide as saucers. 'Oh my!'

Ruby chewed on her lower lip as she remembered her shock the day Marilyn had confessed the truth, dragging Ruby into the one secret she had never revealed to Griffin.

'When Marilyn was diagnosed with cancer, I helped take care of her, and I was there when her doctor told her there was nothing more they could do. When I tried to phone Griff to come home, she stopped me and then just broke down and told me the whole story. Griffin was only five when his father died, but Marilyn refused to tell her old man. She said she didn't want a reconciliation because she couldn't trust him around Griffin. Mostly, though, she wanted to get away from the family fortune. She'd seen what that kind of money did to people, and she didn't want that for her son. When she found out her father had died and left it all in trust to her, she felt like he was still trying to control her, and so she refused to use the money and appointed a lawyer and a firm of accountants to manage the trust. I begged her to tell Griffin the truth, but she was scared he'd hate her for lying to him and she passed away before she could pluck up the courage to tell him. We were just eighteen at the time and Griffin only found out when Marilyn's lawyer came to the house on the day of her funeral and blurted out that Griff was the sole heir to a multimillion-pound fortune.'

Ruby felt her eyes moisten again as her mind went back to that fateful afternoon. In between serving drinks and canapés to the well-wishers crammed into Marilyn's living room, she had kept a constant lookout for Griffin, relieved that he was at least pretending to listen to the earnest expressions of condolences from those attending the sombre gathering. Although he had fixed a faint half-smile on to his face since leaving the cemetery, Ruby could tell from his tight jaw and rigidly held body that he was holding on to his emotions by a thread.

Finishing her circuit of the living room, Ruby's eyes instinctively sought out Griffin who, at six feet and four inches, was hard to miss. When she spotted him standing outside the doorway of the living room talking to a broad-shouldered man in a dark suit, the placeholder smile camouflaging Griffin's grief had vanished, replaced by a stricken expression that froze Ruby in her tracks. The man in the suit had not been at the church, or among the mourners at the cemetery. She would have noticed the unusual wheat-blond hair combed back from a high forehead and the pinch-thin nose. Which meant he must have walked in after she'd tired of answering the doorbell and left the door on the latch.

Griffin was shaking his head, his hands raised as if pleading with the man to stop talking. All at once, Ruby knew who the man was – or at least why he was here – and her heart dropped hard and fast into the pit of her belly. By the time she reached her friend's side, the man in the suit had handed a business card to a visibly shell-shocked Griffin and was heading for the front door, leaving Ruby fighting back guilty tears.

'I had so desperately wanted to tell Griffin,' Ruby sighed, 'but it hadn't been my secret to share. Anyway, after that day, Griffin decided everything was his fault.'

'But why would he think that?' Miss Ida exclaimed. 'His mother chose to keep her secret because she wanted to protect him, surely?'

'He was angry because she'd worked so hard to keep a roof over their heads when she hadn't needed to. In his mind, the only reason his mum sacrificed a comfortable life was because she didn't trust the boy she'd raised or have faith in him to grow into a decent man who wouldn't be spoiled by money. It really hurt him to believe his mum thought so little of him.'

'The poor, beautiful man,' Miss Ida lamented. 'It just breaks your heart! He can't be angry with his dead mother because he loved her so much, but he also can't forgive her – or forgive himself – if that's how he still feels.'

Ruby sat in silence, absorbing Miss Ida's words. 'I'd never thought of it like that,' she admitted. 'I've tried for years to get him to accept that his mum only wanted the best for him. After he learned the truth, he didn't want the money either. He's always hated the idea of one person having so much when so many people are struggling. After everything his grandfather had put his mum through, Griffin detested the idea of his life being defined by the man's fortune and, at first, he was adamant he didn't want the burden of managing it or even deciding how to give it away. He's taken a more active role in the past few years, just so he can keep an eye on what the lawyers and accountants are up to, but he's still trying to find something meaningful to do with it all.'

'It's sad how so many folks dream of making millions when money doesn't buy happiness,' Miss Ida said softly.

Ruby nodded. 'A lot of people would love to have his problem, but inheriting so much money really threw Griff's life into a loop. He's incredibly smart and has the kindest heart but the money has cast a huge shadow, and he can't seem to settle. It doesn't help that every woman he meets falls over herself to be with him! I have no idea what sorcery he works on the poor things, but they take one look at him and within weeks they're picturing themselves living with him in his riverside penthouse apartment.'

'*Every* woman – but not you?' Miss Ida probed.

Ruby laughed and shook her head emphatically. 'I think I'm the only female in London who's immune to his charms – which is probably why we've stayed friends! Besides, I'm not his type. Griffin's girlfriends are all supermodel-gorgeous, petite, dainty little things.'

'I see.' Miss Ida nodded slowly, her gaze moving into the distance as if trying to grasp a fleeting idea.

Ruby smiled. 'To be fair, Griffin has always been there for me too. After my parents died, he picked up the pieces and he always puts me and Jake first. He's like my anchor and I don't know what I'd do without him. I can honestly say I trust him with my life because we're one hundred per cent honest with each other and I know he would never let me down.'

'Then you're a very lucky woman,' Miss Ida said gently. 'But, sweetheart, I hope you open up to love again. You've had your share of heartache, but love is waiting for you if you give it a chance. My late ma used to say that life is like being on a trapeze. If you don't forgive and let go of your hurt, you can't ever reach for your happiness.'

Glancing at the jewelled clock on the wall, she stood up and walked around her desk, bending to give Ruby's shoulder a gentle squeeze.

'I need to check on Narita. Thank you for your hard work and I can't wait to see what the website looks like when it's done.'

'It'll be brilliant, I promise.' Ruby stood up and followed Miss Ida out of her office, clasping the laptop to her chest.

27

One of the few downsides to life on Sorrel Island was its dodgy phone connections, Ruby decided, as she waited for the call to reconnect.

'Hi . . . can you hear me?'

'Yes, now I can.'

As Fi's gravelly voice came back on the line, Ruby continued. 'Okay, so where was I?'

'In the middle of telling me how fab it is to see Mac's portrait coming to life.'

'Honestly, Fi, it's so weird seeing yourself through someone else's eyes. Can you believe that a famous – and incredibly sexy – artist is painting *me*?'

Despite the background hum and the clicks on the line, Fi's sigh was audible. 'Yes, I *can* believe it. D'you know, it's a good thing you're getting to see yourself through someone else's eyes because yours need some very strong glasses.'

Ruby pulled a face. 'I'm not saying I'm ugly. I'm just not your typical girlie girl.'

'Girls come in all shapes and sizes. Look at me – gorgeous as I am, I would kill for your height and amazing abs, and I'm not the only one. I've never understood how you barely exercise and still have a body like a gym bunny.'

Ruby laughed. 'You're as bad as Mac. I don't think either one of you has ever met the word "modest"!'

'Talking of bad, how's London's baddest boy doing?'

'Griffin? He's loving it out here. He met a kid soon after he got here who'd run away from a nearby orphanage. The poor child hasn't spoken a word since he lost his granddad in a house fire, but he heard Griff playing his guitar and took to him. So, Griffin's been visiting the home every day to play for Drew – that's the boy's name – and the other children. It's made a real difference, apparently, because Drew has stopped trying to run away and he even sits with the others for the music sessions, whereas before he refused to engage with any of the kids.'

'And there was I picturing the man lounging on a beach, pulling all the hot birds while you clucked around him like a mother hen,' Fi chuckled.

'*Charming!* Then Ruby hesitated. 'Okay, I may be a bit protective sometimes—'

'Possessive, more like.'

'Excuse *me*! I—'

The crackling on the line intensified and Ruby waited impatiently for it to subside. 'Can you hear me? I need to go in a minute. Kenny's picking Jake up shortly.'

'Never mind Kenny,' Fi said impatiently. 'Tell me more about what Griffin's doing. He's talked to me in the past about setting up a project for disadvantaged kids and he seemed quite passionate about it, so this sounds right up his street.'

'Really?' Ruby said in surprise. 'That's news to me. I've always known Griffin is fantastic with kids, but I must admit he's taking this much more seriously than I expected. I assumed it was about a few singalongs, but he's deep into researching how music can heal trauma and getting pretty excited about the whole thing.'

'Sounds like our Peter Pan might be growing up. Who knows, maybe this is just the start and he'll want his own kids soon and settle down, or even get married – *not* a word I ever thought I'd use in the same sentence as Griffin!' Fi hooted with laughter.

'We live in hope,' Ruby agreed, even as she felt a pang of something she couldn't identify at the idea of a happily married Griffin. Surely the prospect of offloading her best mate and all his complications on to a gullible new wife should have her throwing her wedding hat into the air with joy?

'You still there?'

'Yes, sorry, I think the line dropped for a second,' Ruby fibbed.

'We miss you, but I'm glad you're having a ball out there. Shame I can't leave this lot and join you. I could do with a break, and me and George Clooney might well have hit it off.'

'Dolly Parton meets George Clooney . . . hmm, I dunno about that. Besides, weren't you the one who made me swear after divorce number two that I would stop you if you ever so much as looked at another man? You even threatened to make me sign an agreement in blood – mine, not yours, as I recall.'

'Agreements don't count when it comes to George Clooney,' Fi replied, adding a cheery 'Talk later' before abruptly ending the call.

Even halfway across the world, Fi still managed to get in the last word.

Ruby waved until Jake was out of sight before retracing her footsteps into Paradise Inn. Despite his unexplained absence for most of the week, Kenny had kept his promise to pick up Jake, giving her the rest of Saturday to herself. She walked into the hallway just as Griffin was bounding down the staircase, whistling merrily.

'Morning. You're looking chirpy – are you heading over to Ocean House?' she asked.

'No, not until Monday. Where's Jake?'

'He just left with Kenny. They're spending the morning together on his boat and then Kenny's taking him horse riding near the marina.'

'Ah! Does that mean I have you all to myself, then?' Griffin leered, twirling a non-existent moustache. 'Or are you off to do your modelling?'

'Nope.' She shook her head. 'Not today. Mac's working on the background scenery, so I'm free as a bird.'

'Zeke's on his way over to drive me downtown. Why don't you come with? You said you wanted some more pictures for the website.'

'Now that, my friend, is a great idea,' Ruby agreed. Downtown was one part of Sorrel Island she had yet to explore and, without Jake present, it would be a good opportunity to talk to Griffin about her mixed-up feelings when it came to Kenny.

'I'll fetch my camera and see you down here in a few minutes,' she said happily, scooting past him to run up the stairs two at a time.

28

Downtown was a world away from Sorrel Island's palm trees and pristine beaches. Leaving the now familiar coastal road, Zeke drove them further inland and before long they were on the main road leading to the commercial district.

Ruby opened her window and snapped a few shots as Zeke drove along a busy thoroughfare with narrow pavements crowded with people going in and out of shops selling a range of clothing and household goods.

'This here's Church Square,' Zeke announced shortly after the taxi had navigated the congested roads leading into a busy central square. He pulled up in front of a tall, whitewashed building topped by a steeple and switched off the engine.

'The business district and the harbour are that way,' Zeke said, indicating one of the streets leading from the square. 'If you folks want to walk round Central Park or visit the island museum, take that road over there. It'll take you past Nathan's department store, and you just keep going till you reach the park.'

Clearly having concluded his tour-guiding responsibilities, Zeke switched the engine on again and waited for them to step out of the car on to the dusty pavement. Reaching through the open window for the notes Griffin handed over, Zeke tipped his straw boater, pressed hard on his horn, and pulled out into the heavy stream of traffic.

Although it was warm with bright sunshine, any breeze coming in from the coast was trapped between the surrounding high-rise buildings, making the air feel thick and humid. The noise of the traffic and the crowds of people milling around also came as a shock after the serene beauty Ruby had come to associate with the island.

'Where do you want to go first?' Griffin asked, looking around the busy square.

Ruby was still trying to digest Zeke's instructions, and she slipped on her sunglasses and checked the strap on her camera was secure.

'I don't know, you decide.'

'Why don't we check out the museum and park first, and then double back and head down to the harbour for lunch?' Griffin suggested. 'Miss Ida recommended trying one of the restaurants along the front. Apparently, they're famed for their fresh fish and seafood.'

Downtown was clearly going to involve a lot of walking. Relieved to have swapped her heels for comfortable rubber-soled trainers, Ruby followed Griffin's lead and they strolled out of Church Square and headed down the road Zeke had indicated. Judging from the packed pavements and the loud honking from cars and taxis stuck in slow-moving queues of traffic, the area was popular with both locals and a surprising number of tourists.

After being stopped for the third time by holidaymakers asking for directions, Ruby and Griffin exchanged rueful smiles.

'Isn't it ironic that we look more like we fit in over here than we do at home?' Ruby observed wryly. 'Still, it's a relief to look like everyone else for a change and not be stared at the whole time.'

As they walked past a large department store, Griffin stopped to peer through the window. 'I'm guessing this is Nathan's. Do you fancy going in? From what I can see, it looks more like Tesco than Selfridges.'

Ruby grabbed his hand and pulled him along impatiently. 'Come on, I want to see the museum. I'm hoping they'll let me take some pictures inside.'

A few minutes later, they found themselves at a junction, facing the entrance to a huge expanse of parkland where tall trees and colourful shrubs could be seen behind high railings.

'That must be Central Park.' Ruby looked around, trying to remember Zeke's instructions. 'Look, there's the museum over there.'

This time Ruby took the lead, striding towards the entrance to a single-storey red-brick building. Handing over a few dollars to the sleepy-looking cashier, they wandered through a series of air-conditioned, interconnecting rooms where Ruby took advantage of the security guards chatting among themselves to quickly snap pictures of a few exhibits. As they circled back to the museum entrance, she noticed a small crowd gathered in front of a display and waited for them to move away.

The exhibit, simply entitled 'Legend', was made up of a set of three paintings featuring a young Black couple. In the first painting, the couple were holding on to each other in a small boat being tossed on tempestuous waters. The second painting showed them walking together along a deserted beach, while the third depicted them building a cabin from twigs and giant fronds.

Griffin came up to Ruby as she took a few surreptitious shots of the exhibit. 'Miss Ida told me all about this.' Ruby pointed to a large placard below the exhibit detailing the legend of Sorrel Island, alongside a picture of the now familiar aerial view of the heart-shaped island.

'She's convinced it's true and that this island is magic. Apparently, I'm going to find love here.'

'Stranger things have happened,' Griffin countered, wrapping an arm around her shoulders. 'I'm getting hungry. Shall we head to the harbour for lunch and do the park with Jake another day?'

Leaving the museum, they headed back past Church Square and onwards towards the harbour. The walk, longer than Ruby had expected, took them through the central business district of high-rise glass office buildings with nondescript facades, many of which housed lobbies with cash machines visible through the windows. The restaurants in the area looked rather more upmarket than the family establishments Kenny had taken them to, and clearly catered to a more corporate clientele.

Leaving the built-up business district, they passed through a quiet residential area with streets of apartment blocks, and as they drew closer to the harbour, the apartments gave way to bars and street-food stands. Hearing steel-band music blaring from the open doors of a row of barber shops and hair salons, Ruby stopped to take some snaps while Griffin leaned against a stone pillar with a martyred expression.

'Okay, let's go! I can tell from that face you're starving,' she laughed, linking her arm through his. 'We should definitely bring Jake here before we leave, though. I really hope he's having a good time with his dad, because I was worried Kenny wouldn't show up today.'

'I'm surprised you're still so chilled about Kenny. I thought you'd have torn his head off by now.' Griffin looked at her quizzically, and Ruby grimaced.

'Believe me, the anger is still there, but after all these years it's like there's a layer of ice sitting on top of it. Kenny and I need to have a proper talk and I suppose I've been dragging it out because I'm scared of digging into all those feelings again.'

Griffin seemed to hesitate. 'I'm the last person to judge, but at some point, if you don't let the truth out, the silence will cripple you. Mum kept secrets for years and it caused a mess. If she'd been honest with me about her background, her life could have been so different. Even if she didn't want the money, she would have been able to look me in the eye instead of feeling guilty for so long. Guilt can rob you of living, and just spending time with the kids at Ocean House is making me appreciate that you can't hold on to the past.'

They had stopped to cross a busy road and, struck by a strange note in his voice, Ruby looked at him curiously. 'Do you feel closer to making peace with what she did, and her reasons?'

Griffin scanned the traffic and took her hand as they hurried across the busy intersection, letting go once they were on the other side.

'I don't know, Rubes. It's complicated. The more I deal with the lawyers and advisers to the trust, the more I understand why she ran away from that life. They've been trying for years to get me to put money into stuff I don't believe in or that I know Mum wouldn't have given a crap about, and I've had to educate myself about everything from property law to investment strategy just so I can push back against some of the schemes they come up with. I know it's been years, but I'm still struggling to decide how much money to keep and how much I should give away. What's the best way to even decide who should get some of the money, and how do I keep it from messing with my life and relationships and still look after the people I care about? I didn't earn a penny of this money and yet it rules my life. Yeah, I know I'm privileged and that most people think having loads of money is the ultimate dream, but, frankly, it's been a nightmare.'

'Sorry, mate, but I can't feel sorry for you because you're burdened with a fortune.' Ruby smiled to soften the impact of her words. 'I'm still working out how to pay my credit card bill when we get back from this trip.'

'I know. I'm playing the world's tiniest violin, right?' Griffin gave a bark of mirthless laughter. 'If it helps, I'm trying to focus on the future rather than the past, but I just wish I'd had the chance to talk to Mum about this and tell her that she could trust me to do the right thing.'

Ruby took his arm as they walked and squeezed it reassuringly. 'She *did* trust you, Griff. It was the people who would surround you who she didn't trust – you've seen for yourself how being wealthy has changed the way some people act towards you. Yes, the money has caused a lot of heartache, but you're in a position now to do something good with it and that's what matters.'

'The money definitely hasn't changed the way you see me, though, has it? You still treat me like an irresponsible adult on probation,' he said evenly.

'Is that how I make you feel?' Ruby stared at him, startled by the charge, but his profile gave nothing away.

Then he stopped and turned towards her, his eyes studying hers intently. 'Maybe it's because we've known each other so long, but I don't think you've moved on from thinking of me as anything but a messed-up teenager.'

For a fleeting moment, she saw something in his eyes that sent a shiver down her spine, and the automatic denial died on her lips. For a few moments they gazed into each other's eyes and then Griffin's mouth curved into a wry smile. Linking his arm through hers, he urged her forward.

'Come on, I'm starving!'

29

Ruby could taste the faint tang of salt in the air, and moments later the road sloped sharply downhill, bringing the harbour and the surrounding blue sea into view.

'Oh my God, it's so beautiful,' she murmured, quickly unhooking her camera to snap a series of shots.

This part of the island was a far cry from both the high-rise buildings of the commercial district and the lush serenity of Paradise Inn. The harbour road was busy with traffic going back and forth from the bay, and as Ruby and Griffin made their way down the steep paved sidewalk, they passed a long line of brightly painted corrugated-metal kiosks displaying canned goods and household items for sale. The kiosks appeared to be exclusively owned by women, and when Ruby and Griffin stopped at one to buy a bottle of water, a few women from the kiosks nearby called out greetings in a mixture of English and the local dialect, one or two of them optimistically blowing loud kisses in Griffin's direction.

Approaching a vivid pink kiosk, Ruby's nose picked up a familiar scent. 'Oh my God, fried plantain!'

A large, covered bowl of spicy fried plantains sat on the counter, and hearing Ruby's excited squeal, the kiosk owner, who was bent over a large fryer, straightened and beckoned her over. She scooped a pile of the hot snacks into a newspaper cone and held it out.

'Here you go, darlin'. You make sure to share with your 'usband.' She gave a broad smile as she pocketed the notes Ruby handed over.

'He's not my husband, but thank you,' Ruby laughed. She popped a couple of the plantains into her mouth and savoured their spicy sweetness for a moment before reluctantly offering the cone to an amused Griffin.

The harbour was a bustling hub teeming with fishermen offloading heavy nets filled with crabs, fish, and lobsters while workers lugged crates of produce between boats and vans. There was no shortage of restaurants along the harbour front and after a few minutes, Ruby had had enough.

'I'm hot and parched and I cannot walk another step. Just pick somewhere so I can sit down and have a drink,' she begged.

Griffin nodded towards a double-fronted restaurant with bright blue signage a few metres away. 'Go on then, after you.'

Ruby didn't need to be asked twice and, taking the lead, she hurried up to the front door and pushed it open. Inside, the air-conditioned eatery was blissfully cool, and a friendly-looking waiter ushered them to a table by the bay window.

After taking a quick detour to the spotless facilities to wash her hands and freshen up, Ruby sank on to her chair with a groan. 'My feet are tanked, and my calves are killing me. God knows how many miles we've walked today!'

Griffin picked up the menus the waiter had left on the table and handed one to Ruby. 'I could kill for a cold lager,' he said, flipping over the laminated card. 'What about you?'

'Yeah, that sounds good,' she agreed absently, her attention shifting to the food on offer. Although not extensive, the dishes on the menu sounded delicious, and when their waiter reappeared, Ruby quickly ordered lobster soup with dumplings while Griffin chose the spicy grilled fish kebab and roasted sweet potato wedges.

As soon as the waiter had served their drinks, he walked over to a half-hidden piano in the corner of the restaurant and began to play.

Griffin took a long swallow of his lager and settled back in his chair to listen to the impromptu jazz performance, his fingers tapping on the table in time to the music. He looked so delighted that Ruby couldn't help smiling. Despite his outsize inheritance, Griffin was always most at ease in the simplest of surroundings, and Ruby felt a pang of sadness that his mother had never understood that.

The waiter cum pianist broke off to fetch their food, and as he placed the dishes on the table, Griffin leaned in to read his name badge.

'Hey, Diego, that was fantastic! You play professionally, right?'

Diego grinned. 'Yes, sir. Waiter by day, and musician by night. If you want to hear some live music and do a little dancing, you folks should come by my cousin's bar. I play there a few nights a week – everything from reggae to Latin, and even some rock.'

'I like the sound of that. What's the place called?'

'The Marina Beach Bar, sir. It's close to Sugar Bay. It's a popular spot for the locals, but tourists are always welcome.'

Griffin pulled his phone from his pocket and tapped in the information and Diego's number. While the two men continued to chat about music, Ruby let the conversation swirl above her. Tearing pieces of the soft, warm bread rolls, she dived into the hearty broth of freshly caught chunky fish and succulent seafood. Pausing to take a sip of lager, she gazed out of the window at the activity in the harbour, making a mental note to take pictures of the fishermen after lunch.

A little later, and more than a bit tipsy after a second glass of lager, Ruby slumped back in her chair. Diego was back at the piano teasing out a gentle melody that drifted across the room.

Griffin, having made quick work of the skewers of fish and spiced potatoes, drained the lager in his glass. 'Look at you, all glowing and contented. What's going on in that pretty head of yours?'

Ruby gave him a dazzling smile. 'I don't know about the pretty bit, but I'm just feeling happy. Great food, great music, and—'

'Great company?'

'*Fabulous* company! I can't think of anyone I'd rather share this with. Jumping on a plane and coming all this way to bring Jellybean was so over the top, even for you, but I'm really glad you did, because Jake's right: nothing is ever as much fun without you.'

The music stopped, and suddenly Griffin looked at her with an urgency she had never seen before, and her smile faltered.

'What?'

This time, there was no sign of his customary cheeky twinkle and he leaned forward until their faces were so close she could count every one of his thick, dark lashes. As she stared into his eyes, it was as if she had seen but never quite appreciated how extraordinary they were. The dark pupils emphasised the clear hazel of the surrounding iris, and despite the air conditioning, a slow flush of heat crawled up into her face. As her breath caught in her chest, all at once it felt like everything around her was shifting.

Just as she thought Griffin was about to speak, he dropped his gaze and a tense silence stretched out between them. Then, he looked up and into her eyes.

'So, the thing is – well, I've been wondering if . . .'

'If . . . if what?' Ruby stammered, struggling to get the words out of a chest that suddenly seemed to have forgotten how to breathe.

'Rubes . . . have you honestly never considered—'

'How are you folks doing?' Diego appeared without warning, his canvas shoes treading silently on the wood flooring. 'Can I get you anything else to drink?'

Ruby released the breath she hadn't realised she was holding and shook her head dumbly. Griffin responded with a polite 'No' and then leaned back in his chair with a face that had lost all expression.

As soon as the waiter left, Ruby murmured tentatively, 'What were you going to ask me?'

Griffin gave a tiny smile and shook his head. 'Nothing. Forget it. It was only a thought, but I was being daft. If you don't want anything else, let's get the bill.'

About to insist, Ruby thought better of it and remained silent as she tried to process what had just happened or – more accurately – not happened. Diego arrived with the bill shortly afterwards and Griffin dropped a generous pile of notes on to the saucer, waving aside Ruby's offer to split the bill.

Beaming at the size of the tip, Diego shook Griffin's hand with the warmth of a long-lost friend. 'I hope you can come by the bar before you leave,' he said cheerfully as he walked them to the door. 'You and your wife have yourselves a nice day, sir!'

Ruby and Griffin exchanged looks, but for reasons she couldn't begin to explain, neither one of them corrected him.

30

'Jake, for the hundredth time, put your shoes on properly before you ruin the backs!' Ruby glared at her son in exasperation.

'But it's easier to take them off when I wear them this way!'

'*Jake!*'

'But, Mum, they look better like this.' He twirled around and jumped up and down, his weight crushing the back of his canvas shoes.

'Jake, nobody likes a smartarse,' Griffin said sharply.

'Mum! Uncle Griffin said a rude word!' Jake crowed gleefully.

'Uncle Griffin should know better than that, shouldn't he?' Ruby said pointedly.

'Sorry.' Griffin held up his hands. 'I'll put a pound coin in the swear jar when we get back home, but, Jake, *you* cannot talk back to your mum. She works hard to buy you things and you need to take care of them.'

Jake pouted, but Griffin stood his ground. 'If you want to come with me to Ocean House after your lesson with Mac, then you know what to do.'

'But, Uncle Griffin—'

'Your godfather has spoken,' Griffin growled, contorting his features into an exaggerated scowl.

Jake giggled and pushed his feet fully into the shoes, raising a leg and wiggling his foot as proof.

'You do know he doesn't have a clue why you say "godfather" with a bad Italian accent?' Ruby pointed out as they watched Jake run off to play along the beach. Thanks to Griffin, she had never been forced to experience the full weight of single parenthood. Even when Jake was a toddler, Griffin had often picked him up when Ruby was feeling overwhelmed, sometimes keeping him for days at a time. Along with Auntie Pearl, there was no-one Ruby trusted more with her son.

'Still, you'll make a great father one day,' she added with a smile.

'Well, it's good to know that you don't think I'm a completely hopeless adult and human being,' he said, his expression suddenly grim.

'Of course I don't, and I've never said that!' she protested, taken aback by the sarcasm.

Griffin made a show of plucking a piece of cotton from the front of his t-shirt. 'Yeah, well, that's how it feels a lot of the time. Let's face it, if you're not bollocking me about something or other, you're reminding me of every mess I've ever made.'

Ruby wasn't enjoying being labelled as the joyless headmistress. 'I'm sorry if that's how you feel. If I bring up things from the past, it's only because I want you to be your best. I promised your mum—'

'Trust me, I am only too aware of what you promised,' he interrupted, his face closing in. 'The problem is I'm not a kid any more, Ruby, and it's not your job to be my mother.'

With that, he turned and went after Jake, and Ruby watched him go with a mixture of exasperation and disquiet. Something had changed between them since that strange moment in the restaurant, and the ride back home in the taxi had been conducted in near silence. Griffin had seemed on edge and had excused himself and disappeared to his room as soon as they arrived at Paradise Inn. Later, standing on her balcony reflecting on the day's events, Ruby had seen him walking towards the beach, guitar in hand. There had been no sign of Griffin at dinner time and listening with only half an ear to Jake's animated account of his day out with Kenny, Ruby couldn't stop her thoughts returning to that inexplicable moment in the harbour restaurant.

That morning, although Griffin had joined her and Jake for breakfast, he seemed distracted and had barely made eye contact. The sudden awkward tension between them was subtle but undeniable, and all at once Ruby felt herself in uncharted waters.

Leaving Griffin and Jake standing in the shallows skimming shells into the sea, Ruby sighed and went to find Mac.

◆ ◆ ◆

'Raise your chin higher,' Mac ordered.

Pushing aside her musings about the ever-complicated Griffin, Ruby did as she was told, watching Mac's brows furrow in concentration as his gaze flickered between her and the canvas. *Why can't everyone be as straightforward and uncomplicated as Mac?* she thought wistfully.

'You can take a break for a few minutes if you like,' he offered, and only too happy to drop the pose, Ruby plopped herself down on to the grass. She leaned back on her elbows, stretching her legs out in front of her to ease the muscles still aching from the extensive walking of the previous day.

'Mac, I don't think you've ever told me how you first found out about Sorrel Island,' she asked idly. 'It's hardly on the top ten list of holiday destinations.'

'Hmm?' Tilting his head to one side as he studied the canvas, Mac replied absently, 'My wife's best friend was the one who told us about the island. She was born here, but her parents emigrated to the States when she was a kid.'

Hearing nothing after the word 'wife', Ruby sat bolt upright, her mouth falling open in shock. Her stomach dropped like a boulder in freefall as she stared wordlessly at Mac. *Wife? Of course he's married*, she groaned silently. But then, she thought in confusion, what were all the flirtatious, soulful looks for? Had the delicious tension between them just been something in her own head? Something she'd simply imagined? She could have kicked herself. *Wake up, Ruby! The man is gorgeous! What the hell else did you expect?*

'I suppose I should say ex-wife really,' Mac amended, turning his attention from the portrait to look directly at Ruby, who was close to combusting with frustration at his casual tone. *So much for straightforward and uncomplicated!*

'What do you mean, *suppose*? You're either married or you're not *and* you've never once mentioned that you're married,' Ruby snapped, aware of how accusatory she sounded. Admittedly, Mac didn't *owe* her any explanations, exactly, but given all the time they'd spent together, why had he held out on that one *bloody* crucial detail?

Mac nodded as if he'd heard her unspoken question. 'I guess I haven't mentioned it because I'm not married. At least, not really. We've been separated for almost three years.'

'But if it's been that long, why aren't you divorced?'

'Because she's still waiting on me to sign the divorce papers and I – well, I guess I've been trying to figure out if it's really over.'

It took her a moment, but curiosity soon won out over irrational disappointment. 'So, what went wrong?' Ruby ventured, hastily adding, 'and feel free to tell me to mind my own business.'

Mac smiled wryly, an amused twinkle in his blue eyes. 'No, it's fine. It's not like I haven't quizzed you plenty about your life. Estella – that's her name – and I got married ten years ago. The first few years were great. At least, I thought they were.' He scratched his beard and looked appraisingly at Ruby. 'I gotta tell you that you remind me of her. Same height, similar physique – and you've both got a fantastic facial bone structure.'

Still unsure whether to laugh or wail at Mac's bombshell news, Ruby had no idea how to feel about being complimented and compared to another woman in the same breath. And not just another woman, she reminded herself. *Mac's wife.*

Mac picked up a pencil and sketched a few lines on the portrait. 'You know, my life isn't exactly conventional. I spend a lot of time on the road working, which meant Estella was at home by herself, sometimes for weeks at a time. At first, it wasn't that big a deal. I mean, it's not like she was a lonely housewife or anything – the woman's a sought-after physiotherapist with a wide circle of friends. But over time, I guess being married to someone with my lifestyle started to get to her. She was constantly mad at me for never being around for all the social stuff – you know, weddings, birthday parties, vacations with friends . . .' Mac tailed off into a moody silence.

'That's understandable, surely,' Ruby said hesitantly, surprising herself by taking Estella's side, but Mac shook his head impatiently.

'I'm an artist, Ruby, and my work is my life. She knew that when we got married, and she swore she understood I can't take on commissions and still stay home in New York all year round. She suggested travelling with me at one point, but I figured she'd be a distraction. Anyway, we stumbled along for a while and I thought we were making it work, but then three years ago, after I got home from what I guess was one trip too many, she moved out and demanded a divorce.'

Although he sounded matter of fact, Ruby could hear the sadness laced through his words. Putting aside her own ambivalent feelings towards Mac, she asked gently, 'Didn't you talk to her and try to work it out?'

'Ruby, I'm an incredible artist but I am *not* great at showing my feelings. My old man was hardly a role model for how to be a decent husband, and growing up like I did, when you get disappointed, you just learn to suck it up.'

'And yet you haven't signed the papers,' she pointed out.

'*Touché.*' He grinned unabashedly. 'I guess I've been hoping she'll miss me enough to change her mind.'

'After three *years?*' Ruby couldn't help the scepticism in her voice.

Mac shrugged. 'She hasn't chased me to sign the papers, so the way I see it, she can't have found someone else yet.'

'Which is absolutely the mature way to deal with the situation,' Ruby said caustically. 'Come on, Mac! It must be torture to be always wondering and waiting for the blow to come.'

'It's been tough,' he conceded. 'But it hasn't bothered me these past few weeks like it used to. Maybe it's time to let go of the past and see what the future holds. What do you think?'

'I-I don't know,' Ruby stammered, turning away from his probing gaze to examine the grass with great concentration.

'Well, I'm holding you to your promise to come to the States for the portrait exhibition. Who knows, maybe you'll love New York and decide to stay.'

Ruby flushed deeply at Mac's not-so-casual tone and when she eventually looked up and their eyes met and held, his purposeful look left no room for misinterpretation.

'I think we've done enough for today,' she muttered, and struggled to her feet, wincing at the stiffness in her muscles. Unable to meet Mac's eyes, Ruby ducked her head while making a show of brushing grass off her legs, conscious that this was the second time in as many days that a man was leaving her in a state of emotional disarray.

What the hell is Sorrel Island doing to me?

31

Jake had been chattering non-stop from the moment Zeke picked them up from Paradise Inn and had scarcely paused for breath.

'Calm down, buddy,' Ruby admonished. 'Poor Zeke can't keep up with all your questions.'

'It's alright, Miss Ruby.' Zeke grinned, pushing back his straw boater to scratch his forehead. 'It's good to hear the boy's having such a good time on the island.'

Gripping his seatbelt, Jake twisted in his seat to face the driver. 'Can you ride, Zeke? My dad says he's going to get me my own horse when I'm bigger, and then I can go riding whenever I want!'

Ruby sighed under her breath and glanced at her watch. They were on their way to the marina, and with Jake clearly anticipating further visits to Sorrel Island, she was keen to agree a time with Kenny to discuss the future arrangements for their son. Kenny had resumed his practice of stopping by Paradise Inn to take Jake off for a drive or a meal, and although Ruby was always invited, she had begun to make a point of declining. She was still struggling to accept Kenny's reason for abandoning them and she couldn't help the nagging feeling that there was more to it than he'd admitted. Furthermore, even seeing Jake so happy couldn't wipe away the years of pain caused by Kenny's betrayal. Navigating her wayward emotions when she was around him was growing increasingly stressful and, more than anything, Ruby dreaded triggering Jake's anxiety by revealing her feelings for his father. Today, however, with Sam and the rest of his crew out on the boats, Kenny had been unable to leave the office to fetch Jake and had pleaded with a reluctant Ruby to bring him over.

As the taxi sped along the coastal road towards the marina, Ruby left Zeke to Jake's tender mercies and returned to her contemplation. Kenny was only one piece in the ever more complicated jigsaw of her trip. Days after their trip downtown, things still felt off with Griffin. His visits to Ocean House had become a daily routine and while his grumpiness had disappeared, Ruby sensed a distance between them and a guardedness that jarred with the ease they had always known.

Where she would normally have confided her conflicted feelings to her best friend, it was impossible to do so when he was part of the problem. It would – almost – be worth hearing Auntie Pearl's I-told-you-so if it came with some of her aunt's shrewd advice, although even getting hold of the woman these days, in between her numerous get-togethers with her friends, took some doing.

Thinking about home set Ruby wondering whether she would feel more in control of her life once they returned to London and she fell back into her usual routine. Without the tempting distraction of Mac and his hints at developing feelings for her or the frustration of dancing around her unresolved history with Kenny, surely things between her and Griffin could return to normal. At the same time, it was hard to ignore the quiet voice inside questioning if she could maintain the pretence that nothing had changed.

Isn't there more to dream about and to hope for, Rubes?

◆ ◆ ◆

'A penny for your thoughts.'

Ruby started as Kenny's voice snapped her out of her reverie. They had walked to the marina café from his office and were seated at a table, waiting for Jake to work his way through a double-scoop chocolate ice-cream.

'I think they're worth considerably more than that,' Ruby said with a tight smile. 'Sorry, I got a bit lost in my head . . . there's a lot going on.'

'Anything I can help with?'

She hesitated. 'Actually, I'm glad you asked because we need to talk properly. We have to go back to London soon and—'

'Mum, *no!*' Jake howled in protest.

'We can't stay here for ever, Jake,' said Ruby. 'I have to get back to work, and you need to be in school.'

'But I'm doing my classwork every morning,' he pleaded. '*Please*, Mum, can't we stay here longer?'

'We're not leaving tomorrow, so calm down. Jake, you've always known we were only coming for a visit. We've been here for a while and Auntie Fi needs me back at work – and don't forget Grandma Pearl is all on her own,' she added, shamelessly pulling the granny card.

Kenny cleared his throat, and Jake turned to him hopefully. 'I'm very happy you came here to see me, son, but your mum's right. School is important, and now you know where I am, you can always come back for a visit.'

Crestfallen at his father's lack of support, Jake returned his attention to his ice-cream while Ruby gave Kenny a grateful smile. When he unexpectedly returned it with a conspiratorial wink, she couldn't help the giggle that escaped.

'What are you two planning for this afternoon, then?' She broke off a piece of the spiced bun Kenny had ordered for her and popped it into her mouth.

'Sam should be back by now, so I'll take Jake out on the motorboat. My boy loves the water and it's a fantastic way to see the island.'

'You okay with that, buddy?' Despite her own reservations about sailing, Ruby had no wish to project her fears on to him.

''Course I am, Mum. I'm not a baby!'

There was no evidence of anxiety in Jake's indignant expression and Ruby relaxed, marvelling once again at how much Jake's confidence had grown since their arrival.

Kenny leaned forward to dab a lone raisin sitting on her plate with his finger and her pulse quickened at the oddly intimate gesture. His arm brushed against hers and, caught unawares by the unexpected touch of his bare skin against her own, she felt a shiver run through her. For a moment she stared, mesmerised, as he licked the raisin off his finger, and then scolded herself sternly as she fought to regain her equilibrium. *Don't get sucked in!*

'So, what do you say, Rubes? You sure you don't want to come with us? It'll be fun, and I promise I won't let you drown,' Kenny teased, his dark eyes alight with mischief.

'I do know how to swim, thank you very much!'

'You do indeed,' he murmured. 'I always used to love watching you in action.'

She looked at him askance, and he guffawed with laughter. '*Damn*, Rubes, if looks could kill!'

Her lips twitched and then, despite herself, she found herself laughing with him. For just an instant time stood still and the past six years melted away. Kenny's cheeky sense of humour was another thing that had attracted her to him, and it felt good to let go and relax into the moment.

Leaving the café, they returned to Kenny's office and Ruby perched on the corner of his desk while Kenny knelt to fit Jake's life vest. Tugging the jacket to check it was secure, Kenny stood up and looked enquiringly at Ruby.

'Any plans while we're out?'

She tilted her head quizzically. 'Why do you ask?'

'Just wondered, that's all.' He stared at the toes of his shoes with a hangdog expression so much like Jake's that Ruby bit her lip to hide her amusement.

'I'll be fine. I want to take pictures of the marina. This place is stunning, and I'd love to capture some images of the boats in the sunshine under that incredibly blue sky.'

Tugging his father's hand, an excited Jake led the way out, and Ruby leaned against a concrete post to watch as they headed down the walkway to where the motorboat was moored. While Kenny helped Jake aboard, Ruby removed the cap from her camera and then snapped a few shots of her son at the wheel while Kenny, his arm cradling Jake protectively, checked the instrument panel.

When Kenny unhooked the mooring chain, seeing their faces looking so alike and alight with laughter, Ruby couldn't help smiling. Neither could she resist raising the camera and zooming in to Kenny's face as he held on to Jake before starting the engine. *What if we could be a family again?* If Miss Ida was right and Kenny hadn't moved on, was a reconciliation for the sake of their son so impossible?

Watching the motorboat power away over the foam-flecked waters, Ruby slowly lowered the camera and gave herself a mental shake for thinking the unthinkable. Sorrel Island was wearing down her defences and her judgement, she thought sombrely. For more reasons than one, it was time to return home.

32

'*Ruby!*

Hearing the urgency in Griffin's voice as he shouted her name, Ruby's heart dropped, and she tossed aside her half-read novel and scrambled off the lounger. Raising a hand to shield her eyes as she watched him race across the beach towards her with Jake close behind, she gasped as Griffin picked her up and spun her around before depositing her gently on the sand.

'What the hell is going on?' she asked, her heart pounding as she tried to catch her breath.

'He's *speaking*! Drew is actually *speaking*!' Griffin's eyes glittered with emotion, and Ruby clutched at her chest, her mouth dropping open in shock.

'Oh my God!' she exclaimed. 'Oh, Griff, that's so brilliant!'

Jake rushed up to his mother and hugged her around her waist, jumping up and down.

'You should have seen it, Mum! The director was *crying*.'

Ruby glanced at Griffin, who looked close to following the director's example, and she swallowed the sudden lump in her throat. It didn't take a genius to work out why Griffin had bonded so closely with Drew; they had both been through the trauma of losing their much-loved parent figures. Griffin had put so much time and effort into building Drew's trust and now, seeing his lips tremble with the effort of staying in control, she could tell how much it meant to Griffin to see Drew finally respond. Forgetting the awkwardness of the past few days, she threw her arms around Griffin's neck and hugged him tightly.

'Group hug!' Jake squealed, flinging his arms around the two of them.

Ruby laughed as she extricated herself from the tangle of limbs. 'This is such good news, Griff. All the research you've done has really paid off by helping Drew.'

'It's just the start, though, Rubes,' Griffin said, his face glowing. 'Those poor kids have been through so much, and it's simply incredible how powerful music is in breaking down barriers. It can make such a difference because if we can help them open up, they can start healing.'

'What has *happened* to the Griffin I know, and who is this person speaking with what sounds suspiciously like a sense of purpose?' Ruby teased, impressed nonetheless by the impassioned speech.

'I might surprise you yet. Come on, let's take a walk and I'll tell you all about it. I'm too buzzed to sit down.'

Ruby slipped on her sandals and hooked her arm into his as they strolled along the beach while Jake ran ahead. She listened intently while Griffin described the music session and the palpable shock in the room when Drew uttered his first words.

'So what did he actually say?'

Griffin laughed. '"*I want some water.*" Not exactly profound, but it was music to our ears. I've been chatting to Diego – you remember, the waiter we met at the restaurant? He's agreed to hook me up with some of his musician friends cos I want to fund a programme so they can play regularly for the kids at Ocean House. I've promised the director of the home that I'll be in touch to work on a longer-term project we can launch the next time I'm here.'

'The *next* time . . . !' Ruby echoed. Shocked, she released his arm and faced him squarely. 'Oh my God, you're really serious about this, aren't you?'

Griffin shrugged. 'I don't want to abandon Drew, and, besides, what else am I doing with my time and money? This is something I know could make a difference to those children, so why not?'

She tilted her head to one side and studied him gravely. 'So, what you're telling me, then, is that you're going to be very brave and fly in the teeny-tiny plane again?'

He burst out laughing and flung an arm around her shoulders, urging her forward. 'A wise woman once told me that you need to overcome your fears if you want something badly enough,' he said lightly, before releasing her and dashing over to help Jake, who was attempting to climb a large rock.

A few minutes later, leaving Jake perched triumphantly on top of the boulder, Griffin returned to where Ruby was standing alone, staring out to sea.

'Rubes,' he started hesitantly, 'I feel like things have been a bit . . . off between you and me lately. I'm going to Diego's gig at his cousin's bar tonight. Fancy coming along? We can practise our salsa moves and blow away the cobwebs?'

'Yes, of course!' She smiled, relieved for the chance to clear the air. 'But what about Jake?'

'Miss Ida would be happy to look after him. Or, better still, if Narita's free tonight, she'll be glad of the extra cash. Jake's got a massive crush on her, so he'll be ecstatic.'

'*Really?*' Ruby's eyebrows shot up in astonishment. 'I had no idea! Am I really that clueless about what goes on around me?'

Griffin's lips curved into a faint, enigmatic smile. 'Don't ask questions you don't want the answers to. Come on, let's head back and sort it out.'

33

Ruby adjusted the thin shoulder straps and the low-cut vee of her sleeveless, slim-fitting dress before twisting around to check her back in the mirror. The silky fabric clung to her body and the fringed hem, starting at mid-thigh, revealed the long length of her legs. The vibrant orange colour glowed against the deep bronze of her skin, which had been given an extra sheen from the shimmering body cream she had applied liberally after her shower. She forced herself to stop grinning long enough to slick some bronze gloss over her lips and then danced a little jig of excitement, twisting her hips back and forth to swish the fringes on the dress. She loved dancing, and after weeks of family-friendly activities she couldn't wait to do something grown-up for a change. Furthermore, with their easy banter restored, Griffin was the perfect partner with whom to enjoy a night of uncomplicated partying.

Ruby sat on the bed and slipped on her high-heeled sandals before returning to the mirror for a final check. Flip-flops and trainers were all very well for walking around the beach or sightseeing, but she had missed her heels and the confidence that came from strutting with that extra bit of height. Smoothing back her braids, she picked up her bag and sashayed down the stairs, enjoying the stunned expression on both Griffin's and Zeke's faces as she descended.

Griffin's eyes shot straight to her legs. 'Will you slap me if I whistle? Cos you look seriously hot!'

Ruby opened her mouth to bat away the compliment, and then closed it again and smiled her thanks. A world-famous artist was painting her portrait, after all, so who was she to argue?

◆ ◆ ◆

The evening sun moved slowly towards the horizon, the red streaks in the sky casting a pink sheen across the ocean as Zeke pulled up to the Marina Beach Bar and Restaurant. The exterior of the two-storey structure set back from the beach was lit with strings of fairy lights and, judging by the loud music spilling out of the open front door, the bar was as lively as Diego had promised.

Entering the building, Ruby felt as if she'd been hit by a wall of sound. A live band, with Diego on keyboards, was up on the stage blaring out fast-paced Latin music with a beat so infectious that her feet itched to move. Other than a well-stocked bar across the room and next to a staircase, which presumably led up to the restaurant, the rest of the space downstairs was a huge dance floor packed with people.

Griffin tapped her shoulder, but unable to make out what he was saying over the din, Ruby shook her head with a helpless shrug. Taking her hand, he led her through the crowd to the bar, where he could make himself heard.

'What do you want to drink?' he repeated.

'A rum cocktail would be lovely.' She beamed, hopping up on to a bar stool to watch the skilful, rhythmic moves of the couples on the dance floor while Griffin caught the barman's eye and ordered their drinks. Her feet were tapping in time to the music, and she couldn't wait to join them.

'Here you go!' Griffin planted a tall glass filled with a dark liquid and shaved ice in front of her. Taking a long sip through the straw, Ruby gasped at the strength of the cocktail. After a couple more sips, she felt her inhibitions slipping away like a heavy cloak.

'Come on, let's dance!' she exclaimed, sliding off the stool and pulling Griffin into the crowd. Their salsa classes paid off as she and Griffin danced for almost an hour, stopping only to rehydrate with a steady supply of cocktails.

When the band eventually took a break, Ruby and Griffin were standing by the bar when Diego appeared. After high-fiving Griffin, he gave him a warm hug before shaking hands with Ruby.

'You folks having a good time?' Away from the restaurant and dressed casually in jeans and a black t-shirt, he looked younger than Ruby had first assumed, and she nodded enthusiastically.

'I *love* this place and the music is incredible! You guys are brilliant.'

'Thank you.' Diego grinned, wiping his damp brow with a handkerchief. 'We'll be back on stage in a few minutes.' As if struck by a thought, he turned to Griffin. 'Hey, you play guitar, right? You want to jam with us?'

Griffin looked startled. 'What, really?'

'Yeah, go on, Griff!' Ruby squealed, grabbing his arm excitedly. 'You'll be amazing.'

Griffin stared at her doubtfully for a moment and then his face broke into a grin, and he shrugged. 'Okay, then, why not?'

Clapping her hands with glee, Ruby watched Griffin follow Diego across the floor and climb the steps on to the stage. He shook hands with the other band members and chatted to them for a few minutes before strapping an impressive-looking guitar across his chest.

When the band kicked off again, this time with a Latin rock tune, Ruby sat on a bar stool, whooping loudly when Griffin joined in. After playing a couple of numbers and delivering an impromptu solo, Griffin slipped off the guitar and handed it back to its owner before hopping off the stage to appreciative cheers and whistles from the crowd.

As he approached her, Ruby jumped off the stool and threw her arms around his neck in an exuberant hug. '*Omigod!* I knew you were good, but that was incredible!'

'Thank you, ma'am.' He smiled, taking her hand. 'Come on, dance with me.'

For the next couple of hours, caught up in the music, they danced almost non-stop to a medley of rock, Latin, and reggae, letting the music and cocktails melt away any residual tension until eventually, sweaty and exhausted, they made their way outside for some fresh air.

Slipping off her heels, Ruby hooked her arm into Griffin's as they strolled along the deserted beach behind the bar. She shook back her long braids, feeling the warm night breeze against her heated skin and relishing the sensation of cool sand under the soles of her tired feet.

Exhausted from dancing, and buzzing from the strong cocktails, she dropped her shoes on to the sand and collapsed on to a smooth outcrop of rock, pulling Griffin down beside her.

The strains from the music playing in the bar drifted across as they sat silently watching the receding tide wash on to the sand. The gentle breeze whispered through the fronds of the coconut trees, and the only illumination other than the twinkling fairy lights outlining the Marina Bar came from the stars in the sky and the moonlight reflected on the water.

Ruby leaned her head against Griffin's shoulder with a sigh of contentment. 'Isn't this the most perfectly romantic setting ever?' she murmured.

'It's beautiful. Thanks for coming with me and making this such a great night.'

She raised her head to look at him with a smile. 'Thank *you*. I've had a fantastic evening, and I can't remember the last time we danced so much.'

She should have stopped there, but before she could help herself, Ruby added, 'Just imagine, you could have brought someone out here with you if you didn't keep finding silly reasons to dump your girlfriends.'

'There's nothing silly about knowing when a relationship isn't going to work out,' Griffin drawled.

'Hmm . . . so what about excuses like Melinda's voice being too shrill, or Kaitlyn playing with her hair too much, or . . . what was her name? Oh, yes, *Angie* wanting you to meet her mum after only two dates.'

When Griffin chuckled, Ruby added dryly, 'And let's not forget Shirlee.'

'Oh, come on! That was never going anywhere,' Griffin protested. 'She expected a proposal after our third date! Besides, she's a lovely girl but—'

'But what?'

He suddenly looked sheepish. 'Rubes, you never saw her feet.'

'Her *feet*?' Ruby frowned in confusion.

'Yeah, they're kind of— Well, she has this really long second toe.'

'Are you fuc—' She broke off and took a deep breath. 'Are you *kidding* me? Do you seriously mean to tell me that you stopped seeing Shirlee because she's got a long second toe?'

He looked at her silently, and Ruby shook her head in disbelief. '*Griffin!* Loads of people have that.' She stretched out her leg. 'Look! *I've* got a longer second toe. You've never called *my* feet deformed.'

Griffin peered at her foot and then looked at her curiously. 'That's really weird. How come I never noticed?'

They stared at each other for a moment and then Ruby dissolved into helpless laughter.

'You are *impossible*!' She rested her head against his shoulder, and they sat in companiable silence watching the waves rolling in and dispersing into foam on the sand.

'I still think it's a shame you can't take advantage of this setting with some beautiful island girl,' Ruby said softly, turning to him with a mischievous smile. 'You were seriously turning heads in the bar when you went up on stage.'

'I *am* with a beautiful island girl,' Griffin murmured. 'No-one in there tonight could hold a candle to you.'

Their eyes locked, and Ruby's stomach plummeted as if she'd fallen from a great height. She could feel her pulse racing and, unable to tear her gaze away from his, she panicked, blurting out the first random thought that came to mind. 'So says the man who chases any petite blonde who crosses his path.'

She felt Griffin's sharp intake of breath and winced, instantly berating herself for the chastising note in her voice. *Shut up, Ruby!*

After a moment's silence, Griffin said lightly, 'Listen, don't hate me simply because you're not my type.'

When she didn't reply, he glanced at her just as she was frantically trying to blink back the tears inexplicably flooding her eyes.

'*Ruby?* What's wrong?'

His face darkened with concern as he reached for her, and she shook her head, too afraid to speak in case she burst into tears. *What the hell* is *wrong with you, Rubes?* She and Griffin always teased each other, so why had the banter cut her to the quick this time?

Griffin pulled her close with a muffled groan, wrapping an arm around her so tightly she could feel the hard strength of his chest. 'I was only kidding, you know that.'

She pulled away enough to smile up at him weakly. 'I know, I'm just being an idiot. Neither of us is the other's type.'

Instead of laughing with her, Griffin sighed so deeply that she could feel the warmth of his breath on her face. 'No, you're not being an idiot,' he said softly.

Gazing into his eyes, what had always seemed impossible was suddenly inevitable. Before Ruby could speak, Griffin lowered his head and kissed her. Her mind was reeling as she felt his lips on hers and, at first, confused and scared, she froze. But after a moment, she relaxed into his arms and wound her arms around his neck, pulling him closer as the kiss deepened. His hands slid down her back, caressing her bare skin and drawing her so closely to him she thought she would explode with longing.

It was as if she was outside her body watching herself in Griffin's arms as he kissed her feverishly, and she kissed him back. This time, there was no awkward knocking of teeth and no painful braces.

This time, every single kiss was pure magic.

34

Ruby stretched languorously and rolled over, pulling the thin coverlet over her head. After crawling exhausted into her bed, she had lain awake reliving the previous night. The soles of her feet were on fire after the hours on the dance floor, but while every muscle in her body ached, the delicious soreness proved she hadn't imagined what had happened at the beach bar or afterwards. The events on the beach had aroused feelings neither she nor Griffin could control and the passionate kissing in the back of the taxi had continued in Griffin's room, where they had made love until falling into an exhausted sleep with their arms wrapped around each other. Waking at dawn, Ruby had slipped on her dress and crept back to her room before Jake returned. Now, just thinking of Griffin, she shivered like an infatuated teenager with her first crush.

Too restless to lie still, Ruby bunched up her pillow and propped it against the slatted wood headboard. Lying back, she stared at the ceiling with a smile so wide her cheeks hurt. Jake would be back soon from his night in Miss Ida's private quarters and before he burst through the door, she wanted to replay everything in her mind – from the moment on the beach when Griffin's lips met hers, to kissing in the taxi all the way back home, only coming up for air when the car lurched over the rough stretch of road leading to Paradise Inn. Making love had been a revelation and any shyness she had felt had fallen away as their bodies instinctively found each other. Exploring every inch of her, Griffin's touch, sensual and assured, had unleashed a passion she had never experienced before, and she had given herself to him with abandon, holding nothing back.

How quick she had been to scorn the women who fell for him so easily, Ruby mused with a slight pang of guilt, and yet after only one night here she was, unable to get him out of her mind and craving the sensation of his arms around her. What was he doing now? she wondered dreamily. For one wild moment she was tempted to run to his room to find out and then she remembered Jake and sighed. Another memory poked itself into her daydreams just as her phone pinged with a text message. Sticking her head out from under the covers, she squinted at the screen and squealed. Today was her last sitting for Mac, and she had promised to meet him at the clearing. Already late, she yawned widely and reluctantly hauled herself out of bed.

As she stumbled to the bathroom, Ruby stopped in front of the full-length mirror on the wardrobe door and smiled dreamily at her reflection. Although her braids were tangled and every step taken on her sore feet made her wince, the eyes looking back at her were shining, and her face glowed. Even the throbbing in her skull, courtesy of more rum cocktails than she could count, couldn't change the fact that she was blissfully happy.

Looking distinctly unhappy, Mac pushed the box of pencils into the bulging holdall and tugged the zip across. The carefully rolled-up portrait was now safely inside a long steel tube and his expression was dark as he dismantled the easel and packed it into a waterproof bag, along with the folding canvas stool. With Ruby distracted, and

Mac scheduled to leave the island the next day, their last sitting had been subdued. Now, except for some patches of flattened grass, Mac's makeshift studio had reverted to a natural clearing amid thick green foliage and flowering bushes.

When the silence threatened to continue indefinitely, Ruby piped up. 'I told you we're leaving on Friday, didn't I?'

After a long discussion with Auntie Pearl, Ruby had finally booked their return flights. She had also arranged for Kenny to come over the following evening to discuss future plans for Jake.

Mac's expression didn't budge at her announcement, and Ruby tried again. 'You're happy with how the portrait's going, which is great, right?'

'My work is always great,' Mac said loftily. '*That* is not what concerns me.' He weighed the heavy holdall in one hand before slinging it over his shoulder.

It was hard not to roll her eyes at Mac's theatrics, but Ruby did her best to keep her tone neutral. 'Well, you're clearly upset about something, so if it's not the painting, what's going on?'

Mac frowned as if he'd suddenly been struck by a thought, and he set the holdall down again. Watching him unzip the bag and rummage inside it, Ruby's mind drifted back to the moonlit beach and—

'Did you hear a damn word I just said?' Mac growled, closing the bag, and straightening up. He looked even crosser, and Ruby tore her mind away from her daydreaming and tried to focus.

'I'm sorry,' she said penitently. 'Tell me again.'

For a moment Mac simply stared at her, and then he muttered, 'I *said* I've finished the pencil sketch, but I would have liked more time with you.'

'But when you first asked me to sit for you, you said you'd only need me for a few days. We've spent loads more time than that together,' Ruby pointed out reasonably.

211

Reasonable didn't appear to be doing the trick, as Mac's frown simply grew deeper.

'What *is* the matter?' Ruby demanded, torn between exasperation and concern. 'It's not like you to look so down. You're the one who always says the cup's half full, not half empty.'

'Yeah, well, maybe I need you around to keep reminding me of that.' Mac looked her straight in the eye and folded his arms defensively across his chest.

'Seriously, Mac, what is it?' Puzzled, Ruby gazed at him and he shook his head with a tiny smile.

'You know, Ruby, for such a bright gal you can be pretty dumb.'

Her brows rose in surprise. She wasn't fooled by his bluster, but she *was* at a loss as to why Mackenzie Castro, who was never knowingly short of words, was suddenly so lost for them.

'I'm leaving tomorrow.' Mac spoke slowly and with a pained expression, as if every word was being forcibly dragged out.

'Ye-es, I know.'

'So . . . how about coming with me?'

'*What?*' Ruby stared at him, dumbfounded.

'You heard me. So, what about it, Ruby? You'd love New York.'

'Mac, you've known me for five minutes,' she said gently. 'Besides, I've got a life in London, not to mention an eight-year-old son.'

'New York has a whole bunch of schools, and I could get Jake into one with a fantastic art programme.'

He walked up to where she stood rooted to the spot and grasped her by the shoulders. His blue eyes seemed to pierce through her as he scoured her face intently before moving his hands from her shoulders to cradle her face. Gone was the flirtatious teasing, and in its place was a desperation she had never seen before. Maybe, at another time and place, she might have felt differently, Ruby thought, but even as he bent to kiss her and his lips teased hers

212

apart, she knew it was no use. There was no denying Mac was a skilful kisser and for just a moment Ruby lost herself in the sensation of his mouth on hers, but skill wasn't what either of them was seeking.

Mac raised his head and scrutinised her face. 'No?'

Ruby shook her head with a wry smile. 'Mac, come on . . .'

He grimaced in agreement. 'Yeah, I know. Didn't feel right, did it?'

When Ruby shook her head again, he sighed and dropped his hands to his sides.

'Mac, what's going on?' she whispered in bewilderment. No-one had more self-belief than Mackenzie Castro and she had no idea where this panicked appeal was coming from.

His voice was gruff as he turned away to avoid her eyes. 'You've inspired me to draw like I haven't for years. This portrait is gonna be the best thing I've painted for a long time. I can feel it in my gut – and it's because of you! What if I can't do it when you're not around?'

Ruby released her breath in a long sigh. While she felt bad for him, it was almost a relief to know that even a world-famous artist like Mac could suffer from insecurity. But as much as she had enjoyed their flirtatious banter and would always be grateful that he had chosen her to model for him, Ruby felt no compunction about turning him down. Mac wanted her not because he loved her, but because he thought he needed her.

She gently turned his face towards her and gazed into his eyes. 'You're a wonderful artist, as you never tire of telling me, but you're also a lovely man, and I'll never forget how kind you've been to me and Jake. He's a different boy from the one who came out here and you've been so important in building his confidence.'

'But?'

'But,' she echoed with a grin, 'you're not in love with me and I'm not in love with you, which would be the only reason for me

213

to up sticks to live in New York. Mac, you don't need me to be inspired to paint. I don't know much about art, but I've grown to know you. You're a tough-minded and resilient *legend*, and you are going to create loads more incredible art.'

He looked at her moodily and then after a moment the twinkle returned to his eyes, and he raised his hands in surrender. 'Well, it was worth a try, kid.'

Ruby burst out laughing at his sheepish expression and hugged him tightly. She had spent many hours with Mac, and he had been an integral part of her experience of Sorrel Island. Furthermore, Jake wasn't the only one whose confidence had been boosted by him. While Ruby's childhood scars would never fully heal, Mac's sketches had shown her a beautiful woman with distinctive sculpted features, a powerful yet graceful physique, and luminous, almond-shaped eyes that hinted at a sensuality she'd never known she possessed. Seeing herself through Mac's eyes had been liberating, and he would always hold a special place in her heart. She wished she could find the words to tell him how much he had helped her see beyond the cruel taunts that had blighted her life but, instead, she gave him a final squeeze before releasing him.

Mac stroked her cheek gently, his thumb rough against her cheek. 'I'm gonna miss looking at this beautiful face every day,' he said with a regretful sigh. 'It's been like seeing Estella, but without the heartache.'

Knowing that Mac didn't love her but *did* love his estranged wife made Ruby feel a lot less guilty about turning down his offer and quick to proffer her own advice.

'Instead of signing the divorce papers when you get back, why don't you take them to Estella yourself?' she suggested.

When Mac looked ready to protest, Ruby added firmly, '*Talk* to her, Mac. You obviously still love her, and maybe if you show her that you'll do whatever it takes to fix things between you . . . Well, you never know. Like you said, it's not as if she's been chasing you to sign the thing.'

'But what if she kicks me to the kerb?'

'You've got nothing to lose. If Estella's not up for it, at least then you'll know, and you can move on properly with your life.'

'If she says no, will you reconsider?' he asked hopefully.

Ruby giggled and punched his arm affectionately. 'No, but thanks for asking! You'll be fine, my friend. I know you will.'

Leaving Mac in the clearing lost in thought, Ruby made her way down the sandy walkway to the beach. The great Mackenzie Castro might not be in love with her, but he had still asked her to go away with him, she thought happily. *Not bad for a giraffe!* Suddenly, Ruby couldn't wait to tell Fi about Mac's offer. Perhaps, this time, her boss would be so shocked, Ruby might finally get the last word. After all, how often did a girl get to turn down George Clooney!

35

For the first time since their arrival, the sky was overcast with ominously dark clouds and the breeze felt so heavy Ruby could almost taste the unshed raindrops. Although the rain had held off, there had been occasional rumbles of thunder throughout the day. After the unbroken sunshine throughout their visit, the uncommonly gloomy weather also brought with it a sense of finality.

The routine of the past few weeks was ending. With a pang of regret, Ruby watched the back of Zeke's taxi – carrying Michelle, Derek, Jake, and the kids – disappear down the drive. Having waved Mac off that morning, Derek and his family were leaving the following day, and had taken Jake off for some last-minute souvenir shopping.

While part of her felt sad that their time on the island was coming to an end, life looked unbelievably bright, and Ruby's spirits were buoyant with hope for the future. Since the outing to the Marina Bar with Griffin, she had been floating on a cloud of sheer bliss while still trying to wrap her head around the monumental shift in their relationship. Not that Jake had given her much opportunity to do so. To Ruby's mounting frustration, her son had scarcely left her side for the past couple of days, forcing her and Griffin to make do with goofy smiles, briefly snatched kisses, and furtive lingering touches. Her only comfort was that Griffin seemed equally frustrated.

Under the guise of a good night hug before she propelled a sleepy Jake up to bed the night before, Griffin had whispered urgently in her ear. 'Rubes, this is *killing* me! I can't stop thinking about us and – can't you come to my room later?'

Despite the desperation in his voice, they both knew Jake was a light sleeper and too young to leave unsupervised, and Ruby had simply shaken her head and clung on to him for a few seconds longer. Until they'd had a chance to talk properly, she wasn't ready to disclose their changed relationship to Jake.

Wearing only a t-shirt over her shorts, Ruby shivered as a strong gust of wind passed over her, and she rubbed the sudden goosebumps on her arms. Griffin would soon be back from Ocean House and, with Jake gone for the afternoon, her face lit up at the thought of finally getting time alone with the man filling her every waking thought.

Turning to walk back to the house, she was halfway up the steps when she heard the light toot of a car horn. She looked back and her heart sank at the sight of Kenny's Range Rover sweeping up the driveway. She gnawed on her lip, trying to hide her exasperation, as she waited for him to park at the side of the house. He was dressed casually in jeans, a short-sleeved white shirt, and the ubiquitous baseball cap, and he smiled tentatively as he approached.

'I thought we were meeting tonight,' she said, hoping she didn't sound as dismayed as she felt about Kenny's intrusion into the time she had earmarked for Griffin.

Kenny adjusted the visor of his cap over his eyes as he walked up the steps to join her. 'I know that was the plan, but I've been sitting around getting more nervous by the hour. I was hoping I'd catch you sooner so we can get this discussion out of the way.'

Knowing Kenny felt anxious did nothing to settle Ruby's nerves. Shying away from this moment until now, she acknowledged, had been less about disrupting her son's relationship with his father, and more about wanting to avoid raking up the desperate pain of rejection. But as much as she dreaded the prospect of delving into the past, it was time to face up to it and she nodded brusquely.

'Well, I suppose your timing's good because Jake has just gone out with Derek's lot. Let's go down to the beach and talk there – it's more private than the lounge. Do you want to get a drink first?'

Not waiting for an answer, she led the way inside and into the lounge, taking two bottles of water from the fridge where Miss Ida kept cold refreshments for the guests and handing one to Kenny.

Ruby slid open the French doors and walked out, rubbing her arms as a strong breeze swept across the terrace. As they walked down to the beach, neither she nor Kenny spoke until they sat facing each other on loungers under the shelter of a large umbrella.

Ruby played nervously with the bottle of water she had yet to open as she peeked at Kenny from under her lashes. It was still hard to grasp that the man sitting across from her was the same person she had woken up to every morning for years, sharing a child, a home, and a life.

She opened the bottle of water and took a long sip, then screwed the cap back into place and looked Kenny squarely in the eye. 'Okay, so where do you want to start?'

Leaning forward and resting his forearms on his thighs, Kenny clasped his hands between his knees and held her gaze for a long moment. She looked at him expectantly, but whatever she'd imagined he would say, it certainly wasn't what emerged.

'I love you, Rubes. I want to ask you to stay, but I'm afraid of what your answer will be.' Kenny paused and took a deep breath. 'Leaving in the way I did, I had lost all hope of seeing you again and I can't tell you how much it's meant to me having you and Jake here these past weeks. I know I don't yet have your heart but – well, after the time we've spent together since you've been here, I hope you've come to see I'm not the monster you imagined and that there's enough here for us to build on. Ruby, I know my actions were unforgiveable, but I need you to know there hasn't been anyone for me since – since you. I haven't so much as looked at another woman, and what I'm trying to say—'

Ruby stared at him, wondering if she had been dragged into some alternative universe.

Kenny seemed to take her silence as encouragement because he leaned in further. 'You'd like it out here, Ruby. With your experience, you'd find a job easily – or you could even start your own business. I'd be happy to help. You've seen my house, and Jake loves the island . . . couldn't we try once more to be a family?'

'What, so you can let us down again?' She spat the words out as the anger she had thought was buried exploded with the force of a long-dormant volcano. Hearing his words out loud, whatever thoughts she may have fleetingly entertained about a reconciliation were swept away as the sheer *audacity* of Kenny's proposal sparked a rage she could scarcely contain.

'How *dare* you say that to me after everything you did?' she hissed furiously. 'You *dumped* me *and* your son and disappeared without so much as a goodbye! You sent one letter, Kenny – *one* letter in six bloody *years*! Was that all we were worth? And now – now you have the gall to keep telling me you love me and the absolute *temerity* to suggest we get back together? Have you lost your damned mind?'

Kenny shook his head and rubbed his temples wearily. 'You have every right to be angry with me, but it doesn't change the fact that I'm telling you the truth.'

'Truth?' she scoffed. 'You don't have a clue what that means. You lived with me and pretended to care about me and our son when all the time you were planning to do a runner.'

'You're not being fair, and that's not how it happened.'

For a moment Ruby felt like flying across the small divide of sand between them to physically attack him. '*I'm* not being fair? So, tell me then, where were you when my parents were killed? Where were you when I was so broken that Auntie Pearl had to move in to take care of me and Jake? Where the *bloody* hell were you, Kenny, when I had to raise our son for *six* years without an iota of support from you? *Tell* me that's not what happened!'

He took off his cap and rubbed his jaw, his shoulders slumped. 'I tried, Ruby. For years, I sent you cheques and you never cashed them.'

'Because we didn't need your *money*, Kenny, don't you get it? Jake needed his father and I – well, I learned the hard way that I don't need *you*.'

'I don't want us to fight,' he pleaded. 'All I want is what's best for you and for my son. He's been so happy spending time with me – with us, as his parents. Can't you look past what happened and forgive me? Isn't there any way you can find it in your heart for us to try again?'

The sun had disappeared behind the darkening clouds and a strong gust of wind whipped Ruby's braids around her face. She pushed them back impatiently and stared at Kenny in appalled wonder. The man still hadn't given her a decent explanation for his disappearance and yet he dared to suggest that they simply pick up where they left off – using Jake to plead his case, moreover.

'You leave Jake out of this! This is about you and me. How the *hell* do you expect me to forgive you when I still don't have the first clue about why you *really* left me – because, let me tell you, I don't buy that crap about your head being all over the place.'

Kenny stood up and ran a hand over his hair, his expression one of deep frustration. 'Ruby, I've said I'm sorry for my actions and I mean it. I was wrong and I was weak, but I never stopped loving you or Jake. How could I?'

As her fury slowly subsided and the thick sheet of ice that had protected her emotions for so long melted away, all that remained was a deep well of hurt and the pain of his abandonment that she had carried for so long. She stood up to face him, her eyes filling with tears.

'So then why did you leave me, Kenny?' she whispered. '*Why?*'

Just then, Griffin rounded the corner from the adjoining cove, guitar in hand and whistling cheerfully. As soon as he saw them, he came to an abrupt stop, and his smile disappeared. Wordlessly, his gaze moved from Ruby's tear-filled eyes to Kenny's set expression.

The wind picked up in intensity, followed by a loud growl of thunder. Ruby looked from Griffin to Kenny and shivered at the naked hostility between the two men.

Kenny was the first to break the silence. 'Now, why am I not surprised to see *you* here. It's like you have some weird sixth sense that lets you know the best time to get between her and me.'

Ruby bristled at the sarcasm in Kenny's tone and dashed away the tears threatening to spill down her cheeks. 'You have no right to take your frustration out on Griffin. *He's* the one who's been a father to the kid you ran out on, and he's got nothing to do with any of this. I asked you a question, Kenny, and I deserve to know the truth!'

Kenny looked at her quizzically as if weighing his words and then he nodded. 'Yeah, Rubes, you do deserve the truth. But if you really want to know, perhaps you should ask *him*.'

He nodded in Griffin's direction and Ruby followed his gaze in confusion before turning back to Kenny.

'What are you talking about?'

'Griffin here knows exactly why I left, don't you?' Kenny's voice hardened as he directed a searing glare at the other man.

221

About to explode at Kenny, Ruby glanced at Griffin and her voice froze in her throat. He looked pale beneath his light brown complexion and his head had dropped in the tell-tale sign she knew so well. This was classic Griffin when he didn't want to lie and yet couldn't tell the truth. Suddenly, she remembered sitting opposite him in the diner in Brighton telling him about her plans to visit Sorrel Island, and his strange reaction when she'd wondered aloud why Kenny had left.

'Griffin . . . what's he talking about?' Ruby asked through lips as stiff as cardboard. Another rumble of thunder sounded overhead, and she couldn't tell if the goosebumps on her arms were from the chilly gusts of wind or the sudden dread spreading through her body.

Griffin still wouldn't look at her, and in desperation Ruby swung back to Kenny, who was eyeing Griffin through narrowed eyes.

'Will one of you tell me what the hell is going on here?' she demanded, her heart racing in panic. 'Why would Griffin know anything about what happened?'

Kenny gave a mirthless laugh. 'Because I told him.'

'You did *what?*' Ruby gasped. 'I don't believe you! *When?*'

'I went to see him the day I left,' Kenny said grimly. 'I told him I'd bought a ticket back to Trinidad and I asked him to look after you and Jake. He knew I was leaving that night, and he knew why. Ask him if you think I'm lying. Honestly, I thought he'd told you what we had talked about, but it looks like I was wrong.'

Feeling as if she had stumbled into a nightmare, Ruby spun back to Griffin and shook her head in stunned disbelief. 'You *knew?*'

When he finally raised his head to meet her eyes, Griffin's skin looked grey. 'Rubes, it's not what you think. I wanted to tell—'

Far too hurt and furious to listen to another man make excuses, Ruby cut him off. 'You wanted to tell me *what* exactly, Griffin?

Whatever happened to us having no secrets from each other? I have literally sobbed on your shoulder wondering what was so wrong with me that the father of my child would leave. If you knew the answer, why didn't you tell me? *Why?*

Griffin flinched but said nothing, and suddenly the most intense rage Ruby had ever felt erupted deep inside her.

'How could *you* of all people betray me? Why would you do such a thing? *Answer me!*' she screamed, clenching her fists in devastated fury.

Griffin had been there when Kenny disappeared. He had been the shoulder she'd cried on, the hand she had held on to when she didn't have the strength to put one foot in front of the other. He had been a father to Jake and had even *encouraged* her to come and find Kenny. *For what?* For her to learn the truth that he had known all along?

Griffin's eyes glistened at the naked pain in Ruby's face, but as he moved towards her, she shook her head violently and raised a hand, stopping him in his tracks. Through tear-filled eyes, Ruby watched as Griffin looked at her for a long moment and then, without a word, turned and walked away.

36

A rumble of thunder broke a silence that felt louder than the words Ruby had screamed only minutes earlier. Head bowed, she sat hunched on the lounger she had collapsed on to after Griffin's abrupt departure, feeling too broken even to cry. She focused on the golden grains of sand at her feet as if they held the answer to the mysteries of the past. A part of her was desperate to go after Griffin and force him to tell her the truth, but an even bigger part was afraid that what she learned would make her hate him.

Kenny cleared his throat, and Ruby looked up as he returned to sit on the lounger facing her. His expression held no hint of triumph. Instead, he looked troubled. As well he might, Ruby thought. She didn't know why Griffin had acted as he did, but there was no way she was leaving this island without understanding Kenny's reasons for leaving her and why he had kept his conversation with Griffin a secret.

'Why wasn't I enough for you?' she asked, her tone oddly matter of fact despite her distress. 'You were probably the first man who made me feel like a sexy, attractive woman. Before we met, and for as long as I can remember, I'd been teased and taunted for being tall and gawky. Even today, you wouldn't believe how some people take one look at me and decide I'm intimidating or overpowering or – or aggressive. But then you came along. A gorgeous, sophisticated man, even taller than me and who – shock, horror – actually fancied me!

Remember how I gave you such a hard time in the beginning? Well, that was because I couldn't believe a guy like you could possibly be serious about me. When I fell pregnant, even though you were the one who'd begged for us to try for a baby, a part of me was waiting for you to use it as an excuse to call things off, but you didn't. After Jake came along, I knew things weren't always perfect between us, but you really had me convinced that you loved me.'

When Kenny made as if to speak, Ruby shook her head. 'No, Kenny, let me finish. After everything I've just said, do you have the slightest idea how devastated I was when you suddenly disappeared with no warning or explanation? Can you even begin to imagine how much you shattered the confidence I was finally beginning to feel? I'd never felt good enough to attract a decent guy, and when you left me, you proved I was right. I might have got you, but I wasn't enough to keep you.'

'You *were* enough, Ruby,' Kenny said gently. 'You've always been enough. Sometimes maybe even a bit too much,' he added with a tentative smile that vanished as he took in the raw pain on her face. He reached for her hand and, too exhausted to fight, she didn't pull away.

'Ruby, it kills me to see you like this,' he whispered. 'I never knew you felt this way and I swear to you that I didn't mean to hurt you.'

'If that's true, why did you leave?'

Kenny sighed. 'I left because I wasn't strong enough to stay, and I stayed away because I felt too guilty to return – and too scared of what I'd find, if I did.'

Infuriated, she tried to pull her hand from his, but Kenny wouldn't let her. 'No, wait – please listen to me, Ruby. You are an amazing woman, and any man would be lucky to have you by their side. It's true that things weren't perfect between us, and we both know it wasn't always easy, but I did my best—'

Ruby groaned in frustration. 'How is walking away from your partner and your son in any way doing your best?'

Kenny released her hand. 'It sounds ridiculous, but I promise you it's true. The biggest irony about all this is that you always challenged me to want more from life and to be more in life, but the honest truth is that I couldn't do that with you. I couldn't be a decent partner and a decent father when I felt second best all the time, and it got to the point where I just couldn't handle it any more. I would pick arguments with you just to get you to *see* me, Ruby. If I stayed, I'd have started hating you and then you would have hated me and – and I didn't want that for Jake.'

Ruby's expression mirrored her confusion. 'I don't know what you're talking about! You *never* said anything to me about feeling second best. Is this seriously your idea of an explanation?'

Kenny stood up and shoved his hands into the pockets of his jeans, and when Ruby looked up, there was no doubting the hurt in his eyes.

'That's where you're wrong,' he said bitterly. 'I said it a hundred times and in a hundred different ways, and you refused to hear. You thought I was trying to control you or dictate who you could be friends with, but you never stopped to ask me why *I* felt insecure in our relationship. Do you think you were the only one who struggled with their confidence?'

He raised his head to gaze at the dark, swirling clouds overhead for a few moments and then said sadly, 'I left Jake. Even though I knew you'd take good care of him, abandoning my son was wrong and I've spent every day since regretting it. But whatever you thought or felt, I didn't leave you. I didn't leave *you*.'

'What the hell does that even mean?' The ice in her voice could have frozen water but Kenny just shook his head.

'It means you can't leave something you never had.' He looked at her and tilted his head enquiringly. 'Tell me, Ruby, did you ever love me?'

Stung by the question, Ruby sprang to her feet. 'Of course I loved you! You *know* I did. How can you even ask that?'

'Are you sure? Then tell me why you never wanted to marry me, because I lost count of the number of times I asked you. Please don't tell me it's because you think marriage is just a piece of paper because we both know that's not what you believe. You always loved that your mum and dad were so happily married, and I saw how emotional you would get at your friends' weddings. So, why didn't you want *us* to get married?'

Caught off guard, Ruby stepped back. 'I-I don't know,' she stammered. 'It was— We were happy as we were and everything was happening so fast, and after Jake . . .'

She tailed off and Kenny laughed, but there was no humour in his voice. 'If you loved me, like you claim, tell me why *any* time something upset you, the first person you turned to was Griffin. When I tried to get you to share your problems, you'd go quiet on me and then spend hours talking on the phone with *him*. Be honest. When you found out you were pregnant with Jake, who did you tell first, me or Griffin?'

Blindsided by the question, Ruby simply stared at him. There was no need to reply as they both knew the answer, but she tried anyway.

'Griffin and I were best mates long before I met you, and we share everything – at least, I thought we did,' she added bitterly. 'I told you a hundred and one times there was nothing romantic between us, and that the only time we—'

'Ah, yes, the famous bad kiss story. Look, you can tell yourself all the stories you like about how you are friends who've never fancied each other, but no-one buys it. Griffin gets through women like hot meals because he can't have the one woman he really wants, and you – well, maybe you're so scared of losing him if you join the crowd that you won't face the truth.'

Ruby's hand flew up, but Kenny caught her wrist before it made contact with his face. Outraged, she glared at him, her heart pounding so fast with fury that she could scarcely breathe. Then she shook her hand free and turned away from him, squeezing her eyes shut for a moment while she tried to calm her racing pulse. Kenny's harsh words had struck a nerve and she had reacted blindly, but she was nonetheless appalled at losing control. Attacking him wouldn't change anything that had happened or deflect the real questions facing her. Was Kenny right, and had she been lying to herself all this time about her feelings for Griffin? And if Griffin felt the same, why had he never once hinted at it before the kiss on the beach?

She turned back to Kenny. 'I shouldn't have done that, but what you said was out of order.'

Kenny nodded. 'I'm sorry. Look, you asked me for the truth and I'm trying to be honest with you. That's why I went to see Griffin the day I left. I told him I couldn't take coming second with you any longer and, even though it hurt like hell to leave Jake, it was killing me to watch my woman in love with another man.'

'Kenny, I swear I had no idea—'

He cut her off mid-sentence. 'I know that now, Rubes, but just because you refused to see what's obvious to everyone else didn't make it any easier. I told Griffin I was bowing out and that he should explain to you why I was leaving. I don't know why he didn't, but I suppose it was never going to be easy for him to confess that I left because I knew you loved him more. The first day you came to the marina, I assumed the two of you were together and, quite honestly, I'm shocked he hasn't made a move on you all this time.'

Ruby felt the heat rush into her cheeks and looked away. There was no point now confessing what had happened with Griffin.

'So that's it, Ruby. That's the truth.'

'But why didn't you talk to *me*?' she demanded. 'Why didn't you give me a choice instead of just deciding we were finished?'

A loud clap of thunder struck and rumbled across the rapidly darkening skies. Turning her anger at herself for being so blind back on to Kenny, Ruby's voice rose above the howl of the strengthening wind.

'D'you know what, Kenny? Everything you've said is just a *bullshit* excuse for behaving like a crappy human being! I deserved way more respect than you thinking it was okay to basically give me away to another man like I had no say in the matter!'

Suddenly, it was all too much, and Ruby couldn't even pretend to hide her pain. 'If you even suspected that I-I loved Griffin, why didn't you fight for me?'

'I did fight for you – for *us*, but there's no point fighting fate. At the end of the day, we can't help who we love, right?'

'You didn't fight very hard if you could walk away from your little boy without a backward glance,' she retorted bitterly. She felt a few drops of rain on her arm and went back to the lounger to pick up her discarded bottle of water. About to head back to the house, she turned to face Kenny.

'What you did to me and to Jake was utterly selfish and wrong. I don't know why you'd expect me to even forgive you, never mind consider getting back together.'

Kenny flinched as if she had struck him, but his gaze didn't waver. 'Putting my emotions first *was* selfish, but it's also past time you were honest with yourself. Refusing to acknowledge your feelings for Griffin made it impossible for you to see what it did to me. It's time you and Griffin—'

'There *is* no me and Griffin,' Ruby said coldly.

She might as well not have spoken as Kenny continued. 'You and Griffin – this thing of yours, this game or whatever it is, it's hurting innocent bystanders. Do the world a favour and sort yourselves out, once and for all.'

37

Ruby dumped the bag filled with gifts on the bedroom floor and switched on the ceiling fan above her bed. Following two days of grey skies and heavy rain, the sun was back in all its shining glory. Slipping off her shoes, she lay on top of the covers, relishing the cool air after the hours out in the scorching heat. Two sleepless nights, compounded by an afternoon spent with Jake shopping downtown, had left Ruby exhausted and light-headed.

With only a couple of days left on Sorrel Island, she had bought gifts for Auntie Pearl, Fi, and a few other friends, as well as a colourful brooch for Miss Ida. To Jake's disgust, Ruby also bought a box of coconut candies for Mr Hinton and, less controversially, a t-shirt emblazoned with 'I ♥ Sorrel Island' for Nick, as thanks for his work on Miss Ida's website.

'Mum?' Jake bounded on to her bed, showing no sign of fatigue.

'Hmm?' Too drained to speak and enjoying the cool air circling over her, Ruby kept her eyes closed.

'Can I go with Uncle Griffin to Ocean House? I want to give Drew the present I got him.'

Ruby's eyes flew open, and it took a few moments to get her voice under control. 'I'm not sure, Jake. He might have left already.'

'No, he hasn't,' Jake insisted. 'He said he'd wait for me to get back so we could go together.'

It was hard to argue given that she hadn't exchanged a single word with Griffin since the explosive scene at the beach. She had rebuffed his repeated attempts to talk to her, too deeply hurt, and furious with him for lying. While she knew she couldn't avoid him for ever, for now at least, it was easier to hold on to her anger than to give any credence to Kenny's bitter accusations.

'Mum, *please*!' Jake grumbled, bouncing extra hard on the bed to recapture her attention.

'Stop it, Jake! Just give me a minute,' she snapped.

His face fell, and Ruby was instantly remorseful. It wasn't his fault that she was an emotional mess. She pulled him into a hug and stroked his hair.

'I'm sorry, buddy. I didn't mean to bite your head off – I'm just tired, that's all. Go and find your godfather, and I'll see you later.'

Sorting the papers in Jake's homework folder to pack into the suitcase on his bed, Ruby paused at the sound of a knock on the bedroom door. It was almost dinner time, and she instinctively knew who it was. Her first reaction was to ignore it, but after a day of painful silence, she needed answers.

'Come in,' she called, annoyed to hear a slight wobble in her voice.

Griffin walked in and closed the door behind him, and for a moment they stared at each other in silence. His eyes were bloodshot, and he looked as if he hadn't slept in days. He was also clearly uncomfortable, running his fingers over his hair and then around the inside of the collar of his white polo shirt. *Good*, she thought spitefully, relishing his discomfort, and dragging out the silence for as long as she could.

'Where's Jake?' she asked finally.

'Helping Narita set the tables for dinner. Ruby, we need to talk.'

'That's what I asked for yesterday, but you chose to walk away.'

Griffin nodded. 'I know, but you were furious with me, and Kenny was there, and – I'm sorry, but please can we talk now?'

Ruby studied him for a moment and then dropped the folder she was still holding on top of the open suitcase and sat on the corner of Jake's bed.

'Go ahead, but you've lied to me for six years, so why should I take your word for anything now?'

Griffin flinched. 'I know you might find it hard to believe after what you heard yesterday, but I swear to you that I never meant to hurt you or our relationship.'

Ruby laughed mirthlessly. 'That's the second time I've heard that in the past twenty-four hours. No-one *wants* to hurt me and yet both you and Kenny have done your level best to break my heart.'

Griffin sucked in an audible breath, his expression bleak. 'I wanted to tell you. I *desperately* wanted to tell you at the time, but you were so hurt and sad that I . . . I just couldn't.'

'I think what you mean is you were too gutless to tell me that my partner had left me because of you.'

The muscles in his jaw tightened. 'Yes.'

'So, because you thought I would blame *you* for what Kenny did, you decided to keep the truth from me, is that right?'

Griffin shook his head. 'No. I was prepared for you to blame me if that helped you deal with what Kenny did, but—'

'How magnanimous of you,' she broke in sarcastically. 'Well, guess what, I *do* blame you. Kenny did his fair share of damage, but . . . *you*?'

She leaned forward and dropped her head into her hands, breathing in deeply to calm the fury building inside. She could hardly stand to look at Griffin, but she needed to know the truth.

'I'm trying to understand this, but I really don't. Even if you bottled it at the time, why didn't you tell me later when you knew what I was going through? My God, you even encouraged me to come out here and find Kenny. What did you *think* was going to happen?'

'I hadn't realised until that day in Brighton just how much what happened with Kenny still affected you. You barely mention his name and that was the first time you opened up about how badly his leaving made you feel about yourself. I would have told you that day in the diner, but I wanted you to hear his reasons from him, and not from me. I'm hardly an impartial observer and *that's* why I encouraged you to come. If you hadn't moved on because you still had feelings for Kenny, then I didn't want to get in the way of that.'

'What *I* don't get is why you two men think you can make decisions for me! All I need – needed from you was the truth. It was *not* your place to judge whether or not I could cope with it.'

Griffin looked pained. 'I know that now, and I wish I'd handled things differently. I knew the truth would come out once you were here, and part of the reason I followed you was to be here for you and tell you my side of things.'

Too agitated to sit still, Ruby jumped up and grabbed the folder, mindlessly shuffling the loose papers and cramming them back in again with no regard for order.

'You've had *six* bloody years to tell me "your side of things", Griffin, and I think it's a bit late now. So, let me tell you *my* side. One minute, I was living happily with my partner and baby, and then the next minute, boom! No partner, *and* – to make an awful situation worse – my so-called best friend didn't have the common decency to tell me why my world had suddenly imploded.'

Griffin still hadn't moved from where he was stationed just inside the closed door, and he flinched at the contempt in her voice. Then, as

233

if he had nothing else to lose, he shrugged. 'You talk about the truth and yet you won't admit that it wasn't all hearts and roses with Kenny.'

'We were *happy*!' Ruby shouted, but Griffin didn't back down.

'Maybe that's how you choose to remember it, but I was there, don't forget, and the truth is you never loved Kenny. Not really. You fell for him because he was a tall, good-looking dude with a sexy Caribbean accent who told you how gorgeous you were. He made you feel good about yourself – and that was enough for you to decide he was the man for you.'

'That's so not true!' she gasped.

'Remember this is me you're talking to, and that I know you better than anyone. From all the way back in school you've always been so hard on yourself about your looks. You've got it into your head that being small and cute is what every man looks for in a woman. Kenny was never right for you, and even Auntie Opal and Auntie Pearl told you so. But you ignored all of us and insisted he was the one, and now it's time you owned that.'

'No, Griffin. What I *will* own is that I made a colossal mistake in trusting you, but when it comes to learning lessons, it's better late than never,' Ruby said coolly, refusing to let him see that his words had cut her to the quick. 'What this has taught me is that I can't trust you, which makes having anything more to do with you pointless. So, when you get back to London next week, do me a favour and don't call me or try to contact me or mine.'

Griffin blanched. 'You don't mean that!'

'Oh, but I do,' Ruby replied.

He took a couple of paces forward, staring at her in disbelief. 'Do you know what that would do to Jake? I'm his *godfather*, for Christ's sake!'

Ruby stood her ground and raised her chin defiantly. 'Yeah, well, thanks to you he doesn't have a *father* that lives with him any more, does he?'

'Then that's even more reason why you can't separate us. Jake needs me, Ruby, you know that!'

She glared at him for a moment and then dropped her gaze. As much as she hated to admit it, he was right. It wasn't fair to punish Jake for Griffin's crime, but she wanted nothing further to do with him.

'Fine,' she conceded. 'For my son's sake – not yours – you can arrange with Auntie Pearl when you see him, but I don't want you anywhere near me.'

Griffin ran a trembling hand over his hair and exhaled hard. 'Rubes, *please*! Will you let me tell you why I couldn't tell you the truth at the time?'

'*Don't* "Rubes" me! I don't care to hear anything more from you. Don't you get it, Griffin? *Nothing* you say will make a difference. You let my man walk out on me and leave my son without a father for six years! You saw what that did to Jake – why do you think we're out here in the first place? I can't believe that you, of all people, did this to us. I swore to your mum that I would always be there for you, but I don't trust you any more and I don't want you in my life. So, yes, once we're off this island, you and I are done!'

In the tense silence that followed, Griffin pinched the bridge of his nose as if trying to hold back an overpowering emotion. Shaking his head, he said quietly, 'You know what, Ruby? You can blame me for not telling you the truth, but you can't pretend that I made Kenny leave. Let's face it, if he'd loved you enough, he'd have stayed and fought for you.'

Although it was what Ruby herself had thought, it was devastating to hear him articulate her deep-seated fear that she hadn't been enough to keep a man. A flush of heat erupted through her body until even her cheeks were burning with humiliation.

'How *dare* you?' Her breath sounded loud and harsh in her ears, and her jaw ached from the effort of holding back the sob pressing to escape. In that moment she hated Griffin with an intensity she could never have imagined, and desperate to hurt him as badly as he had hurt her, Ruby scrabbled for something, *anything*, to retaliate.

'You know what,' she choked out, 'you were right not to tell me Kenny had left because of you, because then I could have told you that he needn't have bothered! Why would he think that I would want to be with *you*? You have no goals and no sense of purpose other than seducing women and then making their lives miserable. I had – and have – way too much self-respect to want to be with someone like you!'

Griffin looked stricken, but Ruby was too deep into her own pain to care. 'Do you know the saddest thing about you, Griffin? After *everything* she sacrificed for you, your mum would be so ashamed of what you've become.'

The naked anguish on Griffin's face hit Ruby like a hammer blow. His skin looked drained of colour and although he opened his mouth, no sound emerged. But while a part of her desperately wished she could take back the vicious words, in that instant, her need for revenge was greater.

In silence, Griffin opened the door, and the moment he left the room, Ruby's face crumpled. Feeling utterly wretched and deeply ashamed of what she had just done, she collapsed on to her bed, sobbing as if her heart would break.

38

Much to Ruby's relief, there was no sign of Griffin at dinner that night or at breakfast the following morning. She had no idea how she would have reacted to seeing him, and everything inside her shrank from finding out. After he'd walked out, she had stayed in her room crying until Jake's return forced her to duck into the bathroom, where the sound of the shower could muffle her uncontrollable sobbing. After dinner and once Jake was asleep, she had sat outside on the balcony, silent tears flowing down her cheeks as she replayed their hurt-filled exchange. Aside from her family, Griffin was the most important relationship in her life, but the vile words she had hurled at him had been intended to inflict maximum damage and she knew he would never speak to her again.

Nevertheless, despite her grief at losing her best friend, she couldn't let go of the deep anger she felt towards him, not only for withholding the information she had so desperately needed, but also for dismissing her trauma from the years of cruel taunts about her appearance. Someone like Griffin, who had been born beautiful and simply oozed confidence, had no idea what it was like to not feel desirable and to suffer from crippling self-doubt, she thought bitterly. Even if he'd thought his brutal assessment of why she had chosen Kenny and why Kenny had walked away was true, all he had achieved by saying so was to leave her feeling crushed and exposed.

◆ ◆ ◆

After breakfast, Kenny arrived as planned to pick up Jake for them to spend the last day of the trip together. Desperate to avoid running into Griffin, Ruby stayed in her room for the rest of the day, sorting clothes and packing, in between emailing back and forth with Nick to finalise the last touches to Miss Ida's website.

It was six o'clock in the evening when Nick finally pressed the button to launch the Paradise Inn website live on to the internet, and Ruby lay on the couch scrolling through the beautifully designed web pages. The extensive picture gallery displayed the vibrant colour schemes of the bedrooms in Paradise Inn as well as the stately elegance of the house and its beautiful gardens. Nick had cleverly interwoven snippets of the glowing testimonials from guests across each page and Ruby smiled as she played the video of Mac – looking even more handsome than George Clooney – singing Miss Ida's praises.

If that doesn't bring the punters, then nothing will!

Seeing her spontaneous idea coming to fruition, Ruby felt her spirits lift. The stylish but functional website and user-friendly automated booking system and app would, she knew, prove a lifeline for Miss Ida's business and allow her to keep her beloved home. Scrolling through the photo gallery and seeing the pictures of the marina, downtown, and the harbour, Ruby couldn't stop herself reliving the memories. When she reached the section about the island's nightlife, her fingers froze on the keyboard. The images she had taken at the Marina Beach Bar on her phone camera brought the memories flooding back of the magical night of dancing with Griffin, followed by the most perfect of kisses on the beach, and her spirits plummeted.

As the sun dipped below the horizon and the room grew dark, Ruby forced herself off the sofa. Jake would be back soon, and she needed to share the good news. Picking up her laptop, she ran downstairs in search of Miss Ida. There was no sign of life in the hallway and, fearful of bumping into Griffin, Ruby cautiously stuck her head around the door of the dining room, relieved to see only Narita and a handful of guests. Walking over to Miss Ida's office, Ruby knocked gently on the door, entering as soon as she heard the woman's voice.

Miss Ida was reclining on the sofa, her head propped up against an emerald cushion, when Ruby walked in. The only light in the room came from the tall harlequin lamp and two jewelled table lamps on either side of the sofa. A hint of spice from the kitchen next door wafted in on the gentle breeze coming through the half-open terrace doors.

Miss Ida beamed and sat up. 'Hello, sweetheart, this is a nice surprise. I was just putting my feet up after fixing dinner. Come over and sit with me.'

She swung her legs off the couch, patting the seat beside her, and Ruby obligingly sank on to the cushions and flipped open her laptop.

'The website has just gone live, Miss Ida, and I wanted you to be the first to see it.'

Miss Ida gave a cluck of excitement, leaning in as Ruby clicked through the site. With her fist pressed to her mouth, she shook her head in wonder at the crisp, clear images Ruby had taken of the bedrooms, the gardens, and the private beach, and, as Ruby read aloud the section about the origins of Paradise Inn, and Marty and Ida's love story, the older woman's eyes filled with tears.

'Narita's keen to develop her digital skills and Nick's going to train her to manage the site and the booking system. So, what do you think, Miss Ida?' Ruby closed the laptop with a smile that held more than a hint of trepidation. Despite all the work she and Nick had put into the project, everything rested on whether the person they had done this for was happy.

'What do I think? I think you're an angel sent to me by the gods, and I can never thank you enough.'

Miss Ida's voice trembled with emotion, and Ruby blinked back the threatening tears. It had been an emotional few days and she had cried so much that if she started again, there was no telling if she'd be able to stop.

'Are you okay, sweetheart?' Miss Ida frowned at Ruby's downcast expression. 'I missed seeing you at dinner tonight.'

Ducking her head to avoid the woman's probing gaze, Ruby forced a cheerful note into her voice. 'I'm absolutely fine. I've been in my room most of the day, and I haven't done much to work up an appetite.'

Miss Ida shifted her position to face Ruby squarely, her shrewd gaze making it clear she wasn't fooled. 'Sweetheart, I know heartache when I see it, and you weren't the only person who didn't show up for dinner tonight.'

The concern in Miss Ida's eyes pierced through Ruby's fragile self-control, and tears welled up and spilled on to her cheeks.

Miss Ida murmured with dismay and reached for a box of tissues on the side table. Mortified, Ruby plucked one from the box and wiped her eyes, breathing deeply as she tried to control her battered emotions. For a few minutes they sat in silence, the only sounds an occasional sniff from Ruby and the gentle chirp of crickets through the open door.

'Sweetheart, when you first came here, I told you Sorrel Island is a place of love, and it is,' Miss Ida said softly. 'But love is complicated; sometimes it hurts, and sometimes it heals.'

Ruby grimaced and wiped her nose. 'Well, I think the island gods must be punishing me for mocking them because right now it hurts like hell.'

'Oh no, sweetheart, *never!*' Miss Ida shook her head vehemently. 'The gods are always on our side, but you must have faith in the power of love. I can't tell you how many folks I've seen over the years come here broken inside. Our little island – well, it gives refuge to damaged hearts, just like it saved those lovers fleeing death hundreds of years ago.'

Despite Ruby's efforts, fresh tears escaped her eyes. She dropped her head and whispered, 'But what if you're the one who's caused the damage, and can't fix it?'

Miss Ida put the computer to one side and took Ruby's hand between hers. 'Tell me what happened, sweetheart,' she urged.

In between sobs, Ruby stumbled through the events of the past couple of days with both Kenny and Griffin. By the time she tried to repeat the deliberately cruel words she had aimed at Griffin, Ruby was crying too hard to continue.

'Come on now, let's go outside and get some air. I always find it helps to look to the heavens when things down here get too hard.'

Miss Ida patted Ruby's arm and stood up, leaving Ruby to follow her out on to the terrace. A brightly lit lantern on a small table illuminated the night, and the faint sound of voices and the chink of cutlery could be heard coming from the adjoining railed-off dining-room terrace.

'Shouldn't you be with the other guests?' Ruby gulped, scrubbing her eyes with the damp tissue. 'I don't want to take up your time—'

Miss Ida cut her off with a careless wave. 'Don't you worry none 'bout that. We don't have many for dinner tonight and Narita's taking care of everyone. Besides, I'd better enjoy the quiet before that beautiful website of yours has me rushed off my feet, ain't that right?'

Ruby managed a wobbly smile and the two women leaned against the stone balustrade, staring up at the starlit sky overlooking the darkened gardens.

241

'This place is paradise, and I'm going to miss it so much, even if I didn't find love. You know, I'm so envious of couples like my mum and dad – and you and Marty,' Ruby said wistfully, resting her arms on the balcony wall. 'I can't begin to imagine how the two of you stayed so strong for such a long time, especially with everything you went through just to be together. I don't think I'll ever be lucky enough to find someone who loves me that way and who I can trust a hundred per cent.'

Miss Ida weighed Ruby's words carefully, and then turned to face her. In the lamplight, the tiny wrinkles on the delicately boned face were barely visible, and she could almost have been the young bride of fifty years ago.

'Marriage isn't easy, child, and for any relationship to work, both of you must grow easy with giving and receiving, and always find somewhere in your heart the capacity to forgive yourself and each other.'

'But surely it's easier to do that when someone really loves you?'

'Sometimes even love isn't enough, Ruby. You can love someone hard but you still gotta find your own balance. The kind that lets you hold yourself up without depending on how the other person is holding up.'

Ruby sighed. 'But you knew right away when you met your Marty that he was the one for you. What was it you called him – your heart's twin? Finding a perfect love like that feels impossible to me.'

'There ain't no such thing as perfect, child,' said Miss Ida, brushing away an insect that had landed on her arm. She looked up at Ruby with a wry smile. 'See that? Even paradise has mosquitoes.'

Ruby returned the twinkle in the older woman's eyes with a weak smile. 'So, even soul mates have to work at this love business? I don't think I have the patience or the faith for all of that, Miss Ida. I feel like I – I've lost my balance and . . . it's too hard.'

'Right now, your heart is feeling bruised, but in there' – she pointed at Ruby's chest – 'is the kindest, sweetest heart I know. You loved your little boy enough to bring him to meet the man who had wronged you, and look at what you've done for me since you've been here! Both Kenny and Griffin made mistakes, but they are good men. Now, I can't tell you what to do about your situation, but I know your heart will find the answer when it's ready. Just remember, sweetheart, that not one of us is perfect and even when you love someone, you will make mistakes.'

Ruby smoothed down her braids and blinked fiercely to stop the tears threatening to return. 'But what if I can't forgive? I don't know that I want love if it hurts this much.'

For a long time, Miss Ida stared out into the darkness beyond the terrace, and then she tilted her head up at Ruby with a tiny smile. 'When you get to my age, darlin', you learn that while love can hurt, mostly it heals. On Sorrel Island, we see love as a gift, a magical and powerful gift. If you can open your heart and trust in the capacity of folks to change, you'll find your balance in time, and when you do—'

Ruby opened her mouth, but Miss Ida cut her off with a shake of her head and a knowing smile. 'When you do, Ruby, you'll see that love is a gift you can give yourself.'

39

Ruby pulled open the emptied wardrobes in a final check for any stray items of clothing or – God forbid – cherished toy that she might have missed. Jellybean was safely stuffed into Jake's backpack, and a quick scan of the cupboards and the large chest of drawers confirmed she had removed every trace of their month-long stay in the Cloud Room.

Whether it was the conversation with Miss Ida the previous evening or sheer exhaustion from sleepless nights and endless tears, Ruby had slept through the night and woken up in the morning feeling brighter than she had for ages. The packing was finished, and their bill settled, and she glanced at her watch and sighed with frustration. There were still two more hours to get through before Zeke arrived. Although Kenny had offered to drive them, Ruby had declined, not wanting to upset Jake with emotional farewells at the airport. With nothing else to occupy her mind and distract her from thoughts of Griffin, Ruby slid open the glass doors and went out on to the balcony.

Gazing out at the familiar gardens bathed in sunshine, Ruby breathed in deeply, feeling a sense of peace stealing over her. *The magic of Sorrel Island*, she thought with a whimsical smile. Well, whatever happened going forward, she was thankful to have finally made peace with Kenny.

◆ ◆ ◆

Earlier that day, Kenny had driven over to say his final goodbyes. Jake – his face crumpled as tears poured down his cheeks – had clung fiercely to his father.

Intervening before the boy went into a full-scale meltdown, Ruby knelt and wiped his face with a tissue. 'Why don't you go up to the room and check you've put Jellybean safely into your travel bag while I walk your dad to his car?' she suggested gently.

It would be the last chance she and Kenny would have to speak, and no matter what had happened in the past, he was Jake's father and she wanted to leave knowing they had buried any acrimony between them.

Kenny slowly disentangled himself from Jake's arms and, with a glance at Ruby, he nodded encouragingly at Jake. 'Don't forget we'll see each other again soon and you've got your room waiting for you. Now, your mum's right, son. You don't want to forget to pack Jellybean again.'

Jake's eyes widened in alarm and with a wobbly, 'Bye, Dad!', he turned and scooted up the steps and into the house.

Ruby walked with Kenny down the driveway, and neither of them spoke until they reached his car.

'How are you doing, Rubes?' Kenny played with the car keys, his expression unreadable. Before she could answer, he said softly, 'Jake says you and Griffin aren't speaking to each other.'

So much for trying to hide things from kids. Although it shouldn't have come as a shock that Jake would notice she and Griffin hadn't been near each other in a while, she still felt uncomfortable under Kenny's probing gaze.

'The past couple of days have been a lot, and I still need time to process everything,' she said finally.

Looking troubled, Kenny thrust his hands into the pockets of his jeans. 'For what it's worth, I deeply regret my part in all this. I don't want you to leave without knowing how truly sorry I am for the hurt I caused you and Jake. It's more than I have any right to expect, but I hope one day you'll find it in your heart to forgive me.'

When Ruby bit her lip and said nothing, Kenny nodded in acceptance. 'Look, I understand you've got a lot of thinking to do. Have a safe flight home and thank you from the bottom of my heart for giving me the chance to know my son. I swear to you that I won't waste this opportunity to be the father Jake deserves.'

Ruby turned and started to walk towards the house, but after a couple of paces, she looked back. Kenny's eyes were following her and, seeing the desolation in his expression, she stopped. This time, it was she and Jake who were leaving Kenny, but there were no winners here today, and as she watched him standing alone, Ruby felt a surge of compassion. While Kenny had caused her so much pain, he was also the missing part of Jake that had made her son whole again. Miss Ida was right; love could also heal, and Ruby's love for her son gave her the strength to try to heal the rift with his father.

Walking slowly back to him, she looked into his eyes and in that moment felt the weight of the bitterness that had for so long clouded her feelings about him slide away like a heavy cloak dropping from her shoulders.

'For what it's worth, Kenny, I don't think you're a monster. For a moment, I even wondered if we could find a way back to each other, but then everything I felt when you left us came rushing back. We can't force ourselves together for the sake of our son because, although it might seem like a good reason, it's not the right one, so let's do the right thing. I think it's time we both let go of the past. You've missed so much time with Jake, but I can see how much you love him. I know you want to make up for lost time and we'll work it out so he comes to you for some holidays. If we communicate honestly with each other, I know we'll do what's best for our son.'

Kenny nodded and swallowed hard. His eyes glistened, and seeing the emotion on his face, Ruby knew she was doing what was best for Jake – and for herself. 'You hurt me, Kenny, I won't lie. But I forgive you. I *have* to forgive you, for my own sake and for Jake's, because he needs you. And you should forgive yourself and move on.'

Kenny held out his arms hesitantly and Ruby moved forward into his embrace, suddenly filled with a sense of lightness. When he released her, she pushed back her braids and looked up at him with a shaky but mischievous smile.

'Miss Ida says you're quite the catch here on Sorrel Island, so it's probably time you thought about sharing your life with someone special. From what I've seen of the ladies here, I don't think you'll be single for long if you put your mind to it.'

With a hearty chuckle, Kenny climbed into the car and closed the door. Switching on the engine, he rolled down the window and they gazed at each other, silently acknowledging that the past had finally been buried.

'Take care of yourself, Rubes,' Kenny said softly.

'I will.' Ruby nodded, her eyes misting over as she thought of all the wasted years. 'You were wrong about one thing, though, Kenny. Being with you made me happy, and I *did* love you.'

Kenny tilted his head and smiled a slow, sad smile. 'Yeah, maybe you did, sweetheart. But not quite enough.'

40

While Zeke wheeled Ruby's heavy suitcase to the taxi with an excited Jake following close behind, Ruby went in search of Miss Ida. There was no-one behind the reception desk or in the hallway, and finding Miss Ida's office deserted, Ruby hurried over to the lounge.

She hadn't laid eyes on Griffin since he'd left her room, and Ruby reminded herself that he was no longer her problem, mentally pushing away the question as to why it was easier to forgive Kenny than Griffin.

'Oh, there you are, Miss Ida!' Ruby breathed in relief as she strode into the lounge and spotted her standing by the gallery of Marty's photographs on the wall.

'I was just coming to find you, sweetheart,' Miss Ida said. 'I wanted to give you this to say thank you for everything you've done for me.'

She handed Ruby a small parcel clumsily wrapped in plain brown paper, and when Ruby unwrapped it, she gasped aloud.

'But – but this is Marty's photograph of your first house,' she stammered in shock. 'You can't give this to me, it's—'

'It's exactly why I want you to have it,' Miss Ida interrupted, placing her small hands firmly over Ruby's as she tried to hand it back. 'You remembered what this picture is, and I know you'll take good care of it for me. This was my first home with Marty and now, thanks to you, I'll be able to save our last home together.'

Moved to tears, Ruby threw her arms open and bent to hug Miss Ida tightly. 'Thank you for trusting me with this, and I promise I'll look after it for ever!'

'I know, baby. My Marty would have loved you just as much as I do, and when you get home, you hang this up so you don't forget me or Sorrel Island.'

'There's no chance of that!' Ruby gave her a misty smile and clasped the framed photo tightly to her chest. 'This island has definitely worked its magic on me, and we're coming back as soon as we can. Besides, going forward, I want Jake to have a relationship with his father.'

Miss Ida nodded and then took Ruby's arm. 'Come on, now. Zeke's waiting, and you don't want to miss your plane.'

They walked outside to where Zeke, having stowed their luggage in the boot, was leaning against his taxi and listening to Jake's excited chatter with an indulgent smile. Seeing Ruby and Miss Ida approach, Zeke opened the door and slipped into the driver's seat while Jake ran over to them.

'Bye, Miss Ida,' he said, his voice muffled as he hugged her waist. 'Thank you for looking after us.'

'I'm going to miss you so much, my sweet boy.' Miss Ida clasped him tightly for a long moment, and then she let him go and stroked his hair tenderly. 'You make sure to come back and see me soon. I'll have some pancakes waitin' on you.'

Jake nodded, his small face solemn, and Ruby gently nudged him towards the car. 'Go and sit next to Zeke while I say goodbye to Miss Ida.'

She watched him run around to the front passenger seat and then bent to hug Miss Ida once again.

'Thank you so much for everything,' she whispered, blinking back tears as she kissed Miss Ida's soft cheek. 'I'll call you when we get home, so you know we arrived safely. I'm back at work next week and we'll get started with promoting the website.'

Miss Ida stepped away, and Ruby climbed into the taxi. Zeke started the engine and, as the car moved off, both Ruby and Jake looked back, waving goodbye until Miss Ida was just a tiny figure in a bright cerise dress.

As they headed towards the airport, Jake resumed his conversation with Zeke while Ruby stared out of the window at the familiar scenery. Glimpses of beach and blue sea between the thick trees flashed by as the yellow taxi sped down the highway, and the golden sun followed them all the way.

The plane's engines revved up ready for take-off and Ruby looked out of the window, reflecting on how quickly life had changed in four weeks. She had taken a huge gamble in bringing Jake to Sorrel Island and it could have gone disastrously wrong. But, by taking a chance, she had given Jake a father he could admire and made her peace with Kenny.

But for all the good that coming to Sorrel Island had achieved, the trip had also been the catalyst that destroyed her long and, as she could now admit, ambivalent relationship with Griffin. The passion they had discovered for each other at the Marina Beach Bar had offered the promise of an exciting new future for them, a future now irrevocably crushed by her discovery of his betrayal.

Griffin's lie, compounded by the harsh words he had thrown at her, were bad enough. But the savageness of her last words to him, and the pains he had taken over the past couple of days to ensure their paths didn't cross, made it abundantly clear that he wanted nothing more to do with her, and she had no doubt this was the end for them.

As the plane took off, and the heart-shaped island fell below a thick carpet of cloud and disappeared, Ruby held Jake's hand, unsure if she was comforting him or herself. For just a moment, paradise had seemed within her reach, but now it was time to return to earth.

PART THREE

Onwards

41

'Now, I'm not one to say I told you so, but—' Auntie Pearl stopped to sip her tea, but instead of finishing her sentence she simply pursed her lips and let her silence speak volumes. She was ensconced on the sofa and, despite the central heating on at full blast, wore thick socks with a pink shawl draped over the wool jumper topping her velour tracksuit bottoms.

'Auntie Pearl, all you said was that Griffin following us to Sorrel Island was strange. That's not the same as warning me that he was only coming to save himself after lying to me for years,' Ruby protested, exasperated at her aunt's attempt to rewrite history.

It had taken two days from their return home before Ruby finally broke under Auntie Pearl's insistent questioning. With Jake safely upstairs in bed, Ruby had relayed as much about the events of the past few days as she was prepared to share.

'It *is* the same thing,' her aunt insisted. 'I know the two of you are always in each other's pockets, but I told you that him travelling all that way just to bring Jake's toy made no sense.'

She leaned forward and cocked her head, straining to listen. 'Is Jake asleep?' she whispered. 'This conversation is not for his ears.'

'Yeah, he went out like a light. He's so excited about going back to school tomorrow and is desperate to tell everyone about his trip. Which reminds me, I need to write him an absence letter for Mr Hinton's files.'

'Don't change the subject.' Auntie Pearl dismissed Mr Hinton's needs with an impatient wave. 'So now you know why Griffin followed you, and the reason *that man* behaved as he did.'

'Did *you* know why Kenny left?' Ruby looked at her aunt with narrowed eyes. After Griffin's bombshell, nothing would have shocked her.

'Did I know what? That the man ran off and left his family because he couldn't cope with what he thought was the competition? Of course not! I would have told you on the spot – and given him a big slap!' Auntie Pearl's tone blended virtue with contempt for Kenny, whose name she still refused to speak.

She took another sip of tea and then placed her mug on the side table and looked at Ruby expectantly. 'So, what was Griffin's defence?'

'I don't know. He was too busy pointing out how I only got together with Kenny because no-one else has ever shown any interest in me to actually say,' was Ruby's sarcastic response. 'Oh, and in case I didn't get the message, he made sure to point out that Kenny didn't fight for me because he didn't think I was worth it,' she added bitterly.

Clearly taken aback, Auntie Pearl blinked. 'Are you very sure that's what he said?' she asked doubtfully. 'That doesn't sound like the Griffin I know.'

'That's my point, Auntie!' Ruby exclaimed heatedly. 'He *isn't* the Griffin you – or I – thought we knew! He's known for *years* why Kenny ran off. He could have told me the truth at any time so I could have at least stopped blaming myself, but instead he *lied*, and you know that's the one thing I can't tolerate.'

'Yes, but *why* did he lie?' Auntie Pearl persisted.

Ruby stared at her in frustration, biting hard on her tongue to stop herself screaming. What did it matter why he lied? Wasn't it enough just knowing that he had? Besides, Griffin's words had cut so deeply that Ruby had no intention of ever entertaining anything he had to say again.

To avoid a lecture on speaking disrespectfully to one's elders, she forced herself to respond calmly. 'Auntie Pearl, Griffin and I swore never to keep secrets from each other, so I don't *care* what muddle-headed thinking process told him that lying to his best friend was ever going to be okay, especially when he knows how I feel about dishonesty. Quite frankly, after the things he said to me, I can't bear to look at him, never mind listen to his excuses.'

'If you won't speak to him, then what happens with Jake? The boy worships him!'

'More's the pity,' Ruby scowled. 'Jake can carry on seeing him if that's what he wants, but I've told Griffin he has to go through you to make arrangements because I won't talk to him.'

Auntie Pearl pulled her shawl tighter around her shoulders and shook her head. 'Ruby, the two of you have been inseparable for as long as I can remember. Are you *sure* about this? Don't look at me like that – I'm not saying I approve of him keeping the truth from you, even if it's obvious why he did, but at least hear him out.'

Ruby looked at her with suspicion. 'What's obvious about any of this?'

Auntie Pearl's sigh was deep enough to drown a grown man. 'Darling, just go and talk to the boy and let him tell you himself why he's been such a fool.'

Ruby picked up her untouched cup of tea and took a large gulp of its tepid contents. What her aunt couldn't know without Ruby admitting the cruel words she had flung at Griffin – a detail which, along with the night on the beach, she had carefully omitted from her recital of events – was that Griffin was no more interested in speaking to Ruby than she was to him.

'No, Auntie, I can't do that,' said Ruby, her tone uncompromising. 'Griffin and I are done, and that's the end of it.'

◆ ◆ ◆

'*This* is the end of The Ruby and Griffin Show?' Fi's face screamed pure scepticism as she studied Ruby's set expression. 'I'm sorry, Rubes, but I'm finding this really hard to believe.'

After dropping Jake – along with his absence letter and Mr Hinton's box of coconut candies – at school, Ruby had gone into work hoping to surprise Fi by arriving a day earlier than expected. Now, squashed into her boss's small visitor's chair after a morning wading through hundreds of unread emails, Ruby was regretting having declined the extra day off.

Waving away the offer to view Ruby's holiday photos unless it was over a drink, Fi's only interest was in the finer points of Ruby's bust-up with Griffin. But, after Auntie Pearl's painfully forensic questioning, Ruby was thoroughly sick of rehashing the details.

'Well, it's true. Fi, I really don't want to talk about what happened *or* about Griffin.'

Fi stood up from her perch on the corner of her desk and paced up and down, looking thoughtful. After a few moments, she wheeled around and demanded, 'Is Griffin back in London yet?'

'*Fi!* Which bit of "I don't want to talk about it" is unclear?'

Fi looked at her sternly until Ruby folded.

'I don't know, for sure,' she admitted. 'He was staying on for another week or so to sort out funding a visiting programme for Diego – he's the musician we met on the island – and his bandmates to hold music sessions for the children at Ocean House. Now, can we change the subject? *Please!*'

Fi opened her mouth, but when Ruby's eyes flashed angrily, she closed it again, and raised a hand in surrender. 'Okay, if that's what you want. Since you decided to ignore my offer of an extra day to do your laundry and sort yourself out, I'll catch you up on what's been happening here. We also need to work out exactly what your new role is going to be.'

'Marketing director,' Ruby declared, temporarily forgetting her man-shaped problems.

'Marketing manager,' Fi corrected.

Ruby frowned. 'Head of marketing.'

They stared at each other in silence, and this time Fi blinked first. 'Fine, head of marketing. But if you want that title, you're going to have to put in the work.'

Ruby burst out laughing. 'I'm already the hardest worker in this company by a *very* wide margin, so that makes no sense. Fill me in on what's been happening while I was away. It was hard to have a decent conversation through those crackly phone lines on the island. Priya tells me she's set up a new system to stop people swiping stationery.'

Fi hooted with laughter. 'The freeloaders are fuming, but the funniest part is no-one can complain without dropping themselves in it. She doesn't take any crap from the account managers, and she's sent back several "client entertainment" expense claims, politely asking them to "reconsider". At this rate, she's going to save me a fortune!'

Ruby grinned. 'I told you she'd be great at covering the office manager role, didn't I? Okay, let's talk about my new job. I'm really excited about the possibilities, and I've put together some ideas. Firstly, we'll need a marketing plan aligned to the five-year strategy, especially now we're targeting more international accounts, and I can get started on that. I think we should upgrade the CRM system and invest in a more stable conferencing package. We can't afford dropped connections when we're pitching campaigns to top-tier clients abroad.'

Fi blanched and raised a perfectly manicured eyebrow. 'How much is all that going to cost me?'

'A lot less than losing a major client. According to Priya, Ellie accidentally kicked the procurement manager on the Jacobson account off the conference call she was hosting last week, and a couple of the sales team on the pitch spent half the meeting on mute without realising it.'

Fi looked disgruntled. 'Replacing those systems won't come cheap, and you've already had my most experienced technical guy working for almost a month on a website I can't raise an invoice for.'

'I know, but Miss Ida absolutely *loved* it, and it's going to make a world of difference to her business,' Ruby said enthusiastically. 'Nick's done such a brilliant job with it, Fi. Don't you think he deserves a promotion?'

Taking one look at her boss's expression, Ruby decided not to push her luck. 'Not right away, obviously, but – well, you said yourself he's the most experienced.'

'Yes, and he's paid well enough already,' said Fi in a tone that brooked no further discussion.

She returned to her chair and, gazing at Ruby, her face broke into a wide beam. 'It's good to have you back, Rubes! Tell you what, let's go across the road and talk about this over a pub lunch. I'll pay.'

'Anything to get out of this horrible chair,' Ruby groaned, hoisting herself to her feet. 'I'll get my bag and meet you at the lifts.'

She opened the door and hesitated before turning back. 'Oh, and Fi? Can we agree there'll be no more discussion about you-know-who?'

'I have absolutely no idea who you're talking about,' Fi declared, her expression deadpan. Her ready agreement only served to heighten Ruby's suspicions and she scrutinised her boss through narrowed eyes.

Fi returned the look with a sunny smile. 'Meet you at the lifts in five.'

Unable to think of a comeback, Ruby shook her head and left.

42

Despite Ruby's conviction that she had made the right decision in severing ties with Griffin, it was hard not to feel despondent. Abandoning her salsa class in case she ran into him, she had instead taken up swimming, freestyling across the length of the local leisure centre pool until her arms ached and she was exhausted enough to fall into a dreamless sleep. But life without the charming, funny, insightful, and exasperating presence that was Griffin was undeniably bleak. Whether it was rescuing him from his romantic dramas, discussing the minutiae of their day on the phone, taking dance lessons together, downing drinks while his band played at sketchy pubs, or taking Jake out on trips, their lives had been closely intertwined for many years, and untangling their mutual dependence was proving far more painful than Ruby had anticipated.

Ruby's gloomy mood wasn't helped by the long, drawn-out nights and short December days, or the shops crammed with Christmas goodies and a festive cheer she was far from feeling. Almost every day, as she bundled Jake and herself up into thick jackets and woolly scarves to face the cold, dark mornings, she yearned for the blue skies and sunshine of Sorrel Island.

But while Ruby struggled to adjust to her new normal, Jake had settled back into school with ease. Happily showing off the techniques he had picked up from Mac to his tutors and the other students in Art Club, Jake's confidence had soared. One particular pencil sketch had earned a note of congratulations from Mr Hinton, who, to Ruby's surprise, she found herself warming to. The headteacher seemed genuinely concerned with Jake's welfare, and his approval of their trip – as well as the efforts he had made to ensure Jake maintained his learning while they were away – had shown him in a different light. The only sticking point in their newly established entente cordiale, and one which even the box of candied coconut from Sorrel Island couldn't shift, was Mr Hinton's continued insistence on addressing Ruby as *Mrs* Lamont.

Any fears Ruby had harboured that Kenny would let his son down again had been banished by the constant texts, video chats and phone calls between Jake and his father, and their relationship continued to flourish.

Jake's relationship with his godfather, however, was an altogether stickier proposition and, true to her word, Ruby had handed over control of Griffin's access to Jake to Auntie Pearl. It was always obvious when her aunt was on the phone to Griffin as she would scuttle out of the room, invariably throwing exasperated glances en route at Ruby, who would pretend not to notice. Although Ruby never asked Jake about his outings with Griffin, she gleaned odd bits of information from her son's chatter, even as she reminded herself that she had no interest in Griffin's life.

The bright spot amid all the gloom were the friends she had made on Sorrel Island. Miss Ida was always on hand for a chat and to provide a dose of her own particular brand of Southern comfort. And then there was Mac, now a close friend and trusted confidant. Back in New York, he was making strides with the portrait which he predicted would be among the best of his self-described magnificent inventory. Mac's easy friendship and their late-night cross-Atlantic chats were a soothing balm on the rawness of her split from Griffin, while the artist's renascent romance provided a handy distraction from Ruby's own barren love life.

A couple of weeks after returning home, Mac had finally taken Ruby's counsel to heart and journeyed the ten blocks separating him from his estranged wife's physiotherapy practice, clutching the crumpled but still unsigned divorce papers.

On the phone with Ruby later that night, Mac relayed the details of the first step in his win-Estella-back campaign.

'What happened when you got to her office?' asked Ruby, mentally crossing her fingers. She had been high on romance and brimming with optimism when she'd dished out the advice, and she could only pray it hadn't backfired.

'Well, kid, I gotta say that no-one was more surprised than me when she didn't throw me out. I was kinda nervous, but I made sure to say everything the way you coached me, and the good news is we're now talking. As for the rest, we'll have to wait and see how things go.'

Mac's well-rehearsed speech appeared to have opened the door to Estella's good graces, if not yet her heart, and the reunion had led to dinner and subsequent dates.

But as much as Mac's friendship lifted Ruby's spirits, she grieved the gaping, Griffin-sized hole in her life. The only antidote she knew to heartache was work, and she threw herself into her new role. As head of marketing, she now worked closely with Fi and the other heads of departments, and she had swiftly taken to her increased responsibilities. After wresting an uplift in her budget from an agonised Fi, Ruby had developed a marketing communications strategy and overseen the acquisition of the much-needed new conference system. But, despite the long hours she spent on the business and the welcome healthy salary increase that came with the job, nothing lessened the misery of losing the mainstay of her life.

◆ ◆ ◆

'Hey, Rubes, can you stay behind for a minute?'

Ruby broke off her conversation with Nick and retraced her steps back into Fi's office. Ignoring the pint-sized visitor's chair, Ruby pulled out a chair from around the recently vacated conference table and dragged it over.

Sitting down, her face lit up with an excited grin. 'I was just telling Nick that I spoke to Miss Ida at the weekend, and their Christmas and January bookings have shot up.'

'I'm not surprised, given this bloody weather,' Fi muttered. 'Well, I suppose having my staff work for free has done somebody some good.'

Ruby brushed off Fi's grumbling. 'Nick says Narita has turned into a social media whizz. She set up an Instagram account for Paradise Inn and is posting loads. Her videos on TikTok and the promos she's running seem to be doing the trick, if sales are anything to go by.'

Fi eked out a tiny smile and then said briskly, 'Right, so what I wanted to tell you – confidentially – is that I'm promoting Nick in the new year.'

When Ruby clapped excitedly, Fi instantly raised a warning hand. 'Before you ask, it's not because of his work on Miss Ida's website – although I can't deny it's given us some great PR for our corporate social responsibility report. Nick's a fantastic team leader, and he's really proved himself on the big accounts over the past couple of years.'

'That's so cool – and I won't even say I told you so,' Ruby crowed, elated to see Nick's talent and all-round niceness recognised.

'You are so much more like your Auntie Pearl than you know,' Fi observed dryly as she picked up her pen and a sheaf of papers. 'Okay, that's all.'

Ruby was on her way out the door when Fi stopped her in her tracks.

'So, are we still not allowed to talk about Griffin?'

With her hand on the doorknob, Ruby paused and shook her head dumbly.

'Rubes . . .' Fi started, and then sighed.

Ruby turned around. 'There's nothing to talk about,' she said woodenly.

Fi dropped her pen and sat back in her chair. 'You know, I've mulled over everything you said, and it just doesn't add up. Ruby, is there something you haven't told me?'

Ruby stared at Fi for a long moment and then leaned back against the door.

'Griffin and I kissed.'

Fi flicked a careless hand. 'I know all about that. You were fifteen, drunk, and hanging out behind the bike shed and—'

She broke off at the look on Ruby's face and gasped, covering her mouth with her hand. 'Oh, *crap*! You mean on the island, don't you? You and Griffin *kissed*, like properly kissed?'

Ruby nodded forlornly.

Fi dropped her hand, her red lips forming into a shocked 'O' as she absorbed the information. She scrutinised Ruby's troubled expression and asked carefully, 'And how was it?'

'As Priya would say, bloody amazing,' Ruby said, sounding even more miserable than she looked.

Fi looked at her with wide eyes. 'Well, go on then, *tell* me. I want details!'

'It was absolutely magical,' Ruby said in a dull tone. 'We went out to a club one night and danced for hours. Then we went for a walk along the beach to cool down. It was dead romantic, and at first we were just kidding around and then he said something silly which got me upset, and the next thing either of us knew, we were kissing . . . and kissing . . .' She trailed off with a dejected sigh.

'*Shee-it!*' Fi breathed. 'Now, it's starting to make sense.'

'What do you mean?' Ruby frowned.

'I mean, you idiot, that if you two properly snogged at last – well, then, it's no wonder your guard went right up and you were spoiling for a fight. *Obviously*, you were worried he'd see you as one more notch on his rather impressive belt.'

'I didn't think that at all,' Ruby protested. 'I trust – okay, trusted – him!'

'It doesn't matter how much we trust them, we *all* worry that men only want us for one thing,' said Fi dismissively. 'Are you telling me that somewhere in your complicated-Ruby-thinking you weren't petrified that someone with Griffin's track record might break your heart the same way Kenny did? Isn't all this business of cutting Griffin out of your life just you pushing him away before he gets a chance to hurt you? Maybe I'm wrong, but it sounds a bit convenient that you've suddenly decided you can't trust him because he didn't tell you about one chat with Kenny.'

Ruby winced, her fragile emotions wounded by the unfairness of Fi's assessment. *Why does no-one understand why I made the toughest decision of my life?* To her horror, she felt tears welling and she stared at the pointed toes of her boots, willing herself not to cry.

'You're wrong, Fi,' she choked out. 'I know Griffin's reputation with women better than anyone. *I'm* usually the one putting his broken exes back together after his kiss and runs. Maybe it sounds naïve to you, but I wasn't worried about him doing the same to me. It was bigger than that.'

'Then tell me, Rubes, because I don't understand,' urged Fi. She rested her arms on the desk, her turquoise eyes fixed on Ruby's face.

Ruby cleared her throat, but her voice was still thick with emotion. 'When Kenny left, I went through hell. But, looking back, that was nothing compared to how I've felt since I found out Griffin betrayed me. With him, I felt the safest I've ever felt with anyone. He's been in my life so long that he's like a *part* of me! I trusted him unconditionally, and him breaking that trust has shattered me. I don't think I can ever explain to you how traumatic that feels.'

Fi slumped back into her seat. 'I've been through two divorces, remember, so I know what it feels like to be let down by someone you love. After Duncan did the dirty on me, I honestly believed marrying Frank was the right thing to do, and that it would last for ever. If I'd known the bastard was only trying to exploit my heartbreak for money, I'd have—'

She broke off and took a deep breath. 'This isn't about me. Look, love, Griffin has admitted he was wrong not to tell you, but it's *one* mistake after years and years of – well, whatever it is you two have that none of us quite understands.'

Ruby tucked a stray braid behind her ear and shook her head. 'It's not just one mistake, Fi. It's a monumental breach of trust, and it was precisely that level of trust and honesty between us that made our relationship special. Without it, who we are together is meaningless. Just think about it: if he lied about something so important, what else about us has been a lie? I'm a lot happier on my own – or at least I will be, in time.'

Fi wasn't giving up easily. 'Rubes, I accept Griffin's conduct seems a bit shady, although we don't know his motives since you won't talk to him. But you can't go through life not trusting *any* man because of the actions of one – okay, two – men.'

Focusing on Griffin's duplicity was far easier than delving into the murky tangle of her emotions, and Ruby maintained a dogged silence until Fi sighed in exasperation. 'At least we know where Jake gets his stubbornness. Okay, then, have it your way. Let's pretend this isn't another excuse to justify your reluctance to trust people. Painting Griffin as the devil who betrayed you might make you feel more in control for now, but if you stay stuck in that narrative, he won't be the only one you're hurting.'

Ruby pushed away from the door and turned the knob. 'I'll be fine. I've leaned on Griffin for too long, and I'm following Miss Ida's advice and trying to find my balance. Which means that the only things I'm focusing on are my son and my career.'

Fi conceded defeat with an elegant shrug of her shoulders. 'If you say so. But, as someone who's had to learn the hard way, let me just say that avoiding your problems is not the way to solve them.'

43

Christmas and the new year came and went, bringing rain, fog, and icy snow showers that further depressed Ruby's spirits. The long hours at work were doing little to improve her mood, and the dark winter nights and dreary days plunged her into a spiral of misery that only started to lift amid the first glimmerings of spring.

As the weeks and months passed, Ruby's life slowly fell into a new pattern. Socialising, which had in the past almost invariably included Griffin, was now with Fi and her other friends – with the strict proviso that the topic of her former best friend was not up for discussion. Jake continued to see his godfather regularly, and on his days out with Griffin, Ruby found herself particularly eager to escape the house and her thoughts.

The positive fall-out from their trip to Sorrel Island continued. Ruby's regular catch-ups with Miss Ida had become a highlight of both their weeks, and bookings for Paradise Inn continued to soar, with the website and Narita's social media activity attracting visitors from around the world eager to visit the island and stay in Miss Ida's elegant home. Narita now worked full-time at Paradise Inn, sparing Zeke the pain of seeing his granddaughter follow her parents and leave the island to find work.

Mac was close to finishing the portrait and when he gave Ruby a glimpse of it during one of their video chats, she had been blown away by the level of detail he had captured in her face and the vibrant colours of the island backdrop.

'I still can't get over the idea that people are going to be gawking at a picture of me in a fancy art gallery!'

'They will be viewing a masterpiece by Mackenzie Castro, not *gawking* at a picture of you,' was Mac's pained response.

The portrait exhibition was scheduled for the end of October, and Mac was holding Ruby to her promise to visit New York for the grand opening. With Jake scheduled to spend an extended half-term holiday on Sorrel Island with Kenny, Mac refused to take no for an answer, dismissing Ruby's apprehension with a peremptory, 'My agent will take care of getting you here and everything else you need. Ruby, this exhibition is a big deal,' he added, further stressing her fraught nerves at the prospect of being on show. 'I've done some great work, kid, but this portrait is my best work yet and I couldn't have done it without you. Besides I promised Estella you'd come – she wants to meet you and check out the competition.'

The divorce papers remained unsigned as Mac and Estella continued their slow but steady courtship, and Ruby was equally curious to meet the woman who had captured Mac's heart.

As time marched onwards, Ruby tried to persuade herself she had taken control of the hurt, anger, and betrayal she associated with Griffin. If, from time to time, she felt an unexplained ache in her heart or found herself crying unexpected tears that told a different story, she also grew more adept at convincing herself that she was fine.

Ruby's connection with Kenny, on the other hand, had blossomed into a comfortable friendship. Without the bitterness of the past or any expectation for a future, chatting to Kenny felt easy and, to Ruby's surprise, something she found herself looking forward to.

One such phone call came on a Sunday evening while Ruby was in the kitchen helping Auntie Pearl clear up after dinner. When

Ruby ended the call a few minutes later with a smile on her face, Auntie Pearl glanced at her sharply.

'Sounds like you and that man are getting on well.'

Ruby nodded, wondering how to broach the suggestion that Auntie Pearl consider using Kenny's name.

'It's funny, but I think we get on better now than when we were together.'

Auntie Pearl hung the tea towel she was holding on to a hook and folded her arms. 'Well, you know I'm not one to say I told you so, but I'm pleased you've finally taken off your rose-coloured glasses about the past. That man was never right for you but, for your sake and for Jake's, it's good you've made peace with him.'

'Well, he's taken my advice and started dating, and he's seeing a woman he sounds quite smitten with.'

Auntie Pearl sniffed. 'So now you are the matchmaker for these men? I don't understand your generation!'

'Well, I'm glad he's happy,' said Ruby truthfully, even if she did feel an occasional pang that her erstwhile suitors had moved on. First Mac, and now Kenny, she thought ruefully. *I really have a gift for getting rid of any man who's interested in me.*

Just then Jake burst through the kitchen door and raced up to his mother.

'Hey, buddy, what's up?' Ruby ruffled his hair affectionately. 'Gosh, I swear you've grown a couple of inches in the past few months! Have you finished your homework?'

He nodded. 'I wrote all about different types of boats and printed off some pictures from the computer to stick into my book.'

'Sounds great. I'll take a look when I come upstairs.'

'I told Oliver that my dad owns the biggest boat out of anybody in school,' he added gleefully, and Ruby sighed, unable to deny that this time Jake was probably right.

Before she could launch into a lecture on the evils of bragging, Jake said with a wheedling smile, 'Mum, can I get a dog?'

Startled, Ruby stared at his upturned face. 'A *dog*? You don't even give poor Indie the time of day! You've always said you didn't want a pet because you were afraid it would die, and you'd be upset.'

'Yeah, but things are different now,' he insisted.

Ruby scoured his determined expression, marvelling at Jake's transformation since their trip. His anxiety seemed to have disappeared, and while Miss Ida would no doubt credit the healing power of love, it did look as though both Kenny and the legendary gods of Sorrel Island had been putting in some work on her child.

'Jake, what's brought all this on?' Ruby asked in amusement.

'Mum, you can't *not* do things because you're afraid,' Jake said decisively. 'That's what Auntie Shirlee says, and she's right.'

Ruby froze, her breath catching in her chest. It took her almost a minute to speak and, when she did, her voice emerged unnaturally high. 'Auntie *who*?'

'Auntie Shirlee – you know, Uncle Griffin's friend. So, can I get a dog?'

Griffin and Shirlee?! Ruby's pulse started racing so quickly her heart felt like it would explode inside her chest. *Griffin was back with Shirlee?*

Taking one look at Ruby's stunned expression, Auntie Pearl intervened. 'Jake, your mum and I will think about it. Now go upstairs and change into your pyjamas.'

Vaguely aware of her aunt shooing Jake out of the kitchen, Ruby stood rooted to the spot in disbelief. Blindsided by the revelation that Griffin had moved on – and with *Shirlee* – she felt as if she'd been punched in the stomach. *How could I have got it so wrong?* she wondered in bewilderment. She had dismissed Fi's speculation that Ruby was just one in a long list of women, but clearly it was Ruby who had once again misread the truth of her relationship with

Griffin. Even as the rational part of her brain pointed out that it had been months since they'd spoken and the chances were high that Griffin would be seeing someone else, Jake's words had ripped open the wound Ruby had convinced herself was healing. A wave of anguish swept over her, and she slumped, defeated, against the kitchen counter. Had the passion she and Griffin had found in each other that fateful night at the beach, the magical kisses they had shared and – and *everything* that had happened between them and meant so much to her been nothing more to him than an opportunistic grab, and now water under the bridge? Because if Griffin had moved on so easily that he was already back in Shirlee's arms – and clearly unfazed by the woman's dodgy feet, Ruby thought cattily – then Fi had been right to point out what Ruby should have always known. That Ruby had been simply the latest in a very long line of women falling hook, line, and sinker for Griffin Koinet.

Auntie Pearl cautiously closed the door behind Jake and turned back to Ruby, her eyes brimming with sympathy.

'Now listen to me, Ruby—'

Guessing what was coming, and in no fit state to hear the details of Griffin's love life, Ruby cut her off abruptly.

'I'm fine, Auntie Pearl, honest. Whatever Griffin gets up to is none of my business any more, and I don't need to hear it.'

Auntie Pearl looked distressed. 'But, Ruby—'

Ruby shook her head and bent to kiss her check. 'Please, Auntie, I don't want to talk about him. I've got an early meeting tomorrow, so I'll say goodnight now.'

Willing herself to make it to the kitchen door and up the stairs, Ruby maintained her composure all the way to her room, where her knees buckled, and she collapsed on to her bed. So much for thinking she was over him when there was clearly no expiration date on heartbreak, Ruby thought, as she tried – and failed – to hold back the tears streaming down her cheeks and soaking her pillow.

44

'I'm almost scared to ask, but do you want to come with?'

From her seat at the conference table in Fi's office, Ruby looked up from the marketing analytics reports she'd been reviewing to squint at the square white card embossed with gold letters that her boss was holding up.

'What's it for?' It looked like an invitation, but Ruby was too far away to make out the words. 'If it's another product marketing event, then I've had enough soggy crisps and cheap wine to last a lifetime, so no thanks.'

Fi hesitated, and then read aloud from the card. '*You are warmly invited to the launch of the Marilyn McColl Koinet Music Heals Foundation. Please join us to learn more about the work of the foundation and—*'

It took a minute for Griffin's mother's name to register before Ruby cut in. 'The Marilyn McColl *what?*'

Fi dutifully repeated the words and then dropped the card on to her desk with a sigh. 'See, if you weren't so tetchy about us talking about him, none of this would be a surprise to you. I've known about it for weeks, but I haven't dared say anything.'

Pushing aside the spreadsheets in front of her so forcefully that she almost knocked over her coffee, Ruby stared at Fi in disbelief.

'Hold on a minute, are you telling me you're in touch with Griffin?'

Fi sighed again. 'Yes, but please don't get all huffy and annoyed about it. I respect your decision, but I've known Griffin for almost as long as I've known you and, unlike some people, I can't just cut off my friends.'

Ignoring the dig, Ruby scowled at her in dismay. 'But you're *my* friend.'

'Yes, I am, but you made Griffin my friend too,' Fi said reasonably. 'He's been going through a challenging time, and he needed support.'

Ruby looked stricken, and Fi shook her head impatiently. 'Rubes, you're my mate, and if it was a competition, you'd win hands down. But it isn't, and I can be there for both of you, so please don't make this a thing.'

While it stung to hear Fi had secretly been in contact with Griffin, the part of Ruby that still felt guilty about the damage her vicious words would have caused felt a tiny bit relieved someone had been looking out for him. Not that she would give Fi the satisfaction of saying so.

Fi sat back in her chair, watching Ruby's expression closely. 'Before you tell me you're not interested, you should know Griffin's been working like a maniac to set up this foundation. He was so happy about the impact of the music programme he put in place for the children on Sorrel Island that he was keen to scale it up. He's been collaborating with child psychologists, trauma experts, and even musicians' unions to create programmes that integrate music with trauma and mental health therapies for kids and adults. Honestly, Rubes, it's a fantastic idea and he's pulling it off on an international scale. The foundation has started kitting out five centres so far, including one at Ocean House, and he's planning a whole network of them.'

Ruby listened to Fi's impassioned words in stunned silence. She had always believed Griffin could make good use of both his musical talent and his boundless energy, and it sounded as if he had finally found the path to change his life and make good use of his inheritance. Hearing what Griffin had achieved in such a short time – and in Marilyn's name – left Ruby feeling even more ashamed of using his mother to hurt him.

As if she sensed Ruby softening, Fi rammed home her advantage. 'Look, come to the launch with me, or at least think about it over the next couple of weeks. You don't have to get into a long conversation – just say congratulations and leave it at that. You loved his mum, and it's been, what, nearly six months since the two of you spoke? I'm sure it would mean the world to him to see you there.'

For an infinitesimal moment Ruby wavered, and then she shook her head. 'You don't understand. Even if I wanted to talk to him, I promise you that Griffin would cross the street rather than speak to me again. I said some awful things to him the last time we spoke and, in his shoes, I certainly wouldn't forgive me!'

'Yeah, well, maybe Griffin's more generous and forgiving than you give him credit for. Like I said, not everyone has it in them to cut people off just because they're upset with them.'

Ruby remained silent, refusing to be drawn into another argument about a situation she had tried and failed, more than once, to make Fi understand. Despite herself, Ruby stood and walked over to Fi's desk. She picked up the invitation card and, as she scanned the gold-embossed script, she felt the pricking of tears behind her eyes. Griffin had finally found his way and it was hard to believe that after all they'd been through together, she would play no part in this momentous stage of his life.

'Look, he's moved on. Besides, we all know what he's like when it comes to women,' Ruby said desperately. 'Every woman thinks they'll be the one to change a man, but—'

'But nothing!' Fi cut in. 'You might have known Griffin the boy, but it's pretty obvious you don't have a clue about Griffin the man.'

'That's not true!' Ruby protested.

'I'm sorry, Rubes, but it is. You still see him for who he was back when he was grieving and lost, not for who he is now. He might pretend to be an idle playboy, but the man has been quietly overseeing a multimillion-pound fortune for years that he never asked for and never wanted. He could have gone wild and spent the money on drink, drugs, and debauchery like a lot of trust-fund kids, but he didn't. Personally, if I was in his shoes, I'd be living in Monaco and having a ball – not to mention saving millions in taxes! But that man would never dream of leaving you and Jake. Maybe it's easier for you to stay angry at him about Kenny rather than risk trying to make a relationship with him work, but Griffin is a good man.'

Fi watched the emotions chasing over Ruby's face. 'He's grown up, Rubes. Honestly, I think he's put his past behind him.'

A picture of Shirlee in her lemon-yellow sweater instantly flashed through Ruby's mind and she drew in a sharp breath and tossed the card back on to the desk. *Of course he has – me included!*

'Well, it's about time, isn't it? I hope he'll be very happy.' Ruby forced a smile. Griffin had Shirlee now and was looking to the future, not his past.

Fi looked startled. 'Ruby, what I meant was that if you're worried he's not serious about making a commitment, then—'

'Fi, *stop*! I keep telling you I don't want to talk about Griffin, and you just won't let it go!'

Fi held up her hands in mock surrender. 'Fine, I'll take Priya instead since she's besotted with the man – and don't blame me if they waltz off together into the sunset.'

When Ruby failed to crack even the tiniest smile, Fi leaned forward and said quietly, 'Shout at me all you like, but I see the pain in your face. While you think you're the one depriving him of your relationship, you're also punishing yourself.'

Ruby stalked back to the table and gathered up her papers into an untidy pile. Picking them up, along with her half-empty coffee mug, she marched out of Fi's office without a word.

45

For as long as she could remember, Ruby's maxim had always been *Expect the unexpected.* But, as she made her way home from the station, feeling in equal parts furious at Fi for not understanding her position, and devastated at being consigned to Griffin's past, Ruby's go-to mantra was far from her mind. Which explained why, as she hurried around the corner of the high road into Blossom Street with her eyes fixed on her watch, she was *not* expecting to run slap bang into Griffin, who was approaching from the opposite direction.

He reached for her arm to stop her falling, and as soon as Ruby recovered her balance, she wrenched it away as forcefully as if his fingers had burned through her jacket and branded her skin. The blood drained from her face as she stared at him, drinking in the familiar features while her heart went into freefall. Too late, she remembered Jake had been spending his inset day off school with Griffin, and she had forgotten to ring home to check the coast was clear before returning.

Contrary to Ruby's earlier assertion, Griffin didn't look like someone who would cross the street to avoid her. Instead, he stared at her wordlessly, his hazel eyes searching her face. The tan he had acquired in Sorrel Island had faded to his usual light brown complexion and, for the first time since she'd known him, he had a low-cut beard.

Painfully conscious she was staring, Ruby made to go past, and he reached for her arm again.

'Ruby, wait!'

She stopped and turned, but found herself unable to look at him. They were standing in the middle of the pavement, and he gently steered her to the side and out of the way of the passing pedestrians before he released her.

Desperate to escape a conversation she wasn't prepared for, Ruby cast around and then looked at her watch to avoid meeting his gaze.

'I can't stop. I'm running late already and . . .' Her voice tailed off as she failed to come up with an excuse. She sighed and looked up, and as they gazed into each other's eyes, she was startled to see the tiniest glint of humour.

'Did you get the invitation I sent to your office for the foundation launch?'

'Yes,' she said awkwardly, taken aback by his calm, almost friendly tone. She tried to keep her voice steady as she added, 'You've done an incredible job with the foundation. It must have taken a lot of work to get it up and running so quickly.'

He shrugged. 'Having a portfolio of properties and a ton of money on tap can speed things up enormously. Seeing the impact of what Diego and his bandmates were doing for the kids at Ocean House inspired the idea, and after that it was easy enough to convert some of the trust's buildings into music therapy centres.' He paused and then said wryly, 'Besides, I know Mum would have got a kick out of seeing some of those luxury apartments being used to help regular folk. But the best part for me is bringing tried and tested therapies for trauma victims to a lot more people. So, just as you always said, the money *can* be used for something worthwhile.'

Ruby nodded, unsettled by his proximity and gnawing so hard on her lip that she was surprised it didn't bleed. 'You should feel proud, Griffin. You're changing the lives of a lot of people.'.

He studied her silently for a moment and then remarked with a tentative smile, 'Fi says you've been promoted to a *head of* position. That's brilliant.'

Suddenly it was all too much for Ruby, and she stared down at the pavement. For months she had clung to so much pain and anger that she had no idea how to let go.

'You know, I'm really pleased that you've found your path and I wish you all the luck in the world with the launch,' she said stiffly, her jaw tight with nerves. 'But I can't stand here exchanging small talk with you as if the past six months never happened. Goodbye, Griffin.'

Once again, she made as if to leave, but he stepped in front to block her path. 'Ruby, please. I know I let you down and—'

The pain from the months of heartache, intensified by Jake's recent revelations, turned to overwhelming sadness as Ruby clung on desperately to her hurt. 'This wasn't a case of you arriving late for a movie or forgetting to pick up ice-cream for Jake. Griffin, you willingly lied to me for years, and if that wasn't enough, you left me in no doubt how utterly undesirable I am, and why even the father of my child wouldn't fight for me.'

Griffin stared at her, horrified. 'That's not true! How can you even say that? You're beautiful . . . *stunning*, and I've *always* told you so.'

'Just not stunning enough to keep a man, right?'

Griffin blew the air from his cheeks and shook his head, his hand visibly trembling as he ran it over his hair. 'Rubes, you've got the wrong end of the stick. I never meant you weren't good enough for Kenny. Christ, it was the other way round, if anything! I am so incredibly sorry I hurt you and I'm begging you to forgive me.'

Ruby was also trembling. It was surreal that someone she had known for so long could cause her this much emotional turmoil, and she wondered how she had gone for years without recognising how he could make her feel.

'Ruby,' he said softly. 'Talk to me. You gave Kenny another chance, so why can't you do the same for me?'

She backed away from him until she found herself up against a wall. Closing her eyes for a moment, she breathed in deeply and let the breath out in a long sigh. 'I don't even know why you'd want to talk to me after the vile things I said.'

'Because—' Griffin started, and then gestured helplessly. 'We've been through so much together. I can't bear us not being friends. *Please*, Rubes.'

'I want to forgive you,' she whispered, her eyes filling with tears. This was *Griffin*! Everything in her wanted to say yes, every cell in her body was clamouring to welcome him back into her life.

But when his face lit up and he took a step towards her, the agony of knowing he was now with Shirlee was unbearable, and she held up a hand to stop him. There was no way she could go back to simply being friends and watching him build a life with someone else. She had survived the anguish of the past few months and she couldn't afford to lose herself again, but for as long as she remained connected to Griffin and harboured even the faintest possibility of being with him, she would never find her balance.

Griffin took a step closer, his eyes desperately begging her not to say what he clearly sensed was coming. 'You promised Mum you would always be there for me. What happened to that?'

Ruby could feel the pain of her heart shattering into pieces, but she couldn't risk giving in. Steeling herself against the torment in his eyes, she shook her head. 'I'm sorry, Griffin. I wish I could pretend none of this had ever happened.'

'But?' His voice was flat, and his face ashen.

'But I *can't*. I'm sorry, but I just can't.'

46

With summer approaching, Mac's infectious confidence had transformed Ruby's apprehension about the trip to New York into excitement. Although it wasn't for months yet, and she still felt nervous about the media interest Mac had warned about, she couldn't wait to see the portrait – now varnished and drying in a secure location – in person. Mac and his team were preoccupied with preparations for the high-profile exhibition, which was precisely why – as Mac gloomily explained to Ruby on a video chat one evening – Estella had chosen to invite him as her plus one to her client's California vineyard wedding.

'She knows I'm in meetings all day with curators, organisers, event marketers and even the friggin' designers setting up the lighting,' he groused. 'So, of course, she picks *this* time to ask me to travel across the country to San Fernando Valley for the wedding of some woman she's never even mentioned before! Estella's only doing this to test whether I'll put her first.'

'What did you tell her?' Ruby asked with trepidation. Seeing Mac's disgruntled expression on her phone was not reassuring. He had put so much effort into repairing his relationship with Estella that Ruby couldn't bear to see him destroy all the progress he'd made.

'What do you think I said?' Mac grumbled. 'My bag is packed and ready in the hall. I can't take the chance of losing her again.'

'Oh, Mac, that's brilliant! I'm so proud of you.' Ruby beamed like a teacher watching her student graduate, and Mac gave a reluctant smile.

'What about you, kid? How are *you* doing?'

There it was, that sympathetic voice again, and Ruby's smile faded. The trouble with late-night, wine-soaked phone calls was that you ended up spilling the beans in a way you would never have done while sober.

'I'm fine,' she said in a determinedly cheerful voice, silently vowing to cut down on her drinking. The gut-wrenching encounter with Griffin still haunted her but pretending she could settle for friendship after everything that had happened between them promised only further heartache. 'I told you I've put all that – drama – behind me now, and life is good. Jake's over the moon about going back to Sorrel Island, and Kenny can't wait to see him.'

'I'll be heading back there after the exhibition. I'm gonna need some peace and quiet to work on my next commission,' said Mac. 'And before you ask, I'm taking Estella with me.'

'I'm so pleased,' Ruby breathed. 'At this rate, you'll be burning those divorce papers before the year is out.'

'I'll keep you posted, kid.' He winked, flashing the brilliant smile that still managed to make Ruby feel just a little bit wobbly.

She was about to end the call when Mac said, 'Oh, and Ruby . . .'

'Yes?'

'I've been there and I know it feels tough right now, but things will get better. Sometimes we need to be unhappy for a while to figure things out, but don't let what happened with Griffin ruin you for love or for life. You can't let the fear of falling stop you from flying – hell, look at me! Imagine if you hadn't told me to take a chance with Estella.'

Ruby's eyes misted over at Mac's genuine concern, and she touched his face on her phone screen tenderly. 'Thanks, Mac. Talk to you soon.'

Slipping her phone into the pocket of her jeans, Ruby ran downstairs to the kitchen to find Jake regaling Auntie Pearl with the details of his day out with Griffin. She interrupted the conversation with an apologetic smile.

'It's getting late, buddy, and you've got school tomorrow. You can finish telling Grandma Pearl everything after you get ready for bed.'

Jake pouted, but then took one look at Auntie Pearl and reluctantly nodded. 'Okay, but, Mum . . .'

'Yes?'

'Can you make carrot cake?'

She blinked, taken aback by the random question. When did Jake start liking carrot cake, and why on earth would she bake when she could pick one up from a supermarket shelf?

Jake looked at her expectantly, and Ruby shrugged. 'I've never tried. Why?'

'Cos I ate some today and it was scrummy. Auntie Shirlee made it and Uncle Griffin said it was the best he's ever tasted. So, can you make one for me, Mum?'

Shirlee's in his life now and you're going to have to get used to this, Rubes. Ruby forced a smile and gently steered Jake towards the door. She tried to sound breezy even as a concrete block of despair appeared to have lodged itself in her core. 'I'll think about it. Now, off you go, and don't forget to brush your teeth.'

Auntie Pearl rinsed out her mug and placed it in the drying tray, and then turned around to look directly at Ruby.

'When are you going to stop holding what Griffin did against him?'

'I'm not, Auntie. He's apologised and we've both moved past it. Look, I don't have a problem with Jake seeing him but that doesn't mean Griffin and I have to be friends. I tried, so let's leave it there.'

'I can't leave it when anyone with eyes in their head could see how much you two meant to each other. What are you so scared of?'

'Nothing,' Ruby lied, too afraid to confess how Griffin still haunted her dreams and how she still found her hand automatically reaching for her phone to share a random piece of news with him.

'You know, Ruby, sometimes taking a chance and making a leap of faith can lead to something good.'

When Ruby didn't respond, her aunt slowly shook her head. 'Is this really what you want? *Think*, Ruby! What if he gets serious with someone else – could you live with that?'

47

'She's right, and you couldn't,' Fi said firmly.

Fi's flesh-coloured bandage dress clung tightly to her tiny, curvaceous frame and if the two rounds of drinks already sent to their table in the wine bar was anything to go by, the pricey outfit was well on the way to paying for itself.

Ruby tore her gaze away from Fi's cleavage and the wardrobe malfunction just waiting to happen and picked up her third cocktail.

'I'm only telling you what Auntie Pearl said because I'm over the whole Griffin thing,' she said, after taking a long sip and carefully setting the glass down. She hiccupped gently, slightly regretting knocking back the strong drinks after only a salad lunch several hours ago.

'You might be, but the rest of us aren't. Your relationship lasted longer than both my marriages combined.'

'Well, he's moved on and it's all water under the bridge now.'

Even to her own ears her speech sounded slurred, and Fi pointed to Ruby's glass with a wicked grin. 'I'd go easy on that Sex on the Beach if I were you. Whoops, sorry, is it too soon?' she cackled.

Ruby flushed. '*Fi!* I *didn't* have—' She broke off with a sigh of relief as Priya returned from her trip to the ladies. 'Thank God you're back. Fi's doing my head in.'

Fi was still creased up laughing and Priya sat down and looked from her to Ruby uncertainly.

'What's going on?'

'Ignore her,' Ruby snapped. 'It's probably her dress cutting off the oxygen supply to her brain.'

Fi wiped her eyes with the paper napkin under her glass and shook her head, still chuckling. 'Sorry, Priya, love, I just cracked myself up over something I said about Griffin.'

Priya's brow cleared. '*Oh!* Are we allowed to talk about him now?'

'Yes!' said Fi.

'No!' Ruby growled.

Clearly preferring Fi's response, Priya clapped her hands together. 'Oh good, because I still can't get over how awesome that launch was. You missed an incredible evening, Rubes! There was loads of champagne and this lovely man with long dreadlocks – he was a musician who'd worked with trauma kids in war-torn countries, isn't that right, Fi? – gave this amazing speech.'

'And he wasn't bad-looking either,' added Fi.

'Are you okay there, Rubes?' Priya asked sympathetically. 'You look awful.'

Ruby nodded, too tipsy to take offence, especially when her brain felt anaesthetised after a sleepless night replaying Auntie Pearl's warning on an endless loop.

'There's only one person I know who can put that look on your face, so why don't you just face the truth?' Fi sighed.

Ruby felt her cheeks burn. 'I don't know what you're talking about.'

'I think she means Griffin,' Priya said helpfully.

'She knows exactly who I mean, love.' Fi shook her head resignedly and took a sip of her drink.

'What are you going to do about Griffin, Rubes?' Priya asked gently. 'When Fi and I walked into the launch event, I saw his face. It was so obvious he was hoping you'd come with us, because he looked totally crushed.'

'There's nothing *to* do,' Ruby replied, sounding wretched. 'Griffin's moved on and so have I, so there's nothing more to say.'

She sat in boot-faced silence cradling her drink and after a few moments Fi put down her glass and said decisively, 'Okay, we'll stop talking about you-know-who.'

'Good.'

'On one condition . . .'

Ruby looked suspicious. 'What?'

'If you've really moved on, prove it by going on a date with Barry.'

Ruby stared at her blankly. 'Who the hell's Barry?'

'He's my neighbour – Madeline's – brother. He came round the other day to pick up her spare key when she locked herself out, and I told him about you.'

Ruby choked on the drink she'd been swallowing. 'What do you mean you *told* him about me?'

'He's been through a break-up, and Madeline's worried about him.'

'But you hate Madeline,' Ruby protested.

'I know, but I got a bit carried away when I was trimming our shared hedge with my new secateurs last week, and I need her not to sue me.'

'Well, that's not my fault! Why do I have to suffer?'

'Believe me, if I get sued, you will *all* suffer. Besides, I've met Barry a few times and he's very sweet.'

'What does he do?' Ruby said reluctantly. Knowing how much Fi hated spending money, even the whiff of a lawsuit suggested this wasn't a battle Ruby was likely to win.

'I think he said he's an auditor . . . or was it an actuary? I don't know – something to do with numbers or data.'

Ruby groaned, hearing the trap doors closing over her head. 'Please stop, you're doing a terrible job of selling him.'

'You should give him a chance, Rubes,' Priya piped up.

'Exactly,' said Fi. 'Barry's a lovely man. Very solid. If you're over Griffin, prove it by putting yourself out there and getting back in the game.'

'But, Fi, really . . . an *auditor*?' Ruby pleaded.

Fi tutted impatiently. 'For God's sake, just put aside your silly prejudices and give it a try. For the record, he thinks you sound amazing. Oh God, I'm beginning to sound like Priya – sorry, love, no offence.'

'None taken. Wow, I can't believe Ruby's actually going on a date.'

Feeling like a cornered deer, Ruby downed the rest of her drink and sighed heavily. 'Fine, but I'm only doing this if you both stop going on about – well, you know.'

Fi had been engaged in a silent flirtation with the well-dressed silver fox at a nearby table who had sent the last round of drinks. Seeing him glance over once again, she leaned forward to give him the full benefit of her cleavage.

'*Fi!* I'm talking to you! Do we have a deal?' Ruby demanded.

'What now? Hmm, yeah, sure. Oh, and please don't mess Barry around. I don't need Madeline coming after me for chopping off half her prize roses.'

48

While Barry launched into a fresh anecdote, this one featuring a missing – and apparently crucial – audit file, Ruby played with the straw in her glass and contemplated suing Fi for damages herself. Fixing a smile on her face, she let Barry continue to dominate the conversation as she scanned the tapas and wine bar decorated in various shades of beige. Even sitting on the sofa watching property shows with Auntie Pearl would have been more entertaining, Ruby thought gloomily.

The evening had started on a more promising note when Ruby walked into the bar and spotted Barry seated at the table by the window. Well groomed and wearing a tweed jacket, her first thought was that he wasn't as bad as she'd feared. His face lit up as he watched her approach and, tossing back her braids, she gave him her sunniest smile.

'You must be Barry!' Holding out her hand to shake his, her smile faltered when he jumped to his feet.

I. Am. Going. To. Kill. Fi. was Ruby's second thought. In her heels, she was at least six inches taller than Barry, a key piece of information she knew Fi had deliberately omitted. However, as Ruby soon discovered, whatever Barry lacked in height, he more than made up for in speech. After an hour and a half in his company, not even the jug of sangria she had knocked back could lift Ruby's spirits. After the audit-file story, Barry had moved on to a painfully long-winded anecdote about his 'hilarious' run-in with the head of compliance and Ruby sighed, wishing all kinds of hell on her boss as her gaze wandered again.

Suddenly, her eyes locked on to a pair of dark, sexy eyes belonging to a clean-shaven man sitting a few tables away and looking straight at her. Ruby blinked in shock. *Where on earth had he appeared from?* The man's dark brown skin contrasted with his stylish cobalt-blue suit and white t-shirt, and Ruby instantly perked up. Channelling Fi, she squared her shoulders to better show off the plunging neckline of her dress. It seemed to do the trick as his eyes dropped momentarily before coming back up to meet hers with a raised eyebrow. Then, looking amused, he returned his attention to the woman sitting across from him.

'Are you enjoying that squid?' Barry asked, peering dubiously at the contents of the small earthenware dish sitting on the table between them.

'Mmm . . . It's lovely,' said Ruby, stabbing her fork into a piece of the seafood and cramming it into her mouth. The food was the only decent thing about the date so far, and not even Barry was going to put her off enjoying it.

He spooned a tiny portion of spiced rice on to his plate and stared at it morosely. 'Madeline suggested this place, but I prefer English food, don't you? All this foreign stuff repeats on me.'

By the time Barry had launched into a monologue about the near disaster of a missed HR audit deadline, Ruby was losing the will to live.

'The waiter looks busy,' she fibbed. 'I'll go to the bar and order another sangria. Can I get you anything?'

Looking slightly put out at the interruption, Barry glanced at his almost empty glass. 'Another shandy would go down a treat.'

Ruby was waiting at the bar for her order and enjoying the brief respite from Barry when she heard a deep voice behind her say quietly, 'This place is pretty tragic, don't you think?'

She spun around to find herself facing the man in the blue suit. Up close, his eyes were even sexier, and she could smell the spicy notes of his cologne. He was tall enough to look her straight in the eye, she noted approvingly, and, as if he'd guessed what was going through her mind, he winked cheekily.

She bit her lip, trying not to laugh. 'So why are you here, then?'

'I had it on good authority that the tapas is fantastic, but they didn't warn me I'd have to eat in beige hell.'

This time, she couldn't help giggling, and then she caught herself. 'I really shouldn't be chatting to you. I'm on a date.'

'Blind?'

She nodded. 'You?'

'The same. How's yours going?'

'Let's just say it's reminding me of all the reasons why I hate blind dates.'

Although her drinks were waiting on the counter, Ruby couldn't bring herself to pick them up and return to Barry. Instead, she rummaged in her bag, pretending to look for her bank card, while the barman took the sexy stranger's order.

'I'm Leo, by the way.' His slow smile was devastating, and she resisted the urge to toss her hair.

'Ruby.'

Leo pulled out his wallet from inside his jacket and tapped his card on the payment machine the barman pushed towards him. Before putting his wallet away, Leo extracted a business card and held it out to Ruby.

'If you're still feeling the same way about your date at the end of the evening, please give me a call. Since we've already met, maybe you'd like to go on a non-blind date.'

'Smooth.' Ruby arched an appreciative eyebrow as she plucked the card from between his fingers and slipped it into her bag.

'Nothing ventured and all that. Seriously, you're gorgeous, and I'd love to chat some more.'

Sitting in an Uber half an hour later, Ruby took out Leo's card and fingered it thoughtfully. *It's time to take a chance, Rubes.*

Taking a deep breath, she pulled out her phone.

49

Ruby took another sip of her latte and tried to focus on the conversation. Unfortunately, it was hard to concentrate on Leo's words when his eyes reminded her of pools of melted dark chocolate, and his lips curved seductively around the rim of his cup whenever he sipped his steaming cappuccino. Even the way he broke off a piece of the cookie on his plate was ridiculously sensuous, she thought, observing him surreptitiously from under her lashes.

Leo eyed her thoughtfully. 'Okay, so I'll just come right out and say it. Why was a hot babe like you out on a blind date?'

Ruby choked, bringing her napkin to her mouth just in time to avoid spitting coffee over him.

'You've got a nerve!' she protested, laughing. 'You were on a blind date too! What's your excuse, then? It's not like *you're* hard on the eyes.'

Which was putting it mildly. In a black blazer over a white t-shirt and jeans, Leo looked even more stunning for their coffee shop date than at the restaurant the previous week.

He met her questioning glance with a shrug. 'For the past couple of years, I've been too obsessed with setting up my business to even think about a relationship. But now the company's taking off, my business partner insists I need to get out more, which is why he set me up with his friend, Harmony.'

'*Harmony?*' Ruby did her best, but her lips twitched anyway.

'Are you being name-ist?' Leo sounded reproachful, although his eyes twinkled with humour.

'Just a bit. But seriously, *Harmony?*'

'She's a lovely lady, and she takes both her yoga and her meditation very seriously. Now, I'd love another coffee. What about you?'

Ruby watched Leo make his way to the counter, feeling a glow of contentment in her belly that had nothing to do with the hot drink. *I think you've picked a good one here, Rubes.* Finding Leo was making her evening of torture with Barry totally worth it.

Fi had taken Ruby's flat rejection of another date with her neighbour's brother with surprising good grace. 'Well, you gave it a go, so fair enough. I've agreed to babysit Madeline's cat while she's on holiday in Tenerife, so I'm off the hook for the rose bush.'

Fi's reaction to Ruby's confession about Leo had been much less nonchalant. 'You got asked out on a date *during* a date? Bloody hell, woman, you really *are* moving on!'

Watching Leo returning to the table with their coffees, Ruby felt happier and more confident than she had in months. Phoning the sexy stranger from the restaurant had proved to be a good – no, a *great* – move, and she was enjoying every minute of their non-blind date.

'Just so you know, I was watching while you were at the counter to see if you handed out your business card to another woman,' Ruby said with a teasing smile.

Leo laughed and held up his hands. 'Okay, you've got me there.' He leaned in closer. 'But I promise the only woman in this room I'm interested in is sitting right in front of me.'

Their eyes met and she shivered at the smouldering intensity she saw there.

'I'm really glad you called me, Ruby,' he said. 'Can we do dinner next time?'

'As long as it's not in beige hell, I'd love to.' She smiled. 'But I'm a mum, so I've got to negotiate my time off.'

His brows shot up. 'You've got a child? You didn't mention that.'

Ruby's smile froze. 'Yes, a son. Is that a problem?'

Leo lifted his cup to take a sip, his expression suddenly pensive. 'Well . . .'

When his voice trailed off, Ruby's heart sank. *Of course he was too good to be true.* Leo studied her for a moment, and she lifted her chin defiantly. She and Jake came as a package, now and always.

'It's only a problem if he's a Chelsea supporter,' Leo said finally, his eyes flashing with mischief. 'That, I'm afraid, would be a deal breaker.'

Torn between laughter and relief, Ruby slowly released the breath she had been holding. Leo reached across the table and touched her hand, his expression unusually serious.

'Of course, it's not a problem. I love kids. Look, you've got my number, so please call me when you're free to meet up. I really want to see you again.'

The time flew by, and Ruby laughed more than she had in months.

When, reluctantly, she stood up to leave, Leo kissed her gently on the cheek and she closed her eyes briefly, breathing in his spicy cologne. Resisting the urge to skip, she walked out of the coffee shop on a high. Life was finally looking up! Leo was an absolute dream, and, giddy with excitement, she could have hugged the next passer-by.

That desire evaporated moments later as her eyes locked on to the petite figure advancing towards her, and Ruby found herself face to face with Shirlee.

50

'Oh, it's *you*!'

It wasn't the friendliest greeting Ruby had ever heard, but then Shirlee's frosty expression could hardly be described as chummy. Ruby's euphoria disappeared faster than water down a drain. The gods must really want to punish her because London was a big city, and yet she'd managed to cross paths with the one woman she had hoped never to see.

'Hello, Shirlee. How are you?' Ruby nodded politely, keen to keep things civil. After all, it wasn't Shirlee's fault that her boyfriend had broken Ruby's heart.

For a second, Shirlee looked ready to carry on walking, but then she gave a non-committal shrug. 'I've been keeping busy.'

With nothing else forthcoming, Ruby cast around for a topic of conversation that didn't include Griffin.

'Jake was raving about your carrot cake not so long ago. He'll have you signed up for *The Great British Bake Off* before you know it.' Ruby chuckled, attempting to inject a bit of humour into the awkward run-in, but the woman didn't so much as crack a smile.

Ruby gave up, and was about to make her excuses and move on when Shirlee said abruptly, 'Aren't you going to ask after Griffin?'

Ruby's smile vanished and her hackles rose. 'Actually, no, I'm not. As you know, we're not in touch any more.'

Shirlee's eyes narrowed. 'How come?'

'It's a long story.' *And it's not one I'm prepared to discuss with you!*

'I've got time.'

Barely holding on to her temper, Ruby snapped angrily, 'Look, just because you and Griffin are together doesn't give you the right to—'

'Me and Griffin are *what*?' Shirlee spluttered. 'You *are* joking, aren't you? Where on earth did you get that idea? I'll have you know that I'm almost engaged to Simeon.'

Who the hell is Simeon? Ruby stared in confusion at Shirlee's flabbergasted expression. 'I'm sorry, but I don't understand. Jake says you're at Griffin's house a lot, and I assumed . . .'

She trailed off as Shirlee's face cleared and the woman burst into peals of laughter. 'Do me a favour! Do you honestly think I'm daft enough to waste my time on a man who's so obviously into someone else? God, no, I learned my lesson the first time! Besides Simeon and I are practically engaged.'

Ruby was watching Shirlee's lips move but her brain had frozen at the words 'God, no' and the only information she could process was that Griffin *wasn't* back with Shirlee. But if that were true, why was a woman obsessed with marriage spending so much time with a man who had so callously broken up with her? The question slipped out before Ruby could remind herself that it was none of her business.

Shirlee waved a hand impatiently. 'I work in fundraising, which you would know if you'd ever bothered to find out anything about me. I've been helping Griffin find sponsors and secure long-term funding to expand the foundation's Music Heals centres.'

'Oh!' Ruby said blankly.

'If you must know, Griffin got in touch with me late last year to apologise for having been such an absolute bastard. He knows

I'm great at my job, so when he started the foundation, he offered me the contract to make amends.'

'*Ohhh!*' Ruby breathed.

'Obviously, as he works mostly from home, we meet at his place. Not that it's any of your business.'

Shirlee's blue eyes were like chips of ice and her hostility was almost palpable. Puzzled, Ruby shook her head.

'Um, have I offended you or something, Shirlee? You seem incredibly annoyed with me.'

Shirlee let out a short, humourless laugh. 'Do I? Okay, I've answered your question, so it's *my* turn now. Why exactly did you cut Griffin off?'

Ruby inhaled sharply, taken aback both by the question and the ferocity of the woman's tone. She opened her mouth to tell Shirlee to mind her own business and then caught herself. Shirlee might be annoying, but she was right. It *was* her turn to answer the question.

Picking her words with care, Ruby said slowly, 'I didn't cut him off, at least not in the way you mean. Look, something happened, and it's for the best that we go our separate ways.'

'Griffin told me the two of you two slept together when you were on the island, if that's the "something" you're referring to,' Shirlee said bluntly.

Ruby reeled as if she had been punched in the stomach. Her hand flew to her mouth and the blood drained from her face.

'He did *what*?!' she gasped.

The full truth of what had happened that night on Sorrel Island had remained their secret until, fuelled by too much wine as she tried to drown the gut-wrenching pain of losing her best friend, Ruby had spilled the beans to Mac one night. It seemed she wasn't the only one to have slipped up, she thought in anguish, although why, of *all* the people in the world he could have chosen, had Griffin confided in Shirlee?

Shirlee shrugged. 'To be fair, he was so drunk when he told me that he probably doesn't remember anything he said. I can't believe you just dumped him after that. God, that's so much worse than anything he ever did!'

'Now, hold on a second, you don't know the whole story! Griffin lied to me about—'

Shirlee cut in abruptly. 'Yes, he told me that, too.'

'Well, then, you should understand why I didn't want to—'

'Oh, *puh-leese*!' Shirlee interrupted again, her voice dripping with scorn. She folded her arms and looked Ruby up and down. 'You are such a sanctimonious hypocrite!'

Ruby gasped. '*What?* Wait a minute—'

'No, *you* wait,' Shirlee snarled, the tip of her nose white with fury, and Ruby stepped back in alarm. Although Shirlee was quite a bit shorter than her, right at that moment she looked like an enraged blonde Rottweiler about to pounce.

Her blue eyes flashing fire, Shirlee stepped forward to close the gap and jabbed an accusatory finger at Ruby. 'Aren't you the one who said Griffin was wrong to dump me simply for suggesting we take our relationship to the next level? I sat on your auntie's sofa bawling my eyes out while you pretended his behaviour was unacceptable.'

'I *didn't* pretend,' Ruby argued, keeping a wary eye on the finger. 'I told you Griffin was a pig-headed idiot to treat you the way he did, and I meant it. But that's not the same thing at all.'

'Isn't it?' Shirlee glared at Ruby, her expression daring her to disagree. 'Granted, he knew about your boyfriend taking off, but has it even occurred to you to wonder *why* he said nothing all these years? Griffin has always been there for you, and I've seen for myself how he treats Jake like his own. I don't know where you get off, tossing him aside because he did one thing wrong. If it wasn't right when Griffin did it to me, then what you're doing to him is no better.'

'I'm not doing anything to him,' Ruby denied indignantly. 'You don't get why I was angry with him, Shirlee. He *lied*—'

'Oh, change the record!' Shirlee snapped. 'We *all* lie when we're forced into it. You know your problem, Ruby?'

'You mean apart from being a sanctimonious hypocrite?'

Shirlee ignored the sarcasm. 'You have a very bad habit of adopting a script and sticking to it when it no longer makes sense, and *then* getting on your high horse! First it was the "we had a bad kiss when we were kids and we're mates for life" story, and now it's "he lied to me so I can't ever trust him again".' She exhaled as if she had run out of steam, and then picked up again.

'Are you honestly so obtuse you can't see that everything Griffin has ever done is either for you or because of you? Trust me, when I was going out with him, he never left me in any doubt about who came first. To be honest, if he hadn't finished things, I would have, because I was clearly only ever going to be second best – and I bet you'd hear the same from every girl he's dated.'

Ruby's dumbfounded expression appeared to further irritate Shirlee. 'You're quick to point out Griffin's flaws, but how about turning the mirror on yourself for a change? Griffin might be no angel, but at least he has the balls to own up to his mistakes and try to fix them. He didn't have to find me and apologise, but he did it anyway. The man's got enough money not to have to work a day in his life, but he slogs day and night on projects for the foundation and, quite honestly, he deserves better than the way you've treated him.'

The words felt like a kick in the gut and Ruby stared at Shirlee in dismay. 'But you *know* what Griffin's like!' she exclaimed, desperate to defend herself. 'He's never done commitment. *Ever!*

And when Jake said – well, when I thought Griff was back with you, I assumed he'd moved on as he's always done and—'

'Yeah, well, he isn't back with me,' Shirlee scowled. 'I'm with—'

'Simeon. Yes, I know,' Ruby interrupted. Her head was spinning from the barrage of information, and she desperately needed to process her thoughts – and get away from Shirlee.

Shirlee seemed to have the same idea as she turned on her heel without a word. But then she swung back and heaved a sigh.

'Ruby, I work with Griffin and it's bloody obvious that a big part of why he's been so relentless about getting the foundation up and running is because he's utterly miserable without you. It's none of my business, but I care about Griffin so I'm just going to say this. He hasn't given up on you and, left to himself, I don't think he ever will. But if you've given up on him, the kindest thing you can do is tell him and give him a chance to move on with his life.'

51

The cries of the white seagulls circling overhead were muffled by the brisk breeze blowing in from the sea as Ruby tramped over the uneven pebbles, her calf muscles aching from the unaccustomed exercise. She stopped to take a breath and shake a stone from her sandals and then kept going until she reached the sand. Taking off the sandals, she carried on past the stretch of beach packed with holidaymakers enjoying the sunshine.

When she reached their spot, the cool, foamy waves lapped at her bare feet as she raised a hand to shield her eyes against the sun and scan the rocky beach. Her chest felt tight, and her mouth too dry to swallow, and when she adjusted the light rucksack on her back, she could feel the tension in her shoulders. Having coached Auntie Pearl and Jake until they were word perfect, she could only hope the script had worked. *But what if he doesn't come? What if Shirlee, Fi, and everyone's got it wrong?*

Just when she was about to give up and turn back, she saw him sitting on a boulder further up the deserted beach, bent over his guitar. Her pulse racing, and almost dizzy with relief, she tried to catch her breath. In that moment, she knew beyond any doubt that it was she who'd had it wrong all this time. She bent to slip on her sandals, her fingers fumbling as she retied the straps around her ankles. She started to walk towards him, and then broke into a run as impatience overtook any instinct for caution.

Griffin was strumming his guitar, his eyes on the sea, and as Ruby approached, she slowed down, taking in huge gulps of air to slow her pounding heart. As if suddenly aware of her presence, he looked up and his hand stilled. He watched her silently until she was close enough to touch him, and although his expression was guarded, Ruby caught a flash of fear in his eyes before he looked away.

'Did you bring me here to have another go?' he said in a low voice. 'In case you're wondering, I've finally got the message and I won't bother you any more.'

'Maybe that's not what I want,' she murmured.

A spasm of emotion crossed his face and then his jaw tightened, and he shook his head. Looking down at the guitar, he plucked at a couple of strings. 'What do you want, Ruby?'

How could she ever have imagined being with anyone else? She had been fooling herself for too long, and she was tired of denying the truth.

'You,' she said simply.

He gave a mirthless laugh and tapped the guitar strings. 'If you're here out of guilt because of what you promised my mother, then you can leave. I know what Mum asked of you and, if I'm honest, I wish she hadn't. I'm a grown man and I don't need rescuing.'

'I'm not here because of what I promised Marilyn. I'm here because of what I've promised myself.'

Finally, he looked up and his hazel eyes bored into her. 'And what's that?'

Ruby shrugged off her rucksack and dropped it on to the pebbles with a sigh. This was clearly not going to be easy, but then nothing about Griffin had ever been easy. He was, hands down, the most complicated man she had ever known, and the best way to deal with complicated people was to keep it simple.

So, taking a deep breath, she said, 'I promised myself that if you were here, I wouldn't go another minute without telling you I love you, however terrified I am to admit it.'

He froze. 'What did you just say?'

'*Griffin!* Please don't pretend you didn't hear me.'

'The seagulls are really loud out here, and I didn't quite catch it.'

She glared at him, but his expression remained deadpan. 'I *said*, I came to tell you I love you.'

Griffin tilted his head to one side, his eyes narrowed into slits. 'Love me like a brother or *love* me, love me?'

Feeling so exposed and vulnerable that she could have cheerfully wrung his neck, Ruby replied through gritted teeth, '*Love* you, love you, idiot!'

'That's not a very loving tone,' he said reprovingly. Then, before she could say another word, Griffin laid down his guitar and stood up. She looked up into his eyes and he moved so close that she could have counted every single one of his ridiculously long lashes.

'Oh, Ruby,' he sighed softly, a small smile playing at the edges of his mouth.

'Are – are you going to say something?' she asked, suddenly fearful.

'You mean, something like I love you so much that at times, when I look at you, I can't breathe?'

She nodded, biting her lip. 'Yes, something like that.'

As Griffin looked deep into her eyes, her anxiety melted away. He reached for her, pulling her against him and wrapping his arms around her so tightly she couldn't tell whether it was her heart or his that she could feel pounding.

She lifted her head, and when he kissed her, she wound her arms around his neck, clinging to him fiercely. As the waves crashed on to the rocks and the screaming seagulls circled above, Ruby and Griffin remained locked together and lost in each other.

Finally, she pulled away, her breathing ragged. Griffin held her loosely and nuzzled the warm space under her neck. 'Well done for trying to keep Jake and Auntie Pearl on script, by the way,' he murmured. 'I'm sorry, but knowing how much she hates the beach, it was a bit of a stretch for me to believe she was bringing Jake down here to meet me.'

Ruby giggled. 'Okay, so maybe it wasn't the cleverest plan in the world, but after the last time we met, I was terrified you wouldn't come if I asked. Now, Jake, on the other hand . . .'

'Oh, don't get me wrong, he was very convincing,' Griffin said dryly. 'Oscar-winning performance. Between Auntie Pearl's blatant guilt tripping and Jake tugging on my heartstrings about feeling sad and wanting to go to Brighton with me, I was never going to refuse.'

'He may have had a tiny bit of coaching,' said Ruby, feeling a tinge of guilt for shamelessly using her son. 'But he was so relieved I wanted to speak to you that he was well up for it.'

They perched on a flat outcrop of rock, Ruby's head resting against Griffin's shoulder and their fingers interlaced as they stared out to sea in silence.

'What made you change your mind?' he asked quietly.

Ruby sighed. There was so much to explain that she didn't know where to start. 'Griff, you're the one person in the world outside of my family who I would trust with my life. When Kenny blurted out that you knew why he'd left, especially after you and I had just spent the night together . . . well, it felt like Kenny's betrayal all over again, only much, *much* worse. That's why I was so awful to you when you tried to explain. I was hurting so badly that I hated you, and I needed you to hate me enough to never come back.'

'Well, that was never going to happen.' Griffin kissed the top of her head. 'I've loved you for way too long to stop, and it's hard to think of a time when you weren't in my life.'

He released her hand and turned to face her. 'I wanted you to go to Sorrel Island because I was desperate for us to shift our relationship into something more than friendship. At first, I told myself to give you space so you could hear the truth from Kenny and then, somehow, I'd figure out how to make things right with you. But Kenny didn't seem in any rush to tell you, and then you suddenly started gushing about how much he'd changed and how ecstatic Jake was around him. I know you'd do anything to make Jake happy, and so I panicked. I knew I had to see you in person and sort us out once and for all.'

Ruby scrutinised his troubled expression and nodded. 'Well, I told myself that going to Sorrel Island to find Kenny was for Jake's sake, but it was also because I needed to find out where I'd gone wrong, and what I'd done – or not done – that made Kenny feel he couldn't hack it with me any longer. The truth is that I was stuck in limbo. I couldn't resolve the past without confronting Kenny and I couldn't move on with anyone else when, in my mind, I was the problem.'

'It was Kenny who left, Rubes. It wasn't your fault,' Griffin began, and Ruby shook her head.

'Yes, but there are two people in a relationship. Just because I'd convinced myself that my life with Kenny was happy didn't make it so. It would be easy to paint him as the bad guy, but I'm the one who chose to be with him and to have Jake. Right from the start, you, Mum, and Auntie Pearl saw it for what it was. Deep down, I knew the relationship wasn't right, which is why I didn't want to get married. My heart belonged to someone else, but I was too scared to acknowledge the truth, especially after Jake was born, so I told myself everything was fine until I came to believe it. I guess it's been easier to blame you over these past months than to take responsibility for my own choices.'

Griffin reached for her hand, and she clung on to his and the comfort of his touch.

'Fi said I don't trust people, and maybe that's true,' Ruby said in a low voice. 'But I think my biggest trust issues have always been with myself, and Kenny leaving me the way he did was all the proof I needed that I wasn't enough. For years, I defined myself as the girl Kenny left, rather than appreciating the woman I've become. It's been such a struggle to feel confident enough to accept me just as I am, and if *I* couldn't love myself, I certainly couldn't trust anyone else to love me.'

Griffin pulled her in and hugged her to his side. 'I'm so sorry I kept the truth from you. I didn't know how to disclose that conversation without you hating me. The idea of telling someone I love that the man they think they're in love with has left them because of me was terrifying. If I'd told you what Kenny said, I would have had to confess how I felt about you, and – despite what Kenny thought – I was too scared you didn't feel the same to take the risk.'

'You could have told me later,' she pointed out sadly.

He groaned and squeezed her tighter. 'I know. After what happened to your parents, you had so much to deal with and I thought the best thing was just to be there for you and Jake. But truthfully, as time went on, I was scared to death of losing you, and that kind of crippling fear leaves you stuck. When you told me about your decision to go to Sorrel Island, that was the first time you admitted feeling emotionally stuck too. I honestly hadn't realised until then just how badly the situation with Kenny had messed you up. I didn't try to talk you out of going because you deserved the truth and to be happy, and I knew I had to face my fear of losing you if we were ever going to stand a chance.'

After a moment, Griffin asked, 'Why did you want us to meet here?'

His voice held a trace of humour, and Ruby smiled at him wryly. 'The beach has always been our place, for good or bad. I've behaved badly towards you, and I'm so very sorry for the hurtful things I said. I wanted to make this a good-news place for us today – if you'll have me, that is,' she added humbly.

For a long moment, Griffin looked deep into her eyes. Then, wrapping his arms around her, he held her close and she felt a tremor run through his body.

'I'm yours, Ruby,' he murmured. 'I've always been yours.'

Then he kissed her over and over again, and when Ruby kissed Griffin back, it felt like the most natural thing in the world.

EPILOGUE

The small aeroplane suddenly swooped, and Ruby winced as Griffin, seated next to her, stifled a groan and gripped her hand.

'You are such a baby,' she laughed, and then, as the plane dipped sharply, she squealed in horror, her life flashing before her eyes.

'Now who's a baby?' Griffin said, his smugness somewhat tempered by having to speak through gritted teeth.

Thankful Jake wasn't there to witness their humiliation, Ruby clutched Griffin's hand and tried to focus on her upcoming reunion with her son. The four-hour flight they had taken from New York to Jamaica, five days after Mac's exhibition opening, had been a breeze. But after the delicious food and free-flowing champagne courtesy of their first-class seats, boarding the tiny aircraft carrying them back to Sorrel Island had come as a rude shock – and one not helped by Griffin's unconcealed terror. He had insisted on coming with her, both to attend the launch of the newly completed Music Heals centre the trust had built next to Ocean House, and – as he had bluntly put it – to make sure she didn't end up with Kenny again.

'We should be landing shortly,' Ruby said brightly, keeping her tone upbeat in the hope of persuading Griffin – and herself – that they weren't facing imminent death. 'We'll see Jake soon, and I can't wait to give Miss Ida a massive hug!'

'Just as long as it's only Miss Ida you plan on hugging,' Griffin growled.

Ruby laughed, tickled that Griffin could still feel insecure about her ex. 'You are going to be *such* a crotchety old man one day! Besides, Kenny has his hands full with his new girlfriend. Jake says she's very pretty and an incredible scuba diver – so she's obviously much more his type than me!'

Whatever Griffin was going to say was cut off as the roar of the engines signalled the approaching runway. As the plane touched down on to the tarmac, Ruby squeezed her eyes closed for a moment. The worst part was over, and she couldn't wait to see her son again and take him home. This was the longest she had ever been apart from Jake and, as much as she had enjoyed New York, nothing mattered more to her than holding her little boy in her arms.

New York had been a revelation, as had Estella. Ruby's mental picture of a tall, slender blonde had been confounded by the statuesque redhead with razor-sharp cheekbones and a deep, infectious laugh that immediately captivated her.

Mac's portrait, now known as *Island Goddess*, had received rave reviews from a host of art critics and – as he had immodestly pointed out – cemented his reputation as one of the foremost figurative artists of his time. As the model and inspiration behind the portrait, Ruby found herself – just as Mac had predicted – at the centre of a storm of media attention, spending the better part of two days giving back-to-back interviews.

The rest of the time had been spent exploring the city with Griffin, while a riotous dinner with Mac and Estella at their home had cemented her bond with the artist. Whatever the future held, Ruby knew that, in Mac, she had found a friend for life.

As soon as the aircraft doors swung open, Ruby followed Griffin out of the confined cabin and into the bright sunshine. Looking around the familiar surroundings and feeling the warm rays of the Caribbean sun on her bare arms, it felt just like coming home.

In less than an hour, they had passed through customs and collected their baggage. The moment they emerged into the airport terminal and saw an excited Jake waving behind the barrier, Ruby raced to him, falling to her knees, and opening her arms wide as he rushed into her arms.

'Omigod! You *can't* have grown taller in only two weeks!' she exclaimed, holding him tightly.

As soon as she released him, Jake ran to embrace Griffin, and Ruby stood up to give Kenny a warm hug.

'You're looking well,' she remarked, stepping back, and taking in his spotless white sports shirt and the ever-present baseball cap. He returned her smile, and to her relief the two men shook hands amicably. If the greeting wasn't exactly fulsome, it was cordial enough to pass muster.

Kenny relieved Griffin of the loaded trolley and as they walked out of the airport to where Kenny's car was parked, Jake slipped his hand into Griffin's.

'Drew's not at Ocean House any more,' he announced sadly.

'I know, buddy. The director told me last week that the authorities finally tracked down his parents in Miami, and Drew's gone to America to live with them. But you'll get to see the other kids tomorrow at the launch.'

With Jake in the front passenger seat and Ruby and Griffin in the back, Kenny drove to Paradise Inn, having already agreed with Ruby that Jake would remain with him until they returned to London at the end of the week. As much as Ruby would have wanted to stay longer, she had several marketing campaigns on the go and couldn't afford any more time away from the office.

The car bumped along the familiar rough track leading to Paradise Inn and Ruby felt her heart pounding in anticipation. Jake had been under strict instructions not to disclose news of Ruby's arrival to Miss Ida, and Ruby couldn't wait to surprise her. As Kenny turned into the long drive, he honked his horn loudly several times and a few moments later a small figure in a vivid cerulean-blue dress came out of the house. Ruby grinned as she saw the woman clutch at her chest and her mouth open in astonishment when she spied the occupants of the car, before hastening down the front steps. As soon as the car came to a stop, Ruby jumped out and raced over to fling her arms around a stunned Miss Ida.

'It's *so* good to see you again,' Ruby exclaimed, almost in tears as she held on to the slightly built woman she had grown to love so deeply. When Ruby finally released her, Miss Ida took Ruby's hands in hers and gazed up at her with wide, shining eyes.

'You came back, sweetheart, just like you promised.'

'I did! And look who I brought with me.'

She gestured towards Griffin, who came up to them and bent to kiss Miss Ida on each cheek before gently hugging her. Miss Ida cupped his face between her hands and examined him for a long moment before turning back to Ruby, her dark eyes twinkling with mischief. 'Looks to me like you finally found your heart's twin. What did I tell you?'

Ruby laughed, flushing with embarrassment at the woman's smug expression. 'You're impossible, Miss Ida! But this time I have to admit you're right. So, do you have a room for us now you're a social media superstar and Paradise Inn is world-famous? I couldn't believe that video of you on TikTok!'

Miss Ida chuckled. 'You can blame Narita for that, sweetness. The child is always dreaming up some nonsense, but whatever she's doing is working. Since you made that beautiful website for me, we're always busy and I've hired help to take care of the grounds.'

She bent to kiss Jake and smiled in greeting at Kenny, who was wheeling the suitcases he had taken from the car boot. 'Come on inside, y'all. When Jake came by to visit last week, he let slip about the launch over at Ocean House. I knew you were with Mac for the exhibition, Ruby, but I was hoping Griffin might come over and I kept my best room free, just in case!'

While Griffin and Jake carried the suitcases upstairs and Kenny stayed out front to make a phone call, Miss Ida led Ruby through the parlour and out to the balcony. Moments later, an excited Narita came through with a tray bearing glasses and a jug of Miss Ida's sorrel drink and set it down on a stone table before leaving them to it.

Miss Ida filled a glass and handed it to Ruby, watching her sip the chilled juice and exhale with satisfaction.

'You look happy, sweetheart,' she remarked.

'I am.' Ruby grinned. 'Everything feels so different to how things were when I left the island. Griffin and I are great together, and Kenny has turned out to be a fantastic father to Jake.'

'And how's Mac?'

'Mac is floating on cloud nine! He'll be back here once the exhibition ends in New York, but right now he's basking in all the praise the art critics are heaping on him.'

'He's promised to send me a postcard of the portrait and he says you two talk all the time. Like I told you before, that man sure is taken with you.'

Ruby laughed and shook her head reprovingly. 'Miss *Ida*! Mac and I are such good friends now, and, besides, he adores his wife. Estella's gorgeous and we get on like a house on fire.'

Pouring herself a drink, Miss Ida raised her glass to Ruby with a loving smile. 'I'm so glad you came back, sweetheart. Mac may have painted a masterpiece, but no portrait will ever be as beautiful as you.'

◆ ◆ ◆

The launch of the Ocean House Music Heals centre was an overwhelming experience for Ruby. Inside the main hall of the newly built house next to the orphanage, she and the other guests – including the children from Ocean House, sitting cross-legged in rows – had watched as the director of Ocean House and a host of local dignitaries took turns praising Griffin for his extraordinary gift to Sorrel Island. Choked with pride and holding tightly on to Jake's hand, it had taken all Ruby's willpower not to cry during the emotional speech Griffin delivered before cutting the ceremonial ribbon.

Much later, back at Paradise Inn, where Miss Ida had insisted on hosting an impromptu gathering on the terrace, Ruby and Griffin quietly slipped away, leaving Jake with Kenny, Diego, and the other band members to continue the celebrations.

As they strolled down the walkway to the beach, the sun dipped low over the horizon, spreading crimson streaks across the darkening sky. With the soft sound of waves rolling on to the sand and the gentle breeze rippling through the palm trees and carrying the sweet scents of the tropical night, the beach was a soothing oasis of calm at the end of an emotional day.

After the thrill of New York and the joy of seeing Griffin's dream for Ocean House come to life, everything in her world had finally come right, Ruby decided. Well, almost. Walking hand in hand along the shore, she voiced the question still lingering in her mind.

'You know, Griff, you said Kenny let me go without putting up a fight because he didn't care enough, and yet it took you years before you kissed me that night on the beach. Why didn't *you* fight for me sooner?'

Griffin stopped to look at her, his eyes sober. 'Because I didn't deserve you. You are worth so much more than I had to offer. I was so angry at Mum for keeping her money a secret, and then dying and leaving it all to me. I spent years behaving like a lazy, self-entitled idiot and feeling sorry for myself because my own mother didn't trust me to do the right thing.'

He paused and then sighed. 'I haven't led the most praiseworthy life, and I hate that I messed women around knowing the relationship wouldn't go anywhere because none of them was you. For a long time, it was easier to be with women who didn't push me to be my best self all the time, but that was unkind and selfish of me. Rubes, I knew you cared about me and what you'd promised Mum, but I also needed your respect. Until then, being your friend was as much as I had a right to.'

Ruby squeezed his hand reassuringly. 'I always knew you'd figure your life out eventually.'

'Yes, but until I did, I owed it to Mum to at least monitor what the portfolio managers were doing with the investments and keep tabs on the lawyers. I don't know what my grandfather was thinking at the time he made his money, but the old bugger couldn't have created a more complicated financial structure for his business if he'd tried.'

'I'm so happy you've set up the foundation, Griff,' Ruby said earnestly.

'Me too. Playing the guitar always helped Jake when he was feeling stressed or anxious, but it wasn't until I met Drew and started visiting Ocean House and learning more about music therapy when it dawned on me that I could do something to help other kids, and even adults, who've experienced trauma. Meeting

Diego and funding that first programme at Ocean House cemented the idea . . . and here we are.'

Ruby stroked his cheek lovingly, her fingers caressing the soft beard she was still getting used to. 'I can see you've found your passion, and I certainly can't accuse you of being a wealthy playboy any more. Griff, I'm truly sorry for what I said to you the last time we were here. I know Marilyn would be incredibly proud of the man you've become.'

She reached for his hand and clasped it between both of hers. 'You know, Miss Ida once told me life is like a trapeze, and that I had to forgive and let go of my pain before I could reach for happiness. But after everything that happened with us, I was too scared to let go of the hurt because I didn't trust you to be there to catch me. You asked me once why I could forgive Kenny but not you, and it's because I never loved Kenny the way I love you. But even though everything we've gone through has been so hard, I think it all happened for a reason. Somehow, you and I had ended up becoming emotional crutches for each other as a way of avoiding painful truths. We were both stuck, but now look at us – and look at *everything* you've achieved. We've both found our balance as individuals, and now we can hold each other up the right way.'

She looked up at him, her eyes suddenly bright with happy tears. 'I know I can live without you, Griff, but I don't want to. Ever. What do you say?'

He grimaced. 'I'm doing my best, Rubes, but I'm nowhere near perfect. Can you handle a work in progress?'

'Only if you can too,' she said baldly. 'Perfect is a fantasy, and, besides, I've got no business expecting perfection from someone else when I'm nowhere near perfect myself.'

Studying her expectant expression, Griffin stroked her braids away from her face and shook his head. Panicked, Ruby's heart skipped a beat, but then he smiled. 'In that case, let's start working together on our perfect future.'

Griffin's eyes didn't leave hers as he slipped his hand into his pocket and pulled out a small velvet box. Ruby's pulse quickened as she watched him slowly open it, and she gasped at the delicate floating diamond glittering on a platinum band.

Before she could speak, Griffin took her hand and dropped on to one knee. 'I've loved you since we were awkward, gawky teenagers and there's no-one else on earth who I'd rather have by my side when I turn into a crotchety old man. You're my world, Rubes. Please say you'll marry me.'

Ruby's eyes misted over, and her throat felt too choked to speak. She nodded wordlessly, holding her breath as he slid the ring on to her finger.

'Oh, Griff! It's *so* beautiful!' She looked at him breathlessly. 'We're really doing this? Us, I mean?'

He stood up with a grin. 'We certainly are, beautiful.'

When she beamed without comment, he raised an eyebrow.

'What?' she asked.

'This must be the first time you've actually accepted a compliment from me without pushing back.'

Ruby raised her chin and sucked her cheeks into a mock pout. 'We-ell, when a world-famous artist insists on painting you, and half the American media want to interview you and take your photo, there's got to be a good reason, right?'

'I've been telling you for *years* that you're beautiful,' he protested, sounding so disgruntled that Ruby laughed aloud with delight.

'You were hardly an objective commentator. As my friend, you had an obligation to say nice things about me.'

Griffin kissed her softly. 'And I'll keep saying nice things about you because you are the kindest, sweetest, most incredible person in the universe, and I'm never letting you out of my sight again.'

Ruby glanced down at her feet and grinned. 'Even though I've got a long second toe?'

'We all have to make compromises in life,' he said gravely.

Pretending to be outraged, she aimed a mock blow at him and laughed when he caught her fist and swept her into his arms, holding her as if he would never let go.

Thank you, Sorrel Island. She sighed happily, resting her head against the shoulder of the man she had always loved. The trek halfway round the world was as nothing compared to the journey it had taken to finally recognise her heart's twin and discover a paradise she had known all along.

A MESSAGE FROM FRANCES

I hope you enjoyed Ruby and Griffin's love story and thank you so much for reading. Please take a moment to write a short review – even if it's only a line or two, I would truly appreciate it. If you'd like to try my other books and hear about my future releases, then please follow me on my author page and subscribe to receive my regular newsletters: https://francesmensahwilliams.com/newsletters.

Strictly Friends was inspired by an unfortunate incident on a tropical holiday when I found myself plagued by insects while relaxing by the pool. Just like Miss Ida in the novel, it struck me then that even paradise has mosquitoes! I suddenly had a vivid picture of Ruby and her son, Jake, visiting a tropical island, and the story took flight. It has been such a delight to create the fictional paradise of Sorrel Island and to explore how Ruby grows to love herself enough to finally accept a love she has known all along.

I'd love to hear your thoughts about 'The Ruby and Griffin Show', so please do get in touch with me via my Instagram, Twitter, or website.

Thank you!

Frances x

https://twitter.com/francesmensahw

www.facebook.com/francesmensahwilliams

www.instagram.com/francesmensahw

ACKNOWLEDGEMENTS

When I think back to the start of my author journey, it feels incredible that this is my *seventh* novel! I am so thankful to everyone who has encouraged me, held my hand, bolstered my spirits, and talked me over the many hurdles I encountered to fulfil my dream of becoming a writer.

My deepest gratitude to my agent, Rukhsana Yasmin, for your ever-present shoulder, as well as your sage advice and all-round fabulous agenting.

A huge thank you to my Lake Union/Amazon Publishing family and especially my editor, Leodora Darlington. Your cheerleading skills and genius title suggestions are surpassed only by your kindness and determined support. Celine Kelly, a massive thank you for instantly 'getting' the characters of Ruby, Griffin, and Kenny, and for your superb editorial skills and sensitive guidance.

My love and gratitude to my family and my friends. To my girls, Esther, Seena, and Khaya, your interruptions, hugs, and reassurances made all the difference. To Chux, my treasure, thank you for the years of love and support.

Finally, to you reading this book, my sincere and heartfelt thanks for doing so – and I can't wait to share novel number eight with you!

BOOK CLUB QUESTIONS

1. Who is your favourite character in the book, and why?
2. If you could choose which man Ruby ends up with, who would it be?
3. What feelings did Ruby's deep insecurity about her height and appearance evoke in you?
4. What did you like best about Sorrel Island, and why?
5. Did you feel sympathy for Griffin's dilemma about his inheritance?
6. How big a part do you think miscommunication plays in the story?
7. Did you identify with Ruby's dilemma of balancing her son's happiness against her own when it came to Kenny?
8. What is the most important point you think the author was trying to make in this story?
9. Which scene in the book has stuck with you the most?
10. What do you think about the structure of the book? Did it serve the story well?
11. Is there a character you'd love to lecture? Who is it, and what would you tell them?

12. If this book were a movie, who would you choose to play Ruby and Griffin?
13. Have you read any other books by this author and, if so, how did they compare?
14. Has this book made you think differently about other cultures and their challenges?

ABOUT THE AUTHOR

Photo © 2021 Abi Oshodi

Frances Mensah Williams CBE spent her early childhood between the USA, Austria and Ghana before settling in the UK. An avid scribbler, her acclaimed first novel, *From Pasta to Pigfoot*, was published in 2015 and the sequel, *From Pasta to Pigfoot: Second Helpings*, in 2016. Her third novel, *Imperfect Arrangements* (2020), was followed by the Marula Heights series of standalone novellas, *Sweet Mercy and River Wild*, set in contemporary Ghana. *The Second Time We Met* was published in 2022.

An entrepreneur, consultant, executive coach, and TEDx speaker, Frances is also the author of three non-fiction careers books and managing editor of careers portal ReConnectAfrica.com. She is a passionate advocate for skills development and has written extensively on careers and business relating to Africa and the African diaspora. She has received awards for innovation in business and skills development, culminating in the CBE awarded by Her Majesty Queen Elizabeth II in the 2020 New Year's Honours List for services to Africans in the UK and in Africa.